Royal (GONE) ROGUE

EMMA ST. CLAIR

This one goes out to all the readers who keep sending me raccoon and swan and baby goat gifs. Time to add in some peacocks!

Also and ALWAYS to Rob, who puts up with my shenanigans and scoops me up when I'm a puddle on the floor. Taste the happy!

CONTENT WARNINGS

Because I write light romcoms, I often don't think about including content warnings. Still—I like my romcoms with a side of reality, and I want to help readers feel safe! Here are some topics that are touched on in the book, serious and not-so-serious:

- Losing parents at a young age (childbirth & car accident)
- A father dying of liver failure
- Attack peacocks
- Meddling family members

Spoiler alert: No one dies. There is no sex in this book. You will get a happy ending with no cheating and minimal angst.

FROM THE ROYAL BUGLE, EUROPE'S #1 SOURCE FOR ROYAL GOSSIP

Robot Royal Searching for a Wife?

Who's ready to be a princess? Time to throw your tiara in the ring!

Sources inside the palace at Elsinore have confirmed that Crown Prince Phillip is actively seeking to settle down–though what kind of woman he's looking for remains a mystery. Perhaps best-known for his stiff personality, Phillip (who has been dubbed the Robot Royal) has never been publicly linked with anyone, so this news comes as quite a shock.

"His parents are actively seeking to arrange a match for Prince Phillip," an exclusive source tells us.

Is this why the Duchess of Vendar was recently spotted leaving the palace in tears?

"He didn't want a casual fling," a rebuffed woman, who wished to remain anonymous, told the *Bugle*, "but he also had no interest in discussing anything more serious."

Maybe he prefers the company of machines to humans,

which would be a real shame for the living, breathing females who would love to help make an heir!

Perhaps because Prince Phillip has never officially been linked with anyone, speculation has reached a fever pitch on what he could possibly be looking for in a wife. And if the gorgeous Duchess of Vendar isn't good enough, who is?

Meanwhile, Prince Callum has gone from dishy playboy to seemingly celibate. The Golden Boy hasn't been photographed with a woman since last summer when he was linked with American designer Brit Malloy.

Perhaps the sudden changes in both princes stem from King James's health issues. Though the palace has yet to issue an official statement and refused to comment at the time of publication, our source tells us that the king is gravely ill. King James has made only a handful of public appearances in months, with Prince Phillip assuming his role at diplomatic meetings and public functions alongside his mother, Queen Suzette.

We invite the palace to put all rumors to rest by giving an official statement and we invite you to vote in our poll below on which prince has the best abs! See photos below— hello, Thirst Trap!

CHAPTER 1

Phillip

THE DOOR to my office bursts open, the way it only does when it's my younger brother, Callum.

That is, unless this is the start of a coup, which is highly improbable given the current stability and security in Elsinore. Claudius jumps to his feet, as though he plans to defend me. Even more improbable than a coup. Claudius is a top-notch advisor but in no way a bodyguard.

I glare as Callum sweeps into the room, all bright smiles, indecently short tennis shorts, and sweat-damp hair. He must have come straight from the courts, while I've been at my desk since before the sun rose.

A tale of two princes. Other than our builds—tall and broad, our hair—wavy and blond, and our eyes—a bright blue, Callum and I have very little in common.

Claudius sinks back into his chair.

Callum squeezes the advisor's shoulder before flopping down in the chair next to him. "Claud. Good to see you."

"Please refrain from calling me Claud."

"Sure thing, Claw." Callum picks up a pen from my desk and twirls it expertly between his fingers. "I came by to see if you wanted to have lunch later, but it looks like I crashed a secret meeting."

Claudius and I exchange a glance, because actually—yes. He did.

One I'm still trying to wrap my head around. Even though all of this was my idea, now that it's becoming reality ... I'm more than a little overwhelmed. And definitely self-conscious about sharing the details with my brother.

Callum drops the pen and leans forward, eyes shining. "You *are* having a secret meeting! Brilliant! What are we plotting?"

Before I can stop him, my brother snatches the folder off my desk. With a sigh, I lean back in my chair. The last thing I want is Callum sticking his nose into the delicate matter before Claudius and I iron out all the details. Though I suppose I *am* going to need Callum's nose (and the rest of him) to pull this off.

Callum flips through page after page, looking amused. "Well, this is unexpected. Dear brother, why do you have a dossier of single women throughout Europe?"

When I don't answer immediately, my brother's eyes take on a glint I do not particularly like. It is the same one he had when arranging to send swans to King Rafe and Queen Serafina as a prank.

"Are you planning to star in your own royal edition of *The Bachelor*?" Callum asks.

I frown. Is that some American reality TV show? Claudius

2

coughs and looks as though he's hiding a smile behind his hand.

"You'd make for great television—all stoic and noble while women have catfights in bikinis over who gets to sit beside you at dinner. I love it. Can I be your wingman?"

"Absolutely not. No television. No catfights. No wingmen." I pause. "I'm searching for a wife."

Callum's eyes go wide, and he drops the folder. Papers scatter and Claudius—with an irritated sigh—helps gather them back together.

"Since when do you want to get married?" Callum asks, tucking the last few papers back into the folder. I reach for it, but he pulls it to his chest. "I thought you were dead set against the idea."

"No. I'm simply not interested in any of the women Mum and Dad have been parading through the palace."

"What's so wrong with the women they've suggested, if you don't mind me asking? The Duchess of Vendar wasn't beautiful enough for you?"

"The Duchess of Vendar was indeed beautiful. And she knew it."

Not unlike most of the other "suitable" women my parents have been not-so subtly suggesting, the duchess was titled, entitled, and completely ... wrong. If I'm choosing a wife, I am far more interested in what lies beneath the surface. And so far, the supposedly "good" candidates my parents have suggested are puddle deep.

"She did spend an awfully long time at dinner discussing the evils of open-toed shoes," Callum says thoughtfully.

"I think her passion for the subject rivals Henrietta's feelings about heels. Which is fine for Henri ... considering our sister is barely eighteen. I'd prefer to find a woman who hasn't been handed every opportunity. Someone with a strong work ethic, someone who *isn't* titled."

"I can understand that. The duchess was no good for you. I concede your point. It's just …" Callum shoots a sideways glance at Claudius before meeting my gaze again. He lowers his voice. "I actually wasn't sure you liked women at all."

"Just because I rarely date—"

"*Never.*" Callum coughs into his hand.

"Just because I *rarely* date," I repeat, "it doesn't mean I don't like women."

I do like them … *generally* speaking. I simply haven't met any *particular* woman who interested me beyond simple physical attraction. And I've never wanted a relationship based solely on that. Physical attraction is like low-hanging fruit. Common. Not hard to find. Attraction isn't the problem.

The problem is that I want—no, *need*—something more. I need the kind of woman I will want beside me not just in sickness and in health, but in kingdom-ruling as well. I don't have the luxury of choosing a woman just for myself. I'm choosing a woman for the people of Elsinore too. And so far, no woman I've met fits this description. Not even close.

Callum gives me a lopsided grin, then says, "I thought maybe you were asexual."

He—*what?*

Claudius makes a sound somewhere between a cough and a snort.

"I googled it," Callum continues. "Some people have no sex drive. Definitely nothing to be ashamed of. You know what else is asexual? Zebra sharks. You're a zebra shark! How cool is that?"

I lean forward, resting my head in my hands, taking deep breaths. I slowly count backwards from ten in Elsinorian, then in English, Spanish, and finally Italian. When I look up again, Callum stares at me expectantly. The look on Claudius's face is barely concealed amusement.

"It's nothing to be defensive about, bro. The internet says plenty of asexual people live happy, fulfilled lives. The concept of an heir might be an issue but—"

"I am *not* a zebra shark, nor am I asexual. And please, for the last time, stop using the word *bro*." When Callum opens his mouth again, I pound my fist on the desk. "I don't like casually dating any woman who blinks at me the way you do."

"In case you haven't noticed, I haven't been dating, casually or otherwise, since last summer," Callum says.

It's true, and I *have* noticed. After the arranged marriage between Callum and Serafina of Viore went down in flames (thanks to Callum lighting a match and dousing it with petrol), he's changed. Dare I even say he's matured?

He just called you a zebra shark. Mature is not what he's done.

Right. But at the least, Callum hasn't been spotted with a new woman every week in the tabloids. And he made peace with Serafina and her new husband, Rafe. Though now Callum and Rafe are engaged in a long-distance prank battle that I fail to understand. Pranks in general seem so wasteful of time and resources. But ultimately, this is an improvement on things, so I'll ignore it until it creates some kind of national incident.

"Regardless," I say. "I've chosen to focus on my work and my duties rather than relationships. It doesn't make me asexual. I always planned to get married. The only thing I'm against is marrying a woman ill-suited to the job."

"Ill-suited to the ... *job*," Callum repeats slowly.

"Yes."

"You realize your wife will not be an *employee*."

I scoff. "Of course I know that."

5

"Are you *sure* you know that? Because," Callum goes on, an intense look on his face, "I know you said you're not a zebra shark—but *just in case*—when a man loves a woman and wants to *demonstrate* this love physically—"

Without stopping to consider the repercussions, I toss a paperweight shaped like a sailboat at Callum's head.

He ducks, and the boat lands in the corner of my office beneath the portrait of my stern-faced grandfather, King Gerald.

If possible, Gerald looks even less amused than before.

I'm not usually a violent—or even very physical—person. But Callum knows where to find my buttons and how to jam his thumbs directly into them. Repeatedly.

A zebra shark, I scoff to myself. *Asexual. A wife as an employee.*

Claudius retrieves the paperweight and sets it on my desk. The mast is broken, but I regret nothing. Callum grins and spreads out until he takes up twice as much room as any normal person. I may have to ask someone to disinfect the chair later, given his post-tennis state of sweat.

"Do you two need to take this outside?" Claudius asks drily, adjusting his wire-rimmed glasses.

"No," Callum and I say in unison.

Callum clears his throat and taps the folder he's still holding. "How, precisely, did you and Claudius come up with this list of women?"

"With a specific list of qualities and characteristics I provided," I say, keeping it intentionally vague.

"Demographics, psychographics, personality tests, and background checks," Claudius adds. "I designed an algorithm to—"

Holding up a hand, Callum says, "Got it. You're brilliant, Claudius." My brother swings his gaze back to me, his eyes narrowing. "Just tell me you didn't make a spreadsheet."

I say nothing. Because I did *not* make a spreadsheet.

I made two.

Callum groans, then covers his eyes and groans even louder. "You can't choose a wife based on a *spreadsheet*."

"Ultimately, we didn't use a spreadsheet," Claudius says. "I made an algorithm and plugged the information into a rubric."

"Even worse." Callum pauses. "What's a rubric?"

Claudius sighs. "It's a scoring guide evaluating the final candidates chosen by the algorithm."

Waving the folder just out of my reach, Callum says, "And you really think this is the best idea to choose a wife? A silly rubric? No offense, Claudius."

"None taken."

"I'm sure it's quite a lovely rubric," Callum adds politely.

"Stop saying the word *rubric*," I snap.

"It's a *dreadful* idea," Callum concludes, swinging his gaze to me. "If you'd like, I can set you up with someone within the hour. Even if you are a geeky, too-serious hermit with very little dating experience. You're good-looking. And a prince. Also, a very decent man."

"Tempting, but no. I've made my choice."

"You mean, your *rubric* made the choice. You'd trust a rubric over your own brother?"

I'm not going to even *touch* that question.

Callum huffs. "Fine. So, it's like an arranged marriage—with you and Claudius doing the arranging. By way of spreadsheets, algorithms, and—"

"Don't say it."

"—a rubric. What about love? Attraction? Chemistry?" Callum asks. "Where do those fall on the rubric?"

7

I drum my fingers against the desk. "They don't."

Callum looks like he's about to jump out of his tiny tennis shorts. Before he starts spouting some rubbish about the importance of attraction in the animal kingdom (to all species other than zebra sharks), I speak.

"Love is a choice. A commitment. It develops and deepens over time. Attraction can and will grow in proportion to this deepening connection."

"Next, you'll tell me there's a pie chart or bar graph you've made for this," Callum says with a laugh.

There are actually both. I'm grateful they didn't make it into the folder Callum still has in his lap.

"I don't need to tell you that royal marriages don't always happen conventionally."

"They can still include love," he argues.

"Mum and Dad had an arranged marriage. Love followed."

"Our parents are more of an exception than a rule. My point is that you shouldn't get married out of a sacrificial desire to do what's best for Elsinore," Callum says, and I'm touched by the sincerity in his eyes. Even if I disagree. "We're not bound by some law about how or when to get married. If you don't like the women Mum and Dad are setting you up with, fine. But don't rush this and make a choice based on—"

Before he can say *rubric* again, I interrupt. "It needs to be now. Because we don't know ..."

My stomach twists as I trail off. Callum's shoulders slump as he realizes what I didn't say—we don't know how long our father has left, and our time with him may be shorter than any of us want to admit. Once I am crowned king, searching for a wife will be a task I simply won't have time for. It *must* be now.

All of Elsinore knows father's health has worsened over the past nine months. We've tried to keep the news of his liver failure quiet, but it seems we have someone leaking information from the palace to the gossip mags. It's someone with enough access to have more information than most of the palace staff, but not enough access to know that the doctors have said a transplant isn't an option.

I've attempted to discover who, but so far to no avail. Maybe I can convince Claudius to help. He'd likely bring me a name within a week, though I doubt he'll want to be apart from Viore or his fiancée, Kat, longer than necessary. I'm grateful he agreed to come help with this.

"I understand the urgency," Callum says quietly. "But you can't treat a relationship like one of your computer programs. Plugging in the right line of code isn't going to spit out the perfect woman."

"That is not what I am doing."

"It sure sounds like it is," Callum says.

Claudius pushes his glasses up his nose before speaking. "I believe this match has a high potential for success."

I cling to those words. *High potential for success.* Coming from the advisor whose opinion I value more than anyone in the world, this means something.

But is Callum right? Am I treating the prospect of choosing a wife like fixing a glitch in one of my computer programs? That isn't what I intend.

There's a sharp knock, and my office door opens. A stern-faced royal guard dips his head and steps out of the way as my mother glides into my office.

"Mum," I say, rising from my chair.

Claudius does the same, smoothing a hand over his dark hair as he bows. My mother looks like she's been up for hours, her mint green suit perfectly pressed and not a single

9

hair out of place. And her eyes, ever watchful, take in the room with intense precision.

The folder!

So subtly I'd have missed it if I weren't looking, Callum slides the folder under his thighs and shoots me a wink. I'm so grateful, I won't even be angry about the sweat marks he's going to leave on the folder.

"Good to see you back in Elsinore for once," she says to Claudius, an icy chill in her voice. My mother still hasn't gotten over the former Elsinorian advisor leaving to work for Queen Serafina. "Do sit."

"It's always a pleasure, your majesty," Claudius says, running a hand over his dark hair as he returns to his seat.

Callum leans back so he's looking at our mother upside-down. "Morning, Mum!"

Giving a shake of her head like he's an adorable but troublesome puppy, Mum roughs up his hair. "Good to see you awake at this hour," she says pointedly.

Callum only shrugs. I wait to see if she notices the edge of the folder sticking out from beneath Callum's bare thighs. She doesn't.

She turns her assessing gaze to me. "Is now a good time to discuss the ball?"

It's *never* going to be a good time to discuss the ball in question. I manage a polite smile. "Of course."

As she steps closer, I notice little things I didn't when Mum walked in. She's fidgeting with her wedding band, and what I'm sure is an expensive concealer doesn't quite hide the circles beneath her eyes.

The last year has taken a toll on her. To those who know her well, the weariness and worry in her eyes are always visible. She's thinner than she used to be, probably thinner than she needs to be. The only positive change is that she gave up alcohol, which had become something of a coping mechanism as Father's illness progressed. I know she thought the change was for *his* sake—liver failure and all that—but she needed it for herself too.

Without drinking, however, she needed something else to distract herself from Father's health.

Namely: meddling.

Specifically: in my life.

"We've finalized the guest list. Robert will make an official announcement very soon," Mum says.

If her communications secretary is already planning an announcement, this isn't going to be as easy to get out of as I'd hoped.

Mum adds in a dark grumble, "Hopefully our announcement will get out before word of this reaches the press."

I squeeze my fists underneath my desk. "Could we wait? A few more months, at least." That will give me time to complete the plan Claudius and I have made. To get to know the woman I hope to be my bride and make sure this isn't, as Callum has been suggesting, a terrible idea.

She shakes her head. "No. The date is set. First the ball, and then in August, the wedding."

My head is spinning at the mention of a wedding. And August—that's barely a few months away.

"I know that might seem soon, but I've been working behind the scenes on some of the details. It's the month your father and I got married, and it will be good luck. It will mean a lot to him."

Using Father is like a kind of trump card these days. I can't exactly argue any time she mentions something he would like.

So I focus on the ball instead. "Don't you think the idea is a little ... trite?"

I have a lot of stronger words I'd use for what is my parents' last-ditch effort to force me into a match of their choosing. And though I'm sure her invitations won't read *Ball in Which Prince Phillip Will Choose a Bride*, we'll be lucky if her intent doesn't reach our leak.

"We're throwing a ball to help him find a bride?" Callum asks.

I glare.

"We are," Mum says definitively.

"I think it's romantic. Like a fairy tale," Callum says in a falsely sweet voice. Whose side is he on, anyway?

Hosting a ball for the sole purpose of me choosing a wife is *not* romantic. It sounds more like a livestock auction.

And though the idea for a ball *is* ripped straight from a fairy tale, the original story also had Cinderella's sisters chopping off parts of their feet to fit into the glass slipper. By either count, this is not something we should emulate. No matter how set on it my mother seems to be.

"Your father and I have been more than lenient with the time we've given you. And you've had plenty of opportunities to take an interest in one of the lovely young ladies we've suggested."

Mum picks up the paperweight, frowning at the broken mast. She sets it back down before turning the full weight of her gaze on Callum, who has just opened his mouth, likely to make a smart remark.

"Don't get me started on you, Cal. Your time will come."

Callum's eyes widen and he looks to me for help. I will happily offer exactly *none*. Whenever his time does come, I'll plan a ball—or whatever terrible idea Mum has—myself.

"It's settled. I'll make the announcement this week. The ball will be in two months, and you'll choose a suitable wife from one of the women in attendance. We'll plan for a summer wedding." Mum pauses, as though for dramatic effect. She's got it. With a smile, she says, "Have a lovely day."

When the door closes behind her, Callum leans forward. "Is it just me, or is she growing more terrifying?"

"It's not just you." But it's hard to be angry or upset when I know her intensity is at least in part a coping mechanism as she deals with my father's decline.

"If the rubric fails, take comfort. You'll always have the Cinderella ball," Callum says with a smirk.

"Shut up."

"It won't fail," Claudius says.

I wish I shared his confidence, but this whole morning is leaving me with lingering doubts. And a headache.

Callum pulls the folder out from beneath his thighs and, as I knew there would be, a damp sweat stain mars the front. "Sorry," he says with a grimace, placing it on my desk.

"I'll get it disinfected"—or incinerated—

"So, tell me. Have you narrowed it down to a short list?"

"A very short list," Claudius says. "One woman."

"Impressive," Callum says. "Tell me about her. I'm dying to know what kind of woman captured your attention." He pauses. "Or, I suppose, the kind of woman chosen by your magical rubric."

I expect Claudius to point out how rubrics actually work, but he says nothing, training his gaze on me. I realize that I am the one who needs to answer.

What kind of woman *has* captured my attention?

Callum interrupted this morning before I was able to study the final dossier ... which is in the now-sweat-soaked folder. When Claudius hands me a clean copy, I decide to make sure I send him home with a generous bonus.

"Thank you." I scan the dossier. It is full of concise, bullet-point information and a single photograph.

"Her name is Alessia," I say. *Ah-less-ia*. It is the first time I've spoken the name out loud, and it tastes like music on my tongue.

My finger follows the bullet points down the page. "She is from a small village called Repestro on the western coast of Italy. She didn't attend university and has been working in her grandfather's restaurant for years."

"As a chef?"

"As a waitress," Claudius says.

Callum smirks. "Quite a contrast to the women Mum and Dad have suggested. I approve. What about her family? Any beautiful sisters I need to know about?"

I scowl, already feeling a protective urge that surprises me. Pulling the paper closer, I try to read, but the letters swim in front of me.

"You don't know if she has sisters?" Callum asks.

"I know very little—yet."

But I vow to memorize every bit of information on the page as soon as we're done here, then ask Claudius to find out even more. As much as he can. A single sheet of paper with bullet points is nowhere near enough.

"Her parents are dead," Claudius says, and my head snaps up. "No siblings. It's just Alessia and her grandfather, Enzo. Her paternal grandparents are estranged. They've never met."

A tightness moves from my chest to my throat. Alessia is an orphan. More than that, her mother's death is listed on the paper as Alessia's birthday. Childbirth? Her father's date of death was five years later. And here I am, thinking of time being short with my own father. She only got *five years*. How has this impacted her? How have these losses shaped her into the woman she is now?

Family is something I have no shortage of with Callum and my two younger sisters, Henri and Juliet. And despite Callum's accusations about me being a hermit, I'm grateful for our large, loud family. I always hoped to have my own. As infuriating as he can be, Callum is my closest friend.

Alessia has only her grandfather.

Would she want to leave him? If it were me, I wouldn't. But she could bring him here. We would make a place for both of them.

If she accepts my offer of marriage.

For once, my younger brother probably *is* correct. This idea is ridiculous. Being set up by my parents makes more sense. The ball makes more sense. Even Callum's first thought about me taking part in a reality show probably makes more sense.

Panic seizes me. Machines and computer programs I understand. Matters of diplomacy and policy I've learned.

Relationships, women—these are like subjects I've failed in school. This is why the idea of asking Claudius for help made sense in my head. Choosing a woman based on specific characteristics, then presenting her with a proposal resonates with the logical part of my brain. It reduces a complicated issue into rudimentary math.

Two plus two equals four.

Well-suited woman plus offer of marriage and title equals a happily ever after. Or, at least, a hope for the best outcome.

And yet ... faced with the reality of this woman, of Alessia, it all feels very different.

"This won't work." My voice is quiet as I set the paper on the desk in front of me. When this was an idea in my mind, it made sense. But I think Callum was correct when he accused me of plugging in the right code to result in the right woman.

Alessia isn't a number. Even from this single sheet of paper with the most basic details about her life, that is abundantly clear.

My gaze falls on the single page in front of me. More specifically, to the black and white photograph of Alessia. Perched on a crumbling stone wall on a cliff, she is overshadowed by the sea and sky stretching before her. Her dark ponytail is blowing over her shoulder in wild waves. Her chin is lifted, as though accepting some silent challenge from the wind, meeting it head-on.

Who are you? I find myself wondering as I study the picture. *To have lost so much but not break under the weight of it.*

She also looks nothing like my parents' suggestions—with her t-shirt and dark pants, ponytail, and light—if any—makeup. I see strength and a simple, raw beauty in her dark eyes and the curve of her cheek. Maybe I'm reading too much into the single photograph, but Alessia looks far from broken.

Either way, there is definitely something here, something in Alessia's face that intrigues me. She possesses something else, something more, and I struggle to name it.

Arresting, I finally think. That's the English word for it.

Fiele, an Elsinorian word, is a better fit. It is used to mean beauty, but literally translated, it refers to the captivating light from a distant star.

"May I?" Callum reaches for the page I'm still staring at.

I hesitate only for a moment, giving her photo one last glance, then slide the page his way. "Just keep this one away from your sweaty thighs."

Callum's eyes rove over the paper, and I struggle not to snatch it back.

"She's pretty," Callum says. "She seems very ... *unassuming*. A waitress. Not much family. No higher degree. No driver's license. No social media. No mobile phone? That can't be right."

"It is," Claudius assures, and I wonder at the man's thoroughness.

Callum shakes his head. "Rubrics and algorithms aside, I don't know how you and Claudius possibly chose this *one* woman in all of Europe."

Claudius takes his glasses off and begins cleaning the lenses, looking bored.

"It's Claudius," I say, as though that explains it. I reach for the sheet of paper.

Callum hands it back. "Even so, it seems unlikely that—"

"Shall we discuss the next steps?" Claudius asks, settling his glasses back on his nose.

"Yes, *please*." I tuck the paper in my center desk drawer, watching the photograph of Alessia disappear as I close it again.

"You'll have your own part to play, actually," Claudius says.

"I thought you didn't need a wingman," Callum says with a smirk.

"I don't."

"What *do* you need from me?"

I arch an eyebrow. "I thought you didn't approve of this plan."

"Oh, I don't approve. But I know you've got a good heart in there somewhere, overshadowed perhaps by your logical brain."

"Thanks?"

"You're welcome. If this is the course you're set on, I'm

all in. I'll remain pessimistically optimistic about its success. Sign me up for anything."

"Anything?" Claudius raises his brows.

"Anything," Callum repeats, excitement shining in his eyes.

Which is good, as we're about to throw him into the fire. Or to the wolves. Or both.

"Excellent." Claudius pulls two sheets of paper from his folder and hands one to each of us. He addresses me first. "You will grow a beard."

"I will?"

"And you." Claudius turns to Callum, completely ignoring me. "Will be assuming all of Phillip's duties and engagements while he goes."

Callum blinks down at the paper and looks back at Claudius. "Goes where?"

My words sound like a declaration but feel more like a wish before tossing a coin into a fountain. "I'm going to Repestro to bring back my bride."

Alessia, I think, pulling open my drawer to look at her photograph again. *My bride?*

CHAPTER 2

Alessia

I'M HAVING that daydream again. THE daydream.

The one where a handsome stranger walks into my nonno's restaurant, sweeps me off my feet, and carries me (literally or figuratively—I'll take either) straight out of this village and into my happily ever after. In the fictional world, I feel zero guilt about leaving Repestro and Nonno behind.

Also in my daydreams: stranger danger does not exist.

This recurring daydream is *so* tempting, *so* painfully disruptive to my mental status quo, that I only allow myself to indulge in it once a week. And I already filled my quota, so I'm confused by the presence of the ridiculously handsome man standing inside Nonno's restaurant.

When I blink, he doesn't disappear. And he *should* because men who look like HIM do not belong in my tiny village.

I blink again. Still there.

Maybe he's a hallucination, a result of too many long days on my feet, handing out menus, sliding plates in front of hungry people, and tucking too-small tips into the apron fastened around my waist. It's entirely possible I've developed a new disease, one mutating inside me as a result of boredom, longing, guilt, and the never-fading scent of garlic in my hair.

"Are you going to give him a table, tesoro?" Nonno asks, passing me with two steaming plates of pasta, his chef's coat flecked with sauce.

So then, the handsome stranger is *not* a hallucination or daydream. He is a customer. One whom I've left standing by the door far too long. He's still there—with his broad shoulders, dark blond hair, and the kind of bone structure that should grace magazine covers or movie posters.

Except for the beard. In contrast to his perfectly pressed button-down shirt and khakis, the patchy beard seems out of place.

"Of course. I was just … resting for a moment."

"You—rest?" Nonno chuckles. "More like checking out a handsome man."

"I wasn't—"

Nonno clucks his tongue. "Go on, Lessy. Serve Mr. Handsome."

I give him a dirty look, but he only chuckles, nudging me with a shoulder. Grabbing two menus, I approach the man, keeping my eyes trained on his feet. It's the best policy. I've already gawked at him from a distance. No need to do so up close.

Don't meet his eyes. Don't meet his eyes. Don't—

"I am alone."

His voice is a low rumble that goes straight to the center of my chest like a poison-tipped arrow. My gaze snaps to his.

The blue of his eyes is brighter even than the sea, which shouldn't be possible.

Caspita. The man is more than just handsome up close. Except for the patchy beard. *Focus on the beard!*

I turn away with a quick nod that hopefully says *follow me.* I am currently unable to access the part of my brain necessary for speech.

I am alone, he said. What a strange way to say he needs a table for one. His Italian is slightly accented, clearly not his native language. Despite the fact that Repestro is out of the way and definitely not on most tourist guides, we do see our fair share of tourists—almost exclusively for Nonno's food. But this man is no tourist. I'm not sure who he is, but there's something different about him. And it's not just his good looks.

I lead him toward the bar, where Antonio is wiping down the wood. Antonio's smile fades when he sees the stranger behind me. I can already see Antonio's chest puffing up. Not that he has any reason to feel threatened or possessive. I've been turning him down for as long as I can remember. And I have no interest in a man who—tourist or no—is only passing through.

Before I can set a menu on the bar, the stranger touches my arm. "A table, please," he says, the soft glide of his fingertips making my skin dance.

"Of course." I switch to English, guessing it might be more comfortable. Though he doesn't smile, I see a flash of something like relief in his eyes.

"Need help?" Antonio smiles at me from behind the bar, his teeth too big, too white. Many women in the village have swooned over his smile, but it does nothing for me. I can practically sense the waves of masculine challenge wafting off him as he looks the stranger up and down. The man does not possess a subtle bone in his body.

"I'm fine."

Antonio frowns but says nothing more as I walk to a table in the back corner. The stranger moves past me to get to his seat, close enough that his chest brushes my back. The feeling in my belly is like a cascade of pebbles skittering down a mountain, the warning before an avalanche.

"Sorry," I say again, stepping out of the way and fumbling for an explanation for why I keep losing myself in thought tonight. But I have none.

The truth is that all day, I've been lost in the kind of melancholy I usually fight off with ease. Most of the time I've learned to embrace contentment with my small life, even if, somewhere inside my chest, there's a Belle singing about her provincial life. After years, I've gotten good at shutting her up and settling into the life I've been given. The very blessed and good life. One which has no room for wanting anything beyond Repestro.

And yet, here I am, desperately, inexplicably, instantly drawn to this stranger, whom I have no business even thinking about twice—much less ten or fifteen times.

Oooh, he has nice hands.

Make that *twenty* times.

"No, *I* am sorry," he says, surprising me. He seems more suited to issuing commands than making apologies.

I'd happily be commanded by him any day.

That little voice tells me I've been spending way too much time with Luci.

"What would you like to drink?"

He doesn't answer right away, forcing me to look at him again. While I'm sure the low light only emphasizes the dark circles under my eyes, all of this man's features are enhanced in the flicker of the candlelight. His eyes are somehow even more piercingly, achingly blue, and the cut of his cheekbones is dangerously sharp.

No ring, I notice as he reaches up to scratch at his beard. And no tan line from a ring that's been removed either. A *very* important point.

Not that I need to concern myself with his marital status. In fact, it's the *last* thing I should be concerned about.

"I'll bring you water," I say, starting to back away when he still hasn't answered. "There's a wine list inside the menu."

I'm being a little brusque, but I just noticed Luci and Marco walk inside, followed by a group of tourists, crowding the entryway.

"Water, please."

Something about the please, and the way one corner of his mouth lifts an infinitesimal amount, makes my stomach flip flop. Without another word, I walk away, wondering if I'm imagining the heat of his gaze on my back. I seat the tourists and get their drink orders first. By the time I'm done, Nonno has given my best friend and her boyfriend a table before retreating to the kitchen to cook alongside Marcello.

"And who's the hottie seated at our usual spot?" Luci asks, craning her neck to see.

Of course Luci notices the man I need to forget. I glance over, pleasure blooming in my chest when I see him watching us. Watching *me*.

"A customer," I reply, setting down two waters. "Typical tourist."

I can't meet Luci's eyes. Even at a glance, there is *nothing* touristy about this man. And nothing typical about my reaction to him, one which I can't explain.

It's just attraction, pure and simple. A chemical thing. My

hormones reacting to his pheromones—I think that's how it works.

My hormones clearly need to be kept on a shorter leash.

"Busy night," Marco says, glancing around.

It's the same greeting he uses every time they come in together. Which has been most nights for the last six weeks. Marco should win some kind of award for lasting this long. Luci falls in and out of love so frequently, I'm convinced she's more in love with love itself.

I'm not sure how she isn't bored out of her mind with Marco, because everything that comes out of his mouth sounds like it's being read from a textbook. There is absolutely nothing remarkable or interesting about him. Average looking. Nice, but not noteworthy. But he is a steady presence, and maybe that's exactly what Luci needs.

Plus, she has heart emoji eyes whenever she looks at him, so whatever. If she's happy and he's not a jerk, okay. Six weeks with a guy is practically marriage material for Luci.

"He can't take his eyes off you, Lessy!"

"Who?" I ask, though I know exactly who she means. I force myself not to look again. Better not to know. Better to pretend he's not there.

"The handsome stranger."

"He's looking because he's waiting for me to bring his water, and I'm over here chatting with you."

"No." Luci shakes her head and leans closer to Marco, who is engrossed in reading the menu he probably knows by heart. "That's not the look of a man wanting *water*."

Now, I do glance over. He is watching me, yes, but more like he's assessing me, not mentally undressing me.

Which is just fine! Mental undressing is offensive and demeaning. Still—at least some small part of me wouldn't mind if there were something more heated in his gaze.

24

"And you," Luci continues, grabbing my wrist. "You are interested in him."

"Am not."

"You *are*."

Marco clears his throat. "I think Alessia probably knows how she feels better than you do."

Maybe Marco isn't so bad after all.

"No," Luci says firmly, and I glare. "Alessia knows how she thinks she *should* feel. She is completely out of touch with how she actually does feel because she won't let herself *have* feelings or wants."

Having a friend studying psychology isn't always a good thing. Because Luci completely nailed it. Not that I'll admit to anything. The best policy when she starts psychoanalyzing is complete and total ignorance. Marco and I share an awkward smile.

"Go after what you want," Luci says, pressing a kiss to Marco's cheek. He beams at her. My best friend is impossible not to love. Even if she's very wrong about this.

"Who says he's what I want?"

Luci raises one eyebrow, but there is no need to answer the question. The flush in my cheeks says it all.

"Stefan," I say, which is as good as closing a vault door on the conversation. At least for now. Luci is nothing if not persistent.

She rolls her eyes and mutters a curse on my last boyfriend's great-grandchildren. To be clear—the as-yet-*unborn* great-grandchildren. Stefan is my age, twenty-two, and based on how quickly he swept me off my feet and then departed, he's not interested in settling down to make children or grandchildren anytime soon.

"Get over him."

"I'm over *him*," I say. "But I've learned my lesson about

25

handsome men who hail from other places. Now, what would you like tonight?"

I manage to take their orders as well as the whole table of German tourists before finally grabbing a glass of water for the man I've kept waiting.

If he feels offended by how long it took, he says nothing. I'm a little surprised as I suspect this man is not made to wait for much.

"Thank you," he says.

Even these simple words possess deep authority—*Is he a general? A CEO? A political figure, perhaps?*—but the quick swallows as he drinks seem almost like ... *nervousness.*

I start to wonder why this seems so incongruous, but then I get distracted by the way his throat moves as he drinks. Throats shouldn't be sexy, especially when half hidden by a patchy beard. Neither should hands, but the way he grips his water glass has me wondering what those long fingers would feel like on the back of my neck, pulling me toward him.

I am really *losing it here.*

"I couldn't help but notice you didn't write down any orders," the man says, pulling me out of my racing—and *racy* —thoughts. He gestures to the loud table of tourists. "Were they simple, then?"

I raise my eyebrows. "Maybe I just have a brilliant mind."

He doesn't smile, but interest sparks in his eyes. "What are they having?"

"Are you looking for suggestions? I'm happy to recommend something on or off the menu."

He shakes his head once, with all the decisiveness and authority of a man signing a peace treaty. "No. I mean, yes, I would like your recommendations. But first, I want you to repeat their orders to me."

"Are you testing me?" I ask, crossing my arms.

His lips twitch the slightest bit, but I can't tell if he wants to smile or frown at the question. I'm good at reading people, but this man is like a wall of granite.

"Call me curious."

When I still hesitate, he offers a small smile, one that feels like a challenge. And also like a shot of adrenaline straight to my already overloaded heart.

"Is there some kind of restaurant confidentiality?" he asks. "Like with a physician or lawyer? Privacy laws protecting diners?"

The giggle bubbling up from me is a shock. I do NOT giggle. I smile. I laugh. I seat people and quickly deliver food. I don't do ... this. Whatever this is. Flirting? The concept is almost foreign to me. Somehow, this stranger is making me a stranger to myself.

"There's no confidentiality," I tell him. "It's just an unusual request."

"One which you seem reluctant to grant."

He doesn't call me a coward, not in so many words. But it's all right there as he sits back in his chair, slowly crossing his arms and raising his brows.

Definitely a challenge. Of what? And why?

Sighing, I put my hands on my hips, giving the table a cursory glance. "The man in the blue shirt—the one playing footsie under the table with the blonde who is not his wife— is having spaghetti with Bolognese sauce. His wife, a caprese salad, no oil. The blonde he's cheating with ordered gnocchi with extra sauce on the side."

I continue through the table's orders, including other personal bits as well, like how the dark-haired woman is pregnant, and how the man with the glasses is wagering on the horses and losing. Normally, I don't advertise this bizarre and mostly useless skill I've picked up. But keeping in line with my out-of-character night, I've just gone and showed off.

When I'm finished, my mouth snaps shut. I've said far too much. Why I felt the need to prove myself to this stranger at all, much less in such great detail, I cannot say.

"How can you tell?" He's leaning forward now, eyes sharp, a faint smile making his cheekbones rise.

"About the affair? The rift in the relationship? The gambling?"

"Yes—the gambling."

I glance over at the man with glasses. He's running his hands through his thinning hair again.

I nod to the televisions over the bar. Two have American sitcoms dubbed into Italian. The other has the races.

"When he came in, his mood matched the rest of the group. Jovial, pleasant. He went to the bathroom before I took their orders, and though I didn't see him ask, that third television was playing the news earlier. Now, it's on the horses. And his mood has changed. He's glued to his phone, worried. Probably moving money around as he wagers."

The stranger studies me, and there is appreciation in his gaze now. He doesn't ask how I can do this, and I'm glad because I actually think I would be tempted to tell him.

It started as a game I played, a guessing game. Growing up in a restaurant, I spent much time coloring or reading in a booth. I started to realize I enjoy people-watching more than crayons or stories.

At first, the guesses I made were just that—stories I made up. Fiction. The woman with the long, white braid is bringing food back to her pet dragon. The two children who were so ill-behaved are actually changelings, fae creatures sent to replace the real children. Those children are now in

28

the winter court, a faery prince and princess. The ideas were silly, stemming from whatever book I was reading at the time.

But as I grew older, I realized how many clues people gave away, even to things they didn't want to be known.

Except for some people, from whom I can read very little. Like the man in front of me, who is taking up too much of my time and absolutely too much of my mind. I catch Luci watching me from across the room. She gives me a wink and a big thumbs-up. I shake my head.

"You were right," the stranger says.

"About?"

"Your mind *is* brilliant."

I tell myself not to warm under his compliment, but my cheeks heat anyway. I lift a shoulder. "It's a trick waitresses everywhere pick up."

Slowly, methodically, the man shakes his head. "No," he says, "I don't think they do."

A lock of dark blond hair falls across his forehead. Until his fingers push it back in place, I can think of nothing else but that strand of hair. What would it feel like under my fingertips?

I can't explain the strangeness of this man's gravitational pull on me. But I need to remove myself from it as quickly as I can.

"Have you decided what you'd like?" I ask in what I hope is a polite, professional tone that does not give away my very unprofessional thoughts.

"Tonight, I am interested in what *you* like."

His tone is even and his blue eyes are steady, but his words feel weighted, like he is attaching some kind of importance to a simple dinner order.

"It's hard to say when I don't know what *you* like."

I shove my hands into the pocket of the half-apron around my waist. My fingertips brush against my tips and a spare few hair ties. A pen. A straw. These everyday objects ground me, reminding me of where I am, of who I am.

Of why I need to stop whatever is happening in my head and inside my body.

The man gestures to the tourists. "You made astute observations about them. Could you not guess what I might like?"

No. And that's the problem. I'm picking up little things about this man, but there's something larger I can't quite put my finger on. Or maybe my attraction to him is dulling my senses.

"I'm actually quite busy," I say, "So, if you could just—"

"What do *you* like best?"

His interest in me causes an unwanted flutter in my belly. I ignore it, hoping it will go away.

"I'm biased," I tell him.

His head tilts slightly to the side. "Why?"

"Because this is my grandfather's restaurant. All of the recipes are his, and I love them all."

He nods, as though unsurprised. "If you could choose one item from the menu to eat every day, what would it be?"

"That's a terrible question. I don't want to eat *any* food every day for the rest of my life."

"Fair point. How about now? What do you want to have right now, if you could have anything?"

What do *I* want?

The question irritates me, and my mind flips to Luci, telling me I don't allow myself to feel, to want.

But if I did ...

If I could have *anything* ...

It would be freedom. The freedom to travel the world. To

go to university. To meet someone I loved and have a big, loud family and also still something of my own. Something bigger than memorizing orders and making guesses about the people I'm serving.

None of this is on the menu. I glance over, watching Nonno rubbing his lower back absently as Luci animatedly tells him some story.

A sudden surge of unwanted emotion—longing mixed with regret and a heavy dose of familial guilt—floods me. I start to walk away, and the man grasps my wrist.

His touch is firm and possessive, yet his grip is light. The effect of it ricochets throughout my body in pulsing waves of heat.

"Did I offend you?" he asks. He looks genuinely concerned, which only floods me with more feelings I have no business having.

I twist my arm from his grasp. "I have to help other tables. As for your meal, I'll surprise you."

"Can I ask your name?"

I don't know why, but I feel like I shouldn't tell him. Like I should make something up or, like Rumpelstiltskin, tell him he has three guesses. Only, instead of taking his firstborn child, I'd make him promise to leave and never return.

Instead, I pause, meeting his unwavering blue gaze.

"Alessia. My name is Alessia Maria Elana Rossi Romano."

I expect amusement at my many names, or perhaps curiosity, but he simply holds my gaze. I don't offer up the explanation, which is that when my mother realized she was dying, she gifted me with a whole stack of names. Enough for all the daughters she'd never have—all her hopes pinned on me.

Swallowing hard, I ask, "And yours?"

"Phillip."

31

One name to my five. "Just Phillip?"

His jaw flexes, a tiny motion, but one I don't miss. He's not lying, but he is hiding something. Something big. Something big enough to make me more wary than I already am.

Run! I tell myself. *You should run!*

But my sense of self-preservation is clearly broken because I do not move. I wait for his answer and am rewarded with the smallest of smiles as he says, "Yes. Just Phillip."

CHAPTER 3

Phillip

THE MOMENT I put in the earpiece Claudius insisted I utilize on this trip, I regret agreeing to it. Two of my personal protection officers are stationed outside. Graves—the youngest man on my PPO team—and Martin—the most seasoned—are doing their best to look inconspicuous while watching me through the windows.

Even this is likely overkill. Enzo's restaurant holds no threats, except perhaps one related to eating oneself into a food coma. Wearing an earpiece seems ... excessive. And excessively annoying when I realize who else is speaking to me through the tiny device.

"You were supposed to keep the earpiece in for the duration," Claudius accuses, just as Callum says, "Did she say yes to the proposal? Did you kiss her? Tell me everything."

I groan softly. The restaurant has cleared out considerably

since I arrived, but I don't want to attract any more attention than I have already. The bartender—clearly enamored of Alessia—sees me as a threat and has been shooting me watchful glares. By *watchful*, I mean slightly murderous. Alessia's grandfather and his two friends also keep looking at me curiously. After Enzo brought my food, he sat down at their table, and I know they were talking about me in hushed, rapid-fire Italian.

Point being—to any curious (or murderous) eyes, I don't want to look like I'm talking to myself.

I shift my head slightly toward the wall, hoping this hides my moving lips. "I'm perfectly safe. Graves and Martin are standing just outside. This is unnecessary."

"You agreed," Claudius says.

"Perhaps too quickly," I mutter.

Disappearing from Elsinore was no small matter, and I'm grateful Claudius had a plan, even if I don't agree with all points. Specifically this one. But accompanied by a much smaller detail of personal protection officers and no cell phone to avoid tracking, Claudius insisted on the earpiece as an extra layer of security.

It's one I designed, but more for military and security goals, not this kind of mission. It has a geolocation tracker and utilizes satellite links, not cellular, impossible to intercept. If something were to happen to me, it's not like the almost invisible device would prevent it, but I suppose it makes Claudius feel some kind of national incident is less likely.

I see the point, to a degree. But I didn't want anyone to have a front-row seat (even simply through audio) as I met Alessia for the first time. Not that it would matter. She's avoided me ever since we exchanged names.

"Let's focus on what's important," Callum says.

"Agreed. Update us on your status," Claudius says.

Callum cuts in again. "Did you use any of my tips? How about the knuckle move? That one's a classic."

In the two weeks I spent preparing to briefly disappear from Elsinore, my brother made it his personal mission to supply me with advice on women. Callum's Charm School, he called it, and it was every bit as dreadful as it sounds.

Callum may have dated far more than I have, but this does *not* make him a fount of wisdom on the subject of how to woo one. Callum has never had to try. Not with his winning smile, his confidence, and his title. He could have the manners of a honey badger and still get any woman without any effort.

If he ever meets a woman who doesn't immediately fall under his spell, I'd love to watch him use the tips he gave me. Then we'll see how Callum's Charm School works.

I lift my water glass in front of my mouth and mutter, "No. I did *not* have a chance to drag my knuckles across her cheek while Alessia was taking my dinner order."

"You're at the restaurant right now?" Callum sounds shocked.

"Where did you think I would meet her? She's working tonight."

"I thought you'd show up and sweep her away to some-where private or romantic—like I suggested."

I considered it. I have backup plans upon backup plans. But I wanted to come here first, to meet Alessia and observe her in her own daily life. To see her as more than the summation of all the data points from the spreadsheets and Claudius's rubric.

To make sure I felt something.

"I wanted to meet her here first," I say.

"And?" Both Callum and Claudius ask at the same time.

And … Alessia is more than I expected. Much more.

More beautiful. More brilliant. More … *fiele.*

And she's avoiding me like I'm carrying a new strain of Spanish flu.

"She is unexpected," I finally answer.

Callum chuckles. "Now, there's a loaded answer. Details, please."

"Do you not like her?" Claudius asks carefully.

That's not it at all.

Despite our brief interactions and having to settle for observing her from a distance, I do like her. I *more* than like her.

And therein lies the problem.

I hoped for physical chemistry—and there's that in spades. To the point I couldn't answer when she asked what I wanted to drink.

It's not only her beauty, which is understated but made me catch my breath when I first saw her. In a simple t-shirt and pants, hair pulled up in a loose ponytail with no makeup, Alessia somehow outshines all the women Mum and Dad brought to the palace.

Something within Alessia seems to shine straight through, something electric and fiery and real, highlighting her big, dark eyes, her full lips, and the curve of her cheeks.

As I've watched her tonight, I've seen her kindness and humility, her ability to make anyone smile. She's vibrant and passionate. Whip-smart, with the kind of keenly observant eye that reminds me of Claudius. It's clear everyone here who knows her already loves her, and those who don't—the few tables of tourists passing through—are quickly won over by her. Including me.

But Alessia also seems deeply sad. Or perhaps deeply lonely? When she's not serving tables with a smile or making someone laugh, her face falls. Her shoulders slump—but only a little, as though even in these moments, she's aware enough to keep this secret longing hidden.

I find myself wanting to pull her into my arms, to hold her close and ask what she's thinking about in those moments when she looks lost. Somehow, within a few hours' time sitting at this table sipping water and watching, I've become completely invested in her.

Which ... was not the plan. It was not the backup plan or the backup to the backup plan.

I know Callum would tell me this is brilliant, that it's exactly what I wanted—a real connection rather than a logical match chosen by a rubric. But *that*—I knew how to handle.

This? I'm completely out of my element and all my plans have dissolved into dust.

Now? This idea seems preposterous and maybe even insulting.

Wrong—it's very, very wrong. Even if Alessia herself is *right*.

When this was more of a legal contract, a logical proposal to present, it felt manageable. If Alessia said yes, I'd take care of her grandfather financially. I'd take care of *her*. She would be my wife, my partner, and hopefully one day, this could blossom into love. Or at least, friendship and mutual respect.

But that was before I saw Alessia.

Before the thud of my heart became a pounding drum in my ears drowning out every other sound.

Before my words vaporized in her presence.

Before a light touch from her lit up nerve endings I didn't know I had.

It sounds ridiculous, I know. I would have scoffed at the idea. What are the chances that the one woman Claudius chose in the way he did would be the first woman to cause this kind of reaction in me? Unlikely. Impossible. Maybe it's the mere power of suggestion—my subconscious knowing Alessia is my choice for marriage and somehow fulfilling this in actuality.

That must be it.

Whatever the reason, now the plan that sounded practical —if also awkward and a little strange—is purely impossible.

Now, the words are gone. They are all wrong. I can't explain how watching Alessia all night has made this clear, but whatever I wrote, whatever I planned, it isn't right.

"Are you still planning to ask her?" Claudius says.

I watch Alessia make the German tourists laugh as she walks their group to the door. She has to feel me watching her, she has to know. And yet she intentionally won't look my way.

"I don't know."

Claudius makes a thoughtful hum, but Callum groans.

Callum sighs. "It's the beard. I told you the beard was a bad idea."

"It's not the beard," I murmur.

"It's uneven and hides your jawline. Women love a good jawline. You've got one, and you're hiding a valuable asset."

"It's not the beard," I practically growl.

But I find myself scratching my jaw. I *do* hate the beard. It grew in unevenly and looks messy. I hate messy. Plus, no one talks about how itchy beards are. Or how hot in the summer months. The first chance I get, I'm shaving it clean off.

"The beard was the quickest and easiest adjustment we could make to his physical appearance to help Phillip stay off the radar."

"Oh, he'll be off *all* the radars," Callum says. "Including the built-in radar women have to notice a sharp jawline."

I weigh the merits of taking out the earpiece and dropping it in my water glass.

Before I can think of any other response, I become aware of a voice calling from across the restaurant. It takes me another few seconds to realize the voice is addressing *me*.

"You, boy!"

I don't register that the man is speaking to me at first. But then one of Enzo's friends gestures to me and pats the seat at the table next to him with a smile.

The shiny dome of the man's head gleams in the light like a bald beacon. "Come," he says in heavily accented English. "Sit."

Has anyone ever called me *boy*? Or given commands that could be given to a dog? I am fairly certain the answer to both is NO.

It is ... oddly refreshing.

"What's happening?" Callum demands. I don't answer as I stand.

"Who's speaking to you?" Claudius demands, and I wonder how much this earpiece picks up.

"I'm fine." I try not to move my lips as I speak, so it sounds more like *I'n fine.*

"Is that German?" Callum asks. "I did hear people speaking German a moment ago."

"*Ein fine* in German means *a fine,* as in, a single fine," Claudius says. "It probably means he's fine. Or ... he received a fine?"

"It could be code. Did we ever come up with a safe word?" Callum asks. "Phillip, cough once if you're okay. Twice if you're under duress."

I wonder how many coughs would communicate *I'm going to murder you when I get back home.*

"I *am* fine," I say, running a hand over my mouth.

39

"They might be telling him to say that," Callum says. "Should we call in security? Is it time to pull the plug on Operation Bad Beard?"

I'm almost to the table but manage to mutter, "Shut. Up."

I hear what sounds like rustling and grunting on the other end—perhaps a scuffle?—but thankfully, no more words for the moment. I'd like to think that was the sound of Claudius removing my brother from the room. But my brother has a lot more muscle mass as well as years training in fight tactics, so I doubt I'll be so lucky.

Alessia's grandfather joins the other two men at their table as I do, smiling at me with warm brown eyes, crinkled at the corners. He puts a hand on my shoulder and squeezes.

"How was your meal?" he asks in English as I sit down.

"Delizioso. Grazi."

"Why are you speaking Italian to the Germans?" Callum asks, and I grit my teeth.

Still smiling, Enzo introduces the other two men as Sal and Gianni. Sal is the one who called me over, and up close I can see a small gap between his front teeth that makes his smile more endearing. Gianni has small, dark eyes and silver hair cut so close to his scalp that it stands up like a bristle brush. His frown is intense and intimidating.

Gianni scoffs and says something in such rapid Italian, I miss it. Something about a horse? Or perhaps a mule?

Alessia's grandfather pats my hand. "Don't listen to a thing he says."

"What did he say?" I ask. "My Italian is not the best."

Sal laughs. "You don't want to know, boy."

"It's nothing," Alessia's grandfather says, waving a dismissive hand while glaring at Gianni.

In my ear, Callum laughs and says, "I think he just called you a donkey."

40

"The backside of a donkey," Claudius corrects.

I do my best to tune them both out.

"Tell us what brings you to Repestro," Enzo continues.

I came to ask your granddaughter to marry me.

I swallow and try not to fidget. Asking Alessia's grandfather for his blessing was always part of the plan, even if I did so after broaching the subject with her. Maybe to some, this is an outdated custom, but to me, it is a way of showing respect and honoring her family.

But I'm not about to ask now.

"I am staying just to the north," I answer, giving the name of the slightly larger town about twenty minutes up the coast. Both Sal and Gianni *boo* until I add, "I came because I heard good things about the food here."

Enzo beams, and Sal slaps me on the back. I am relieved when my security officers don't come blasting through the door at the physical contact. I'm not sure how closely they're watching, but in Elsinore, no stranger would be allowed this kind of casual contact.

Gianni's frown deepens. This time, when he speaks, I pick out enough of the words to know he's asking what I did to offend Alessia.

So, I'm not the only one who noticed her avoiding me.

Enzo only *tsks* and replies quickly, saying something that sounds like, *You know how she is*, which sparks my curiosity.

Does she tend to avoid men? Did her remarkably keen insight reveal that I am here for reasons beyond the food? As extensive as Claudius's research was, there are so many aspects to a person that cannot show up in a dossier.

Enzo and Sal pepper me with more questions that I answer as best I can without lying or revealing anything more than I need to. I explain I work in technology—which is true when I'm not attending to my royal duties—and that I am on a trip to get away from it all.

"No wife?" Enzo asks.

I shake my head.

"No girlfriend?" Sal's smile is hopeful.

"None."

Enzo and Sal share a look, and Gianni's frown deepens. I follow the gist of his words. And the gist is that something must be wrong with me if I look like this and am still single.

Callum laughs in my ear. "I think he just called you hot. Guess the beard works for some people."

"You know," Enzo says slowly, as if an idea just occurred to him, "my granddaughter is also single."

Gianni grunts, and Sal beams. "What is it they say—single and ready to mingle?"

Enzo shakes a finger at his friend. "No one says that. And there will be no *mingling* of any kind."

Enzo says the word *mingling* like it means something else. Sal giggles, his eyes crinkling at the corners, and Gianni huffs, muttering something under his breath.

Enzo turns back to me, his expression serious. "But yes—Alessia is very much single and available for non-mingling activities."

Callum is practically braying with laughter in my ear. If one of us is a donkey, it's definitely my brother.

"She is beautiful, no?" Enzo asks.

I can only nod because that word doesn't even begin to describe her.

The kitchen door swings open, and Alessia walks out, glancing around the restaurant, now empty except for this table. When she sees me sitting with her grandfather and his friends, her whole body goes still. Then, her eyes narrow, and she strides toward our table.

As though they've been caught, the men straighten in their chairs, and Enzo shushes them. They remind me for a moment not of older men, but of children up to no good when their mother walks into the room.

I cannot tear my gaze away from Alessia as she approaches. She stops behind Gianni, arms crossed. Her deep brown eyes crackle with fire, her cheeks are flushed, and her hair is mutinously trying to escape the elastic holding it back.

"Well, isn't this cozy," she says. "You and the nonnos."

Until her glare lands on me, I don't realize I am smiling. I immediately force my face into a neutral expression.

"We're closed," she says to me in English.

"Ah, tesoro." Enzo clasps my arm. "The boy is with us."

Her eyebrows slowly lift. "The *boy*?"

Sal laughs, then reclines in his chair, leaning toward Enzo. "Ah, your Alessia is a smart girl. This is no boy. He is *all man*. A *single* man, Lessy."

Alessia's glare shifts to Sal, and I'm able to breathe again.

"Come, sit for a moment," Enzo says.

Alessia rolls her eyes, but when Gianni—whose tight expression softened remarkably at her appearance—pulls out a chair for her, she sits. Arms still crossed, she turns the heat of her glare on Enzo.

"Don't think for a moment I'm blind to what you're trying to do. It won't work," she says in quick Italian.

Unlike Gianni, her syllables are crisp and clear and I have little trouble understanding her. My stomach sinks a little at the words. Until Callum murmurs, "Methinks the lady doth protest too much."

I can only hope.

"Me?" Enzo presses a hand to his chest and feigns outrage. "What am I doing except extending the arm of hospitality to this young man?"

"I thought he was a boy."

Sal laughs, while Gianni goes back to shooting dark looks my way.

"Boy, man." Enzo waves a wrinkled hand. "The important thing is the strength of his arms."

My arms?

"His arms?" Alessia's brows shoot up, but I don't miss the way she looks me over.

"I hope you're flexing," Callum says. "A perfect opportunity to deflect her attention away from the bad beard and onto those guns."

I finally think I understand the prank war between my brother and Rafe.

The moment I'm home, I'll be launching my own campaign against Callum. Perhaps I could even team up with Rafe. Or get ideas from Claudius. He takes any task he's given seriously. After suffering through this with my brother, I think Claudius would be more than willing to give some ideas.

The important point is: I'm going to make my brother suffer.

"Yes, his arms." Enzo cups his hands around his mouth, not that he needs to do so, and shouts to the man behind the bar. "Antonio! The bags?"

Antonio's hostility rivals that of Gianni as he walks to our table carrying several large cloth totes. Stopping behind Alessia's chair, he sets the bags down with a thump and puts both hands on her shoulders.

He meets my eyes over her head. The man is clearly staking a claim.

The sight bothers me more than it should. When Alessia gives her shoulders a firm shake and wiggles out of his grasp, the tightness in my chest eases. Alessia's eyes meet mine, and I have to look away, afraid of what emotion my face might be displaying. Jealousy, most likely. And it's the first time I ever recall feeling this emotion.

Enzo gets to his feet with a slight groan, then makes his way over to the bags, picking them up and boxing Antonio out of the way with his body.

"His arms will help with deliveries," Enzo says, gesturing to me.

"I can help," Antonio offers, stepping around Enzo. "I'm always here to help. Every night, I'm here."

"What's wrong with Antonio's arms?" Gianni asks in English this time. "His are good arms. *Village* arms."

Antonio pulls his shirtsleeves up, revealing his biceps. Alessia drops her head into her hands, and Sal giggles.

Enzo waves Antonio away. "Get home to your mama. There's a bag in the fridge just for her. Go on," he adds when Antonio hesitates.

Giving me another look I know serves as a warning, Antonio sighs, then stomps back toward the bar, tossing his apron on the counter before disappearing through the swinging kitchen door.

"Come, boy," Enzo says, giving my sleeve a tug.

I stand, and Sal eyes me appreciatively.

"He has more than just arms," Sal says. "He's got the whole present."

"Package," Enzo corrects. "I think you mean he has a good package."

Now it's not only Callum laughing in my ear but Claudius too. I'm not sure I've ever heard the advisor laugh, and it distracts me for a moment from the embarrassment at hand.

"*Nonno!*" Alessia hisses.

"What?" Enzo says, then gestures to me. "The boy has a perfect package. No?"

I've endured many uncomfortable public events. But never have I felt the depths of embarrassment I do now.

Alessia's cheeks are crimson. "The phrase is *the whole package*," she says, then mouths, *"I'm so sorry"* to me.

I'll take her attention, even if it's under humiliating circumstances.

Enzo waves a hand. "That's what I said! He's got a whole, good package."

She groans and gets to her feet. "That is *not* what you're saying. And please, *please* stop saying the word package."

Alessia bends close to her grandfather and speaks in passionate, quick Italian until he starts to laugh. Sal, who has hardly stopped giggling since I came over, laughs even harder. Gianni continues to glare.

Tears spill down Enzo's cheeks, and he finally slumps back in his chair. His watery eyes, crinkled at the corners from his wide smile, meet mine.

He clears his throat before speaking, still on the verge of laughter. "We need your whole package"—Alessia slaps a hand to her forehead and says what sounds like a quick prayer—"to help my granddaughter with deliveries."

I don't know what kind of deliveries, but if it means spending time with Alessia and escaping from this present humiliation, I'm there.

"I would love to help," I say, reaching for one of the bags.

Alessia snatches both of them first. They appear to be heavy, but she steps out of reach. "I've got it. I do this every night alone. I'll be *fine*."

She glares at her grandfather before heading to the door. I hesitate, unsure if I should follow. Everything in me says I should, but the last dark look she shoots me clearly says I should stay back.

"Go on, boy!" Sal says, waving toward the door.

"Maybe the boy is afraid," Gianni says, his accented English almost as difficult to understand as his Italian. "Strong arms. Weak heart."

Enzo clucks his tongue. "My granddaughter might make you give chase. But she is a prize worth catching."

With a quick nod, I bolt for the door. I push through into the warm summer evening, as a cheer erupts from inside the restaurant, and I chase after Alessia.

CHAPTER 4

Phillip

ALESSIA IS HALFWAY down the deserted block and shows no sign of slowing. In fact, I'm pretty sure her pace picked up the moment I hit the sidewalk.

"Alessia!" I call, but she continues forging ahead. For someone much shorter than I am, she possesses a remarkably quick stride.

"Alessia Maria Elana Rossi Romano!" I shout, and this makes her halt.

It also makes a few dogs bark nearby, and a light flicks on in the cottage I'm standing outside.

Alessia turns slowly, her eyes wide.

"Bonus points for remembering all her names," Callum says in my earpiece.

I memorized each and every one the day Claudius gave me the dossier. I've been whispering her many names under my breath like a prayer or song lyrics. It is a wholly different experience shouting her full name in this dark, sleepy village. I want to say it again—this time as a whisper in her ear while I hold her close. I swallow.

The surprise on Alessia's face morphs, and her features harden. If I thought Gianni's glare in the restaurant was intense, it has nothing on hers.

Even furious, she looks beautiful.

"You can't just yell in the street!" she whisper shouts. "People are sleeping!"

"People *were* sleeping!" a voice calls. A woman with a long, gray braid leans out from an upstairs window. "Does your nonno know where you are, girl?"

Alessia sighs. She shoots another glare at me, then an apologetic look at the woman. "Yes, Maria. I'm just trying to tell this man to go home. He won't stop following me."

Maria squints down at me, and my skin feels hot. I search for the words in Italian to explain I'm not some stranger chasing after Alessia before this woman comes down with a cast iron skillet or a hunting rifle.

I'm still struggling with words when the woman—Maria, I guess—pulls a pair of reading glasses from her nightdress and leans further out the window. Dangerously far. Almost unconsciously, I step closer to the building in case I need to break her fall.

Maria smiles, then waves dismissively. "Ohhh, yes. We've all heard about him. The tourist with the perfect package!"

I die just a little bit right there on the sidewalk.

In my ear, Callum snorts, then says, "That's it. Operation Bad Beard has been officially renamed. From henceforth, we shall call it Prince Perfect Package."

I'm grateful when my brother's laughter gets cut off, and I can only hope Claudius kicked him out of whatever room

49

they're in, listening to my miserable and seemingly unending humiliation.

How did Maria even hear about what Enzo said? The conversation just happened minutes ago. Does gossip travel *that* quickly in this town?

If so, the gossip sites in Elsinore have nothing on the rumor mill in Repestro.

"Let him carry a bag, girl," Maria calls. "Let him carry *you* if he asks. He looks like he could manage. It could be fun. You could definitely use some fun."

Alessia's cheeks burn red. "No, Maria, I don't—"

Maria waves her hand again, more of a shooing motion this time. "Go on. Playing hard to get isn't all it's cracked up to be. Trust me."

A second head pops out of the window, and a bearded man squints down at us. He harrumphs and turns toward Maria.

"Playing hard to get gave you all this," he says, gesturing to his bare chest, wide and blanketed with silver hair. "Now get back to bed, woman."

Maria laughs, waves to Alessia, and ducks back inside.

"Goodnight, Lessy," the man calls down.

"Goodnight, Ernesto," Alessia says quietly.

As he closes the window, I hear him mutter, "His package doesn't seem all that perfect to me."

I squeeze my eyes closed and clench my jaw. Could this evening have gone any more poorly?

Alessia clearly wants nothing to do with me, and the occupants of the town—at least those I've met—seem determined to humiliate me while trying to force her to spend time with me. This was a mistake. What's more—I really want a chance to get to know Alessia more. My disappointment at my utter failure has less to do with not fulfilling my goal and more to do with my personal feelings about *her*.

At the sound of a *thunk*, I open my eyes. Alessia has dropped one of the bags at my feet. Her expression is hard to read, but it's not angry. She's not ignoring me or sending me away. The small smile barely lifting one corner of her lips affects me far more than it should.

"Might as well make yourself useful." Her tiny smile grows by an infinitesimal amount. Before I can respond, she's off, dark ponytail swinging as she calls over her shoulder, "Try to keep up, *boy*."

———

I follow Alessia from home to home as she drops parcels on porches like she is the fairy godmother of delicious food. The analytical side of my brain keeps worrying about things like refrigeration and spoiling, but I'm trying to ignore it.

"Do you do this every night?" I ask as we turn a corner and walk to another quiet street. My voice sounds obscenely loud.

"Most nights," Alessia says, which sounds more like she means *all*. "Nonno and I like to share the extras."

We've stopped at no less than six houses already, and my bag is still heavy. Alessia must know as well as I do that these carefully packaged and labeled meals are in no way *extras*.

She and her grandfather are intentionally feeding less fortunate families in the village on a nightly basis.

This is one detail that escaped Claudius's very thorough follow-up dossier I requested about Alessia. What he did make note of were Enzo's financials. And they are not great.

At least, not good enough to account for what these "extras" must cost. This is frankly irresponsible.

It's also admirable.

Alessia stops in front of a cottage with a worn wooden door and two lights—one burned out, the other flickering. Shadows pool at her feet as she reaches into the bag she's carrying. The moonlight paints her cheeks, somehow making her more beautiful.

"Whose home is this?" I ask.

Alessia places two parcels on the stone stoop. "The Costas. They have three young children."

"Ah. How lovely."

She snorts, then covers her mouth, barely stifling a giggle. "You'd say something quite different if you met them."

"Are they *not* lovely?" I ask.

"No," Alessia says, still laughing a little. "They're little monsters. I babysit them once a week and barely make it out alive each time. If you ever have the misfortune of seeing them in the village, run."

"How will I recognize them?"

"Believe me, you'll know them when you see them." She pauses, looking down as she folds up her now-empty bag. Without moving closer, she slides it inside the bag I'm carrying. "Although you may not need to worry about it since you won't be here long."

I swallow, and Alessia turns her whole body toward me, meeting my gaze head-on. Her dark eyes are mesmerizing, pinning me in place and forcing me to suck in a breath.

"You *aren't* staying long, are you?"

It sounds like a challenge, and I swear, I can feel both Alessia and Claudius waiting for my answer. They've been utterly silent since Alessia invited me to join her. Which likely means Claudius has Callum's mouth duct-taped or simply had him tossed from the room.

What I wish I could tell from Alessia's question is whether she wants me to stay. I clear my throat, which seems to have locked up tight. "I'm not entirely sure yet. My plans are ... flexible."

"They absolutely are not flexible," Callum corrects, startling me. So—he's not duct-taped. "You must be on the royal jet in sixty-one hours and twenty-three minutes to save me from the dinner with the foreign advisors."

Leave it to Callum to be counting down the minutes.

One of the integral parts to this plan working—aside from me finally revealing who I am and the purpose of my visit—is the length of time for which I can conceivably be gone without notice. It would be an absolute state of emergency if my absence were to be discovered. Callum is covering for me, saying I'm not feeling well but not sick enough for the royal physician. So far and to my surprise, this has worked.

Alessia studies me. "You don't look like the kind of man whose plans are ever flexible."

I shouldn't be surprised by her insight, given what she noticed at the table of German tourists. I wonder how much of me she does see.

"You seem like the kind of man who has very firm plans, in fact."

"Quite correct."

"And those plans involve returning quickly with a fiancée," Callum says. "Let's get on with it."

If I could remove the earpiece without Alessia noticing and crush it under my heel against the cobbled sidewalk, I would.

She tilts her head, and though I love having her gaze on me, I also must resist the urge to squirm at her scrutiny.

"I expect that you have people depending on you, which would prevent you from taking indefinite time off. Your responsibilities matter to you, and as such, your 'flexible' plans won't allow you to stay in Repestro long." She arches an eyebrow. "Am I close?"

Too close. Yet … I'm very sure she has no idea who I really am. And she'd never guess why I'm here. This is the perfect opportunity to say something truthful.

But I don't. Even though the longer I go without telling Alessia who I am, the harder and larger and more difficult this truth becomes.

"Keen observations. You are quite right."

If she only knew how well I already know her. I've studied and memorized all the details from the longer dossier Claudius composed. Which suddenly feels like I'm cheating on the most important exam of my life.

I've always valued honesty. Yet, here I am, hiding so much from Alessia. How would Alessia respond if I told her I've been studying her from afar, memorizing the key details about her life?

A dark curl blows across her cheek, and my mouth goes dry. The urge to brush away that strand of hair is almost overwhelming now, my fingers twitching against my palm as I stand here like some kind of statue.

The air between us dances—alive, electric. I almost wonder if she's thinking about kissing me. But after a moment, she steps back, the moment passing.

"We've got a few more houses to go. You look tired, Just Phillip. I'd guess you're a morning person."

I fall into step beside her, close enough that our arms almost touch. "Wrong."

Her head whips my way, her long hair brushing my arm. She looks skeptical. "Really? You're not a morning person?"

54

"Well. I do like mornings, yes. I'm up early. But I tend to be very busy late at night."

Her eyes widen a little, and I realize how that might sound. I am not a man who blushes—something which I'm very grateful for—but if I did, I would be a tomato right now.

"With machines, not people," I add, picturing my second office, which adjoins my bedroom, filled with computers and devices. With my royal duties during the day, nights are the only time I can still indulge my interest in technology.

Alessia chokes out a laugh. "You're getting busy with machines late at night?"

Good grief. I've made it worse.

"No! Not like—*no*."

Alessia laughs harder, bending over and clutching her waist.

"Forget sixty-one hours," Callum says, laughing in my ear. "You'll be on the royal jet headed home in thirty minutes."

"It's not whatever you're thinking," I say.

"I am trying not to think *anything*," Alessia says, straightening and wiping her eyes. "I'm definitely trying not to form a mental image."

"I work primarily in developing smart technology, though it's more of a hobby at the moment." Now that Father's health has declined, the time I've had to work on anything has diminished almost to nothing.

"What's your official job, then? Let me guess—government intelligence? You're a spy."

I hesitate. "It's a … family's business."

Callum laughs in my ear. "Now you sound like you're in the mafia. Brilliant."

"Are you in the mob, Just Phillip? Perhaps a contract killer with a heart of gold?"

I chuckle. "I have never taken a life. And I'm not so sure about my heart."

"So, that's a no to the mafia? Or just no to being a mafia hit man?"

"No mafia."

"But you don't want to discuss your family business?"

"I'd prefer not to at this time. But you're welcome to ask me about other topics."

I wait for her to ask why and press for an answer. Or even to ask me *why* I won't answer. Instead, she switches directions.

"How many languages do you speak—that is, when you're not busy with machines or the non-mafia family business?"

"Four. Elsinorian is my native tongue. Then English, Spanish, and Italian—in order of my proficiency. You?"

"Not quite as impressive. Italian and English. A little Spanish. Are you from Elsinore? I don't know much about the country, I'm sorry to say."

Probably better she doesn't, or else she might have recognized me. "Yes. I live there with my family."

Her head rears back a little. "Your *family*?"

"My parents, a brother, and two sisters," I clarify, leaving out all the other staff and employees who *also* live in the palace. "I'm not married. I wouldn't be here with you like this if I were."

"Good. I mean, not that we're ... I mean, this isn't some kind of—"

"Date?" I smile. For the record, Alessia when she's flustered is adorable.

"Yes," she says.

"Yes, it is a date?"

Alessia shakes her head, grinning, and nudges me with her shoulder. "For English not being your first language, you're quite good at word play. *Yes*, I meant date. And *no*—that's not what this is."

"What would you call it? Perhaps ... a precursor to a date?"

"That would imply a date will follow," she says, shooting me a quick gaze that's teasing. "And I make no promises. We can call it a stroll, perhaps? Or maybe a grocery delivery."

"It's certainly the best stroll I've ever been on," I say. "If that's what we're calling it. And I'd really like to stroll and deliver groceries with you again. You say you do this every night? Same time tomorrow?"

Alessia stops in front of a doorway, this one with fresh flowers trailing from a pot outside. She reaches for my wrist and then leans closer, rummaging through the bag. I resist the urge to lean closer, and instead, relish in the way her fingers still circle my wrist and the way the ends of her pony-tail tickle my arm.

Finally, she finds the parcel, stepping away to place it by the door. When she turns back to face me, she puts her hands on her hips.

"Just Phillip, are you asking me on a date? Because I have a policy against dating men who don't live in my village, much less ones who don't live in my country."

"But we aren't talking about dating; we're talking about strolling. What's your policy on strolls? Because I'd love to join you again tomorrow night."

Alessia hesitates. Her weight shifts from one foot to the other. She bites her lip and looks down at the sidewalk between us. My heart seems to contract and hold—waiting, waiting, waiting.

Finally, she looks up. When her brown eyes meet mine, I feel as though I've stepped straight off the edge of a cliff.

When she smiles, I hit the cool water below, completely submerged, weightless.

"I think my policy could allow for another stroll," she says slowly. "At the very least, it is nice to have your arms to carry the bags."

"So, you'll have me just for my arms?"

She smiles. "Your company is not altogether horrible."

"'Not altogether horrible,'" I repeat. "I'll have that printed on my business cards."

"Aw," Callum whispers, a jarring reminder that I'm not fully alone with Alessia. "Look at my big brother, flirting. Who knew he could!"

"Did I upset you?" Alessia asks. "You look annoyed."

"I'm not annoyed with you," I say, wondering how I can make Callum suffer later.

"Good. Because we still have packages to deliver. Now, come on. We don't have all night."

With that, she turns, her dark ponytail swinging, and starts off again.

It's not a date. It's not even quite a yes. But as I hurry to catch up with Alessia, I realize I've never looked forward to anything more.

CHAPTER 5

Alessia

LUCI FINDS me the next night in the walk-in freezer, pacing and wringing my hands like some kind of melodramatic, popsicle-loving heroine.

"I knew you'd be here." Luci's smirk quickly turns into a frown as she rubs her arms. "Brr! Why does your special thinking place have to be subzero?"

"It's the one place in the restaurant where Antonio won't follow me," I say.

Once, and only once, Antonio accidentally locked himself in the walk-in freezer after a few too many glasses of wine. Nonno found him the next morning, and if my grandpa hadn't come in early for a shipment, Antonio might not have been so lucky. When I need a moment to myself, I prop a bag of flour in the doorway and pace. Cold air is clarifying for my thoughts.

Usually, anyway. Tonight, my thoughts remain cloudy. Like a thick fog where my visibility is limited. All I can see is Phillip.

It's almost time for our second date—*stroll*, I mentally correct, *NOT a date*. Only a few patrons are left, and Phillip is already here, sitting with the nonnos.

I'm excited.

I'm anxious.

I'm regretting all my life choices. Most especially this one.

"Why are you in here when you could be somewhere warmer, making out with the handsome stranger who can't take his eyes off you?"

"Gah!" I throw both hands up and go back to pacing. "Stop giving me bad ideas!"

Especially when I've already thought about bad ideas since the moment Phillip walked into the restaurant last night. As he walked with me to deliver food—*more* bad ideas. His presence completely throws me off balance and off my game. Not that I *have* game. Or, if I did, my game would be something like Keep Away (From Me). At the very same time, being around Phillip is somehow steadying. He's inquisitive and thoughtful, a good listener, and didn't lay on the charm too thick—even while he made his interest clear. I can't imagine feeling safe walking late at night alone with any other man I'd just met.

Which makes Phillip the wild waves of the sea and a lighthouse offering safe passage.

I barely kept myself from kissing him when Phillip walked me home. Essentially, the second we got to the door, I waved erratically, said goodbye far too loudly, and bolted inside.

Tonight? I'm not so sure I'll have such restraint. And with Luci planting a garden of bad ideas sure to bloom in my head …

Luci's smile widens. "Who says they're bad ideas? Or, who says being bad isn't sometimes very, *very* good?"

"Out." I point to the door. "You're ruining my ice palace. I need a brain break, and you're in here breaking my brain."

The teasing glint fades from Luci's eyes, replaced with something softer. "Aw, Lessy."

"Oh, no you don't," I say, crossing my arms. "I don't need your … whatever this is. It looks like pity."

Growing up in a nosy village as the orphan girl who lost her parents far too young, I am very well-acquainted with pity. Love and kindness, I appreciate. But anything that looks even faintly like feeling sorry for me—NO. It sets my teeth on edge and makes me stabby.

"It's not pity," Luci says. "It's *concern*. It's *love*."

"Take your concern and love, plus your bad ideas about kissing Phillip—"

Luci barrels toward me, and I back up. Because when she gets fixated on an idea, she goes feral.

Before I can escape, she grabs me in what I like to call a Luciana Signature Attack Hug. Her arms pin mine to my sides, and she hooks one leg around one of mine so I'm unable to run. I'm practically holding up all her weight. Thankfully, my friend's size is the opposite of her emotions.

Her feelings: huge.

Luci: tiny.

"You," she says fiercely somewhere near my collar bone, "are allowed to dream."

"I know I—"

"Shush! This is *my* time, down here."

"Not *Goonies* again," I groan.

Luci is obsessed with the actor Sean Astin. She's been methodically making me watch anything he's ever had even a tiny role in, from *Stranger Things* to *Mom's Night Out* to all the

Lord of the Rings movies and everything in between. Now, anytime Luci has something important to say, she quotes Mikey from *Goonies*.

"Luci, please. I don't have time for the speech."

"Shh! There's always time. You don't let yourself dream, and it's time to stop holding back."

"I have plenty of dreams."

"Yes, but you don't allow yourself to think those dreams could become reality. You wanted to go to college, but you didn't."

"I'm taking online classes!"

Luci scoffs. "Like one a semester. At this rate, you'll have a degree when our grandkids are getting married. And that's another one! You're a romantic but pretend you're not."

Can't argue there.

"You want a family and kids so badly."

Also very true. Maybe because I grew up almost solely with Nonno, I envision a big, loud house full of big, loud people. *My* people. I see Nonno there, laughing, with a child on his knee while another few run around, possibly chased by Sal or Gianni, who is the gruffest softie I've ever met.

But this dream has a prerequisite: a man I love right beside me, managing and relishing the chaos together.

I want it all so badly, it burns when I think of it. I'm burning now, and I half expect Luci to notice the heat coursing through me since she's still plastered to my body like a too-tight jacket.

"You don't even have a cell phone!"

"What does that have to do with this? I hate cell phones. Everyone is glued to them and they cause cancer and—"

"The studies are inconclusive on that. It's relevant because you don't have a cell phone in order to sever any link to the outside world. Just in case you might decide you want to leave Repestro for it."

Okay, fine. My best friend *might* have a tiny point here, though I've never thought about it that way. Perhaps not having a cell phone *is* my way of wearing blinders, of keeping my world small.

Luci squeezes me a little tighter. "You know I love you. I want to see you happy—truly happy. Not just pretending that limping along is the same as building a life you actually want. You can't find happiness if you don't allow yourself to hope for it. To dream of it. To take brave risks to get it. You know that you're the bravest person I know."

I sniff, only then realizing I'm crying. "I'm not brave. I had to call Nonno to kill a spider in the shower yesterday."

"I know. I heard you screaming from Marco's house."

"Shut up."

"Make me." Her grip tightens, forcing a wheeze out of my chest. I might have inches and pounds on my tiny friend, but we both know she could take me.

We're both quiet for a minute.

"He doesn't live here, Luci. It's Stefan all over again."

"That man out there sitting with the nonnos is nothing like Stefan!"

It's true—Phillip is nothing like my ex, whose red flags all should have been obvious to me. I'm usually so good at reading people, but I was blinded by the man from Spain with his dark hair and deep voice and way of making me feel beautiful and wanted—until he made me feel the exact opposite.

After he left with no warning after stringing me along, his selfishness and narcissism were all too clear.

But after knowing Phillip for only twenty-four hours, I know he's nothing like Stefan—except in the one area it matters most. Phillip sat quietly, patiently, all night waiting to talk to me. Phillip won Nonno over—something Stefan never did. Sal too—though Gianni will be a harder nut to crack. Phillip delivered food to the village with me and agreed to another non-date, doing the same.

Everything feels different with him, including my own reactions, which are far more than physical. My attraction to the man goes so far deeper than the surface, it's almost subterranean.

Which makes this all the more terrifying.

"He's leaving," I whisper.

"So, go with him," Luci counters.

"You know I can't." Even if he asked. And it's been one night. Why would he ask?

"You won't turn into a pillar of salt if you set foot outside of the village. And Nonno would be furious if he knew you're staying here for him, giving up your dreams for him."

She's right. I *know* she is. And I suspect Nonno knows my dreams are bigger than this tiny village. But I also can't help but feel like it would break both our hearts if I ever did leave.

"You're thinking too far ahead," Luci says. "For now, for tonight, think only about the man out there—"

"Who might be a serial killer or a criminal on the run, hiding out so he doesn't have to pay off his gambling debts in Monaco. I still know almost nothing about him."

"There is something very wrong with your brain, Lessy. No. He could be the start of your happily ever after."

My chest constricts at those words, folding in on itself like it's facing imminent collapse.

Happily ever after. Is that something I can even have outside of my one allowed daydream per week?

Does *anyone* ever really get that?

Nonno's happily ever after looked like losing his wife to

cancer, then his daughter to childbirth, and his son-in-law to a car accident not too many years after. It looked like being saddled with the care of a young girl when he had already raised and lost his daughter.

Not that he would ever admit he minded the burden or thought of me that way. I don't think I'm the only one pretending to be content with the lot I've been given. I think we're lying about some of the most important things, to ourselves and to each other.

"Happily ever afters aren't real," I whisper.

Hope disappoints, I think.

Love hurts.

"Not like the fairy tales," Luci concedes, finally loosening her freakishly strong grip on me enough to meet my gaze. "Of course not like that. Real happily ever afters are messier and involve fights and making up and heartache and happiness all tangled up. They are real. Just not like the books. And you'll never experience the beautiful parts and the messy parts unless you take a chance."

I know my best friend is right. I *know* it.

But I also know my reality, and the tiny flame of hope in me dims when I think of Nonno alone in the tiny cottage we currently share. Nonno trying to manage the restaurant and all he does without me. Nonno with all his family *gone*.

Luci puts her hands together, pleading. "Get to know this man who is clearly interested in you and, statistically speaking, is probably not a serial killer," she says.

"If you tell me once more that it's *my time down here*, I'll lock you in this freezer. I'll do it. Don't think I won't."

Luci's tiny but strong hands grip my shoulders, giving me a little shake. "What would Sean Astin do?"

"Easy. He'd sacrifice himself for the greater good and get eaten by a demogorgon."

Luci groans, dropping her hands to cover her face dramatically. "We never should have watched *Stranger Things*."

"Hey—you're the one with the Sean Astin obsession. It's not my fault."

"You're wrong though. Because this is what Sean Astin would do—he would take risks for love. Give the man a chance." She says it like we're bargaining, like this is a negotiation.

Well, too bad for her. Like they're always saying in American movies, I don't negotiate with terrorists.

"We'll see."

"We'd better." Luci squeezes me once more in a tight hug and steps back. I swear, my ribs might be bruised. "Now, if you don't mind, Marco is waiting, and I think my nipples have frostbite."

———

As Phillip and I hike, other than the occasional owl's hoot and our footfalls on the rocky path, the loudest sound is his labored breathing. I smile, then glance over my shoulder where he trudges behind me. I find it ridiculously amusing that this big, strong man is struggling with a little hike.

"Are you okay back there?" I ask.

"Just … not used to … hills," he pants.

"I thought Elsinore was a mountainous country. Don't you share a border with Switzerland?"

"I live in … a valley."

Taking pity on him, I pause along the narrow trail. When Phillip catches up to me and leans on a scrubby tree for support, the grin he shoots me is sheepish.

"Enjoying this?" he asks.

I laugh. "A little. It's fun to see someone so fit struggling with something simple."

The grin he gives makes me regret my compliment. It's the kind of smile it's hard to come back from. The kind I wouldn't mind seeing every morning for the rest of my life.

Which is exactly the kind of thought I can't have right now. I blame Luci—planting her garden of bad ideas in my mind.

"You think I'm fit?"

Not answering *that* one. "Need me to carry the bag for you?" I ask in an extra sweet voice.

He narrows his eyes, pulling the bag behind his back. There's only one bag tonight, and he insisted on carrying it. "No."

"Suit yourself." I turn away, starting the climb again. "Come on, Just Phillip. We don't have all night."

He groans, but I hear him following behind me. We don't talk again—probably partly because Phillip really is struggling as we climb the narrow, steep path—but it's not an uncomfortable silence. With a warm breeze blowing my hair off my neck, the moonlight kissing my skin, and Phillip nearby, I feel more at peace than I have in a long time.

Before we started up the hill and Phillip lost his ability to speak, I pestered him with questions. I told myself it was because I was looking for red flags or reasons *not* to be interested. Instead, I found his love for his family endearing, and though he lost me the moment he started talking about technology, I'm impressed with his geeky side. Not that I have any interest in such things (see: aforementioned lack of cell phone), but it's clear he's very bright.

Other than the bullfighter-sized red flag of being from another country, the biggest issue I've found is the way Phillip dances around the specificity of what he actually does for a living. I know based on the two bodyguards who have been shadowing us—which I haven't brought up yet but plan to—Phillip is someone important.

Maybe he simply wants to be liked for who he is as a person, not for what he does or where he works.

Maybe he's a disgraced heir, and though I didn't recognize his face, I'll know his last name and not want anything to do with him or his family.

Maybe I should listen to Luci and take a chance.

"Where are ... we ... headed?" Phillip asks, just as I reach the top of the hill.

I turn at the edge of the clearing, waiting for Phillip to join me. "This is the DeSanti homestead. They've lived here decades and have been harvesting this vineyard for just as long." My words, despite themselves, turn bitter. "At least, until the vineyard owners died and some British conglomerate purchased it."

"They didn't still need workers?" Phillip asks.

"They brought in their own."

It's one more blow to Repestro's economy. What was—before my time—a small but thriving village has been in a slow decline. Maybe *decay* is a better word. Nonno's restaurant is the only business truly making money.

Tourism is our best option to revitalize, but it would take businesses and money—plus, something to draw people here. It's hard enough even *keeping* people here. Mostly, children grow up, go off to universities or other cities for work, and never return. With rocky cliffs rather than beaches, Repestro will never have the draw like the Italian Riviera or Cinque Terre, which bring tourists in droves. Our one beach is small and difficult to climb down to, with strong currents not safe for weaker swimmers.

Repestro is dying. This is why every night, I deliver food

Nonno makes to various families in the village. I told Phillip these were extras, but he's smart enough to know there's nothing *extra* about them. Not for Nonno, who cuts into his profits by intentionally cooking and baking more than he needs to, and not for the families who don't know what extra is. We have little to give, but we do what we can.

"Here we are," I say, turning toward the house, which is little more than a shack.

The wood may be rotting and the stones crumbling, but there are signs of life and care. A wreath woven from wildflowers hangs on the door, which is painted a bright, cheerful blue—even if it looks ready to fall off the hinges. I can't imagine how much longer the DeSantis can hang on this way. The thought makes me ache.

I wish I could do something, something more. Something bigger. I'm doing all I can, but it's not enough.

I avoid Phillip's gaze and begin to pull parcels out of the bag.

"Let me." His hand covers mine and gently takes the parcels I'm clutching.

Our eyes meet in the darkness, and there's something so kind in his, so genuine, that I cannot hold his gaze. I look down, watching as he bends to carefully place everything by the door. I squeeze my eyes closed, trying to steady my breathing, which has become strained.

Phillip's fingers brush mine. "Alessia," he says softly.

I didn't think my chest could grow any tighter, but it does. "Yes?"

"Open your eyes."

When I do, Phillip's smile is gentle. He nudges my hand with his. I glance down and see a tiny pink wildflower held between his fingers.

"Did you steal this from the wreath on the door?" I ask.

"Maybe."

I try to keep my voice light, though the moment feels heavy. "I didn't take you for a thief."

Of anything but my heart, which I think he stole the moment I first saw him, despite trying to hold myself tightly in check.

He shrugs, lifting the flower toward my ear. "May I?"

My heart beats wildly, battering my ribs. I clench my fists to keep them from shaking. "Yes."

I close my eyes again and suck in a breath as Phillip gently places the flower behind my ear. Without my sight, I'm more aware of my other senses. The sound of Phillip's breathing, steady and slow. My own heart beating wildly in my ears.

The scent of him—warm and spicy, strong and masculine.

The soft brush of his fingertips as they graze my ear, then trail down my cheek, as gentle a caress as the wind.

And he'll be gone just as fast as a breeze. Here, then gone, I remind myself. But myself isn't listening.

Phillip's fingers trace a light path down my jaw. I want to grab his hand and hold it in place against my cheek. I want to step into his arms and lose myself in the moment. I want to lift up on my toes and kiss him.

I want too many things I can't have.

He drops his hand, and the moment passes. When I sway on my feet, his hand wraps around my shoulder, steadying me. I open my eyes, finding his gaze heavy on me.

"You must be exhausted," he says, a crease forming between his brows.

"I've been on my feet all day. I think I got a little lightheaded." I am lightheaded, but it has nothing to do with being tired or spending too long on my feet.

70

No, it has everything to do with the man whose hand I don't want to ever let me go.

"Would you like me to carry you back down?" he asks, lifting a brow.

I step away because I must. I need to clear my head. And yet, when Phillip's hand lets go of my arm, I want to weep. I force a teasing smile on my face. "You could hardly make your own way up the hill, Just Phillip. How could I expect you to carry me down?"

Before he can answer, I snatch the empty bag and start down the path at a quick pace.

Phillip has a much easier time going down. The trail is only wide enough for one, and I try to regain control of myself as we descend back toward the village. When we reach the bottom, we both stop, standing awkwardly on the sidewalk.

Phillip rocks back on his heels, his hands in his pockets. "Is this the end of our *stroll*?"

I should say yes. I should let him walk me to Nonno's door and rush inside again before my body can betray me. "It doesn't have to be."

"I don't want it to be."

I incline my head and start walking, Phillip matching my pace. "Do you do a lot of *strolling*, Just Phillip?"

"Hardly any. Which may make me rubbish at it."

"You're doing just fine."

Almost as an afterthought, like he forgot to ask or somehow already knew the answer to his question, Phillip asks, "What about you? Are you a frequent *stroller*?"

I snort. "No. There aren't many people to *stroll* with in the village or even nearby. And even if there were ..."

I can't finish THAT sentence, which would have ended with something like *none of them would compare to you.*

"Why don't you *stroll* more often?" I ask, feeling silly that we're talking so obviously about dating without saying the word.

Phillip considers. I like this about him—he rarely answers without first thinking about his words.

"I'm very busy, and I haven't met anyone who made me want to stop being busy long enough to do so." Another pause, this one even longer. "I'm not a casual stroller. I want strolling to mean something."

Okay, now my body's on full alert. Because we *are* strolling. Right now, at this very moment, strolling right down the main road in the village. And, according to what he just said, he hasn't previously met many women who have made him want to do so.

And he's here. With me. Now.

Though, what we're talking about is actually *dating*. Maybe even relationships—not strolling.

Is that what we're really doing—going on a date that I've insisted we call something else?

And is Phillip saying that after not finding anyone he wants to date, he does want that with me?

I really wish I hadn't insisted on calling this a stroll, because now I'm unsure. I don't want to read more into this than I should. I mean, I *think* I know what Phillip is saying. But it's hard to believe that he's interested in a lowly waitress in a tiny village he stopped into just for a good meal. That ... doesn't happen.

As though sensing the way my brain is overthinking and in desperate need of a subject change, Phillip asks, "Where are we going now?"

"To my favorite spot in Repestro, which is another uphill walk. If you think you can make it after all the hiking, heavy breathing, and flower stealing."

"Are you going to carry me if I can't?" he asks.

"Nope." I look pointedly behind us. The two men trailing us duck into the shadows. They're quick, but not quick enough. "But I bet your bodyguards can."

Phillip's eyes widen, and he glances back. The two men—not the same two I noticed the night before—are out of sight at the moment, but our village is too small to be able to hide something like bodyguards.

"You noticed?" he asks.

"They're very good." I grin. "But so am I. And the village is small and nosy. I think *everyone* noticed two oversized strange men shadowing you. Why do you have them? Or, rather, why do you *need* them?"

Phillip rubs the back of his neck, looking down. "Let's just say my family is overprotective."

"They must also be very wealthy. Or important. Or both. I mean, if you have a team of—what is it, four—guards with you?"

"You really are observant." Phillip smiles quickly, but it fades almost as fast. "They're personal protection officers. And because I'm set to take over the family business when my father … retires, they are non-negotiable."

It's obvious that he doesn't want to talk about this. What's more—he seems sad talking about taking over the family business. Not at all the way he looked talking about working with artificial intelligence and developing smart home systems. That seems like his passion. Whatever business his family's in, it's not what Phillip would do if given a choice.

But it doesn't sound like he has one.

Join the club!

"Come on," I say, linking my arm through his. It's a bold move for me, but I get the feeling confessing even as much as he just did was a bold move for him. We start off again, heading toward the cliffs where I end many days, staring out over the sea.

"I'm sorry I'm being so deliberately vague," Phillip says.

"Clearly, there are some things you don't want me to know." I pause. "At least, not yet."

"And you're okay with that?"

Am I? The curious part of me, the part which loves making guesses about strangers who walk into the restaurant, wants to pick Phillip apart to uncover all his secrets. The rest of me, which would like to enjoy this moment, is more than okay not being privy to whatever he's not telling me.

"Not forever," I tell him. "But for now."

The only problem with this particular philosophy, I realize as Phillip takes my hand in his, linking our fingers and making my heart skip like a stone over water, is that *now* might be all we ever have.

CHAPTER 6

Phillip

I HATE when things don't go according to plan. Especially human things. Give me a computer glitch or a bug in a program—I'll happily go through lines of code or metadata until I locate and repair the issue.

When things go awry and there is a human component, however, my skin starts to itch and feel too tight. I'm less certain of where to begin looking for the problem, much less finding a solution.

And when the human component malfunctioning is ME, I'm at even more of a loss.

I was supposed to tell Alessia the truth: I am the crown prince of Elsinore and I came to ask for her hand in marriage. And have I said any of that?

No. No, I have not.

Not even close—even though I've spent the whole night

on this uncomfortable stone wall, my backside falling asleep as Alessia and I have talked about everything from our favorite movies to the fact we both wish we had a dog.

Now would be a perfect moment to tell her the truth, and yet, instead of confessing, I'm holding a sleepy Alessia to my chest, stroking her hair as the sky grows lighter behind us. Her hair is soft yet wild, which reminds me of her spirit.

"We should go," she says through a yawn, making no move to get up as I slowly drag my fingers through her hair.

"If you were going to turn into a pumpkin, you would have done so already," I tease.

"True."

"Will your nonno be angry I kept you out all night?"

Alessia huffs a small laugh without opening her eyes. "He'll probably throw some kind of party. You seem to have won him over quickly. How did you do that, by the way? He's usually very protective, not trying to set me up with men I barely know. Especially after ..."

She trails off, and a crease appears between her brows. I move my hand from her hair, smoothing away the worry line with my fingertip. She sighs and snuggles closer.

"An ex?" I ask, the mere idea rousing an unfamiliar jealousy I hope doesn't come through in my voice.

"Yes."

I slide my hand back into her hair, lightly massaging her scalp. Though I've wanted to kiss her many times tonight, I've refrained. It only makes this simple physical contact feel more intimate.

"Do I need to send my PPOs after him?" I keep my voice light, though the thought of anyone hurting Alessia makes me feel anything *but* light.

She laughs. "No." A pause. "Would they?"

They wouldn't, as they're on my protective duty. But one phone call and—

"Anyway. He was just a jerk. Nothing special. He led me on, and then he left."

I process this for a moment. "Is he the reason for your policy on not dating men outside Repestro?"

"You remember I said that. I'm impressed."

I remember lots of things when it comes to Alessia. Probably more than I care for her to know. "Hard to forget, seeing as I also fit that description."

Her eyes open, and she tilts her head to meet my gaze. "You are not like Stefan."

"You hardly know me."

"But I feel as though I do," she says, and I have to agree.

Alessia feels like a gift I've yet to unwrap, but somehow also like a comfortable pair of gloves, worn into a perfect fit. It doesn't really make sense. And yet—here we are.

Alessia closes her eyes again. "I know you love your family, even if you don't want to tell me what kind of business they're in. You're responsible and thoughtful, patient and humbled, despite whatever your high-level position is."

"You're being too generous," I say, feeling a prickle of self-consciousness at her kind words.

"I'm just stating what I see in you. You might still be a mystery in many ways, but I know this—the only common trait you share is being from another place."

And this is a significant point. I will return to Elsinore tomorrow. I swear I can hear Callum's countdown timer ticking, even though I left the earpiece at my hotel last night, insisting to Claudius my PPOs were enough to keep me safe. I half expect to find him and my brother back at the hotel when I return.

Alessia sits up, blinking sleepily as her hair falls over her face. She twists it on top of her head, securing it with an elastic she had on her wrist. I watch her movements, which are simple, yet somehow alluring.

"I should head home for bed." She smiles. "Or breakfast. Breakfast, then bed. Will you walk me?"

"Of course." I take her hand again, our hands sliding together like they've done so hundreds of times, yet the contact makes my skin hum. We start down the narrow road back to the village. It's a short walk, and I keep my pace slow to make it longer.

"Tell me—why don't you want to be in charge of your family business?"

The question startles me. "What?"

"I could tell when you spoke of your family that you're close. But you seem sad whenever the topic gets near work."

Do I?

I shake my head. "I will take over for my father in the next …" I clear my throat. "Soon. I'm not sure when. A year. Two. Or less."

"And you don't want to?"

"I don't have a choice or the luxury to think about what I want. I've always known this would be my role, and I've accepted it. The change is just happening sooner than I thought it would."

"And?"

Alessia is a little too insightful. I'm impressed, but also feel pressed to answer questions I'd usually avoid even thinking about.

"I've always known what this role would cost me," I say slowly. "But any woman who wants to be with me will have to choose this as well. I regret that I come with such a huge burden."

Alessia is quiet for a moment. When she speaks again,

her tone is lighter, as though she's trying to cheer me back up. "I'm sure it comes with perks as well—this important family business you can't discuss."

"It does. I'm just not sure it's worth the cost."

I'm not sure I am worth the cost.

We reach her grandfather's cottage with its white stucco walls and red-tile roof. I wouldn't be able to pick it out from the row of almost identical homes except that Alessia has planted window boxes and pots dripping with pink blooms. Even if she hadn't told me last night about her love of gardens, I would have known from Claudius's dossier. I feel better about all the things I know about her now that I've learned of them from *her*, not just a piece of paper.

Yes, but what will she think when she does know?

And when are you going to explain this to her? How will you tell her you've studied a report on her like she's a subject in school?

My stomach dips as Alessia turns toward me in front of the scarred wooden door.

"Well, here we are," she says, her smile looking more sad than happy.

At least she hasn't bolted inside like a frightened lamb the same way she did last night. I'm not sure what changed between her resistance the first night to her openness now, but I'm grateful I seem to have earned her trust.

Not that you deserve it considering you're lying with every word you say that isn't the truth.

Guilt seeps through me, a stinging poison. But when Alessia links her other hand with mine, staring up at me with heavy-lidded eyes and an adorably sleepy smile, it eases the sting. I can forget, at least for now, what feels every moment like a grander deception.

"Thank you for allowing me to take you on a stroll," I say,

my heart clenching like a fist at the words, which sound like the start of a goodbye. I don't want a goodbye.

Alessia smiles. Her ponytail blows wild around her shoulders in the breeze.

"I can definitively say this is the best stroll I've ever been on," she says.

"I agree. Totally worth giving up sleep and losing all feeling in my bum." I make a dramatically pained face and shift on my feet. "Perhaps permanently."

She laughs, the sound tugging straight at my heart. "Will your bum recover?"

"Unsure. I'll have to let you know."

"Please do," she says, her eyes shining. "I'm quite invested in your bum making a full recovery."

Silence falls between us, as we succumb to an awkward, loaded tension hanging in the air.

What would this be like if I weren't a prince but just a man getting to know a woman to see where it leads? I almost never allow myself to indulge in thoughts of what *isn't*. What-ifs are a waste. My reality exists only in what IS. And yet, those two days in Repestro and every moment with Alessia feels like living out one big what-if.

My gaze drops to Alessia's lips. Is a kiss something Alessia would welcome?

Is it wise when so much is still left unsaid on my part?

When I glance back up at her eyes, she's looking at me with intense longing. I'm not the only one thinking about what-ifs. Or kisses.

My heart thuds faster. I take a small step closer. So does she. As she drops my hands and reaches up to wrap hers around my neck, my breath quickens. Her fingertips play with the hair at the nape of my neck, and I wrap my hands around her waist, tugging her closer, closer, closer still.

When her warm brown gaze falls to my mouth, I dip my head. I hear a sharp intake of breath as her eyelids flutter closed. I move still closer, hearing nothing but the steadily increasing tempo of my heart.

Just before our lips touch, something stops me.

That *something* is my conscience.

Can I really kiss her if I'm not being completely honest with her?

After she's placed so much trust in me—especially knowing how her trust has been broken before—would she ever forgive me?

I hesitate, pulling back. Her eyes open, and whatever she sees on my face makes her brows furrow.

"Phillip? What is it?"

"Alessia, there's so much I haven't—"

The door flies open as I'm mid-sentence and Enzo steps outside, nudging right between us like some kind of herding dog separating the sheep.

Was he ... listening just inside the door?

"Buongiorno!" Enzo beams at us both, his teeth white against his weathered olive skin. Then he turns and shakes a finger at Alessia before kissing both her cheeks. "Out all night. A regular troublemaker."

"Yes, that's me. A real rabble-rouser," Alessia says.

But when he turns just to me, Enzo winks. "Come, come. I have caffè for you."

Indeed, the air is fragrant with the scent of coffee, rich and dark. I have to duck inside the doorway of the house, and it takes my eyes a moment to adjust. The cottage is one main room—small but tidy, with salmon-colored tile floors and comfortable seating. The kitchen is crammed in the back corner, barely more than a gas stove, sink, and a sliver of countertop.

"This way"—he points to me with a wink, then turns to

Alessia— "and it's straight to bed for you. Can't have you dropping another plate of gnocchi."

"That was one time!"

"And I'm still mourning. It was the best gnocchi I've ever made." Enzo continues his herding, shooing Alessia toward a dark hallway to the right while waving me toward the kitchen area.

"All your gnocchi is the best gnocchi." Alessia meets my gaze. "Just Phillip, thank you for a lovely *stroll*."

Enzo's laugh is loud, echoing against the tile floors. "Is that what the kids are calling it these days?"

"Nonno!" Alessia throws a pillow at him, her cheeks turning pink. "Be good!" To me, she says, "Have fun!"

My eyes trail after her until she disappears and Enzo points me toward a door at the back of the kitchen.

"We're out back," he says.

We?

CHAPTER 7

Phillip

I DUCK through an even lower doorway, past an ancient-looking washing machine in a room hardly big enough to hold it, and out another door leading onto a sunny patio overflowing with flowers and herbs in pots. More touches of Alessia.

Sal and Gianni are already seated at a crooked wooden table, but my gaze is drawn to the view beyond the low stone wall. I step closer, looking out. The cottage is built almost on the cliff's edge, giving it a perfectly unobstructed view of the sea beyond. The sun has fully risen now and the sky is a beautiful, cloudless blue, a few shades lighter than the dark waves far below.

"Beautiful." The word escapes my lips almost involuntarily.

I'm surrounded by beauty in Elsinore—the palace itself

and the surrounding lush valley and massive mountains whose tips remain snow-capped for much of the year. But there's something powerful about such a view, especially juxtaposed with the simple cottage.

Enzo claps a hand on my shoulder. "Sit, sit."

Sal pulls out the chair next to him, beaming, and, as usual, Gianni shoots arrows at me with his eyes. I have to wonder how long they've been here. All night, perhaps, waiting for Alessia?

"I'm sorry for keeping Alessia out. Did you wait up?"

"No matter." Enzo fills my cup from a small, silver pitcher. I can't remember the name, but I remember Claudius having one. The steaming coffee he pours into the tiny cup smells as rich as espresso from a coffee shop.

"One or two sugars?" Enzo asks, pushing the cup and saucer toward me, then a small bowl with sugar.

I shake my head. "È perfetto," I tell him. "Grazi."

"Oh, now the boy thinks he speaks Italian." Gianni blows out a puff of air, and Sal gives his arm a light squeeze before saying something in a hushed whisper I don't quite catch.

"No matter how much he fusses, Gianni is soft in here, where it counts." Enzo pats his chest, right over his heart. "I may be Alessia's nonno by blood, but we are all her grand-pas. Drink."

I'm used to sipping tea through the morning until it goes lukewarm on my desk. But this is clearly meant to be enjoyed quickly, while hot. I drain the cup, savoring the richness.

I meet Gianni's eyes before looking back at Enzo. "She is lucky to have all of you."

Sal pushes a plate my way with a few flaky pastries. "Eat, boy."

"Good, no?" Enzo asks. "Zia Agnesia makes them. They're as sweet as she is salty."

84

"Delicious, thank you." I stick to English now because Gianni's glare tells me not to attempt Italian again.

From a small, frosted window right near the table, I hear the unmistakable sound of a shower starting. I force my gaze to a small heart scratched on the tabletop so my thoughts don't wander toward Alessia on the other side of that wall. I trace my finger over the rough lines of the heart.

"Alessia did that when she was six," Enzo says. "I made her pull weeds on Antonio's family farm for a week."

I don't want to ask more questions about Antonio, though I have many. His interest in Alessia seems as clear as her disinterest in him. Still—some deep part of me I'd rather not examine too closely doesn't like thinking of Alessia and Antonio having history, even if it's not a romantic one.

My feelings must show on my face because Enzo chuckles and pats my hand. "Don't worry. She doesn't return his affections. Never has. Lessy, despite what she might pretend, is a romantic at heart." He taps the carved heart on the table. "When she decides to let someone in, she won't settle for less than love."

If this is true, Alessia certainly *wouldn't* have been open to my original proposal, which was little more than a legal contract. A business deal, really—practical, logical, and definitely not remotely related to romantic love.

I hate even thinking about that idea now. How was I so foolish to think that she—or any woman—would respond to something like that? Actually, a bonnet of women would jump at the chance, like all the ones my parents tried to push on me.

But not Alessia. For her, this is all wrong. Guilt rubs like an itchy wool sweater, one that's a few sizes too small. I do my best to shrug it off because I'm here now, and I've already discarded my first plan. Now, I just need to find a new one.

I clear my throat, but Enzo speaks before I can. "Let's talk about why the crown prince of Elsinore is in Repestro and what his intentions are toward my granddaughter."

The pastry falls from my fingers. When I glance around the table, I'm met with smug expressions from Enzo and Sal, and—no surprise here—a glare from Gianni.

I turn to Enzo, unsure of what I'll find in his expression. "How long have you known?"

His brown eyes remain warm, crinkling at the corners when he smiles. "Since you walked in the door of my restaurant. You think that excuse for a beard would fool anyone?"

He takes a large bite of his pastry. Crumbs dust the white stubble on his chin as I work to process his words.

"Does Alessia know?"

"No!" He shakes his head. "And no one outside of this patio does—yet. I know your face, but Sal is the one who reads all the gossip."

Sal smiles. "My Rosa got me hooked on those horrible magazines. She loved reading about royals and movie stars. I still read the websites."

"Blogs," Gianni corrects.

"Yes, yes—blogs, websites, whatever." Sal waves a hand, and then his eyes harden. "I hate the paparazzi. Vultures, all of them. But reading these articles … it reminds me of *her*."

Gianni reaches over, squeezing Sal's hand. Enzo passes him a napkin, and Sal nods, smiling even though his eyes are damp. I'm struck by the depth of these men's friendships and their care for one another.

"And I read because *he* reads," Enzo says.

"I do not waste time on such rubbish," Gianni says.

I'm with Gianni—these sites are rubbish. Paparazzi *are* horrible, and at any given time our legal team is threatening several with lawsuits. But the idea of Sal reading them to remember his wife is sweet. Achingly so.

It does make me wonder what opinion they must have of me. The gossip sites refer to me as the Robot Royal, though it didn't catch on as well as Callum's Golden Boy moniker. Thankfully.

Enzo again seems to sense what I'm thinking. "Don't worry. We never believe the things we read. Well—*most* things we read."

"Ninety percent of those stories are pure fiction," I tell him.

Sal giggles. "So, you don't have a robot girlfriend?"

This draws a belly laugh out of Gianni. I didn't think the man capable of laughter, and I enjoy it far more than his glares. Even if it's at my expense.

I scoff. "I do not have a robot girlfriend."

Gianni's expression darkens again. "What about that duchess?"

"I thought you didn't read them." Sal nudges his friend, and Gianni grunts.

I shake my head. "No duchess. No girlfriend. I wouldn't be here otherwise."

"And why *are* you here?" Gianni asks.

"The prince is here to find a wife," Sal says. "Because your father is ill, no?"

I swallow. Okay, maybe the fictional percentage is much smaller than I thought.

"Stop prying!" Enzo turns to me. "You don't have to tell us. But is it true?"

"Which part?" I ask, trying to tread carefully through this minefield of a conversation. I don't know how much I should tell them, especially since I'm still keeping so much from Alessia.

"How is your father's health?" Sal asks, just as Enzo says, "Are you looking for a wife?"

Gianni contributes nothing, but his arched eyebrow is an unmistakable challenge.

I draw in a slow breath. "My father is not well. His liver is failing and ... we don't know how much time we have."

I've never had to say the words like this—lining up the facts in a neat row to be examined. It hurts.

Enzo reaches over, squeezing my hand. Sal whispers what sounds like a prayer under his breath, and Gianni tosses me his napkin, though I'm not crying.

"I am sorry," Enzo says.

I nod, surprised by the swelling of emotion in my throat. "Thank you."

Enzo pats my hand once more before letting go. The three men resume staring, though Gianni's glare is a little softer now.

Right—I still need to answer the *other* question, the one about marriage. I lean forward, resting my elbows on the table, meeting each of their eyes in turn. First Gianni, then Sal, and lastly, Enzo.

"It is true that I am looking for a wife. I would like to get married while my father is here to see it." And, more immediately, before my mother forces me to pick a wife at her ball.

Sal beams. "And you have chosen Alessia!"

Enzo watches me carefully. "Is this true?"

"It is." I pause, swinging my gaze back to Enzo.

Gianni's frown deepens. "Are you visiting other places, other women—trying them on like clothes?"

"No." It's at this moment I realize that even if Alessia doesn't want to marry me or if Enzo sends me away now, I don't want to see anyone else on Claudius's list. Alessia is it.

"She is my only choice." I turn to Enzo. "If she wants it, and with your blessing, of course."

In my world, a royal world, discussing marriage between two people who barely know each other (or who haven't even met) wouldn't make anyone blink. No one at this table is blinking either. Apparently, the nonnos aren't shocked.

But I can't read their reactions.

Gianni speaks first, his tone only mildly scornful. "You think Lessy wants to marry you?"

"No. I barely got her to agree to go on a stroll with me," I admit.

Gianni smiles at this. "Good for her."

Sal shushes his friend, and Enzo takes another sip of his caffé. "And you want my blessing to ask for her hand?"

I glance down at the half-eaten pastry on my plate, my stomach churning. "Not today. I'd like … time with her. But I want to be honest with you about my ultimate intent."

"So fancy," Gianni says. "'Ultimate intent.'"

This time, Sal gives him a light smack on the back of the head and the two begin bickering in Italian.

"What, then, is your plan? How will you win over our Lessy?" Enzo asks.

Gianni and Sal stop fighting, and once again, I'm facing the scrutiny of three men. I've withstood hostile negotiations with other princes, prime ministers, and diplomats that scared me less.

"I don't know." The honest truth. With the plan thrown away and my time running out, I don't have the first clue. "I'm open to suggestions."

"I have many ideas." Sal rubs his palms together with delight, but Enzo waves him off.

He looks me over, leaning back in his chair. The moment

stretches, and I feel sure he's going to tell me to head back to Elsinore immediately.

"Six weeks," he says. "Six weeks, you work for me. Then we will see how our Lessy feels about you and if I can offer my blessing."

Six weeks is an interminable amount of time to be gone. And it's running right up against the date for my mother's ball.

"He can't stay," Gianni says. "He's busy with princely things. And his father's health. He must go back."

The voice of reason in my head agrees with the grumpy grandpa. I must go back. Tomorrow. My stomach twists at the very idea. Through the tiny window, I suddenly hear the sound of Alessia singing—loudly and off-key—as the shower cuts off. Sal chuckles.

"She is beautiful but not a songbird," Sal says.

"And she cannot cook," Enzo says.

"She is perfect," Gianni says, glaring at the other two.

"The boy must know her faults if he wants to marry her," Enzo says with a shrug. "Lessy is also stubborn. And does not like change."

"Leaving here would be a massive change," I point out. "Would she even consider it?"

If not, there is no point in me staying. Even if I could somehow agree with Enzo's terms. Which ... I can't.

"She would." Enzo nods slowly. "She would for love."

My smile is forced. "Then I should go home. Six weeks is hardly enough time for love."

Enzo leans close, his gaze soft. "No. You look at her the way I looked at my Gracie. The way Eduardo, Lessy's father, looked at my sweet Talia. It is quick, yes, but it is the start of love. It does not come in only one speed."

He sits back, a satisfied smile on his face. He seems so certain. But Enzo is wrong about love.

Isn't he?

Love isn't a thing you accidentally fall into, like a pit you stumble into in the dark. I've always thought true love begins with mutual respect and develops slowly, like wine aged in a barrel, as I told Callum before I came here. As Father has told me so many times.

When he and my mother met for the first time, they were already betrothed, an arrangement by my grandfather, King Gerald. They were strangers entering into a commitment of the most serious kind by way of mutual agreement. They've held fast to their vows, and what I'm sure were shy, uncomfortable gazes at first have been replaced with pure adoration. I thought it would be the same for me.

My feelings for Alessia came as a surprise. And yes, I've reevaluated and scrapped my original plan. But I still wouldn't call this love.

It's just ... it's only ... it is ...

I take a sip of coffee, contemplating, trying to locate the right response to Enzo, if there even is such a thing.

Is it possible I've been wrong about love?

"Will you stay?" Enzo presses. "You have not given an answer."

Even the thought of leaving has me gripping the edge of the table like it's the edge of a cliff.

"He won't agree. The boy must run his *kingdom*," Gianni scoffs, saying *kingdom* as though he thinks I'm running some kind of pyramid scheme.

"I will stay."

Even as I say the words, I know they are right. How I will pull this off—of that, I'm not sure. I also don't know why my heart is beating so wildly in my chest or why I suddenly feel so hot, despite the breeze.

Enzo's smile is blinding. "Then, it is settled. Six weeks, you will work for me. Then I will grant my permission and bestow my blessing. Assuming, of course, Alessia agrees."

Sal chuckles. "And *that* may be the real challenge."

A door closes somewhere inside the house, and I start to get up. "First, I must tell Alessia who I am."

All three men rise at once, shouting various forms of *No*. Enzo grabs my arm.

"No, no, no," he says, pulling me back down into my seat.

"Not yet," Sal says.

"Patience, boy." Gianni shakes his head like he's never encountered such stupidity. "Putting the horse inside the cart."

"The cart before the horse," Sal corrects.

I frown at Enzo. "But she needs to know. She may not want to even date me when she knows who I am. Much less consider an offer of marriage."

"You must give the truth some time," Enzo says. "That's why I stopped you earlier, before you could confess."

"And before the boy could kiss her." Sal grins at me conspiratorially. "He had his ear pressed to the door."

"And you were watching through the window," Gianni says.

Enzo waves them both off. "You must wait."

"But why? I need to tell her the truth. Otherwise, it will all be a lie." The secrets I'm keeping feel larger and heavier every moment I'm with her. "Love and lies don't go together."

Enzo is still shaking his head. "She will *never* give you a fair chance if she knows who you are." With a sigh, he leans back in his chair and rubs his face. "Alessia has lost much.

Some would turn bitter, but she has not. She has, however, built iron walls around herself."

"Especially after that Voldemort." Sal's whole demeanor changes.

"Voldemort?" I ask.

"He who shall not be named," Enzo says.

"Mortacci tua!" I'm not exactly sure of the translation of what Enzo says, but something to do with ancestors.

I assume they mean Stefan. "The last thing I want is to be like him. Which is why the truth matters."

Enzo is still shaking his head. "You are not a Voldemort. But if you tell her now, she won't be ready to accept it. She will tell you to go. I see how she looks at you, boy. But I know my Lessy and her stubbornness. Don't think of it as lying. You're *withholding*."

"Are they really so different?" I ask.

His lips purse. "They are like ... cousins?"

"Step-cousins," Sal says.

"I say tell her," Gianni says. "Rip away the bandages."

"That's just because you don't want her to go," Enzo says, frowning. "But our baby bird has stayed in the nest too long. She won't leave without a push." Enzo grabs my hand, and I'm surprised by the force of his grip. "Promise me. You'll give her a little time. Blame me if you must. But *promise*."

Before I can respond, Alessia steps out on the patio. She's barefoot, wearing a rumpled t-shirt and what appear to be oversized boxer shorts.

"My ears are burning," she says. "Are you talking about me, Nonno?" She's toweling her dark hair dry, and her skin is scrubbed clean and bright.

I try not to stare at her bare legs, and my mouth goes dry.

Tell her the truth.

Wait.

93

Withhold.

Tell her.

When no one speaks, Alessia pauses, frowning as she glances around the table. Her gaze lands on my hand, clasped tightly in Enzo's. Her frown deepens.

"What's going on out here? What did I miss?"

Enzo's smile rivals the sun as he gives my hand one last squeeze that feels like both encouragement and warning.

"Lessy, you are looking at the restaurant's new dishwasher."

FROM THE ROYAL BUGLE, EUROPE'S #1 SOURCE FOR ROYAL GOSSIP

Royal Gone Rogue!

Something's rotten in the state of Elsinore. More specifically, someone is *missing* in the country of Elsinore.

According to exclusive sources inside the palace, Crown Prince Phillip has not been seen in 10 days and appears to not be in residence at the palace, or perhaps even in the country.

Robert Vitalla, the spokesperson for the Royal Family declined to comment, dismissing the rumors as ridiculous. However, Prince Phillip has been noticeably absent from public functions with Prince Callum appearing in his stead.

Some have speculated that the crown prince's absence is related to his search for a wife and perhaps he has eloped. Are the women of Elsinore not enough for Prince Phillip?

In the crown prince's absence, Prince Callum has been stepping out and stepping up. But is the spare able to truly fill his older brother's shoes?

"It's certainly a different side to the Golden Boy," a royal correspondent told the *Bugle*. "He has matured a lot in the last year."

It may be true that Prince Callum has made changes, but he still has room to grow. He bungled several public engagements this week, including calling the wife of Zeldaire's foreign minister a pig in their native tongue.

Experts say the flub was likely because the Zeldaire words for *pig* and *pretty* are so close. One linguist we spoke to said, "I'm sure Prince Callum meant to say she was pretty. The two words are quite similar, and it's easy to see how a mistake would be made."

Though if Prince Phillip were here, it's a solid bet Elisnore's negotiations would be moving forward instead of backward with Zeldaire.

When asked at a state dinner about his older brother's whereabouts, Prince Callum turned on his characteristic charm, asking, "Am I not good-looking enough to be his replacement?" We remain mum on the answer to *that* question.

King James's health still remains a concern, though nothing further has been learned. The same source from the palace reports that most days, the king doesn't leave his bedroom.

Share your answer in the poll below! Who's hotter, Prince Phillip or Prince Callum?

CHAPTER 8

Alessia

LUCI BLOWS into the restaurant like a cyclone and practically bowls me over where I'm preparing tables for dinner service. The restaurant is nearly empty, but a few regulars linger at the tables. These days, it seems like half the village is here for the gossip, not the food.

"I missed you," she says, kissing both my cheeks and then hugging me tightly.

"It was only five days." But in truth, I missed her too. While Luci was gone on a getaway with Marco, I had no one to talk to about Phillip. Not that I would have had time since I spent most of my days with him.

Now that I'm faced with my bubbly best friend, I'm not sure where to start or what to say.

"So much has happened!" Luci steps back, taking me by

the shoulders and studying my face like we've been separated for years. "I hear you have a *boyfriend*. Good for you."

"Yes." I step away, straightening a chair that doesn't need straightening before I move to the next table, avoiding Luci's eyes. "I guess I do."

We haven't used that term or made any kind of commitment. But every morning, I wake to find Phillip having caffé with the nonnos on the patio. He spends most of the day in the restaurant with us, though more and more villagers have been showing up, asking for Phillip's help with various odd jobs, like he's now the village's unpaid handyman.

But my boyfriend? I'm still not sure.

Luci follows because she is an expert tracker where juicy secrets are involved. And she's sniffing out my desire to avoid this topic.

"You *guess*? What does that mean?"

"We just haven't defined things in a specific way."

Or discussed the herd of elephants in the room, made up of all the other things we haven't discussed. Every time Phillip looks like he's going to say something about his family or work or why he has two personal protection officers on him at all times, I shut it down. I'm not ready for the inevitable reality crashing down on me, confirming what I already know—this can't work long term. Even if he's not Stefan, not even a little, Phillip will still have to leave at some point to go back to … whatever it is he does.

The less I think about that, the better.

"Hm." Luci grabs a few rolls of silverware and begins setting the tables as I clean them. "A non-boyfriend wouldn't babysit the Costa-monsters with you."

"True." Phillip wanted to spend the morning with me yesterday. I agreed—not telling him until he arrived that it was my morning to babysit the three Costa children.

"I'm honestly surprised he survived," Luci says with a laugh.

Phillip more than survived babysitting the Costas. I've never seen the three children take to anyone so quickly. Of course, *taking to* Phillip looked like all three climbing him like an olive tree, one pouring a large dose of lemon juice into his water, and another cutting off a lock of his hair.

By the end of the two hours, Phillip looked shell-shocked and exhausted. But he was still smiling as we walked back to Nonno's.

"Still want a big family?" I teased, hoping my tone hid my curiosity.

I still remember the way he looked as he met my gaze. "Only if I have the right woman beside me."

I mean ... he just HAD TO give me the best answer possible, didn't he?

Assuming I'm the right woman he means. I am, right? I feel like his actions all point to yes, but with words, it's all still very nebulous.

Because you won't let the man tell you anything, a nasty little voice tells me. A nasty but accurate little voice.

The sooner he tells me everything, the sooner I'll have to choose between Phillip and this life. MY life.

This instantly silences the nasty little voice. Because it knows that I'm right.

"Did he give you the flower?" Luci asks.

Smiling, I touch the delicate bloom Phillip tucked behind my ear earlier. "Yes."

"That's definitely a boyfriend thing."

Phillip has taken to leaving me flowers in tiny jars, both at the house and at the restaurant. Daily. Sometimes more than one jar of flowers a day. My room at home is now like a miniature garden, which I love. He also has been slowly and steadily adding to the actual garden on Nonno's patio. Roses and plumeria in clay pots, but also rosemary and basil too.

Romantic *and* practical—be still my heart!

Then there are the messages scrawled in his blocky script left in surprising places—in a drawer in the bathroom, clipped to the laundry hanging on the line, inside my apron. They are not poetry or love letters, but happy little notes. One simply said *hi* with a smiley face. I can't explain why that one made me smile so big. Another said, *I've never met a woman whose beauty rivaled a summer sky.*

That one made me roll my eyes. I mean, such a total line!

And yet … I've been carrying that note around in my pocket ever since.

Nonno must be feeding Phillip insider tips during their now-daily breakfasts because a slice of my favorite tiramisu appeared in the restaurant fridge with my name on the box. Yesterday, a complete box set of my favorite young adult fantasy series appeared by my bedside. *Signed* by the author.

Two days ago, I found a new pair of Converse on my bed to replace my worn favorites. But rather than being plain black, these are a deep blue, reminding me of Phillip's eyes. He even tried giving me a mobile phone, which is the only gift I've rejected.

I'm becoming quite spoiled. Not just by the gifts and gestures, but by the man who is steadily making me lose my head.

"I heard he rehung Zia Agnesia's front door," Maria adds as Luci and I start prepping a table near the couple.

"Did he, now?" Luci asks.

Zia Agnesia is no one's actual aunt. But as the oldest widow in the village whose children have grown and gone, we've all adopted her. Still, it was Phillip who noticed her crooked door and took it upon himself to fix it, not any of the villagers. Maybe he'd never washed a dish before, but the man knows his way around a toolbox.

"I wish he'd get to my shutters next," Maria adds.

Ernesto *harrumphs*. "I told you I'd fix them. Keep your Mr. Perfect away from my shutters and my wife, Lessy. Him and his toolbox."

I roll my eyes but smile at Maria. "Phillip isn't the village handyman," I say, moving on to the tables by the door.

"And how is he with his hands?" Luci asks in a low voice.

"Luce," I warn.

At least she had the decency to ask this question quietly, though I think I heard Maria chuckle behind us. The woman's hearing likes to go in and out, but it always seems to be IN when there's even the tiniest crumb of gossip.

"What? It's me! You can tell me anything. *Anything*," Luci says more pointedly, making sure I don't miss her wink. "You know I tell *you* every detail."

"Sometimes *too many* details," I tell her, remembering the time she tried to draw me a full-body diagram of her ex-boyfriend's moles because she said they were laid out like the Big Dipper.

Shudder.

"Well?" she asks, nudging me with her hip and placing a few rolls of napkins down on a table. "At least tell me how he kisses."

I wipe down one of the wooden tables like I'm trying to slough off the top layer of wood. "We haven't kissed yet."

Luci's jaw goes slack, and she grabs my arm. "You're telling me that man in there—the one with the intensity and the smolder, the one who took a job washing dishes just so he can be near you—hasn't even *kissed you?*"

"We're taking things slowly."

"Is this something you mutually decided? Or are you pumping the brakes?"

"It's mutual," I say, which is basically true. We talk. We flirt. We dance around things like kissing and when he's leaving and what his big, secret family business is. "Look— my speed is not your speed. You are a Ferrari. I am a bicycle."

"Even bicycles move forward, Lessy."

"Sometimes bicycles can be fast," Maria chimes in from across the room.

"And they're good with hugging the curves of the road," Ernesto says, eliciting a giggle from his wife.

Luci snorts, and I groan softly. My stupid cheeks are flaming.

"I'm being smart," I say. "He's still going to leave. Slow is good. Slow is safe."

"And you know he's leaving because you've talked about his plans."

More like ... I assume it and refuse to talk about it. "Not exactly."

Luci dramatically falls down into a nearby chair. "Che cavolo!"

Maybe I'm NOT so glad my best friend is back. I slump down in the seat across from her. "Luci, I still don't know what he's holding back. The idea of kissing him feels ..."

Like something I'm really eager to do. But also like a strangely massive line to cross, even my best friend thinks there's something wrong with me.

"It feels like something I can't do until I know everything," I finish.

Luci sighs heavily. "So, you don't want to lock lips or any other body parts until you know if he's an oil baron or part of the mafia."

"Pretty much. Though he did say he's not in the mafia."

"But do you not know these things because you aren't asking or because he's not telling?"

A couple walks inside the restaurant, saving me from answering one more invasive question I'd rather not. For now.

I stand. "I've got to get back to work." Her mouth opens, and I point a warning finger at her. "And don't you dare ask me what Sean Astin would do."

"Fine. Get back to work and back to avoiding," Luci says, narrowing her eyes. "But that will only work for so long with me. You know that."

I do. And I also know it will only work so long for me and Phillip too.

"What are you doing, Lessy?"

Gianni's voice makes me jump, and I bang my head on the swinging kitchen door I was hiding behind. I didn't expect anyone to catch me watching Phillip wash dishes. Nonno insisted that he and the nonnos deliver food tonight, leaving Phillip and me to clean and lock up. They've been gone for at least half an hour.

I jump back, the door swishing shut behind me. Gianni gives me a stern look, and I try not to squirm under his glare.

Because I wasn't doing anything wrong! I was just ... admiring the view.

Did I know that watching a man wash dishes could be sexy? No. No, I did not.

But that was before I saw Phillip with his sleeves rolled up, suds on his hands (and even a few scattered in his hair), scrubbing pots in a way that emphasizes the muscles in his forearms. Yes—there are muscles in his forearms. I'd need an anatomy chart to know for sure, but I think I'm seeing completely new muscle groups there.

Further study on the subject is most definitely needed. But not while being watched by a man who is like a second grandfather to me.

"Did you forget something?" I ask Gianni.

"Yes," he says, but doesn't elaborate.

"And what did you forget?"

"You like the boy," Gianni says.

I groan and press a hand to my eyes. It seems that everyone, all the time, ONLY wants to talk to me about Phillip. After Luci bombarded me with questions and opinions earlier, this feels like too much.

Although I can count on Gianni to be the one person not practically tossing me into Phillip's arms or telling me I should have kissed him by now.

Nonno and Sal have always been the sunshine to Gianni's rain cloud about *everything*, but especially me dating. After Stefan, it only got worse.

"I know you don't like him. Could we just not talk about this now?"

I expect a gruff agreement. Followed perhaps by a list of all the reasons Gianni doesn't think Phillip is enough for me. To which, I'll defend the man whose character I respect more and more the more I get to know him. Or maybe I'll just let it go tonight. I'm not sure I have the mental energy.

But instead of listing the evils of Phillip, Gianni says, "He makes you shine."

This … I was not expecting, and I have to swallow past a growing lump in my throat when Gianni wipes his eyes. Is he … *crying?*

"Any man who makes you come alive is a man I like. Too

long, you have been in the shadows. He is worthy of you, tesoro mio."

This is not what I expected. But it's true. Sometimes you can only see the truth of a thing when you are on the other side of it. Since Phillip has come, I've seen just how shadowed my life has been, how right Luci was when she accused me of not really living.

Now, with Phillip, I feel alive.

With a firm nod, Gianni says, "Yes. He is your farm boy."

"My ... what?"

"Your farm boy. From The Princess Wife film—you know, the one with the man who has too many fingers. You say, 'Farmboy, wash this dish!' and the boy says, 'as you wish' when he really means 'I love you.'"

I don't know how to respond to this—to the fact he's seen *The Princess Bride* (one Luci made me watch even though Sean Astin isn't in it) or that Gianni is comparing Phillip and me to Wesley and Buttercup.

"I'm hardly a princess," I say, struggling to find some kind of protest. Because I'm not ready to call this *love*. Even if I suspect that's exactly what it is.

Gianni looks suddenly flustered, then gives his head a little shake. "Any kingdom would be lucky to have you. So would any prince."

I'm about to tell him I'm not exactly living in some kind of fairy tale when he takes me by the shoulders and gives me a surprisingly strong shove right into the kitchen.

CHAPTER 9

Alessia

PHILLIP TURNS from the sink as I'm trying to keep myself from flying into the stainless steel prep table. His eyes dance with mirth as the ladles hanging from a rack jangle together. After the brief but impactful conversation with Gianni, my insides feel just like those ladles—totally shaken.

"Why, hello," Phillip says casually, as though my dramatic entrance was completely normal. He wipes his hands on a dish towel, and like everything with him, it's a surprisingly sexy movement. "Was that Gianni I saw?"

"Yes. He forgot … something."

"Ah." Phillip crosses his arms and leans back against the counter. "I saw you peeking in earlier. Have there been complaints about my job performance?"

I nod and somehow manage to keep a straight face.

"Quite a few. And you know how seriously we take clean dishes."

"I do. Would you like to inspect my work?"

"I think I've seen enough. You look like you're doing a very thorough—"

"Come here."

They are two simple words, but Phillip's tone carries the kind of command I find myself responding to almost instinctively, walking closer as my heart thuds.

I jolt when he takes my hand and tugs me to the sink. His hand is still slightly damp, but firm and strong as he settles me in front of the industrial sink, my hips pressed to the edge as I stare down at the soapy water. My mind is on *anything* but dishes.

I hate when he lets go.

But then Phillip puts a hand on either side of me, gripping the sink and trapping me in front of him.

My eyes squeeze closed for a beat, then two. I try to steady my breathing and keep my heart from fully escaping my chest. Phillip's body is warm, though he keeps a careful distance between us. I can barely feel the brush of his chest on my back.

"What do you think?" he asks, leaning just his head forward so his lips are close to my neck.

I want to arch into him.

I also want to run screaming from the kitchen.

"Is it that bad?" Phillip asks, and I'd forgotten his question altogether or even what I'm supposed to be thinking about. "I suppose I'll have to go to remedial dishwashing school."

His breath ghosts over my skin, and I tremble. The thing is—all the dishes are already put away. The main washing sink still has warm, soapy water, but his job is done. There is nothing to look at except ... water. But do I point this out and stop the charade we're in?

Absolutely not. I am COMMITTED to this moment.

"You might. I've heard nothing but good things about those who graduate from remedial dishwashing school. That's a very bright future right there."

He hums, a sound low in his throat or maybe in his chest, because that's where I feel it.

"Or," he says in a soft voice, tilting his head so his mouth is even closer to me. "You could give me some pointers. Teach me how to really scrub. How much soap I'll need. When to let plates soak for a while."

This is *dish* talk. Not *sexy* talk. There's not even a hint of double entendre I can pick up on with his words.

But the *delivery*!

His voice is low and rough, and my body is reacting like it's hearing ALL kinds of hidden meanings.

When he leans closer still, his chest now flush with my back, my breath catches. Phillip takes one hand off the sink, reaching down and dragging his fingers through the soapy water. Slowly, deliberately, he slides his fingertips over my cheek, leaving a trail of bubbles. I can feel them on my skin, as light as a chaste kiss.

But definitely not as satisfying as one.

"There," he says. "Maybe this will give you a better frame of reference to judge my work?"

"This *does* help." I attempt a teasing tone and instead sound like I'm practically panting. "I'm seeing things much more clearly now."

"And what do you see, Sia?"

The nickname Phillip has been using for me sounds like music, a gentle and melodic caress. If his lips moved any closer, they would be pressed to my ear. The torture is simply delicious. I want it to end—in a kiss, obviously—and I also *never* want it to end.

Just when I feel ready to implode or do something reckless like turn around and press my mouth to his, Phillip leans forward again, this time dipping his whole hand in the sink. Even though I'm watching his every movement, I still gasp when he flicks water on me.

"You lose points for sloppy technique," I tell him. "The water should stay *in* the sink."

"Is that so? I'm not so sure."

Once more, his hand dips into the water, then flicks water my way. More this time. Enough to run down my neck, dampening my shirt collar.

Wherever this playful, flirty side of Phillip came from, I am really digging it.

I drop my hand and palm a handful of bubbles, then lean back and swipe them over his beard. The bristly hairs tickle my palm, and Phillip traps my hand there, holding it against his scratchy cheek.

"That was a bad idea," he says.

"I disagree. I think I should do it again."

And as I'm reaching for more bubbles with my other hand, Phillip grabs the nozzle over the sink—a high-powered sprayer attached with a long, metal hose. He steps away and, without warning, douses me with water.

Though I'm sure he's used the sprayer before, he may not have thought through exactly how different it is turning this on a person, not a dish. I'm soaked in an instant, water pooling in my sneakers as my shirt and pants stick to my skin. I gasp because the water is also freezing.

Phillip immediately drops the sprayer, his eyes huge. "Oh—Alessia, I'm so sorry. I didn't realize it would be so—"

I grab the closest thing, which is a metal mixing bowl, scoop up water from the sink, and toss it right in his face.

Phillip stands there, stunned, blinking the water from his eyes. It runs down his cheeks and drips from his beard. His blond hair looks darker now, and it's hard not to stare at the way his shirt quickly gets plastered to his chest.

We stand this way for a few seconds like two snakes, coiled and waiting to strike. More delicious tension sparking, more wanting.

I wonder just how close I can dance to this flame without being burned.

"You really shouldn't have done that." His voice is calm —*too* calm.

My stomach flips, then turns inside out. "You started it."

"Did I?" Phillip takes a step forward.

"Absolutely."

Another step. "I can't recall."

My insides are a quivering mess, and my outsides aren't faring much better. I can't hold back a smile, though Phillip's face is a mask of deadly seriousness.

"Don't come any closer." I grab the nozzle now and point it his way.

"You wouldn't."

I barely press the lever, sending a light spray toward him, landing just short of his feet. A warning shot. Phillip lowers his brows, his eyes narrowing.

"I don't think you will," he says, watching me.

Rather than answer, I tilt the nozzle up, and this time the water arcs straight into his chest. After only a second or two, I stop, but he's drenched. We are now a matching set.

He presses a hand to his chest, gasping and stumbling to the side like he's been shot.

I know it's just water. He's not hurt. Still—some

misguided caretaking instinct makes me drop the sprayer and reach for him.

"I'm sorry! Are you—"

I don't get to finish my question because he picks me up, throwing me over his shoulder like a sack of flour. I squeal, wiggling, though Phillip is tall and I don't exactly want him to drop me on the tile floor.

"What are you doing?" I demand, swatting at his back. "Put me down!"

"I will," he promises, but as he moves closer to the sink, I realize I should have been more specific about *where* he puts me down.

Because it's a restaurant sink, wide and deep. Definitely big enough to fit a person my size.

"Don't!" I practically squeal as he reaches the sink and starts to bend.

He pauses. "No?"

"No! Please. I think we're even."

"Are we?"

"Yes?" I'm laughing now, uncontrollable giggles that only stop when Phillip slides me slowwwwwly down his body until my feet touch the floor. I grip his biceps for stability.

MOSTLY for stability.

I'm breathless from the contact of my curves against the hard planes of his body. But when my weight fully sinks into my feet and my wet shoes make an awkward squelching sound, I start to giggle again. Phillip's smile is wide, his blue eyes like the ocean on a perfect day. His smile is blinding.

"Just when I think I'm getting to know you," I say, too aware of the way his hands still rest on my hips, heavy and strong. "You go and surprise me again."

As I watch, Phillip's smile fades, a hard-to-read mask

taking its place. I almost fall over when Phillip says, "You never kiss me."

"I—*what?*"

He blows out a breath, shaking his head slightly. Sliding his hands from my waist to my hips, he says, "As a greeting. Everyone kisses everyone here to say hello. But you don't kiss me."

Oh. *OH.*

He's right, though I hadn't thought about it until right now. I rarely think at all about the way Italians all kiss each other on the cheek. At least, I didn't consciously think about it. Maybe it's because I wasn't sure what the customary greeting in Elsinore is.

Or maybe I just didn't want to give myself away. Kissing Phillip on the cheek, even as a greeting or goodbye, wouldn't feel like just any kiss. Because NO touch with him feels like anyone else.

"I simply didn't think of it," I explain.

His eyes narrow. "You kiss all the nonno's cheeks. Marco's. Antonio's. But never mine."

"Just Phillip—are you jealous?"

It's hard to tell with the beard, but I could swear his jaw clenches. "Maybe."

We're still standing so close. I slide my hands up his arms to twine them around his neck. He blinks in surprise as I rise up on my toes to press my lips to his face. His beard is scratchy, but my lips find the soft skin of his cheek.

"I'm sorry for not greeting you properly," I whisper against his skin.

As slowly as I can and keeping my lips almost touching him, I switch to the other cheek. I press my mouth there, letting my lips linger. His eyes are closed, and I think he's stopped breathing. I'm tempted to turn my head ever so slightly and capture his lips.

Luci would. She'd be making out on the prep table.

But I'm not Luci. I'm me. And I'm still a bicycle, not a Ferrari.

I sink back down on my toes, watching Phillip's face. His eyes slowly flutter open, and he stares at me as though mesmerized. First at my eyes, then down to my lips. I have never been looked at in this way before, like I am both a puzzle and the key to solving it.

The tension in the room seems set to combust. Or maybe I'm about to combust. For a moment, I think Phillip will kiss me. I think I finally want him to kiss me, even with all the unknown risks he still carries.

And then a photograph on the wall behind Phillip catches my eye. It's of Nonno in this kitchen years ago, an apron in place and a wooden spoon in hand.

I step back. Phillip's hands fall away from my waist. "Walk me home?" I ask, even though he's been doing this every night since Nonno somehow convinced Phillip—a man who I'm positive has never washed a dish before in his life— to work in the kitchen.

"Always," Phillip says, and I try not to be sad at the one word I know simply can't be true.

CHAPTER 10

Phillip

"DID YOU HAVE A GOOD NIGHT, SIR?" Graves swivels around from the front passenger seat, looking as hopeful as a puppy when he sees his owner carrying his leash.

For such an intimidating man—his shoulders are broader than my own and his neck could command its own province —Graves harbors a secret romantic soft side. One I've only learned about on this trip. Because of the nature of this particular job, the barriers between my PPOs and me have all but dissolved. The four-person team now acts not only like my security, but my drivers, and, as in the current moment, like the therapists I definitely didn't request. Mostly with Graves and Martin, who are typically the ones going with me to Repestro.

"Yes."

Every night with Alessia is a good night, each better than

114

the last. So long as I ignore the guilt, throbbing like a bruise being continuously poked. Guilt for leaving everyone but Callum and Claudius in the dark about my whereabouts. Guilt for the worry my parents must feel. Guilt at forcing Callum to shoulder my duties.

And, most especially and painfully, guilt for not telling Alessia the whole truth.

Martin's cool, gray eyes meet mine in the rearview mirror as he pulls onto the road leading out of Repestro. "Did you tell her yet?"

"No."

"You really ought to stop putting it off," Martin says. "A relationship shouldn't be founded on lies."

"Thank you, Dr. Love, for your insight," I say, unable to soften the edge to my voice.

First, because I don't need love advice from a twice divorced and currently single man on my protection team.

Second, because I agree.

"Who's Dr. Love?" Martin asks.

"You don't know Dr. Love?" Graves asks. "She's an advice columnist from America. Snarky but smart advice." Graves turns to me again. "You should write her. I bet she'd have excellent advice."

"If she's truly good at her job, she'd agree with me," Martin says.

My phone buzzes, and I glance at the screen to see Callum calling. I've been avoiding his calls for days, resulting in a million texts filled with complaints and gifs from *New Girl*, one of my brother's favorite shows. The influx of texts has not made me any more eager to have a real conversation. At the moment, however, his timing is impeccable.

"I need to take this," I say, pushing the button to extend the glass partition between the front and back seats.

"Hello, Cal. How's life in Elsinore?"

"Horrid," he answers. "Living your life is *horrid*. I've never been more grateful to be the second-born son."

"Oh, it's not so bad."

"Says the man currently out of orbit and living his best life with the woman of his dreams. Did you hear that I called the Zeldairian foreign minister's wife a pig by accident?"

"It really is unfortunate that *pig* and *pretty* are only distinguished by a single letter. Could have happened to anyone."

"It's never happened to *you*," Callum says. "Anyway, I'm rubbish at all this policy and politics. When are you coming home?"

An excellent question. "Unsure."

Callum groans. "Still? If you'd only employed more tips from Callum's Charm School—"

"Then I'd be back already. Without Sia."

"Sia, hm?" Callum's voice sounds warm now, and I can picture him smiling as he spreads out in a chair somewhere, taking up more room than is possibly needed by any human.

A sudden pang of homesickness slices through me. Who'd have ever thought I would miss Callum? Not I. But I do, and it's a pleasant surprise.

"Tell me about her," Callum says.

"I've told you."

"In texts, yes. You've given me little that I couldn't read in Claudius's dossier—she's smart and beautiful and wonderful. Blah blah blah. I'd like to hear you talk about her in more specific terms. Personal terms. I think you owe me. And I need a break from thinking about my duties—sorry, *your* duties. I'm currently talking on a burner phone in some closet I've never seen before in a servant's wing. Mum will likely fit me with a tracking device whenever she finds me. And you too—especially you—whenever you get home.

Anyway, spill. Give me a reason to live, a reason to see meaning in life again."

"So dramatic," I say, but I'm smiling.

In truth, I do owe him. I'm incredibly grateful for his help. Though my brother is far more charming than I am and excellent in social situations, the more formal meetings and negotiations have always been the bane of his existence. Not to mention fending off Mum and Dad, who I know must be flaming mad. I took a risk in staying. I assumed that Mum and Dad would rather not have the country discover that I've disappeared. They can't exactly employ troops to bring me home without causing a national incident. Especially not with the leak we've had in the palace.

Callum is making a big sacrifice so I can stay—taking up my duties and also assuring Mum and Dad of my safety. What's more—he's not doing it to gain something in return. The least I can do is indulge his curiosity.

"What do you want to know?" I ask.

"Anything. Everything. Tell me about what it's like to live as a commoner and about the woman who made the perfect prince go rogue."

I start with what's easiest, telling Callum about living a simple life— washing dishes and delivering food and by all accounts, pretending at being an average, everyday man.

"It's been enlightening," I tell him.

"Dishwashing and manual labor are enlightening?"

"Actually, yes."

Alessia aside, my time here has changed—or *is changing*— me in ways I can't yet name fully. I've seen people who have very little live joyfully, shouldering one another's burdens. It will impact me as I consider how to best serve Elsinore and what kind of policies and programs might be efficient and effective.

I also can't stop thinking of ways to help the struggling economy of this one village, but I don't mention this to Cal.

My brother laughs long and loudly when I tell him about ruining a cast-iron skillet that had been in Enzo's family for generations. How was I to know cast-iron shouldn't go in an industrial dishwasher? I don't skip the embarrassing details, like how the whole village keeps trying to not-so subtly push Alessia and me together, or how many of them still refer to me as Mr. Perfect.

"Little do they know you're *prince* perfect."

"Some of them do know," I admit.

At this point, I think the older half of the village knows. I'm not sure if they've recognized me or if the grandpas have been talking. Thankfully, Luci is gone with Marco, because from what I know of her, Sia's best friend is very nosy.

But so long as I'm the one who tells Alessia ...

"I hope they're good at keeping secrets," Callum says. "Because if word gets out about you being there—"

"It won't."

The village is actually full of *terrible* gossips. But they have also managed to stay incredibly tight-lipped about this. I think it's for Alessia's sake—clearly the nonnos aren't the only ones who think she'll kick me to the proverbial curb when she finds out who I am.

"And you're sure about her?" Callum asks. "I mean, I guess that's a silly question. What else but love could make you forsake your duties?"

Love. It's a word I thought I understood until her. "I'm sure."

"I just never pegged you for instalove."

"It wasn't that."

"But you said you knew the first night," Callum says.

"I knew I felt something more than expected, that she was more than expected. But it wasn't instalove."

"You should have seen Claud's face, by the way. So smug. So proud of his precious rubric. I told him if this works out, he should turn it into a digital matchmaking service and make millions. He refused even to let me try it. In any case, instalove or love in ten days, four hours, and thirty-seven minutes—whatever. It's love."

I won't argue his point, even if it feels strange to say it to anyone but Sia. And I can't do that if I haven't told her who I am.

"You're still tracking the minutes, I see."

"I've switched from a timer counting down to a stopwatch counting up the minutes. And yes, I'm tracking down to the minute until you're back home. Any ideas on how soon that will be? No pressure, but do remember I'm currently hiding from Mum in a closet filled with mothballs and cleaning supplies."

"How's Father?"

There's a pause. "No changes to report."

Callum sounds like he's hedging around the truth. I frown.

"Any worse?"

"You know I'll let you know if he takes a turn. Meanwhile, Mum sent out the invitations to the ball."

That information settles like an anchor in my stomach. "I guess she's pretty certain I'll return, then."

"I think she thinks pushing ahead with it is like her insurance that you'll come back," Callum says. "Though it's not like the invitations say the ball is specifically *for* you. Still— the rumors are flying."

"And what, exactly, are the rumors?"

Callum laughs. "You really are out of touch."

"I am, and it's wonderful. When I return, I highly recommend disappearing for a while. That is, if Mum doesn't attach a tracker to you."

"She won't let either of us out of her sight ever again. But let's see—the rumors. Our leak has apparently shared that the ball is to find you a bride. But a few of the other news outlets are reporting that you've run off to get married and that the ball will be to introduce your new wife. Which, hopefully, is exactly what the ball will be."

Let's hope so.

Callum pauses. "I don't want to put a dark cloud over your happy time, but what if she *does* find out and doesn't want that royal life? The longer you stay, the more attached you get, and then ..."

The more crushing Alessia's rejection would be.

"If she says no, there's always the life of a zebra shark." I try to keep my voice light. But there's nothing light about it.

Because if Alessia doesn't want me or doesn't want me because of my title and my life, I can't imagine being with anyone else.

_____

"Form a well in the flour," Enzo instructs, leaning into me as he examines the giant pile of flour in front of me.

We're at his kitchen table for a cooking lesson. And even though it's morning, the room is stuffy. We need to open a window. Or maybe if one less person were watching over my shoulder...

I've got all three of the nonnos giving me advice on how to make pasta. Sal, across from me, and Enzo and Gianni flanking either side of me. At least for now, Sia is sleeping.

But any minute now, she'll probably emerge to watch me fail at pasta making.

"Like this?" I ask, digging into the center of the pile of flour.

"No, no—that's more like a pit. A *well*," Enzo says.

Gianni chuckles, a low rasp. "More like digging a grave."

Sal giggles, and I wipe sweat off my brow with my forearm. I'm trying to enjoy this--shouldn't cooking be fun? But I'm not used to being ordered around. Or being so bad at something. I mean, I'm struggling to make the right kind of indentation in flour. I'm not sure the power of all three nonnos combined can help me.

"Like this." Enzo steps directly behind me, his front pressed to my back. He pops his head around under my armpit and puts his hands directly over mine. Using my hands, he forms what looks just like what I did before. "A well. See?"

I *don't* see. And I'm more concerned with how close he's standing, and how weird this is. It *is* weird, right?

I glance up to see Sal laughing silently but so hard his face is like a tomato and tears roll down his face.

Enzo keeps directing my hands with his, praising me though he's doing all the work. Then he fills in the well, piling more flour on top, and I want to groan.

"Now we do it again. One more time together," he says.

With his worn hands cupping mine, I start making another dip in the flour, hoping it's correct. To be honest, I'm not sure cooking is ever going to be in my skill set if I can't make a correct well in flour. I will say the task is harder, not easier with a little Italian man pressed up against my back, directing me like a fully grown human puppet.

"That's it," Enzo coaxes.

"It's like *Ghost!*" Sal sputters, finally finding his voice as he clutches his stomach.

"What's a ghost?" Gianni demands.

"The movie!" Sal says. "Mr. Perfect is our Demi Moore, and Enzo is Patrick Swayze."

"He's what?" Gianni cups his hand around his ear, like his lack of understanding is because he can't hear Sal. I don't understand either, but I can hear just fine.

"Good," Enzo says, ignoring his friends as they switch to Italian and what sounds like a heated debate. "Now the eggs."

Trying to crack six eggs with another person's hands covering yours goes about as well as could be expected—shells go everywhere, and one yolk escapes the well, rolling down the side of the pasta and glomming onto the wooden table.

"Maybe if you step back and let me do it myself ..." I suggest.

"No, no! We can do this," Enzo says.

Gianni walks around the table to where Sal is now humming. I recognize the song, I think. "Unchained Melody?"

When he reaches Sal, Gianni puts a hand on his chest and starts singing in a deep baritone. He has a beautiful voice, rich and surprising. And as soon as I hear the words, an image comes to mind. I haven't seen the movie *Ghost*, but I suddenly remember the iconic—and very sensual—scene.

NOT the kind of scene I want to be reenacting with Sia's nonno.

"One more egg, then we stir," Enzo says, handing me an egg as he starts to hum.

As I crack the egg, his humming becomes full-on singing--offkey--and then his hands are on my hips and we're swaying. The other two nonnos are now waltzing through the small living space with Gianni still crooning, and I'm just about to ask Enzo for some space *please*, when Alessia walks through the door from the hallway, rubbing her eyes.

She comes to a stop, then rubs her eyes again. I expect her to ask about why Enzo is still spooning me or the dancing or maybe even the singing.

Instead, she says, "You're teaching Phillip to cook?"

Her voice sounds choked and raspy from more than just sleep. Finally—*finally*—Enzo steps away, kissing both her cheeks and giving her a hug. He murmurs something in her ear as Gianni holds out the last, long note. Sal claps and whoops as he finishes, and I join him. With a crooked smile, Gianni takes a little bow.

"Boy! Come, come," Enzo calls, waving me toward Alessia, who is smiling, but has her arms wrapped around her middle. She offers me a sweet smile.

"What about the pasta?" I ask.

Enzo claps his hands. "Bah! Another time. Too much work makes you dull. You and Lessy need a break. Day off!"

As I open my mouth to ask if he's sure, Enzo winks and lumbers back to the table, where within just a few moments, he's incorporating the eggs with a fork, making the whole process look easy.

Sia leans close. "He never teaches anyone to cook," she whispers.

"It didn't quite work. I think I'm in need of a lot more lessons."

Stepping closer, she links her arm through mine and leans her head on my shoulder. "It means something that he took time to teach you at all. It means he approves."

I don't have time to process this, because Enzo makes a rumble of disapproval. "Go, children! Time is a waste!"

"We're going! Give me a minute to wake up." Sia yawns and turns to me. "I need caffé and a change of clothes. And some time to think. I don't know what we should do. I don't take days off."

Gianni launches into another song, this time in Italian, and Sal begins dancing again. No waltz this time, but something more modern involving a lot of hip thrusts. Sia covers her mouth, stifling a laugh.

I give her a gentle nudge. "Why don't we spend the afternoon in Repestro, and then you can come up to my hotel. I'll take you to dinner—a proper date."

Sia frowns. "Aren't you sick of our village yet? You've spent every day here for the better part of two weeks."

"Just the restaurant and walking through the village. Your thinking place. I would like to see other places that are special to you. Places you love, places that matter to you."

Alessia thinks for a moment, then her small smile widens into a grin so wicked, it makes my heart leap. "I hope you have a bathing suit."

CHAPTER 11

Alessia

PHILLIP DOES NOT, in fact, have a bathing suit, which is the ONLY reason I'd ever willingly rummage through Nonno's underwear drawer where he keeps his bathing suits.

"How could you come somewhere like the coast of Italy and not bring a bathing suit?" I ask him while brushing past a fistful of briefs for anything swim-related and remotely close to Phillip's size.

Phillip leans in the doorway, sliding his hands into his pockets. "I didn't think I'd have time to swim," he says simply.

What did he think *he'd be doing?* Phillip's answer about why he's even in Italy—for a work break—is just vague enough to stoke the fire of my curiosity. Of course, I've been doing my best to ignore ALL curiosity with regard to things he's not telling me.

But it's becoming harder to do. The more I get to know him, the more I want to know. Even if I *don't* want to know.

"You *can* swim, yes?" I ask. "The current is very strong. And we know you can't climb hills so I need to make sure you can handle it."

Almost before I can register the movement, Phillip steps close, crowding me against the dresser. "Are you questioning my physical prowess, Sia?" he murmurs.

There is nothing I question *less* than Phillip's physical prowess. Especially now that his chest is pressed up against my back like he's a new jacket I'm trying on. My breath hitches, and the only thing that keeps this from being an incredibly sexy moment is the fact that my hands are currently inside Nonno's underwear drawer.

"Maybe." My voice sounds embarrassingly breathless.

"Then I guess I'll need to prove myself," he says, his breath tickling my neck and making all the tiny hairs there rise.

I'm seconds away from combusting when Phillip has mercy on me and steps away, returning to the doorway. "I played water polo in school," he says.

And now I'm imagining his big body cutting through the water with smooth strokes and strong arms. I should have known. He's got the broad shoulders and tapered waist of a swimmer. A *competitive* swimmer.

I love to swim, but my hips and backside are definitely the broadest part of me, tapering up to a chest I only wish had a fraction of what Luci has. I may swim proficiently, but I do NOT have a swimmer's body.

"It's not often I get to swim in the sea. Will you keep me from drowning if I need help?"

"I think I could probably save your life. *If* I wanted to."

"You'd be sad to lose me."

I would. "Nonno would be sad to lose his dishwasher. So hard to find good labor." I look at him. "Especially free labor. Nonno said you wouldn't accept payment."

He doesn't so much as bat an eye. "I don't need it. Find anything?" Phillip asks.

Honestly, no. Phillip is tall and water-polo broad and muscular. Nonno is short and round and soft. Even the stretchiest swim trunks I've found so far would fall right off Phillip's lean waist.

My fingertips brush against something solid at the back of the drawer—an oversized matchbox. Why is Nonno keeping this in here?

I slide it open and freeze. Inside the compartment are a few matches and two rings—my mother's and my grandmother's. My hands tremble a little as I trace my grandmother's single gold band, then examine my mother's. It has a single, round solitaire. Simple, unassuming, beautiful—all qualities Nonno has assured me she had. And has told me I inherited as well.

Grief envelops me in a sudden and suffocating embrace. It takes effort to move air in and out of my lungs.

"What is it?" Phillip asks, and I'm grateful for his words yanking me back to the room. "Sia?"

My throat is tight, my eyes damp. Phillip steps close when I don't answer, cupping my hand inside his as he peers into the matchbox.

"Was this your mother's?" His voice is a soft caress.

I nod. "And my grandmother's. She died before I was born."

Phillip slides an arm around my shoulders, and I throw myself against him, clutching him in a hug tight enough to rival one of Luci's. I keep the box carefully tucked in my palm as Phillip strokes my back and hair, dropping a kiss to the top of my head.

"I'm sorry, Sia. So sorry."

I sniffle, trying desperately to contain all kinds of moisture so I don't do something embarrassing like leave tears—or *worse*—on Phillip's shirt. "It's okay. It was a long time ago."

He's quiet for a few breaths. "Time helps. But I don't think it heals. Not like they say."

"No," I agree. "It doesn't."

I sense a shift as his hands clutch me, as though now he's the one needing comfort. I nuzzle shamelessly into his chest, seeking and finding comfort as I breathe in his warm, masculine scent. With my free hand, I stroke his back, willing Phillip to tell me whatever is making him suddenly cling to me like a vine.

"My father is dying," he says, finally, his voice ragged.

I manage to set the matchbox on the dresser behind him so I can hold onto him with both hands. Tightly. He shudders once, then sighs, his hands resuming their soft slide up and down my back. One tangles in my hair.

"I'm so sorry, Phillip."

"Thank you."

I'm relieved he doesn't try to tell me it's fine. How could it be?

But a lingering question fills my mind. It's one I don't want to think about and definitely don't want to ask. But I must.

"Shouldn't you be with him? Instead of being here with me?"

Don't go, don't go, don't go.

I have to be the most selfish human on the planet for even thinking this. It only reveals how attached I've grown to

Phillip in an absurdly short time. Even without knowing all the details of his life.

Even knowing he will leave.

Slowly, carefully, Phillip pulls back, only enough to meet my gaze. Blue may be a cool-toned color, but his eyes are warm.

"You are reason enough to stay."

Oh, my heart. My silly, secretly romantic heart.

I want to smile. I want to cry. I want to climb into Phillip's arms.

"But—"

Phillip cups my face in his hand, and I lean into his palm like a desperate house cat.

"He is stable for now. But yes—I must return soon."

There is a question in his eyes. And on his lips, as they part, then close. Then part again.

Ask me, I think. *Ask me!*

He doesn't, even if I swear I can see the question in his eyes. I hope he can read the answer in mine. Because, despite the fact that leaving Nonno still feels impossible and heart-wrenching, it would be a yes.

For Phillip, I would say yes.

Phillip presses a soft, lingering kiss to my temple that does wonders to snuff out my disappointment. Given the topic at hand, this kiss has zero business sending a thrill through me. Clearly, I've got some mind-body disconnect going on here because the thrill is there. It is real. And it has me feeling stupid things and wanting to say and do even stupider things.

Needing to break this tension before our first kiss happens while Nonno's tighty-whities are hanging out of the drawer, I step away.

And that's when I see a familiar scrap of fabric at the very back of the drawer. Exactly what I need by way of distraction from this moment, which has quickly become a little too real.

A wicked smile curves over my mouth, and I manage to tamp it down before I pull out the faded zebra print Speedo and hold it out to Phillip. "This might work. If you aren't allergic to spandex."

CHAPTER 12

Alessia

IT'S NOT until we pick our way down the rocky cliff to Repestro's best (and most private) beach that I realize my mistake. Because when Phillip pulls off his shirt and drops his shorts without an ounce of hesitation, I'm faced with the REALITY of Phillip wearing Nonno's old Speedo.

The joke's on me.

I always thought the phrase *swallow your tongue* was disgusting in addition to being physically impossible. But I understand it now. Because I completely choke at the sight of Phillip in Nonno's tiny trunks.

I've also lost my ability to blink. Or breathe. Or stop staring at the glory that is Phillip in a minuscule piece of stretchy fabric.

Just my luck—he notices me staring.

I mean, OF COURSE he does. I'm standing a few feet

away with my jaw practically unhinged as I take him in. And the normally reserved man has absolutely *zero* reservations when it comes to his body. Not even one shred of self-consciousness.

Nor should he.

"What?" he asks, setting his hands on his hips, which makes his muscles flex. The tiny tilt of one corner of his mouth is the only clue that he knows exactly what he's doing.

"You picked out the suit. Do you not like it?"

I avert my eyes, forcing them toward the horizon where the choppy blue sea meets the cloudless sky.

"It's adequate."

Adequate? Adequate is not in the right hemisphere for what Phillip in this suit is.

Illegal. Indecent. Scandalous. *Delicious*.

"Does it cover me sufficiently?"

Is he serious?

Apparently, he is fully committed to pretending he doesn't know what effect this is having on me because he takes a slow turn, arms spread wide. I can't keep my gaze from him.

The man is *perfection*. Seriously, was he designed by a computer model and spit out of a high-tech 3D printer? Maybe that's it. He did say he develops smart technology. Maybe he *is* tech.

Because no human man should have this kind of body—all tawny gold skin and perfectly cut muscles. I feel like I should be covering my eyes, watching only between a crack in my fingers. But I'm not. I'm just flat-out staring.

Does the suit sufficiently cover him? NO.

His broad, bronze shoulders ripple as he turns. He stops, propping his hands on his hips again. I can't stop staring at the dusting of blond hair in the center of his chest, disappearing over the building block ridges of his abs, then reappearing a little darker just above his bathing suit. I force my eyes to skip over the bathing suit itself and what it does—and does NOT—hide, letting my gaze trail down his legs. Have I ever really looked at a man's thighs? Not like this, I'm sure. I want to smooth my hands down his legs, to feel the muscles jump beneath my palms, the tickle of coarse hair. I'd like to trace the faint tan lines I see above his knees.

"Well? Am I all good?"

"You're all *something*," I mutter, too low for him to hear. Then, louder, I add, "It's fine. You're covered … sufficiently."

Not even close, but that's my own fault.

"Are we going to swim?" he asks, still with that tiny fraction of a smile on his face.

My head snaps up, and I fumble with the button on my shorts. "Yep."

I step out of my shorts and pull my shirt over my head, forcing my eyes toward the ocean and not the landscape of Phillip's perfect body. But when I'm down to nothing but my black two-piece bathing suit, built for swimming and not for showing off, I find Phillip is now the one staring. The intensity in his gaze makes my stomach do a barrel roll.

"What?" I ask, mirroring his earlier stance with my hands on my hips. This is no time to be self-conscious—even if my body is *nothing* like his. I am built how I am built, my body strong and curvy and not going to change. Phillip's heated gaze seems perfectly happy with what he sees.

"Am *I* sufficiently covered?" I ask.

"You … I …" He trails off, then swallows hard, the fire in his eyes igniting into a blaze that feels at once like desire and a challenge.

Though my soft curves couldn't be more different than

the hard planes of Phillip's fit frame, I refuse to cower or hunch or hide. I guess I don't need to worry because Phillip looks ready to *devour* me.

The thrill of his heated gaze makes me grin. "Race you!" I call, already turning toward the water.

I take off at a sprint, ignoring any lingering self-conscious thoughts of what my backside looks like while running in a swimsuit. If Phillip doesn't chase me after seeing whatever jiggling is happening back there, it says more about him than me. I wouldn't want to be pursued by him anyway.

You want me? Then you better want my curves.

My feet hit the water, slowing me just enough that Phillip almost catches me. His fingertips brush my lower back, but I dive into the surf just out of reach.

The water is icy cold, a delicious shock against my heated skin. Just what I needed to reset my brain. What I told him earlier is true—this stretch is dangerous for people who don't swim well, with a steep drop-off and strong currents. But knowing Phillip played water polo gives me confidence not to worry about him as I continue kicking and propelling myself through the water.

I feel the gentle pound of surf on my back as I pass under the wave break and out into deeper, calmer water. When my lungs are burning, I burst to the surface, gasping as I brush wet hair from my forehead and cheeks. Whipping my head around, I look for Phillip, expecting to see him swimming after me.

I am alone. I turn, then turn again, treading water as I scan the choppy surface of the water. There are only waves and a gull swooping and diving.

Where is he? I didn't know my mind could imagine so many terrible things in a few seconds' time. Maybe he got a leg cramp. Or a shark—rare but present in these waters—came after him.

"Phillip?" A sudden panic seizes me. "Phillip!"

I twist, squinting against the sun and the sting of salt in my eyes as I search for any sign of him. I shouldn't have gone so far out without first seeing for myself that he could swim well.

Phillip's head breaks the surface a few meters away, and my heart dips with relief. His eyes are wild, and as his gaze lands on me, the relief on his face matches my own. His grin is huge, and I swear, I feel it all the way down to my cold toes.

"Sia."

He swims toward me, those strong arms cutting through the water with powerful, fluid strokes. I haven't moved, save to keep treading water, kicking to keep myself afloat. He bobs up, our faces close. My pulse thrums through my veins.

"I thought I'd lost you," Phillip says, looking desperate and relieved at once.

"I'm here."

His hands find my waist under the surface of the water, his rough palms scooping me up, drawing me closer. I gasp when our bodies line up beneath the surface. Something about the heat of his skin contrasted with the cold ocean, makes my skin prickle with sensation.

My hands grip his shoulders—his large, lovely shoulders. I'm still kicking slowly, instinctively, but there's hardly a need when Phillip is doing all the work to keep us afloat. I have never felt indebted to a sport until now.

Water polo—I thank you for making this moment possible.

I expect Phillip to release me as his expression calms, but the fear and panic dissolves into something more heated. His hands clutch me firmly. I'm hyperaware of the strength in his big hands as they tighten around my waist.

I slide one hand along his shoulder to his clavicle, tracing it with a finger. He sucks in a breath.

"Let's move where I can stand," he says.

No argument here. He releases me with one hand, the other tightening around my waist as he manages to move us a few feet closer to shore. My feet are still not touching the bottom, but Phillip stands and returns his attention to me as the waves gently lap at us.

He draws a hand up my spine, his touch sure and firm. But with the way my whole body breaks out in goose pimples, it might as well be a single feather brushing lightly. His gaze roves over my cheeks, dipping down to my mouth, then lower as he seems to trace every bit of my skin above the surface of the water.

He finishes his perusal, and our eyes meet again.

"Is this okay?" he asks, and I nod so vigorously, he chuckles.

"More than okay."

"I am not ... misreading?"

"I think you're reading me just fine." I slide my hands from his shoulders to the back of his neck where I let them tangle in his short hair. I almost confess that his touch has become almost an insatiable craving, and I feel like I'm a starving woman set in front of a buffet of delectable food. But I feel foolish letting him see the depth of my desire.

Also, Phillip is SO much better than food.

"Good."

He nods, then brushes wet strands of hair away from my cheek, tucking them behind my ear. When his fingertip grazes my jawline, I shiver.

"I'm not used to this," Phillip says, and vulnerability coats his words.

I wait for more, but he only blinks at me, his eyes roving over my face like it's the first time he's ever seen me.

"Used to what?"

He considers, tilting his head as his hands flex against my skin. "Used to feeling too much. To this kind of connection."

"Good," I say, and the look on my face must reveal my jealousy at the mere idea of Phillip like this with anyone else because he shakes his head.

"I don't just mean in a romantic way. I'm ... I'm not sure I've ever had this with anyone."

His confession feels like a prize I've fought for and won. But it makes me a little sad for him too. "Not even your family? You speak of them like you're close."

"We are. But I think I've always been holding back somehow. Even when I didn't mean to. Being with you, being here —it's helped me to see what I've been missing."

I'm not sure how to respond to his confession. And he seems to have more that he wants to say. So, I wait.

"I don't trust easily," he continues a moment later, his blue eyes intense. "Too often, people have the wrong intentions for wanting to be close to me. And I've been sheltered in some ways."

I glance toward the beach, where his PPOs—who no longer hide since the whole village knows they go where Phillip goes—are walking along the sand, always with an eye toward us. Today, it's Graves (the young one) and Martin (the one who looks like he could kill someone with any ordinary household object).

What if they're *always* with him, not just now? Exactly *how* sheltered has Phillip been?

Phillip clears his throat, meeting my gaze again. His eyes are filled with something like wonder. "I never knew it could be like this. I didn't expect it, maybe didn't even believe in it."

Neither did I.

Tightening my arms around him, I nestle my face in his neck and hug him like I did in Nonno's room, only a little less desperately. Phillip tugs me as close as we possibly can be.

He sighs, tilting his head and pressing his nose to my temple. "This is ... everything."

It is. I could live out here like this. Phillip and I, our own little island. Just the two of us with the sea and sky and one another.

My heart constricts as reality intrudes into my daydream. *This is temporary,* I remind myself. *He isn't here forever.*

But you could go with him. IF he asks.

I want to tattoo this moment on my skin, to let it mark me forever, to give me something I can point to later and remember if this doesn't last. If Phillip leaves without asking me to come with him, or if, when push comes to shove, I can't bring myself to leave Nonno even if Phillip asks.

It's this desperation to cling to NOW, this sense of what's truly at stake that makes me lift my head. Our gazes collide, and the urge to kiss Phillip is too strong to ignore. Whether this is all we ever have, or if this is the start of something too huge for me to comprehend right now, I am done holding back.

I lean forward, closing the distance between us. His eyes darken, dropping to my mouth, then back up to my eyes. Our lips are millimeters apart when he pulls back.

"Wait," he says.

Talk about romantic buzzkill.

But none of the heat has left Phillip's eyes.

"Before anything more, I need to tell you what I haven't. There are things you should know before ... this."

NOW? He wants to do this *now*?

I mean, sure—I want to know. I DO. I also appreciate the depth of character he has, where he doesn't want to move on and mislead me or keep me in the dark. I absolutely want him to sit down and spell out every single detail of his life.

But I also REALLY want to kiss him. What's more, I want —no, maybe NEED is the word—to kiss him *before* whatever bomb he's about to drop.

Based on his expression, it's quite the bomb.

Now it's my turn to make him wait. I give my head a little shake. "Answer me this—have you ever lied to me?"

His brow furrows. "I haven't been forthcoming."

"That's not what I asked. I'm not talking about omissions. Have you told me an outright lie?"

He thinks for a moment, and then his answer is firm. "No."

"Have you misrepresented yourself in some way?"

He hesitates on this one. "No, but without knowing everything, it's just as—"

I put a gentle finger to his lips, which doesn't help with the whole needing-to-kiss-him desire, but it does stop the flow of words from his mouth.

"What I mean is, have you been misrepresenting the core of who you are? Your character. Who *you*, Just Phillip, are in here." I drop my hand to the center of his chest and press my palm flat over his heart. "Whatever details you haven't told me, they are not *who you are*. Those are a job, a title, or a circumstance you were born into. Who your family is and

139

what you do for work—those things do not *define* you, even if they are big parts of your life."

While I watch, his face sobers, and he swallows. Under my palm, his heartbeat picks up, and the expression in his eyes softens.

"You might be the only one in the world to really see me."

"Then everyone else in the world is missing out."

He closes his eyes and releases a shuddering breath. His hands move up and down my back so tenderly, as though I truly am precious to him.

When his eyes open again, the serious expression is back, and as much as I love his need to be honest, at this exact moment, I want to drop-kick his honesty and need to suddenly confess his truths into the middle of the Mediterranean.

"I just want to make sure—"

I interrupt him. Again. My tone is a little sharper, my words a little faster. "Are you married? Seeing someone else?"

"No." His expression turns fierce. "I would never."

"Then, Just Phillip, I need you to kiss me *before* you tell me whatever it is you think I need to know. If there's no other woman, if you haven't lied, if you've been wholly your-self aside from sharing the particulars of your job or family or whatever I don't know—then I want to kiss you. Just you, Phillip, just like this. As we are *now*."

My words feel monumental. I know that I am choosing to intentionally stay in the dark. Whatever Phillip has to say could change everything. Based on this conversation, it abso-lutely will change everything.

But right now, under the summer sun with the icy ocean and his warm skin against mine, I am choosing simple. Uncomplicated. Temporary.

I am choosing Just Phillip.

Before I can rationalize my way out of it, and before Phillip comes up with another reason to hold back, I slant my mouth over his in a searing brand of a kiss I immediately know I won't ever come back from.

CHAPTER 13

Phillip

IT IS NOT unusual for me to struggle with words, especially when I'm skating by on my marginal Italian or mostly better English. But as Alessia's mouth meets mine, the existence of words at all seems to disappear.

There is only *sensation*—the pillowy softness of her lips, the urgency as they move against mine, the sweet taste of her mouth balanced by the tang of salt water. Her hands drag through my hair, up the back of my scalp, and I feel it everywhere. I feel *her* everywhere as our mouths move, discovering, teasing, taking, demanding, offering.

The kiss has two sides, somehow both sweet and tender while tinged with desperation, heavy with *want*. My breath comes in ragged pants, my heart is thrashing against my ribs, and my skin feels like fire is dancing along its surface. I've kissed women before, but ... maybe

I haven't. Because this kiss is so much more, so complete, so heady, and so much deeper than physical. I'm instantly aware of how insignificant any other kiss has ever been.

How insignificant any other *woman* has been.

Alessia has utterly wrecked me in the very best way possible.

As is the story with Sia, this is wholly unexpected. It is so much *more*. I shouldn't be surprised; after all, this is how it's been with us from the start. I came planning to make an offer of marriage based on logic and reason and—yes, a rubric—hoping love would follow. The script got flipped, so I still haven't mentioned marriage, but I think ... I think I might have fallen in love.

My body's response to having Alessia pressed close, her lips on mine, seems in full agreement with this new plan. But my mind refuses to quiet now that rational thought edged its way in.

I was nervous to come to Repestro, concerned about the outcome and how Alessia—a complete stranger—would respond to a proposal. I am not nervous now. I am *terrified*. Because as I'm holding her, feeling things I've never felt before, I'm aware of several very important things simultaneously.

First—I still haven't told her the truth. And *not* telling the truth feels far too much like lying, no matter what she just said.

Second—this feels far too fragile, too good to be true, too easily lost in a blink.

We can both feel it—the fragile state of limbo we're in. I think this is why Sia insisted on kissing me before I could tell her the truth. Later, things may change. As much as it pains me to even consider, Alessia may not want to leave. In fact, after spending time here with her and Enzo, I doubt she'll leave him.

Which may make these final moments without the truth the last happy moments of my life.

Alessia pulls back, studying my face with a furrow between her brows. She cups my cheek. "You're shaking."

Am I?

"Is it too cold?" she asks. "I'm used to the water temperature, so I didn't even think about—"

"It's not too cold."

Alessia's gaze moves over me with such care and concern, somehow in a way no one has ever looked at me before. Her fingertips trace over the ragged excuse for a beard covering my jaw, slipping down my neck. I've never wanted to shave more.

The need to confess the truth to Alessia presses hard against me, an urge even stronger than the one I have to capture her mouth with mine again.

Biting her lip, she asks, "This isn't ... too much?"

Oh, it's too much. But in the best way possible.

"If anything, this is not nearly enough."

With one finger, she lazily traces my collarbone. The smile on her lips is playful, teasing. "Good. Should we maybe ... do it some more?"

I shift my hold on her, sliding my hands down to her lower back, keeping her right up against me. "Sia, I still want to talk. I need to tell you everything."

When her gaze meets mine, my throat constricts, feeling suddenly too small for the unfamiliar emotions lodged there. What if—after all this—she can't stomach the idea of being with a prince? Of becoming a queen in the near future? Or even at the most basic, moving and leaving Enzo behind?

Now that I've met them both and spent time here, I can't

see him leaving Repestro. Not with Gianni and Sal and the restaurant.

And I'm honestly not sure Alessia will want to leave. Even for me.

"What's the rush?" she asks, and I can see how hard she's working to keep things light, to push off the inevitable. "You said you aren't married. That's good enough—for now."

I shake my head. "You deserve the truth."

"I'm not saying I don't want to know. I do. But maybe I don't want to know *right this second*. I'm far more interested in … other things." Her gaze falls to my mouth again, and she lifts one finger to trace my lips.

She wants the dream to last. And I can't fault her because so do I.

Tilting her head, she drags her fingertips roughly across my scalp as she kisses me again, and I groan, tightening my arms around her waist.

"Sia," I growl, and she murmurs something in Italian against my lips.

"I like you growling my name," she says. "You're always so in control. So measured and thoughtful. I love that about you, but it's also nice to see that control slip."

It's more than *slipping*. From the moment I met her, every ounce of my good sense and my logic, and yes, even my control, has all but evaporated like morning fog in the heat of the sun.

It feels good. SO good. And yet … I cannot allow myself to completely lose who I am. She *must* know.

But first, she has to stop kissing my neck like this.

Giving her no warning, I dip down below the surface, grabbing her by the waist. Bursting out of the water I toss her as far as I can. Her scream dissolves into laughter just before she hits the water with a smack.

I reach her in long strokes as she surfaces. I grab her again and pull her up, planting a quick kiss on her smiling lips before I throw her again. This time, likely because it wasn't a total shock, she tucks her body and manages a graceful flip in mid-air.

Again and again, I toss and retrieve her, both of us laughing until we're breathless, kissing until my lips are numb.

The sun is hot, the water cold, and Alessia in my arms is simply perfect. I think this is the best day of my life—so far.

I'll tell her tonight, I promise myself. *I'll pamper her like she deserves, like a true princess, and then, I'll tell her the truth.*

When we both tire of the water and her lips are starting to turn blue, we climb out of the ocean onto the beach. Only then do I see the Costa children, giggling and running up the step path—carrying all of my clothes.

"Come back!" I shout.

Alessia only laughs, tugging her shirt down over her wet bathing suit as she wrings out her hair.

"I guess being their favorite new person doesn't make you immune to their pranks," she says.

I glance up in time to see the little girls tossing my clothes right over the side of the cliff, over white-capped water crashing over the rocks.

I shake my head. "You were right. They are monsters."

Alessia grins, giving my body a cursory glance. "Hope you aren't feeling shy. It's quite a walk through the village."

CHAPTER 14

Alessia

FROM THE MOMENT we climb into the sleek black car driven by one of the two PPOs, Phillip shifts. It's subtle but as real and tangible as the exquisite leather seats and tinted glass. I see it in the confident set of his shoulders, the sharp awareness in his eyes, even in the assured way his arm curls around my shoulders in the backseat. It reminds me of my very first assessment of him when he walked into Nonno's restaurant.

Phillip exudes confidence and power—even if he's dressed in a baggy pair of Nonno's pants that come just below his knees and a shirt too small to button.

He speaks to Martin, the older PPO who's behind the wheel, in what must be Elsinorian. I don't need to know the meaning of his words to have a visceral response to Phillip's deep voice speaking unfamiliar syllables coupled with his deep confidence and authority.

The sense of commanding power is like a pheromone, even if it's also a stark reminder that Phillip doesn't belong in my little world. I've managed to shove reality aside most of the time, but now it's smacking me right in the face.

"What's wrong?" Phillip asks, drawing me closer as he raises the partition to give us privacy from Martin and Graves.

I gesture to the tinted glass. "This!"

"You want me to lower it again? I was trying to keep Graves from talking our ears off, which is usually what he does when we're driving back to the hotel. But if you want to …"

I have zero desire to talk to Phillip's protection team at the moment—though at another time, I'd be happy to get to know them. I'm sure they have stories I'd *love* to hear.

Phillip's finger hovers over the button, and I grab his hand, tugging it toward me. "It's not that. It's just all *this*. I forget, you know?"

"Forget what?"

"I forget that you're not just a simple dishwasher from my village. It's fine. Don't mind me," I tell him, squeezing his hand. "You've gotten a good feel for my world. I guess it's only fair I get to experience a little of yours."

Phillip studies me, and I get the sense that he's on the verge of telling me everything. And again, I'm not quite ready.

But then he flashes me a sweet smile and says, "I hope you're ready to be pampered because that's my plan for the rest of our date."

I can't say that I've ever been pampered, unless I count being fussed over by the nonnos my whole life, which I instinctively know is nothing like whatever has put this gleam in Phillip's eyes.

"You already have a plan? We didn't find out we're spending the day together until this morning."

"I always have a plan," Phillip murmurs, and before I can think of a good response to that, he captures my mouth in his, making me glad for the partition after all.

———

"You can't be serious." I gape at Phillip who is, admittedly, serious much more often than not. But he can't be serious about THIS.

"What, exactly, is the issue?" Phillip crosses his arms, leaning in the doorway of the ridiculously enormous hotel room—*my* hotel room.

It's just one bedroom in a suite, one of multiple suites we have access to because Phillip has rented the *whole top floor of the hotel.*

And we're not talking like, a normal hotel. Oh, no. This is one of those swanky affairs for celebrities and socialites. Not that I'd know. But in the little traveling I've done with Luci, the places we've stayed have NOT looked like this. They smelled like feet and cheese—and no combination is quite as bad as cheese-feet—and looked like an apt location to film a horror movie.

Here, everything is gorgeous and shiny and like I couldn't afford to replace it if I broke it. I've tried to avoid touching anything, as there's probably a person whose job it is to wipe down all fingerprints from every shiny surface.

And this room—*my* room—is filled with flowers, first of all. Not just a nice arrangement or two, but I count half a dozen at a glance. In cut-glass vases, which might actually be crystal. And then, there are the clothes. An entire rack of them—everything from sundresses and casual tops to what can only be described as ball gowns. I pull open a drawer and, yup—it's filled too.

With underwear and bras.

My gaze shoots to Phillip, who rubs the back of his neck. "I had help from Luci," he says, then quickly adds, "Lest it seem creepy that I went underwear shopping for you and knew your size."

"I ..."

Creepy isn't the word. IS there a word for this kind of thoughtful excess?

No. There are zero words.

I make a noise, because that's about all I can do, and then slam the drawer shut.

"I told you I wanted to pamper you." Phillip smiles like this is nothing.

Maybe to him, it is nothing. Maybe ... he's wealthier and more important than even I suspect. And that thought makes me feel like I need to breathe into a paper bag. If there are paper bags in here, they're probably designer.

I manage to locate my voice. "This is more than pampering. It's too much."

"It's not enough."

THAT simply isn't true, but Phillip's tone tells me I won't win this argument. The look in his eyes, which is something like adoration, assures me that he believes this—even if he's wrong.

"Is this how you treat all the women you date?" I mean the question to be teasing, but it comes out sounding far too insecure.

Phillip frowns. "I told you I haven't dated much. And I can assure you—I have done nothing of this sort for any woman, ever." He meets and holds my gaze, that same confident, authoritative tone taking over. "Nor do I *intend* to do it for any other woman. Ever."

I mean, how can I argue with that?

Because what he's implying—or what I think he's implying—is huge. And I don't think I'm missing his meaning. It's just hard to believe.

As though he can sense my overwhelm, Phillip takes two steps into the room and cups my cheek with one hand, wrapping the other around my waist. "The last thing I want to do is make you uncomfortable, Sia. But if you don't think you're deserving of this, you're wrong."

I smile, leaning into his palm. "You're sweet. And thoughtful. It's just ... I don't *need* all this."

Phillip is quiet for a few beats, then he pulls back, cupping my face with his hands. "Sia, let me spoil you. Please. It is my pleasure. And it's so much more enjoyable knowing you're the kind of woman who doesn't require it and would never demand it. Will you deny me this?"

When he puts it that way ...

But then I think about the DeSantis and others in Repestro, living on so little. I think about Nonno's cottage where I've spent my whole life. It would fit in this whole suite several times over.

"Phillip, the cost—"

He places a soft kiss on my lips, just enough to make my argument vanish as my mind starts to wander to other places.

"Please don't think about the cost," he says, finally pulling back and leaving me in a post-kissing haze. "I know you don't *need* this. It's why I gave you simple gifts in Repestro—flowers I picked by the roadside or books I knew you'd like."

"The books were signed by the author. Not exactly simple."

He ignores this. "I love that you aren't swayed or motivated by money." He pauses. "But I do *have* money. And tonight, I would like to spoil you with it. The fact that you don't chase after it only makes me want to give you the world."

My head is spinning, and Phillip takes me by the shoulders, turning me so I'm facing the luxurious room. He wraps his arms around my waist and leans forward, resting his chin on my shoulder. His breath and the tickle of his beard on my neck make me shiver. My eyes flutter closed.

"I'll treat you as my queen, Sia," he murmurs against my neck. "As long as you'll let me."

I'm hardly a queen, I want to say, but I'm honestly tired of protesting. If Phillip can afford to do this and wants to do this, why can't I just let go and enjoy it? Even if it feels so strange.

Probably just as strange as it felt for him to wash dishes for no pay in Nonno's kitchen.

But if you have a future with Phillip, it won't just be for tonight, a nagging little thought reminds me. *This would be your new normal because this is HIS normal.*

Okay, I definitely don't want to consider that right now.

I CAN'T consider that right now.

"Please, Sia? For me?"

It's hard to protest when Phillip is begging me to enjoy it, his breath against my skin a very persuasive argument.

The dresses really *are* gorgeous. I've never had a really nice dress, nor an occasion to wear one. Plus, there's a large soaking tub in the en suite bathroom calling my name. After spending my whole life using the cramped shower at

Nonno's where I'm constantly slamming my elbows into the walls, a giant tub looks like heaven.

"Thank you," I whisper.

"You are more than welcome. Now—please take your time getting ready." Phillip places a last, too-quick kiss on my cheek and releases me, walking back to the doorway. "I have dinner plans for us, and I need to take care of a few things first. Not the least of which includes finding some clothes that fit." He tugs at the collar of Nonno's shirt. "If there's anything you need, just shout. Or call down to the front desk." He points to a phone next to the bed.

I can't imagine needing anything else. But a part of me wants to test this. What would happen if I called down and asked for a Toblerone?

"How much time do I have?" I ask.

"How much time would you like?"

"Maybe an hour." I glance through the open bathroom doors at the tub. It has jets! And is that a bottle of wine next to it? "Maybe ... make it two."

CHAPTER 15

Alessia

I PERFORM A VERY scientific study about how long it takes for skin to prune while soaking in the massive tub. It takes thirteen-and-a-half minutes for skin to start to prune. By twenty-five minutes, the wrinkling is at a maximum volume. I stare at the tips of my raisin fingers, telling myself to get on with getting washed up and ready.

Instead, I have another sip of wine. It's a crisp chardonnay, my favorite—even if Nonno says chardonnay is the most boring of all wines. I wonder if he or Luci told Phillip which wine I prefer. And what kind of shampoo I like and where I buy my soap. Because Phillip even had a bar of Zola's lemon and lavender sheep's milk soap waiting in the tub for me. She makes it on her farm and only sells it in the village.

The thoughtfulness behind all of this threatens to overwhelm me. After finishing my glass of wine, I hold my breath underwater until my chest aches, then come up for air, gasping but feeling somehow more centered.

When I climb out finally, my skin is pink and soft from the heat and being well-scrubbed. I slide into the bathrobe hanging by the door, which feels like wearing a cloud. I've never understood the idea of people stealing bathrobes from hotel rooms, but if the robes are this nice, I totally get it.

I stare at myself in the giant mirror above the double sinks, giving myself a stern look. "Enjoy this," I tell my reflection. "Let him pamper you."

But I don't really need the rebuke. I *am* enjoying it. Unless I allow myself to think about how different this feels from my normal life. Earlier today, when Phillip told me about his father, I would have said yes had he asked me to come home with him.

If he does ask, though ... is *this* the kind of life I'd be living?

I can do so for a night. But could I do this for longer?

Channeling Luci, I shove that question right out of my mind and focus on getting ready.

I always wondered if expensive products would really make my hair behave. Turns out, yes. Yes, they do. All my wild waves needed was a deep conditioner that probably cost eighty euros and some kind of cream that smells heavenly and smoothed my hair into perfect, soft curls.

Each and every dress fits perfectly. I try them all on, of course, saving my favorite for last. I pull on the turquoise dress that first caught my eye. It slips over my curves like it was tailored to my exact measurements.

The back of my neck starts to prickle as I look in the mirror. What if ... what if it *was* made for me? There isn't a tag. Does that make this custom? Couture? I'm not even sure I know the difference between the two.

What I *do* know is that this level of pampering wants to lull me into a content acceptance. It whispers *just relax and enjoy. Drink another glass of your favorite wine and smell the flowers. Relaxxxx...*

But a still-sentient part of my brain is trying to shake me awake. I can't let the extravagance lull me into a luxury-based hypothermia. First, you stop feeling the shock of it all. Then you settle in and get used to it, feeling like this is where you belong.

Then you die.

Sheesh! Shut up, inner voice. You can't kill my vibe tonight.

I'm just debating whether or not I should put on the matching jewelry I found on the dresser when there's a knock at the door.

"No rush, but everything is ready whenever you are." Phillip's voice is slightly muffled through the door. "Do you need help with anything? Like maybe ... a zipper needing to be zipped?" he says, a teasing lilt to his voice.

I grin. "Nope. I chose one with a side zipper. I'm all set."

"Too bad."

The low rumble of his voice, even through the door, makes my pulse race.

"Give me five more minutes?" I slip the necklace around my neck, fumbling with the clasp. I can't identify the light blue stone hanging in a platinum setting, but I have to assume it's real.

"I'll be on the terrace," he says. "Pretending I'm not dying to see you."

"Please don't die."

"Then please don't make me wait too much longer."

I hear his heavy steps as he walks away.

My hands shake as I slide in the earrings. "Just costume

jewelry," I tell myself. "Not expensive gems worth a small fortune."

The necklace hangs heavy around my neck, the weight itself a good indication there is nothing *costume* about these jewels.

Everything about this night is excessive. Completely and utterly so. Ridiculous, even. I may be a simple woman with simple taste, protesting all of this in theory, BUT I'm still grinning like some kind of fool as I take a last look in the mirror.

Drawing in a deep breath to steady my fluttering nerves, I step out of the room—and gasp.

Because somehow, while I was busy getting wrinkly in the tub and enjoying pricy hair products, the suite has been transformed.

Candles are everywhere, their flames dancing. Strings of lights criss cross overhead, tiny bulbs like glowing stars. The balcony doors have been thrown open, revealing what's more like a terrace, big enough to hold flowering plants and topiaries. A wrought iron table in the center holds more candles and roses at its center. Silver domes cover two plates, like something I've only seen in movies.

Phillip steps into view on the balcony, then perks up as he sees me. "Sia," he says on a shuddery exhale. And I'm so distracted by the hungry look in his blue eyes and the cut of his perfectly tailored dark suit as he crosses the room, I miss the very obvious update to his appearance until he reaches me.

Then, I gasp for the second time in two minutes. Because Phillip *shaved*. And his bare face without even the slightest hint of stubble is glorious.

Gone is the patchy beard, revealing golden skin and a strong, square jaw. The man was unfairly handsome before, but now, he's been upgraded to *impossibly* handsome. Perhaps illegally.

As he reaches me, stopping just a foot or so away, I also notice there's no tan line, which confirms something I suspected the first night I met him—the beard isn't his usual look.

"Is that a good gasp or a bad gasp?" he asks, running a hand over his face and looking adorably self-conscious.

"I'm just shocked. I wasn't expecting it. But it's good. Not that the beard was bad, but—"

"It was definitely bad. My brother tried to tell me. I couldn't stand the itching," he says.

I reach a hand toward him, then pause. "May I?"

"Please."

His eyes close as I trace his jaw with my fingertips. His skin is smooth and warm, and when I place my hand against his cheek, he leans into my palm, smiling, still with closed eyes.

"What made you decide to shave tonight?"

He opens his eyes, meeting mine. "I didn't like how it felt while we were kissing." He pauses. "I wanted to feel your skin on mine. Which, now that I'm saying it sounds ..."

He chuckles, but there is nothing funny about what his words are doing to me. "It sounds like you maybe want to try kissing without the beard," I suggest, biting my lip.

His smile, against a backdrop of smooth, golden cheeks and a sharp jawline, is LETHAL.

"I absolutely do. But later."

I raise a brow. "Later? Are you sure you want to wait?" I'd be offended, thinking maybe I somehow imagined the combustible chemistry of our kisses early, except for the heated look in Phillip's eyes.

His gaze falls to my mouth, darkening further. "No. I'm

really not. But I think if we start kissing now, dinner will be cold by the time we stop."

Agreed. Even if kissing Phillip will always trump dinner.

Phillip sucks in a breath and allows his gaze to roam over me. "Sia, you are beautiful. *Fiele*."

He doesn't offer up the meaning of the word, but his expression says it all. I've never felt so beautiful, so adored.

"The dress really is gorgeous." I smooth a hand down the silky material. "Thank you."

"I do like the dress, but it isn't nearly as lovely as the woman wearing it."

Although he looks half ready to throw me over his shoulder and carry me back to some cave (which would be a luxury cave with designer rocks and custom torch mood lighting), Phillip holds out an arm. I slide my hand through the crook of his elbow.

"This feels like a dream," I say.

"A good one, I hope."

I don't point out that all dreams, good or bad, end when you wake up. Because I am not going to let myself think— much less *talk*—about endings tonight. No—I am simply going to enjoy the fairy-taleness of it all and ignore whatever might come after.

"It's wonderful, but I don't feel quite like me," I tell him.

Phillip smiles at me, his gaze tender. "You are beautiful in your work apron, beautiful when your hair is damp from the sea, and you are beautiful in this dress. You bring beauty wherever you are because it comes from inside."

"Thank you," I whisper, feeling a tiny pinprick of tears I also don't want to allow tonight. Even if they're happy tears, which these most certainly are. Needing a change in subject before I do something stupid like confess I might be falling in love with him, I ask, "What kind of elves did you hire to help with the lights?"

"No elves. Graves and Martin helped."

I choke on a laugh. "Your personal protection officers helped hang twinkle lights?"

I can maybe picture Graves doing so, because the man has that gentle giant thing going on. I've caught him smiling a few times while watching Phillip and me. I'd bet money on the man being a romantic.

But Martin hanging twinkly lights? I can't picture it. Or— I can picture it, but he's glaring daggers at Phillip the whole time.

"They are as proficient wielding a string of lights as a weapon," Phillip says. "Part of the job requirement. But I'll have you know I did most of the work."

"You can wash dishes *and* hang lights. A regular Renaissance man," I say, fighting against a rising tempest of emotion in my chest. I'm feeling too many things and feeling all of them WAY too much.

"Only for you," Phillip says as we step out on the terrace. There are more twinkle lights here, lightly bobbing in the breeze. Faint music and the sound of cars and people talking filter up from below, making this balcony seem somehow more intimate by contrast.

"You know what I just realized?" I ask, turning to face Phillip.

"What?"

"It's *later*."

Grabbing him by the lapels of his perfect suit, I pull his mouth down to mine in a kiss that I hope says *thank you, this is an amazing night*, and *I might just be convinced to run away with you and have your babies*.

But maybe Phillip was right to suggest we wait. Because

kissing without the scratch of his bristly beard hairs is even better than it was earlier, and now I'll never want to stop. His smooth cheek, smelling of aftershave, brushes mine in a delicious meeting of skin on skin.

He pulls me closer, his fingertips gripping my hips. I may have started this kiss, but Phillip takes control until my lips are tingling, my fingers are numb where they're still clutching his jacket for dear life, and I'm pretty sure I've confirmed the existence of several previously undiscovered galaxies.

Kissing this version of Phillip, the commanding one with a cleanly shaven jaw, makes my knees go weak. I'm grateful for the way he's holding me because otherwise, I'd be a boneless puddle on the very plush carpet.

Slowing things down, Phillip backs off enough to press kisses to my cheeks and forehead, then lifts my hand to his mouth, keeping me pinned in place with his intense gaze as he kisses my knuckles.

Do knuckles even have nerve endings? They must because they're sending a signal to the rest of me.

"Well? Was it better without the beard?" I ask, keeping my voice light.

"To be perfectly clear, I would be more than happy to kiss you under any circumstances. But yes—I much prefer without the beard."

Phillip pulls out my chair and I wobble a little in my heels, plopping into my seat with all the grace of … well, someone completely without any at all.

"Are you okay?" Phillip asks.

I manage to locate my speaking abilities again. "Yes. Just not used to heels."

As he takes his seat, he smiles, and the fondness in it tugs at a new part of my heart. "Ah. One of my sisters has rebelled against heels. She's made it her personal mission never to wear them. She tried to instate a no-heel edict."

His smile widens, like the story is that his sister discovered a cure for a rare disease, not that she tried to be the fashion police. I love seeing his brotherly concern.

"Which sister? And remind me how old they are again?"

"Henrietta. Though she prefers Henri and gives bonus points to people who pronounce it like it's French. *En-ree*," Phillip adds, in a French accent so sexy I have to clench my fists under the table. "She's eighteen and Juliet is seventeen."

Whenever he speaks about his sisters, his eyes fill with warmth—the blue of a mellow, tropical sea. I lean forward, elbow on the table (manners be damned) and rest my chin in my hand.

"Do you miss them?"

"I do. Though most of the time, they're away at school. We enjoy our summers and holidays together." Taking a deep breath, he says my name in the way one does when they're about to say something you definitely don't want to hear. "Sia."

Whatever he's going to tell me will be like the carriage turning back into a pumpkin at midnight. I know it. I clutch the napkin in my lap, twisting it in my fingers. Despite my desire to get rid of the secrets still between us, at the moment, I'd rather lift the dome off our food than pop the lid off Pandora's—or Phillip's—box of secrets.

"It's time you knew everything. So you can decide if my life is something—or if I am *someone* you still want."

I'm already shaking my head. "Phillip, the details I don't know, important as they may be, are not *who you are*."

Phillip's jaw clenches, and I wonder how often I've missed being able to see the movement before he shaved.

"Unfortunately, in this case, these things really are a matter of who I am."

My heart thunders in my ears, and I do my level best to capture a memory of this moment, the Before. Just in case things don't go so well in the After.

"Maybe, like the kiss, this conversation could be filed away for later?" I suggest, but Phillip shakes his head.

"It's time," he says.

A throat clearing at the door to the balcony interrupts. I could kiss Graves. (On the cheek, of course.) Only, more than apologetic for interrupting, he wears the kind of serious regretful look of a man about to deliver some really bad news.

"Sorry to interrupt, sir."

"Does it have to be now, Graves?"

Graves glances at me, then back to Phillip. "I'm sorry, but yes."

They switch to Elsinorian, and I think I pick up on the word *father*. My stomach tumbles, and I clutch my napkin tighter in my hands. Phillip rises quickly, concern etching his features. He gives my shoulder a quick squeeze as I try to stand.

"Stay," he says. "Eat. I'll be right back."

I wait for more reassurance, like *this won't take long* or *nothing to worry about* or *whatever this is, it won't change everything all at once*, but Phillip only offers a tight smile and the briefest of kisses on my cheek.

When he goes inside, he closes the balcony doors behind him. They're glass-paned, but the gauzy curtains fall shut, meaning I can only see vague shapes moving inside.

Should I eat? I stare down at the silver dome covering the plate. My stomach makes an embarrassing sound I'm glad it held back while Phillip was here, but then it twists with worry as I think about his father.

A voice calling up from somewhere below pulls my attention to the railing. "Lessy!"

Frowning, I stand. That sounds like Luci. But surely, it can't be …

"Alessia!"

I place my hands on the stone railing and lean over just enough to look down. "Luci?"

My best friend is standing on the sidewalk below the balcony. Marco is beside her, looking a bit embarrassed by this whole scene. The streets aren't too busy, but there are a fair number of people passing by and with three flights between us, Luci has to shout with hands cupped around her mouth.

"What are you doing?" I demand.

"I'm so glad I found you!" she says, putting a hand to her chest. She's breathing heavily, as though she ran here all the way from Repestro. "This place sure has a lot of balconies."

I glance back at the closed doors. "Have you been shouting up at all of them?"

"Yes!" she bends over, putting her hands on her knees for a moment, and Marco rubs her back with one hand, waving to me with the other.

I wave back. "Luci—why are you here?"

She stands back up. "We came to tell you—ooh! Lovely dress! And the jewelry! Those stones could blind me even from there!"

"Thanks, but I know you didn't come here to check out my dress. Is it Nonno? Is he okay?"

"He's fine." She waves a hand. "Lessy, it's about Phillip."

My stomach is an anchor, plummeting to the cold dark

ocean floor. I give the doors another look. No sound, no movement behind the curtains.

"What is it?"

"When you said he was from Elsinore, it made me think of something, but I couldn't quite remember. Then I overheard a conversation between the nonnos. I googled Phillip and Elsinore, which we really should have done ages ago." She gives Marco a light shove. "I've been distracted."

Marco looks well pleased with himself.

I lean farther over the balcony. "Luciana! Get to the point!"

She pauses, and though my friend is all about making entrances and exits and high drama, she's clearly *still* trying to catch her breath.

"For heaven's sake, Luci, did you *run* here from Repestro?"

She shakes her head, but Marco is the one who answers. "We've been running around the outside of the hotel, shouting up at balconies. But she's been hyperventilating like this since she realized you're dating a prince."

Marco's words hit me in stages. Or, rather, the word at the very end of his sentence hit me in stages. A ... *prince*. I am dating a *prince*.

The moment the word sinks in, it's so obvious. Phillip is a *prince*.

All of the pieces fit. The way Phillip speaks, the way he carries himself, the ease with which he gives orders. The PPOs. My dress, and all the luxurious things in my room. The fact he has a whole hotel floor to himself. The family "business."

Phillip is a prince.

"Marco!" Luci wails. "I wanted to tell her!"

"Oh, sorry." Marco does actually look apologetic. "But I didn't tell her everything. You can still tell her the rest."

"The rest?" My voice is so faint, I'm not sure it reaches them down below, but Luci is already speaking.

"He's not *just* a prince of Elsinore. He's the *crown* prince. And his father's health is poor, which means any day now—"

I finish her statement because my brain already came to all the conclusions my best friend is trying to share with me. "Phillip will soon be king."

I slump against the railing, letting my brain fully process this information.

The man I'm currently on a date with, the one who I opened up to against my better judgment and my protective instincts, the man I'm *falling in love with*, is not just a prince but will soon be a *king*.

Which means ...

No. NO. That's absolutely as far as I can follow this information.

"LESSY!" Luci shouts from below. "Do you know what this means?"

I ignore her, glancing around the balcony, looking for an escape hatch. Or a ladder. A parachute. Anything to get out of here before I have to face Phillip again.

PRINCE Phillip.

My fight or flight instincts have been reduced simply to flight and flight NOW.

"Just think," Luci calls. "You could be Princess Alessia."

Nope.

At one end of the balcony, there's a trellis just beyond the railing with some climbing vines. I walk over, yanking on it to test the structure's sturdiness. Seems okay. And this isn't a huge hotel. We're only four floors up.

"You'd be Queen Alessia!" Luci shouts, clearly not reading the room.

I kick off my heels, remembering Phillip's story about his sister and her no-heels edict. I snort, a hysterical laugh bubbling up out of me. It probably was an actual edict, like a *law*, she tried to pass.

"Unless their laws would make you a consort, which I don't understand. Sounds like a fancy kind of royal escort to me. I'll look it up."

"No need! I'm coming down!"

"You're WHAT?!"

I hike up my dress and kick one leg over the railing.

"Lessy, no!"

"This isn't a good idea," Marco calls. "Perhaps you should reconsider."

I'm reconsidering, all right. Thinking back over every interaction I've had with Phillip. *Prince* Phillip. *Crown Prince* Phillip. Should I have been bowing or curtsying all this time? Exactly how many rules of etiquette or actual rules have I broken since I've met him?

And Nonno had him washing dishes! No wonder Phillip was so bad at it.

Wait—Luci said she overheard the nonnos talking. Did they *know about this?*

I feel so incredibly stupid. Like the butt of some cosmic joke—no, more like the butt of a *royal* joke.

Fabric rips as I swing my other leg over, the slit in my dress becoming a few inches slittier as I balance precariously on the other side. Luci darts around below me, holding her arms out like she could catch me or perhaps just break my fall.

I inch toward the trellis, telling myself this escape plan is totally fine. With the way the hotel is built into a hill, it's not as high over here. I should be able to work my way down. Luci and Marco can give me a ride back to Repestro, and I won't have to face Phillip.

"Lessy, stop it! You climb right back over the railing this instant!"

"Make me," I mutter, reaching out to grab the trellis.

The vines are a thorny variety, but I ignore them as I manage a firm handhold and ease one foot out, then the other.

"Ow!" Thorns prick the bottoms of my bare feet as I start to move down the trellis.

I ignore Lessy's shouting below. Ignore the rational part of my brain saying this is the worst idea of all the ideas I've ever had. Ignore the guilt when I think of what Phillip said before Graves called him inside.

"So you can decide if my life is something—or if I am someone you still want."

He'd been so sure knowing who he was would change how I felt about him.

And I'd been just as sure that whatever truth he told me, it wouldn't change who he is and therefore how I felt about him.

I pause, now a few feet down, my head below the balcony railing now. I can see the twinkle lights and the table set for dinner.

He did this. He did this for you.

I close my eyes, pressing my head forward to rest on part of the trellis without the thorny vines. Forcing myself to breathe in deep and slow, I focus on slowing my heartbeat. On shutting down that part of my brain that's reacting with panic, not logic.

I don't want to be a princess. Or a queen.

But I do want Phillip.

The man behind the title is worth all that comes *with* the title.

Isn't he?

Yes.

As terrifying as the prospect is, as many questions as I have about everything, as much as I would never have considered this had I known who he was when he walked into Nonno's restaurant, I can't give up on Phillip because he's a prince.

I open my eyes and begin carefully picking my way back up the trellis.

"Oh, thank God," Luci calls.

But then several things happen at once.

I grab a very thorny section of vines and feel a deep prick, the terrace doors fly open with Phillip shouting my name, and the top of the trellis wrenches free from the wall with a horrifying groan.

CHAPTER 16

Phillip

"ALESSIA!"

I'm alarmed by the empty terrace, but even more so when I catch sight of Sia's face—on the other side of the railing. I don't have time to wonder what she's doing or how she got there because just then, the vine-covered structure she's holding onto pulls away from the wall.

She screams, and I sprint for the railing. Graves and Martin shout behind me, but I ignore them, slipping out of my suit jacket as one of them grabs for me. I hop over the railing in a split-second, assessing faster than I move.

"Phillip," Sia says, her voice laced with panic. "Be careful!"

She's hanging over the side of a building and is worried about me?

"Just don't let go," I tell her.

"Sir! You can't do this!"

Graves reaches over and makes a valiant attempt to grab my hands. I move quickly, lowering myself so I'm holding the bottom of the railing, both legs dangling.

The balcony below is smaller than mine, but it's empty. I swing my body and use the momentum to propel forward as I let go of the railing.

I land in a crouch, dimly aware of shouts from my men above and shouts from what sounds like a gathering crowd below. There are flashes—lightning? No, *cameras*—as I dart to the edge of the railing where Alessia is hanging on to the trellis, her eyes panicked.

"Hang on," I tell her, leaning over the railing to grab her.

There's a thud behind me, and Graves is suddenly here, offering me a curt nod as he steadies the trellis. This won't keep it from completely coming loose, so I still need to hurry.

I manage to grab Alessia's torso with both hands, praying the railing will hold my weight as I lean over. She has a firm grip on the trellis.

Our eyes meet. "I've got you, mi bellina." The panic in her eyes subsides. "Trust me."

"I do," she whispers.

She lets go.

It's harder than action movies make it look to hold an entire person's weight like this, and I'm grateful for the disciplined training I've done for years that allows me to pull Alessia over the railing and into my arms.

There are cheers below and clapping, along with more flashes of phones or cameras. I ignore them all as I hold Sia to my chest. Her hands clutch my shirt, yanking me even closer. My heart slows only as Sia breathes, as I feel her warmth, as I hear her sigh of relief.

She's here. She's safe.

171

And so quickly, she's become the one steady thing in my life. Even if everything else just went sideways. I press a kiss to the top of her head.

"Thank you," she breathes. "Thank you."

I have a thousand questions bounding around inside my skull, but for the moment, it's enough that Sia is in my arms.

"Lessy!" a voice calls from below.

"Is that Luci?" I ask, frowning.

Alessia tenses, and with no small amount of reluctance, I loosen my grip, stepping back enough to examine her face. She looks uninjured but tense and shaky. Her eyes slide away from mine.

"She's here with Marco."

The questions hit like a sudden deluge of rain. Why was Sia dangling from the edge of the building? Why are Marco and Luci here at the hotel?

And why is Alessia suddenly having trouble meeting my eyes?

"Are you okay?" I ask.

She nods quickly—too quickly—and sighs. "I'm not splattered on the sidewalk—"

She must catch my grimace because she stops.

"Sorry. Too soon for jokes about my demise?"

"It will always be too soon for that."

A throat clears, and I glance over to see Graves, who can't seem to decide where to focus his gaze. "Uh, sir. We really must go."

I'm not sure if he means we must leave this balcony or get to the airstrip. A plane will land any minute to return me to Elsinore where my father has taken a turn for the worst.

I brush the hair back from Sia's cheeks, and her eyes finally meet mine again. Despite what just happened and the adrenaline still pumping through me and likely through her as well, we need to talk. And there's no time to do so gracefully, to tell her all that I need to say slowly, giving her time to react.

Par for the course, my plans have gone up like a house made of matchsticks and doused in petrol. I can't tell Sia who I am over the gourmet dinner upstairs now growing cold. She won't have time to get used to the idea of me being a prince while I'm still washing dishes in Enzo's restaurant.

After I get on the plane, my time here will be over. And I have no idea what that means for us.

I swallow past a sudden knot of emotion in my throat. "Yes. Sia, I need to—"

"Sir," Graves says, a little more insistently this time.

I shoot him a glare, but then see hands holding up phones, just beyond the balcony doors. Clearly, this room is occupied. Graves does his best to block them with his big body, but their cell phones extend above his shoulders.

"Vainto," I mutter, turning my body so Sia is hidden behind me. But that only puts her closer to the railing and I see more people, more phones held up by the crowd gathering below.

Martin appears inside the hotel room, throwing open the balcony doors and urging us inside with a flick of his wrist. "We need to get you out of sight," he says with a frown more sour than his usual, like he swallowed a bowl full of lemons rather than just one slice. "You're all over social media. We have to go before you're mobbed."

"Can you walk?" I ask Sia, and she gives me a look.

"You're the one who has trouble with a little hike," she says. Her smile is a flash, there and gone. "Now come on. Before Martin really loses it."

Taking my hand, she tugs me through the balcony doors, where a man and woman in nightgowns stand against the wall, kept back by James, another of my PPOs. He must have requested that they put their phones away, because they just watch, smiling, as we walk through their hotel room.

"Sorry for the trouble," I say, and Sia spits out something in rapid-fire Italian that has them both grinning as we exit.

"What did you say?" I ask as we make it to the door, where Graves makes us pause so he can exit first.

"Oh, just something about the brave prince rescuing his damsel in distress."

My head whips her way. "You know?"

She nods, but before I can ask more questions Martin ushers us into the hallway, which is becoming crowded with people. Most have phones up and are filming.

"Keep your heads down," Graves says, doing his best again to be a protective wall as he steps in front of us.

"I'm sorry about all this," I tell Sia, not sure if I mean the fact that strangers are filming this whole event in violation of our privacy or ... just the fact that I am who I am.

"And everyone gives me a hard time about not having a cell phone," she mutters as someone takes a photo with flash.

Martin grabs the phone and crushes it beneath his boot. The man starts to protest until Martin pins him with a look. "You'll be compensated," he says. But his words come across more like, "Say another word and it will be your face under my boot."

The man nods and ducks back inside his room. We say nothing else on the brief climb up the stairs, and a few minutes later, we're in the suite. A woman wearing a dark dress and a hotel name tag glances at us quickly, then away as she rolls a suitcase toward the door.

"You're leaving?" Sia asks.

I nod, then pull her into her room—not that she'll get to

use it again. Someone has already put most of her clothes in garment bags lying on the bed. She glances around the room, blinking rapidly as I fumble to locate words in English. Or any language for that matter. At the moment, I'm mute.

Sia squeezes my hand. "Is it your father?"

"My brother called. Father is fighting some sort of infection and they aren't sure ..."

The words catch in my throat, and Sia pulls me into a tight hug. I can't help but hope it's not a goodbye. It feels like a goodbye. It feels like—

"Let me go with you."

I pull back, stunned. Her beautiful face is serious, but her eyes are soft.

"Weren't you even going to ask me?" she says softly.

"I was, but I didn't think you'd go." I clear my throat, glancing away. "Not when I hadn't even told you who I am."

"You tried." She smiles.

"How did you even know? Or *have* you known this whole time?"

Sia shakes her head. "Definitely not. Though it seems clear Nonno did."

She looks at me, waiting. I nod. "But I didn't tell him."

She rolls her eyes, staring up at the ceiling. "Of course. Sal and his gossip sites. Anyway, Luci drove up here with Marco to tell me."

"Ah. And then you climbed over the railing and ...?" I raise a brow.

"I might have panicked when ..." she trails off, looking at me apologetically.

"When you found out I was a prince." She doesn't have to answer. I see the apology on her face. "That bad?"

"Just a lot to take in."

"Better or worse than if I were a mafia boss?"

She grins. "So much worse."

I chuckle, but the lightness of the moment is short-lived when Martin knocks once and sticks his head in the doorway. "The plane is here. We really must go."

When the door closes again, I take Alessia's hands in mine. "You really would come with me?"

"You really want me there?" she asks, seeming unsure for the first time since I've known her.

"I'll always want you with me."

Her smile is soft but strong. "Then I'll go with you, Prince Phillip."

FROM THE ROYAL BUGLE, EUROPE'S #1 SOURCE FOR ROYAL GOSSIP

Prince Phillip Rescues a Real-Life Damsel in Distress

In an unbelievable turn of events, Prince Phillip played the hero last night after he leapt from a balcony to save a woman hanging from the side of a hotel in Tarquinia, Italy.

It's unclear what the Robot Royal has been doing in Italy or how the woman fell over the railing, but there's no mistaking the fact that he saved a life. It's also impossible to miss the intimate way he's embracing the mystery woman in the photos.

Has this prince finally found a wife?

Though she's wearing what appears to be thousands of euros worth of jewels in these photos, taken by hotel patrons, upon closer inspection, we see no evidence of a ring.

Witnesses reported that the two seemed cozy, holding hands and even kissing. Just moments after the near-fatal rescue, Prince Phillip's security team escorted them to a local airstrip, driving a two-car detachment through streets crowded with onlookers hoping for a chance to see the prince. Other than his time at Hillwell, the prestigious all-boys school both Princes Phillip and Callum attended, the royal family has never been spotted with such little protection.

A member of the hotel staff told *The Bugle* that the prince and his mystery woman have been getting cozy for days in the luxury hotel suite. And now, it appears she's heading home to meet the royal family.

Might we be hearing wedding bells soon? Could the royal ball announced just a week ago be an engagement ball?

Time will tell, but rest assured *The Bugle* will keep you up to date with any new developments. Maybe next we'll be seeing Prince Callum settling down. See the slideshow of The Golden Boy's string of past girlfriends.

CHAPTER 17

Alessia

RATHER THAN A PRIVATE plane ride to Elsinore, I feel as though I've flown through some kind of wormhole and emerged into another world entirely.

I woke up this morning in the same bed I've slept in since I was a girl. The same uncomfortable mattress too, because Nonno and I are both too cheap to purchase new ones even if we both groan about how they feel like they're stuffed with hay bales or rocks. And now, I'm sitting in a buttery leather seat of a private jet, still wearing a (now-ripped) gown and jewels whose cost I cannot fathom, holding the hand of a prince.

I gasp as the plane dips with no warning, my fingers digging into Phillip's hand. He leans closer, pressing a kiss to my temple.

"We're having a little bit of turbulence, your highness," Graves says.

"I think he's aware," Martin says drily as the plane shudders again.

Phillip leans closer, pulling his hand from my death grip before dropping both hands to my hips. I suck in a breath. A slight smile tugs at the corner of his mouth as he buckles my seatbelt.

"For safety," he says, his hands lingering.

"You're trying to distract me."

"Perhaps." He arches a brow. "Haven't you been doing the same?"

I shouldn't be surprised that he noticed the way I talked incessantly through most of the short flight. Asking for a tour of the plane (it has a full bedroom and a bathroom with a shower!); asking what each and every button does (the seats recline fully and are heated!); asking how I should greet his parents (with a simple curtsy).

The plane jolts again, and I squeeze my eyes closed. Phillip presses something into my hands. I glance down and stifle a laugh.

"Your family even puts their crest on the air sickness bags?"

Phillip grins. "We prefer the term barf bag, and yes—it's very important that our crest be on everything. Right down to every square of toilet paper in the country."

"Are you serious?"

He holds it together for only a few seconds. "Of course not. And this"—he points to the paper bag in my hands—"is utterly ridiculous."

The turbulence starts in earnest then, and I forget about Phillip's very effective distraction techniques and instead do my best to act like a rational human instead of shrieking like a terrified banshee. Phillip curls an arm around my shoulders and leans close, singing an Elsinorian lullaby in a low baritone.

I don't understand the words, but his singing voice is incredible. I only wish I could enjoy it.

"We're about to touch down," Phillip murmurs a few minutes later. He gently pries my fingers from his bicep and curls his hand around mine.

"Oomph!"

There's a hard bump, then another quick one. Now we're slowing, and I cannot wait to get off this flying metal tube. This fancy, *royal* metal tube.

I'm sure I've left fingerprint bruises all over Phillip's arms, but he doesn't seem to mind. I'm still clutching the air sickness bag, thankfully, it's still unused.

But only BARELY. I don't want to get into gross details, but let's just say it was a very close call.

As we disembark and my feet touch asphalt, I could cry happy tears.

Phillip touches my cheek. He's frowning as he drags a finger across my skin, and I can feel the slickness there. I guess I *am* crying.

"Are you okay?" he asks.

My head is fine, my heart is feeling all warm and melty from his touch, and my stomach is—well, better not to think about it for the moment. I'm sure it will settle. For now, I stuff the air sickness bag in my purse.

"Just happy to be here," I say, and this earns me a quick kiss.

Phillip turns to his security team. "Thank you for your service. You should all take some time away." He frowns. "Graves. Are you okay?"

Graves looks about as green as I feel. "I'm a sympathetic

barfer." His eyes bounce to me and then quickly away. He grimaces, then covers his mouth with his hand.

"I didn't even throw up," I protest.

"But you still look like you might," Graves mumbles from behind his hand.

"Come on." Phillip sighs and links our fingers, tugging me toward a waiting black car with a uniformed man standing by the open door.

"Don't we need to get our bags?" We didn't have time to go back to Repestro for my things, but all of the clothes and items Phillip purchased for me at the hotel were packed up by hotel staff. I didn't so much as lift a finger.

"They'll be brought inside," Phillip says.

"I don't mind carrying my own bags."

Phillip drops a quick kiss on my lips, looking tempted to linger. "I'm sure. But you won't be carrying bags here."

And so it begins—the royal treatment.

Technically, it began when we boarded the jet. Or maybe when I slipped on the gorgeous dress and jewelry back at the hotel. But now, in Elsinore, at the palace, I'll get a real taste of what this life is like for him—and what it would be like for me.

It starts with not being allowed to carry my bags and will end with ... what?

Phillip immersed himself in your world, I tell myself. *You can do the same.*

"Will you make sure I don't make some kind of etiquette mistake?" I ask as we slide into the back of the car. "I don't want to embarrass you by using the wrong fork or something."

He grins. "You're concerned about using the wrong fork?"

"It's a thing in all the movies and books. Apparently, knowing which fork to use is the epitome of class."

"I've never stopped to think about forks."

"Because you know which fork is the correct fork. It's second nature to you. Meanwhile, I'm going to use the salad fork for dessert. Or a soup spoon to stir my coffee."

Phillip still looks amused, and I'm glad to see something other than concern in his eyes. Though I'm really not kidding about this fork worry.

"And then you'll be sent to the dungeon," he says.

"Does the castle *have* a dungeon?"

"I guess you'll find out," he says as the car pulls away from the airstrip and starts down a winding drive through lush trees and rolling hills.

There is not, in fact, a dungeon.

And it's a palace, not a castle. Which is a fancy term for an absolutely enormous estate that looks very castle-like. Made of gray stone, it's four stories high with wings shooting off in every direction. There are even a few towers. Most of the windows are dark, but many are lit, glowing warm and bright through the darkness.

"I'll give you a tour as soon as I can," Phillip says. He pauses, pulling his phone out of his pocket to glance at the screen. "Or I'll make sure to arrange one."

Arrange one.

A tiny pinprick of worry needles me. It makes sense that Phillip might not have the availability to give me a tour. He's been gone for two weeks. In addition to his father's health, I can only imagine the kind of work he needs to catch up on.

Actually, I can't imagine. Because what does a prince DO all day?

I silently count the windows on the back of the palace as we approach and give up at thirty-eight. I'm not even a fraction of the way done.

"How were you allowed to leave for so long? Was it a

princely sort of leave of absence?" I ask, twisting my hands in my lap.

Phillip doesn't answer right away. "I wasn't technically supposed to be gone. Only Callum knew I left."

I spin to face him fully. "You didn't tell your parents?" He shakes his head, and that pinprick of worry becomes more like a stab. "Are they going to be angry with you? With me?"

He squeezes my hand. "Any blame will fall squarely on me. As it should. But it will be fine."

Easy for him to say. I suspect forgiveness will come easy for the crown prince. But will I be viewed as some kind of money-grabbing royal chaser? Or blamed for his decision to stay away while his father is sick? I can only hope not.

Leaning closer, he presses his lips to mine in a soft kiss as the car slows, waiting for two tall, intricate iron gates to open. The driver rolls down the window, waving to the guards standing on both sides of the gate who give sharp salutes.

I lean closer to Phillip, feeling the phone in his pocket buzz again and again until he sighs heavily and pulls it out. He scrolls one-handed through notification after notification. Finally, he turns it off and sets it on the seat next to him as the car reaches a circular drive near stone steps and two large doors.

A grinning man, who must be Callum, bounds down the steps as the car stops. He's similar to Phillip in build and coloring, but Callum carries himself completely differently—open and easy, just like his smile. He yanks Phillip from the car and into a back-pounding embrace.

Callum winks at me over Phillip's shoulder as I climb out of the car with Phillip's jacket. Callum says something in Elsinorian and then switches to English.

"You've made it," he says. "I've never been so glad to see you, brother."

"Tired of all the responsibility?" Phillip asks, extricating himself and smoothing a hand down his shirt.

"Obviously. I'm quite ready to stop being a lesser, more flawed version of you. But also, I missed you. Shocking, I know. But true." Callum turns his attention to me, hugging me just as effusively as he did his brother. "I'm so very pleased to meet you, Alessia."

Phillip tugs me away from his brother, nudging Callum roughly back. "That's enough of a greeting, I think."

Phillip curls an arm around my waist possessively, which seems to delight Callum. He rubs his hands together. "This is going to be brilliant. Alessia, your pictures don't do you justice."

Pictures?

He must see the look on my face because his jaw goes slack. He recovers quickly. "The two of you made quite the sensation tonight. I can't wait to hear the full story about the heroic rescue later."

The doors burst open and two young women I assume are Phillip's sisters come practically sprinting out. They're both blonde—one with long hair who looks simply delighted to see us and the other with a chin-length bob looking somewhere between delighted and furious. From what Phillip has told me, I immediately peg the first as the younger of the two, Juliet, and the one pretending to be angry as Henrietta.

Henri, I mentally correct. It's shocking how immediately I feel the NEED to be liked by Phillip's sisters.

"Phillip!"

I step out of his embrace just as they reach him. It's a good thing I did, because the two girls throw themselves at

Phillip, causing him to stumble back. He hugs them both with his eyes closed, and my throat gets tight as I watch.

I feel a little like I'm watching a foreign film without subtitles. Even though everyone is speaking English, probably for my benefit. This kind of familial closeness is something I only have with Nonno, and it's just not the same. I'm both filled with warmth at the bond they seem to share, but it's coupled with an irrational jealousy and longing for something I've never had.

It's been years since I've chewed my nails, but I find myself viciously tearing at my thumbnail. I force myself to curl my hands into fists and wish this gown had pockets. Phillip keeps a hand on each of his sisters' shoulders.

"You left!" Juliet says. "I can't believe you left without telling us!"

"Without even bothering to say goodbye," Henri adds. "Or clue us in on the big secret. I can't believe you don't trust us."

"You told Callum," Juliet whines, but she seems barely irritated, while I can hear the hurt in Henri's voice. "Everyone knows he's got the biggest mouth in Elsinore."

"I'm sorry I didn't tell you. The information needed to be kept to a small group." Henrietta opens her mouth, clearly to argue, but Phillip adds, "A *very* small group."

A second car pulls up, and the PPOs step out, grabbing matching black duffle bags from the trunk.

Henri crosses her arms and shoots a glare their way. "Graves," she says in a sneering tone. "Of course *you* were involved in this."

The big man's neck goes red all the way to the tips of his ears. He dips his chin. "Your highness."

Phillip steps close to me, pressing a warm hand to my lower back. "I'd like to formally introduce you all to Alessia."

The look of unbridled affection in his gaze makes my heart feel toasty warm, even as I want to wither a little under the weight of his siblings' stares. But only for a moment. Callum's giant smile returns. Juliet has tears gleaming in her eyes. Henri has stopped trying to pretend to be mad at Phillip and is smiling.

Juliet steps forward and hugs me with an unbridled force that rivals Luci's even before I can move. My arms are pinned to my side as she squeezes me.

"You're so beautiful," she whispers into my ear, her voice raw and fierce. "I'm thrilled to meet you, Alessia."

"Stop hogging her," Henri grumbles, jostling her sister out of the way to hug me with only a little less violence than Juliet. "Lovely to meet you. Don't worry; we'll make sure you have everything you need."

"That's my job," Phillip grumbles.

Henri gives me another squeeze, then steps back, raising an eyebrow at her brother. She sniffs and hooks an arm through mine. Juliet immediately moves to my other side, doing the same.

"I'm still mad at you," Henri says. "And anyway, some things are best handled by ladies."

Phillip gives his sister a long, doubtful look. "We'll see."

"I think we're overwhelming Alessia," Callum says, and again, all eyes are on me.

"She'll get used to us," Juliet says. "We'll be besties in no time."

"Are you feeling okay?" Henri asks, tilting her head to study me. "Or are you naturally this shade of green?"

Ugh. How embarrassing. My cheeks flush, but I guess I'll take red over green. "I'm still feeling a little motion sick from the flight."

"Get her some crackers." Henri snaps her fingers at

Graves, who is the only one of the PPOs still standing nearby. His jaw tightens.

"He's a PPO, not a kitchen maid," Phillip says. "We'll have someone else find something. Graves, you're released. Get some rest. Go home. You're on break for a few days."

Graves nods, and heads inside, leaving Henri to scoff at his retreating back.

"I'd like to see Father if we can move this welcoming party inside," Phillip says. "Alessia? Are you okay to wait a few minutes? And then we'll see if we can find something to settle your stomach."

"Of course."

My stomach will hold out. It makes a gurgling noise and sweat pops out on my forehead. It will *probably* hold out. Between the nerves and the turbulence, I'm not totally sure.

We move inside the palace, and I do my best not to stare at everything with wide eyes. But I've never been in such a grand building. Everything, from the golden wall sconces to the detailed wood trim to the rugs and the paintings and portraits on the walls, speaks of a rich history (emphasis on the *rich*).

The walk is silent, the mood much more somber than before. Though I'm grateful for how quickly Henri and Juliet have taken to me, I would feel better on Phillip's arm, with his quiet strength to draw from. I can see the tenseness in his shoulders grow as we move deeper into the palace, climbing a second set of wide stairs, before stopping outside a set of double doors with four guards positioned on either side. They don't make eye contact with any of us, and Callum glances back with his hand on the knob.

"Ready?"

No. Absolutely not. I am the furthest thing from ready.

Phillip must see something in my face because he delicately removes me from his sisters' clutches. I'm surprised they don't protest, but maybe my nerves are obvious to everyone.

Phillip takes my hand in one of his and touches my cheek gently with the other. "I told you—I've got you."

I nod, exhaling a slow breath. "Okay."

"They'll love you," he says. "As I do."

My whole body freezes at his words. Did he just tell me he loves me?

Or was that just one of those phrases that sort of slipped out?

Phillip doesn't seem to realize the significance of what he said, even as his siblings are smirking and elbowing each other not so discreetly.

I don't have much time to overthink it because Phillip gently tugs me into a room about half the size of the main living area, with a grand bed along one wall. It's ornate, with a carved wood headboard and thick posts stretching high above toward the vaulted ceiling. The man in the bed still retains something regal about his countenance, even though his color is decidedly yellow and he looks exhausted.

While on the plane, Phillip mentioned his father is dealing with liver failure and is ineligible for a transplant because of some rare clotting condition. He's been receiving some treatments and so far, has been fairly stable. I'm sure Phillip would never have left if his father looked this bad.

Callum's siblings group together at the end of the bed, while a woman who must be the queen sits in a tall chair, holding her husband's hand. She stands when she sees Phillip, brushing her hands down what looks like a perfectly pressed blue suit.

I remember probably too late that I'm supposed to curtsy, and I do something between a curtsy and a bow, still clutching Phillip like a lifeline. Juliet snickers, and Henri elbows her.

The queen reaches for Phillip, her eyes sliding right over me like I'm empty space. He lets go of my hand to embrace her.

Whatever she says to Phillip, it's in Elsinorian. She steps back, giving Phillip a closed-mouth smile as she looks him over. In a much cooler tone in English, she adds, "We'll discuss your unexpected absence later."

Maybe it's not meant as a barb, but it lands like one. Not for the first time, I question the wisdom in my being here.

"Finally—I'm not the only one in trouble," Callum mutters, earning him an elbow from Juliet and an arched brow from the queen. But it draws a small smile from me—perhaps his intention given the cheeky grin he shoots my way.

Phillip steps closer to the bed, bending down to kiss his father's cheek and whisper in hushed tones. I'm grateful when Henri hooks her arm through mine, pulling me closer. I feel less out of place standing shoulder-to-shoulder with Henri, Juliet, and Callum, but still not like I *belong*. Especially not with the way the queen still hasn't acknowledged me.

But right now, the focus is Phillip's father, not me. I'm here for Phillip, not in the normal meeting-the-family capacity. Still, it's hard not to fidget while I stand here—the stranger in the room during an intimate family moment. My stomach is still protesting, churning as though I'm still in the air and not in a bedroom in a palace. I don't dare grab for the barf bag and draw attention to myself.

Callum clears his throat dramatically as Phillip straightens, stepping back. "Since Phillip is taking forever with this —Mum, Dad, I'd like to introduce Alessia, Phillip's fiancée."

Henri and Juliet gasp in unison and Phillip's jaw goes

slack, and his eyes find mine, looking as shocked as I feel. The queen momentarily loses her stoic mask, her eyes widening as she takes a step closer to me. "Fiancée?" she asks.

With a final lurch, my stomach gives up its commendable fight, and I vomit all over the queen's very expensive shoes.

CHAPTER 18

Phillip

WHEN YOUR IDIOT brother does something as asinine as introducing the woman you've spent a few weeks and exactly half a date with as your fiancée, it's hard to know where, precisely, to go from there.

Thankfully, I don't have to make too many immediate choices because the room erupts into chaos after Alessia erupted on my mother's shoes. Servants rush in to help Mum and clean the rug. The royal physician tells us all to leave and we all ignore him. Graves, who apparently heard my words about taking a break as a suggestion, not a command, appears with crackers and ginger beer.

"I can take Alessia to her room," he offers, even though he looks a little green.

"I'll do it," I say, meeting Alessia's watery eyes.

She shakes her head once, firmly. "No. You need to stay with your family. I'll be fine. I'm so sorry."

"Please, don't apologize. I'm the one who's sorry."

And I am. For the whole situation, start to finish.

At the same time, I can't find it in me to be sorry she's here with me. Which I'm sure makes me the most selfish prince on the planet.

"I'll find you," I promise, kissing her on the forehead. She nods meekly and follows Graves out, looking relieved to escape.

A servant has put the soiled shoes in a plastic bag, which leaves Mum in just her stockings. Somehow, this diminishes the power behind the glare she throws my way.

"We'll talk later," Mum says.

Stern looks just don't work as well paired with stocking feet. She leaves the room, flanked by Henri and Juliet, who make a good show of fussing over her. Callum grins at me, and I know it's because usually, he's the one getting the warning looks from Mum.

He wouldn't be smiling if he had any idea what he's done. "You and I need to have a conversation."

His grin widens. "Can't wait."

The sound of laughter startles me, and I glance at the bed to see Father wiping tears from his red cheeks. Callum and I immediately move to either side of his bed.

I take his hand. "Father?"

His laugh turns to a cough, and Callum hands him a water glass from the bedside table. I'm leaning forward, reaching out to help him drink when Father raises one white brow as though daring me to try and help.

This—the laughter, the look he just gave—it's a relief, honestly. I had no idea what to expect when we arrived. Though he looks far worse than when I last saw him, he's still *here*. I was afraid he'd be like my grandpa, who spent months in bed, a silent shell of himself before he passed. I was eight, but the memory holds strong.

"They say laughter is the best medicine," Father says, his hand shaking a little as he hands the water glass back to Callum.

"Nothing like a little vomit to lighten the mood," Callum says. I glare, and his expression turns sheepish. "Right. And I hope Alessia feels better."

"Alessia," Father repeats, smiling. "So *that's* where you've been. Off finding a wife."

"That's not exactly ..." I start, but Father's eyes mist over with tears, and I let myself trail off.

I need to clear this all up. But maybe not at this *exact* moment.

He squeezes my hand. "I am so very happy for you. It's the best news I could have hoped to receive."

Right. So, now is DEFINITELY not the right time.

"I'm so glad," I tell him, my voice sounding only a little bit strangled by the guilt of perpetuating this lie. I've gone from one lie—or, at least, the omission of truth with Sia—to another. This time to my own father.

"I'm sure your mother is already planning the wedding. Or she will be once she gets cleaned up." Father starts to laugh again, and it's hard to worry about the whole engagement misunderstanding when he seems so pleased. "I expect to hear all the details in the morning."

———

I've barely dragged Callum into my office when I spin to face him. "Do you have any idea what you've just done?"

"Sorry if I stole your thunder with the announcement," Callum says with a shrug. "But Alessia looked so uncomfortable, and you hadn't introduced her. I was trying to be polite."

I shake my head. "I'm not upset about that."

Seeing Father look so much worse than when I left made me feel horrible about being gone. And, I admit, for a moment, I got distracted.

"Then why *are* you so upset?"

"Because you introduced Alessia as my fiancée."

"Yes," Callum says slowly.

"You said that we're engaged."

I begin to pace. Has my office always been so cramped? Everything feels different. Or perhaps *I* feel different.

"I'm sorry," Callum says, still looking confused. "Were you waiting to make a more formal announcement? I just thought with Father being sick, you'd want to tell him and Mum straightaway."

"I would. If we were *actually* engaged."

This statement takes a moment to land. When it does, Callum drops into the chair across from my desk, dragging his hands through his hair. "You're not engaged?"

"No. We were in the middle of our first date when I got word to come home, actually."

Callum drops his hands. *"First date?* I know you said you were working in her grandfather's restaurant, but I assumed you were also at least taking her out, wooing her. What have you been doing with all this time?"

Learning to cook. Spending time with the nonnos. Delivering food to villagers. Playing handyman in the village. Enjoying a life free from all things royal. Getting to know a woman as simply a man, not a prince.

And also ... falling in love. I have no question in my mind

that somewhere along the way, even in such a short time, I have fallen in love with Alessia.

"I've been taking things slow."

"Of all the times to take things slow." Callum groans and covers his face with his hands before sitting up and staring at me with disturbing intensity. "You do remember that there is a ball coming up in a few weeks, correct? One where Mum hoped to peddle you off to any eligible woman. I'm sure she'll gladly shift it to an engagement ball, but she's not letting you off the hook. And with Father ... taking things slow isn't something you have the luxury of, I'm afraid."

I know Callum is right. I'm sure the moment Mum got cleaned up, she started planning. She's probably already in her office, crafting an announcement. Especially now that photos and videos from earlier have hit social media. Mum probably has her communications secretary in her suite right now, crafting an official announcement to release in the morning.

I'll need to be sure I get ahead of *that* story.

"You truly aren't engaged?" Callum asks.

"Why did you think we were?"

"She came home with you. I guess with the whole plan, I just assumed if she came with you, you'd already asked and she said yes."

I sink into my chair. Callum and I stare at each other across my desk.

"I'm truly sorry," he says, and I can see by his face— serious for once—that he means it.

"Apology accepted."

"Just add it to the list of one more thing I've mucked up." His smile is rueful, and his tone bitter.

I blink, studying his face and noticing for the first time the circles under his eyes and the droop of his shoulders.

Now that I'm really paying attention, he does look exhausted. His hair needs a trim (as does mine) and there are dark circles beneath his eyes. Even his skin seems paler than when I last saw him.

"I'm sure you haven't mucked anything up." *Too badly,* I don't add. Because it would feel too much like kicking a puppy at the moment.

"The plan is still to propose though, right?"

"Yes." Though I've hardly had a spare moment to consider where or how or when.

"Should we call Claudius and request his help? I'm sure he'd come up with a brilliant plan for how to fix this."

Tempting. But I shake my head and get to my feet. "No more plans."

Callum grabs my hand before I reach the door. I stop, and he studies my face, still holding my hand in what feels like a pretty uncharacteristic move.

"You love her," he says. Not a question.

"I do."

In the next moment, he's out of his chair and hugging me. "I'm so happy you've found love," he says. "My robot royal brother isn't a zebra shark after all."

I was about to thank him, but I punch him in the ribs instead.

CHAPTER 19

Alessia

QUICK RECAP: I threw up on the QUEEN.

And I'm ... engaged?

Bravo to me, I guess. I've accomplished a lot of things in one day.

Graves hovers in the doorway like a massive, muscly, overprotective mother hen. "Are you sure you'll be all right?"

I'll be honest—I'm grateful for his familiar, though slightly scary face. Though we've never spoken before tonight, the beefy PPO feels like an ally. He's also clearly a not-so-secret softy.

"I'm fine, thank you. I've got everything I need."

More than I could ever need—that's for sure, I think, glancing around the simply massive suite. A pajama set is laid out on the bed for me, and I'd be willing to wager my suitcases (full of clothes Phillip purchased for me) have already been unpacked in the ornate wardrobe along one wall or the walk-in closet next to the bathroom.

"Thanks for these, by the way," I say, shaking the cracker packet at him.

The tips of his ears go pink. "Of course. Someone will be stationed just outside."

I start to protest that I don't think I need my own PPO, especially not here. But maybe that's to keep me from getting out rather than to keep anyone from getting in?

"Welcome to Elsinore, Alessia," Graves says before closing the door and leaving me completely alone.

And do I *ever* feel aware of it.

At home, Nonno was always within earshot. We could talk through the walls or else I'd hear him shuffling around the house, singing or humming to himself. Here—everything is too large, too formal, too fancy. Unfamiliar. Silent. Strange. When I stop and listen, I hear no sounds at all.

I also have no idea where I am in the palace or how to find Phillip. Am I allowed to wander freely? I'd probably end up lost if I did.

Still—I crack open the door and find a man with dark red hair and a matching beard just across the hall in similar dress to the men posted outside the king's door.

"Do you need something, ma'am?" he asks in lightly accented English.

"Am I ... allowed out?"

He frowns. "You're a guest, not a prisoner, ma'am."

"Right." I hesitate, glancing up and down the long hall-way, trying to remember which way we came. Everything looks the same. Expensive. Old. Unfamiliar. "Well, I'll stay for now. Thank you."

"You don't need to thank me, ma'am."

"And you don't need to call me ma'am."

I offer him a small smile, which he does not return, and I find myself missing Graves. He must be excellent at what he does to be one of only four men Phillip took with him, but at the same time, Graves is so very *human*. The man across the hall has already gone back to studying the gilded wallpaper like it contains a secret code that *must* be deciphered. I'd even take Martin over Redbeard out there.

I eat the entire sleeve of crackers, suddenly realizing I'm ravenous, then change into the pajamas on the bed. The loose, silky top and pants are hunter green and even *feel* expensive. With literally nothing else to do, I slip into the massive bed where my thoughts spiral into a tangled knot of worry.

I really, really wish I could call Nonno. Literally, it's the first time in my life I've missed having a mobile phone. It's only been a few hours since I borrowed Phillip's phone to let Nonno know about the sudden change in plans, but I already miss him.

Even if he did know who Phillip was and kept it from me. We'll have another conversation about that later. But for now... I just ache for the sound of his voice and that familiar piece of home.

Then I'd call Luci because only she would understand my embarrassment about vomiting on the queen's shoes. When she hugged me goodbye at the hotel, she whispered in my ear that she was proud of me and Sean Astin would be too.

"You're just like Samwise, not letting Frodo go to Mordor alone," she said.

I can't imagine what she'd say about the engagement confusion. Luci would probably tell me to just go with it. But I don't even know if Phillip *wants* to be married. Or if he has to marry a woman of a certain station. Can he even *marry* a commoner?

Also, can we find a term other than commoner? Because it makes me feel twitchy.

Untitled person? Non-royal? Regular person? Totally average? Peon? Peasant?

Maybe I don't mind *commoner* after all.

As far as whether he's allowed to marry someone without a title, he must be able to. I can't imagine him staying in Repestro the way he did if there wasn't a possibility of a future between us. We hadn't gotten to that point yet, but Phillip was incredibly intentional with his time and with me.

Plus, Callum announced the engagement (which doesn't exist) in front of his family, which he wouldn't have done if it weren't allowed. Right?

Though it did cause quite the stir.

But also—WHY did Callum think we were engaged?

Phillip and I haven't even confirmed if we are officially IN A RELATIONSHIP.

I mean, we are. Right? He's spent almost two weeks living in a tiny village working as a dishwasher even though he's a prince for the sole purpose of getting to know me better. All those weeks suddenly look new and different knowing who Phillip is.

A prince—washing dishes. A prince—having coffee with Nonno on our tiny patio. A prince—pursuing *me*.

I'm dating a prince.

(IF we're dating.)

A *prince*.

And according to rumors, we're not just dating but *engaged*.

Phillip is probably clearing that up right now, and I'm grateful I'm not a part of THAT conversation.

A knock on the door yanks me out of my thoughts. I hesitate for a moment, hoping it's Phillip even though the brisk knock sounded more feminine.

Oh, please let it NOT be his mother the QUEEN.

I open the door to find a woman with wispy gray hair, a wide smile, and a tea tray. She says something to me in Elsinorian and pretty much barrels her way into the room. Across the hall, Redbeard doesn't so much as blink, so she must not be a threat. Not that she looks like one, unless the tea service is some kind of weapon in disguise.

Still prattling on in a language I don't understand, the woman sets the tray on a table in a seating area with two stiff-looking sofas. She asks me a question, blinking as she waits for me to respond.

"I'm sorry, but I don't speak Elsinorian," I say in English.

She laughs, then waves a hand as if to say *no matter*, before continuing on with her chatty conversation as she pours a cup of tea. I'm a coffee drinker, but the tea smells like mint, and the cookies on a gold-rimmed plate look delicious despite the whole sleeve of crackers I just consumed.

How I can go from throwing up to wanting to stuff my face with crackers and cookies, I'm not sure.

But I'm going to embrace it because hungry is better than nauseated.

I sit down on the sofa, eyeing the cookies. "Thank you."

She pushes the plate my way, still babbling on and on, and I really wish I could understand because she's giving off this warm, motherly vibe I'm ridiculously soaking up. Her soft tone and the cheer in her smile makes me a little teary.

Even though she might be a total psychopath telling me her plans to poison me with the tea and cookies and dump my body over the palace wall.

Now, there's a lovely thought.

She says something again that ends in a question, and I look up to see her holding out a little envelope.

"Oh, thank you." I take it, noting my name written in formal script. The paper feels thick and weighty.

The woman gives a little wave and curtsy, still chattering like a jovial squirrel as she lets herself out of my room. Only then do I descend on the plate of cookies, which taste like almond heaven and are lightly dusted with powdered sugar. (And which probably are not poisoned.) I pull out the note after taking a sip of tea, which isn't so bad though it's not coffee, and find a note from the queen saying she hopes I feel better.

Now I feel WORSE, actually. I should be the one writing HER a note. There's probably a stationary set in one of the three desks—yes, there are *three desks*—in this room. But I don't know the etiquette for writing an apology note to royalty.

Dear your majesty, her royal highness, the queen,

I am henceforth deeply filled with sorrow by the unfortunate incident involving my vomit and your shoes. I'd offer to replace them, but I likely cannot afford to, so I hope this humble apology will do. Good day. *insert curtsy*

Sincerely,
Alessia

Yeah. Not happening.

There's a heavy knock at the door. Phillip steps inside the room, and relief instantly washes through me. I don't hesitate, jumping off the sofa and throwing my arms around him.

His big hands span my back, enveloping me in instantaneous comfort that makes my eyes prick with tears.

When did this man become someone who can infuse me with such an immediate sense of security?

"Hey," Phillip says, and the rumble of his voice only makes the whole damp-eye situation worse.

"Hi." I press my cheek tighter to his chest, soaking him up like he's the sun and I'm a cave-dweller emerging outside for the first time in a decade. I'm *starved* for him. In fact, I might stay permanently attached.

Forget being his fiancée—I'm more like a new, living sweater he can never remove.

He chuckles, pulling me tighter. "I've missed you."

"It's been an hour."

"Less. But it feels like more."

It does. Which doesn't make any good sense, but time seems to bend in strange ways with Phillip. Like the way, in a few short weeks and only half of one real date, he's completely won my heart. No sense denying it.

No matter—he's here, and his warm scent and his strong hands surround me, the thump of his heartbeat like my compass's true north.

When I'm sure I won't embarrass myself with tears, I lean back, staring up at his handsome face. I'm still surprised to see him without a beard, and I can't stop myself from tracing his smooth jawline, which I'm still getting used to.

"I can grow the beard back if you miss it," Phillip says. The only hint he's teasing is the glint in his eyes.

"You know, I think I'd like you either way."

"Just *like* me?"

I can't hold back my grin. "Maybe I'm downplaying. Just a little."

"Just a *little*?"

"Stai zitto," I say before pulling his mouth down to mine.

I meant to just give him a quick kiss, but it quickly turns into something deeper. Maybe Phillip needs this connection as much as I do. It's sort of desperate and wonderfully messy, with our heads turning the wrong way and our teeth clacking together. A giggle tries to escape but is quickly drowned out by desire. I love feeling Phillip out of control like this.

His mouth transports me. I'm not in a foreign country, in an unfamiliar and intimidating palace, unsure of my place. I'm home. The cliffs above the sea and Nonno's sun-drenched patio in the morning and in the ocean, with Phillip's strong arms holding me above the waves.

Phillip has somehow colored all those places, all those memories. He is home.

Just Phillip.

But no—he's NOT Just Phillip, is he?

I pull back, breathing heavily as the reality of it all hits me like the force of one of Luci's hugs. I remember who he is, where we are, and the embarrassing reality that the last time I saw him, I was throwing up on his mother's shoes.

"I brushed my teeth," I say. The bathroom was stocked with all the same products as the hotel and more. I made use of the toothbrush before putting on these pajamas.

It takes a moment for understanding to hit him, and he smiles. "I can taste the mint." Phillip licks his lips, and I'm almost drawn right back in. "And ginger?"

"I had tea and cookies after I … you know. On your mother's—the queen's—shoes."

"Right." Phillip shakes his head, like he's trying to clear it, and I'm glad it's not just me thrown off by the kiss. His brow furrows. "Are you feeling okay?"

"I think I'm supposed to be the one asking you that. How's your father?"

Phillip's smile shocks me. "He likes you."

"What? How could he like me? The only thing he knows of me is my weak stomach."

Which, based on the feral rumble it makes, is apparently no longer weak and definitely ready for more sustenance than cookies and crackers. Phillip's smile widens, and he glances behind me.

"I see you've had some of Bertie's famous cookies. But we need to get you real sustenance. Our date was interrupted," he says, turning his attention back to me, his deep blue eyes drawing me in. "What do you say we continue it?"

"I'm in my pajamas," I protest.

Phillip pulls back, giving me an unabashed once-over. There's not much skin on display, yet somehow his heated gaze makes me feel stripped bare.

"I rather like them."

His tone sounds more like he's saying he'd like to get me *out* of them. Which is most definitely out of the question at the moment.

I wrinkle my nose. "But can I walk around the palace in pajamas?"

Phillip's eyes dance. "You just told a prince to shut up moments ago. If you can get away with that, you can get away with pajamas."

"You knew what I said?"

"My Italian isn't *that* bad," he says in Italian, as though to prove the point. "Plus, Gianni told me to shut up a number of times. Now come on. Let's stop by my room and I'll get my pajamas so we match, and then we'll finish our date with a meal."

With a quick kiss, Phillip laces our fingers together. Just before opening the door, Phillip adds, "And then maybe we can discuss our accidental engagement."

Right. THAT.

CHAPTER 20

Alessia

"ARE you sure we're not going to get in trouble?" I ask, not for the first time. I think it might be the third, actually.

I lean my elbows on the gorgeous white marble island, watching Phillip pour batter onto a large griddle. I quickly realize it probably isn't polite to lean elbows on the counter and fold my hands in my lap. I REALLY need some kind of royal guidebook.

But rules are forgotten as Phillip gives the batter a good stir, which makes his fitted white shirt pull tight across his chest. Phillip making food while in pajamas at almost midnight is even sexier than Phillip washing dishes. No—it's definitely sexier.

His mouth lifts on one side in a jaunty smirk. "I'm the crown prince of Elsinore. Who would we get in trouble with, exactly? And for what?"

"For being in the kitchen past hours?"

"Did you see a sign with kitchen hours posted on the door?"

"No ... but to be fair, I was a little distracted by the *size* of the kitchen."

The room we're in is the size of Nonno's restaurant with several commercial-sized ranges and ovens, plus a walk-in refrigerator, freezer, and pantry. I know my grandpa would be torn between scoffing at all the luxurious appliances and gadgets and totally jealous of them. All the appliances are updated and modern, but the age of the building can be seen in the worn wooden floors and exposed brick behind one wall. I'm sure there's a dining room where Phillip's family take their meals, but the island is lined with stools and there's a long table with ten chairs near a bay window over-looking the gardens below.

"You should see the main kitchen," Phillip says.

My mouth drops open. "There's more than one kitchen?"

"Three." Phillip tilts his head, thinking. "No—four. This is just the one used to prepare regular daily meals for my family."

My family. It's so casual how he says it. No airs at all about it being the *royal* family. I guess it would just feel normal if it's what you grew up with.

Still—*four kitchens!* Not even a little normal.

Phillip flips a pancake, then another until each one on the flat griddle is a perfect golden brown. They're slightly lumpy and misshapen because these are flavia, Elsinore's version of pancakes. Phillip described them as light and sweet with fruit compote dropped into the center as they're cooking. (Hence the lumps.)

It's a very hands-on process and watching Phillip work

has helped me relax. Though if he doesn't feed me some of these flavia soon, that may change.

"So, you *had* cooked before you came to Repestro. Just not ever *washed* a dish."

"Hmph. Regardless of my dish-washing prowess, flavia is the only thing I make. It's tradition, and Mother taught us all when we were children."

"Tradition, like for a particular holiday?"

"Not so formal as that," he answers, using a spatula to transfer the golden-brown flavia to a plate with the others. "Just something our family does."

The idea of being brought in on a family tradition makes me feel warm and happy. My stomach rumbles. Warm and happy and still *hungry*.

I'm hoping he'll start dishing them out, but instead, he gives the batter a quick stir, making no move to serve any of the flavia.

"You've already got two dozen. How hungry do you think I am? Or how much do you think I can eat?"

"I don't think there will be any leftovers." Phillip smiles, carefully adjusting the temperature and spreading butter over the griddle before pouring a dozen more. With a tiny spoon, he drops fruit compote into the center of each, then pours a little more batter over the top.

"Now," he says, wiping his hands on his apron, "would you like to try your first Elsinorian dish?"

I'd eat an actual *dish* at this point. "Please."

I expect him to fix a plate, but instead, Phillip plucks a single flavia from the heaping platter and walks around the marble island toward me. He holds out the flavia toward my lips, then pauses, perhaps seeing the feral look in my eyes.

"Don't take off my finger," he warns. "You look a little hangry."

"Try a *lot* hangry. But I'll be gentle." *Probably.*

He hums a response and then lifts the flavia right to my lips. I wrap my hand around his wrist—partly to steady myself and partly to keep him from taking away my food— and take a small bite.

His eyes don't leave mine, only dropping to my mouth for a moment as I chew, letting the flavors explode on my tongue. The orange marmalade filling is tart—a perfect balance to the dough, somewhere between a crepe and a pancake, light and sweet.

It's delicious and would be even if I weren't hungry enough to eat an old boot.

"Mmm." I lick my lips and take another bite, still grasping Phillip's wrist. Under my fingertips, his pulse is racing.

"Mmm indeed," he says, eyes darkening as his gaze falls to my mouth.

I would love nothing more than to stack a plate high with flavia and go to town, but the way Phillip is looking at me stirs a different kind of hunger. The two hungers are currently battling for dominance, and it's hard to say which will win.

"Don't you want a bite?" I ask, taking the last piece from Phillip's fingers and holding it up to his mouth.

"I think I'll need more than a bite." He holds my gaze, smoldering at me as I lift the flavia to his lips.

He's careful as I feed him but then nips lightly at my fingertips and licks a tiny bit of marmalade off. "Delicious."

Oh, caspita.

Before I can respond, Phillip tugs me up against him, lifting me from the stool and depositing me on the kitchen counter. So much for impolite elbows. Now my whole bum is on the cold marble. I don't need a royal etiquette book to tell me this is most DEFINITELY against royal rules.

But I don't care. Not when Phillip looks at me like this. Longing flares in his eyes as he steps close and fuses his lips to mine.

He tastes like tart fruit and the sugary sweetness of the flavia. I can't get enough, running my fingers through his hair and angling my head to meet him kiss for fiery kiss.

It's cathartic—a kiss to soothe my worries and fears even as it ignites hope and desire and wonder.

Phillips's big hands come down on the countertop, just outside my thighs, caging me in. I cling to him, one hand still in his hair while the other moves up and down his back, relishing the way his muscles flex and jump at my touch.

"Sia," Phillip whispers against my lips, the desire in his voice making me feel wild and uninhibited.

And *safe*.

As much as Phillip stokes my passion to uncharted levels, I still feel completely secure with him. As though in his arms I am free to lose myself because I know he'll watch over me.

But what if the thing I most need protection from is the very life he's bound to here?

I smell the smoke at the same time as the kitchen door bursts open and Phillip's siblings pour into the kitchen. Phillip and I pull apart, and he groans, dropping his head to my shoulder.

"Hello, everyone," he says drily. "What impeccable timing you have."

"You're burning flavia?" Henri admonishes, immediately moving to scrape off the smoking, ruined flavia from the griddle.

"Treason," Juliet says, snagging a small rubbish bin from under a counter. She holds it while Henri dumps the torched flavia.

"Such a waste of resources," Callum agrees, grinning while he takes over at the stove, giving the batter a stir. "Though I can't say I blame you for being distracted, brother."

Phillip only grunts, but when he lifts his head to meet my gaze, he's smiling too. "Now do you see why I made so many?"

Is this a typical thing for them—midnight flavia in the kitchen in pajamas? I can imagine the headline in a magazine article now: *Royals Are Just Like Us—Eating a Late-Night Snack in Their Pajamas!*

Callum has on dark gray joggers and a T-shirt, while Henri wears plaid flannel pants and a hoodie and Juliet sports a silky pink top and matching shorts.

I should probably feel more embarrassed getting caught making out on the kitchen counter in a palace.

Their palace.

But everyone seems to be pressing on like it's no big deal, teasing and bickering like any normal family does.

"We'll have to make a new batch since you destroyed these," Callum says cheerfully. "Give me your apron."

Phillip presses a quick kiss to the corner of my mouth, then steps back, helping me back onto my stool. He yanks the apron over his head and tosses it to Callum. Juliet pulls eggs from a basket on the counter and Henri hands Callum the milk before disappearing into the pantry.

"You had the heat too high," Callum complains, fiddling with the temperature.

"It was fine," Phillip says, rounding the counter to stand shoulder-to-shoulder with his brother. "Check the first batch. See? Perfect."

"Let me try." Callum grabs a flavia from the top of the stack, dodging and weaving as Phillip tries to knock it out of his hand. Callum succeeds in popping it into his mouth whole.

"Okay. I'll give it to you," Callum says, still chewing. "These are slightly better than the burnt ones we just tossed in the trash. But they're not as good as mine."

"It's the same recipe!" Phillip protests.

"Maybe so, but each chef imparts his—"

"Or her!" Henri adds.

"Or *her* special something. And my special something happens to be better than your special something."

"I don't think Sia would agree," Phillip says, and suddenly every pair of eyes is on me.

"I ... like your special something," I say, the words coming out as more of a question than a statement, which has Callum teasing Phillip all the more as the two verbally spar about their kitchen—and general—prowess.

"They're always like this." Juliet plops onto the stool next to me and nudges my shoulder with hers in a way that instantly makes me feel like we're sharing a secret. "Just wait."

"For what?" I ask.

"For starters, this," Juliet says, as Henri sets a jar of Nutella down on the counter with a thud and a triumphant look.

"No!" Callum and Phillip both protest.

"Don't be such haters," Henri says.

"Nutella does *not* go in flavia," Callum says, reaching around his brother to smack Henrietta with the spatula.

"Ow!" Henrietta retaliates by grabbing a dish towel and snapping it at Callum. "Nutella goes in crepes, which are basically the same thing."

"Take it back," Callum says. "Crepes are nothing like flavia! Flimsy, watery, weak excuses for pancakes."

Henri shakes her head. "I love crepes. They're not weak; they're *delicate*."

"Whatever," Callum says, then turns his attention to me. "Don't listen to a word she says."

Henri shoots me an exasperated look, and asks, "Where do you stand on Nutella?"

"I'd eat it on anything or straight out of the jar if I could," I tell her. Phillip shakes his head at me, but I don't miss how he adds Nutella to several of the flavia on the griddle, with Callum half-heartedly fighting him off.

"Don't be fooled, Alessia. Flavia is the only food Phillip knows how to cook," Callum says. "He tends to stay as far away from the kitchen as possible."

"Actually, Phillip has been working in my grandfather's restaurant."

This pronouncement is met with complete silence. You'd think I just told his siblings that Phillip worked as a pig farmer.

"No," Juliet says. "I don't believe it."

"I was a dishwasher," Phillip says, sounding prouder than anyone has probably ever sounded about this particular job.

Henri stares at her oldest brother like he's an imposter. She turns to me. "He washed dishes—really? Phillip?"

"Really. Though he did break a few."

"Hey! I only broke one dish," Phillip protests, but he's smiling and still looks all-too pleased with himself.

"And two wine glasses. And a cast-iron skillet."

"Were you counting?" he asks, pressing a hand to his chest like he's appalled.

"I had to take it out of your pay."

Phillip rubs his chin. "Hm. I wasn't getting paid."

"Then, I guess you owe us."

I'm about to make a joke about him needing to come back

to work off the cost, but then my stomach falls. Will he even be able to return to Repestro *ever*?

This is one of many details we didn't get to discuss. I definitely don't want to talk about it now.

"I still can't picture Phillip washing dishes," Juliet says.

"He'll have to clean up tonight, just to prove his mad dishwashing skills are real," I suggest.

Phillip groans, and his siblings cheer.

"I knew I liked you," Callum says, giving me a wide smile. It's so similar to Phillip's, though Callum seems to give them out a lot more freely. He's like a version of Phillip lite.

"I like you too," Juliet says, nudging my shoulder again as Phillip and Callum start arguing about the dishes. "You know, Phillip has never dated anyone seriously. We all weren't sure if he'd end up some kind of monk king. I'm so glad he found you. I can't wait for you to be my sister-in-law! How fun will that be!"

I give her a small smile, which is all I can manage due to the extreme emotional reaction happening in my chest right now. Both because I feel like I'm lying by not telling her the whole truth, and because I've never had anything like this—a big family. Siblings. This kind of bickering and love are like two sides of a coin.

Nonno and the grandpas and Luci are my family. But this is something different. Something I've never had and never admitted how much I've wanted. I think it's why I always thought I'd have a big family—to give my own children the siblings I never had.

Right now ... my longing to be part of this is almost overwhelming.

But it's not *real*. Or, at least, it's not what they think. Because we aren't engaged. We've had two interrupted dates

—both of them today. A handful of (admittedly amazing) kisses—also all today.

And I'm really scared that our fledgling, baby relationship may not survive the pressure of all this.

Being with a crown prince will absolutely mean I have to leave home, leave Repestro, leave Nonno. The thought of abandoning him fills me with crushing guilt.

Which leaves me ... where, exactly?

At the moment, it leaves me in denial. I haven't outright lied to his family, and suddenly I understand how Phillip must have struggled the past few weeks—not lying per se, but also hiding a very big, very critical truth.

"Do you have a big family?" Juliet asks, her blue eyes watching me curiously.

"No."

The word comes out choked, almost like a sob and I *cannot* cry right now. Even if I'm a massive ball of emotions, feeling at home while missing home, wanting to be included while also struggling to see how I can ever really fit here.

When Henri tosses a handful of flour in Callum's face, it's just the distraction I need. It's impossible not to laugh at Callum, who freezes, his whole face covered in flour. Henri slips off her house shoes and bolts around the island barefoot.

Phillip steps in to start the next round of flavia, almost like this is a typical occurrence.

"Dear sister, where are you?" Callum asks in a threateningly sweet voice. He walks like a flour-doused zombie, with his arms out in front of him, fingers wiggling and leaving a trail of flour behind him.

. . .

"Oh, Henri..." Callum calls, using the French pronunciation Phillip told me Henri prefers.

"That won't work," Henri says, then slaps a hand over her mouth.

"Ha!" Callum lunges toward the table, opening his eyes and blinking rapidly, his lashes looking as though they've been dusted with snow.

"You'll wake Mum," Phillip warns, but he's smiling.

Also, he must be joking because there's no way his mother would hear us.

Henri tries to leap from the table, but Callum catches her, pinning her to his chest while she kicks and squirms. He sneezes, releasing a cloud of flour.

"Ew!" Henri squeals. "You snotted me with flour!"

"Oh, I'll do much worse," Callum says.

Henri struggles harder, and Callum walks forward, easily keeping his sister in his grasp like she's a tiny kitten and not a fully grown young woman.

He stops near the mixing bowl and holds out a hand. "Two eggs, please."

"You wouldn't dare," Henri breathes, going still.

"You started it," Callum says. "Eggs, Phillip."

"Nope." Phillip doesn't look up from the flavia, and I notice he makes at least half a dozen with Nutella. "I'm not getting involved."

Leaning over the island, Juliet hands Callum two eggs, a wicked smile on her face.

"Thank you. I shall remember your act of service," Callum says.

"So will I," Henri says, glaring at her sister.

"Must we—" Phillip starts to say, but he's interrupted when Callum unceremoniously smashes the two eggs right on top of Henri's head.

She gasps. I wince, watching yolk running into her hair, tiny bits of shell mixed in.

"You are the very worst," Henri says.

Callum kisses her on the cheek, leaving streaks of flour behind. "I don't know. I'm not the one who ghosted our family for weeks and kept a secret from you. For once, I'm actually *not* the worst brother."

"Phillip is forgiven," Juliet says, throwing an arm around me. "He brought us Alessia."

And now I'm right back to being an emotional mess.

"Who's ready to eat?" Phillip asks, switching off the stove and smiling cheerfully.

Food ends the argument. I'm shocked when Callum sets Henri down and she immediately grabs a plate rather than seeking revenge or washing the egg out of her hair. The siblings line up around the island.

I stand to join them, but Phillip holds up a hand to stop me. "I'll fix yours. How do you want them?"

"They're best with Nutella, obviously," Henri says, and it's hard to take her seriously when she still has egg in her hair.

"Just butter is best," Juliet says.

"Phillip is a purist and eats them plain," Callum says, and the others groan. "I prefer mine drizzled with chocolate syrup."

Phillip raises an eyebrow at me. "What will you have?"

"One of each," I tell him. "I suppose I should try them all so I can make an informed decision."

"Chocolate syrup," Henri mutters, loading up her plate. "And you give me a hard time about Nutella."

"Hey, Hen. You've got a little something in your hair," Callum says while drizzling chocolate syrup over the giant stack of flavia on his plate.

Henri lifts her chin and sniffs. "I'm leaving it. Raw egg is a natural conditioner."

"Really?" Juliet perks up at this.

"Really."

Juliet turns to me. "Egg me."

"What?"

She grabs two eggs and places them in my hand. "Egg me. My hair could use a good treatment."

"Um ..." I glance at Phillip, who shrugs, a small smile lifting one corner of his lips. "You're sure?"

"Someone egg me too," Callum says around a bite of flavia. "I've been swimming a lot lately and the chlorine has wrecked my hair."

This family is ... *absurd*. Nothing like I'd expect of royals. And I really, really love it.

"Come on," Juliet says, angling her head forward. "You know you want to."

I absolutely do. But instead of cracking both eggs on her head, I put one in each hand and smash an egg on her head at the same time I smash the other on mine.

It feels disgusting, but when Juliet looks up at me, grinning as a trail of yolk moves slowly down her forehead, I find I don't care.

"Brilliant," she says.

I hear the sound of another egg cracking and look up in time to see Phillip smashing one on his own head as he smashes another on Callum's.

Callum stares at his brother in shock, even though he asked for it moments ago. I slap a hand over my mouth to keep from giggling, but Henri and Juliet don't hold back, howling with laughter. Henri, clearly still seeking revenge, adds a second egg to Callum's head. He doesn't even flinch.

"If we add milk and sugar, your head could be the next batch," Henri says.

"Ew!" Juliet says, but Callum only chuckles, still giving Phillip a look I don't quite understand.

"He's different," Henri says to me, leaning close as her brothers make their way to the table, yolk dripping down their heads. "I don't know what you've done to Phillip, but it's brilliant."

I smile, even as worry twists into a tight braid in my chest. Because if Phillip is different, I don't know who he was before. Or *how* he was before. And will he just return to whoever he was now that he's back in his normal environment?

I don't know Prince Phillip of Elsinore, and I get the sense I haven't really seen him yet.

I know Just Phillip, the stranger who made me break all my own promises to myself.

Tomorrow, I think, watching Phillip slide a plate of flavia in front of me. *I'll worry about this tomorrow.*

For the moment, I want to relish this moment—eating Elsinorian pancakes at a table surrounded by princes and princesses, all wearing egg on our heads.

CHAPTER 21

Phillip

WHEN I JOLT AWAKE, my brain immediately tries to identify what woke me so suddenly. A nightmare? A noise? Before I've really gotten my bearings, blinding light sears my eyeballs as my mother throws open the heavy drapes.

I groan. She smiles. People often talk about crocodile tears, but perhaps don't make enough of crocodile smiles. And the smile on her face at the moment is quite reptilian, especially for someone wearing heirloom pearls.

"Oh, you're awake," she says, like she wasn't very obviously *trying* to wake me up.

"I am now."

"Late night?" Mum asks, flinging open the next set of drapes with relish. One might even say with *glee*.

The good thing about my mother is that her moods are

easy to read. The bad thing is that this morning, her mood is the kind I usually try to avoid at all costs.

But I think I've used up my allotted days of avoidance being in Repestro. And last night was a freebie, thanks to Sia's unfortunate stomach issues. Now, it's time to face the music, as they say. Even if the music sounds like the theme song to the movie *Jaws*.

Rubbing my eyes, I sit up and swing my feet over the side of the bed. "It was a late night, yes." When Mum raises her brows, slowly and deliberately, I shake my head. "I spent some time with Callum and the girls. Catching up."

"And your fiancée? I assume she was there as well."

Nothing like an immediate reminder of the confusion I need to set at rest today. "Yes. She was getting to know everyone. We had fun."

Fun is not very high on Mum's priority list, if ever at all. And the word doesn't accurately cover last night. I can't remember the last time I enjoyed my family so much. It was even more enjoyable because Alessia was there.

And perhaps most important of all, she seemed to belong. She fit with us—teasing Callum and listening to my sisters' stories. Not minding the egg on her head and holding my hand under the table. According to her sleepy admission when I kissed her goodnight, she said she felt as though she belonged with us.

It warms my heart.

There's a knock at the door. "Ah—that will be my secretaries."

The warmth is quickly replaced by a metaphorical ice bucket dumped over my head. "Your secretaries are here *now*? I'm in my pajamas."

But Mum is already opening the door to allow Gertrude—her private secretary as prim and proper and stuffy as her name suggests—inside. Gertrude is followed by Robert, her communications secretary, and then Allen, my private secretary. Plus a whole group of servants with rolling carts with drinks and breakfast.

Suddenly my private bedroom feels like a surprise party I'd rather do anything but attend.

"Come. Sit. Lots to discuss," Mum says, waving me over to the seating area opposite my bed.

I guess we're doing this—a meeting that feels rather like a passive aggressive punishment whilst I'm in pajamas. Brilliant.

Gertrude sniffs as I sit down in a chair across from her and my mother. Behind Gertrude's wire-rimmed glasses, there is an awful lot of judgment happening because of my white t-shirt and flannel pants. Robert looks amused by the whole thing (though it can be hard to tell with the bristly mustache that covers his mouth), and Allen with his scarecrow-like frame is wholly focused on piling his plate high with bacon.

"Had I known we were holding a meeting, I would have gotten dressed."

After showering. And brushing my teeth. And mentally preparing for the very sudden return of my duties. Which suddenly feels like an almost unmanageable weight to shoulder.

"Perhaps you would have had time if you hadn't slept in so late," Mum suggests.

"What time is it?"

"Eight-thirty." She spits the words like they're poison, as though eight-thirty is an abomination, like I've spent through an inheritance or bungled some foreign diplomacy.

Gertrude sniffs again, and I find myself longing for Enzo's

caffé rather than the milky tea a servant pours for me before slipping out of the room.

"So much to discuss," Mum says with forced cheerfulness. "Where shall we begin? Allen, why don't you give Phillip a rundown on everything he's missed when he disappeared for weeks without so much as a word?"

Setting down his plate of bacon with an unabashed look of longing, Allen pulls out a thick folder and hands it to me.

"Let's begin with some of the larger fires we need to put out, shall we?"

———

Through the entirety of the meeting—which is far more boring than I remember these kinds of meetings being—I find my mind wandering to Alessia. Hopefully, my sisters have found her and are giving her a tour or something.

Did someone bring her breakfast?

Did she sleep well?

Is she thinking of me as well?

"Phillip?" Mum's voice cuts through my wondering.

"A dinner next week with the prime minister—yes. I understand."

"Good." Her smile is thin. "I wasn't sure you were paying attention. Perhaps it was the late night."

I don't point out that I often have late nights, they're just usually spent in the adjoining room I think of as my personal office. I showed it to Alessia yesterday when we stopped by so I could change into pajamas. It's the one room in the house with nothing remotely kingdom-related, filled instead with computers and the kind of tech gadgets that make Callum's eyes glaze over but would make any true geek's day. Alessia seemed impressed—more by my knowledge of something wholly unfamiliar to her than an actual interest in tech. Considering she doesn't even have a phone, I shouldn't be surprised.

Speaking of—I should make sure to get her a phone, even if she doesn't want to keep it. I'm sure she'll want a way to contact Luci and her nonno ...

A throat clears, and I realize that I've missed a whole portion of the conversation. Gertrude eyes me with a frosty glare, but I'm surprised Mum's gaze is soft. She sighs.

"It's so nice to see you in love," she says. "I wasn't sure it would ever happen."

Awkward. That kind of statement is the equivalent of a mother licking her fingers to rub a smudge of dirt off her child's face. Thankfully, Allen has finally been released to his bacon and only has eyes for it, while Robert is typing something into his computer. And it's not like anything could impress Gertrude *less.*

"And this is a great segue into the next order of business, which is your engagement and the wedding." Mum folds her hands in her lap, smiling. "When would you like to visit the treasury to pick out a ring? I noticed Alessia wasn't wearing one, and you know the kind of rumors that can spark."

I'm freshly acquainted with rumors, thanks to Callum blurting out what he said last night. "Actually, her grandfather gave me her mother's ring. But I need to—"

"A sentimental piece—how lovely. Such a shame about Alessia's family," Mum says, and I shouldn't be surprised she already knows Alessia's history. I'm sure she had someone prepare a dossier last night. "But it was a smart move having her spend time with your siblings last night."

"It's not a chess game," I say. "And actually—"

"Though you left quite the mess in the kitchen. My staff was most displeased."

We didn't leave that much of a mess, and I doubt the staff complained. As promised, I did dishes while my siblings watched me like I was some kind of street performer, clapping and making jeers and catcalling. Juliet even made popcorn, though it was more for show than eating, since we were all stuffed to the gills with flavia.

But in any case, I need to steer this conversation back to the point I need to make—one I'd rather make with just my mother and not all the staff present.

"Could we discuss the engagement privately?"

Mum gives the three secretaries a quick nod, and they politely pack up, Allen commandeering another whole plate of bacon as he goes. I have to wonder where in the world all of the calories he consumes *go*.

The door closes behind them, and now, we're alone. Somehow the pressure to explain the situation feels even weightier now than it did before. Mum clears her throat. I clear mine. She smiles. I take a sip of tea, which makes me miss Enzo's caffé and an entirely different kind of morning on a sunny patio overlooking the sea.

But missing the nonnos reminds me of why I returned. "How is Father? I didn't get a full report, only what Callum relayed to me about some kind of infection."

Her features tighten almost imperceptibly. "The physician has him on a course of antibiotics, which seems to be working. Other than that, not much has changed."

Her shoulders start to quiver first, then her head drops forward into her hands. I'm beside her on the couch in an instant, pulling her into a hug. She feels so small in my arms, so frail. Not at all the woman who fired into my room this morning like a cannonball. I remind myself that underneath her tendency to micromanage and overstep, Mum is a wonderful mother who cares very much for my siblings and me. She is a doting wife to a slowly dying husband. And a queen.

At times, especially this past year, it's been hard to see her as anything *but* the queen. I've had to shoulder a lot, but she's had to shoulder more.

"The physician doesn't know anything," she says, sniffling. Her whole body quakes in my arms. "We could have weeks or we could have another year or two. They just don't know! And you *weren't here*."

She pounds a fist against my chest, and as she sobs, I wrestle with fresh guilt. It moves through me like a dark shadow, twisting into every crevice of my being until light seems far away.

I feel as though I've been selfish, a quality I despise in myself even more than others.

"I'm so sorry, Mum. I didn't plan to be gone so long. I hoped you wouldn't even notice my absence."

"Wouldn't *notice?*" She pulls back, staring up at me with shock. "Phillip, you hold everything together. I'm not sure you realize how integral you are to this family." Cupping my cheek, her gaze softens. "We were lost without you. And not just because you're the crown prince. Because you're *you*."

Now I'm the one fighting back tears. These are the kind of words someone in my position often longs to hear—that my value as a man isn't simply tied to my title or what I do. Even from my mother, I need to hear this.

And yet it guts me to feel like I disappointed my family.

I kiss the top of her head. "I am truly sorry for putting you through that. I stand by my choice to go, but I didn't mean to cause stress or hurt you."

She pulls back, regaining her smile and a little of her composure. "Well, at least your trip was successful. You returned with a fiancée. This has really brought fresh life to your father. Perhaps as much as or more than the antibiotics."

Right. About that …

Why can't I find the words? It's not hard to say—*Callum made a mistake. Alessia and I aren't engaged.*

Not difficult.

And yet, I cannot make myself confess. Possibly because I've already disappointed my family with my disappearance. Father did seem in good spirits last night. How will he react when he learns the truth?

The other thing holding my tongue is the fact that I wish it *were* true. I wish the engagement *were* real.

Mum stands, smoothing down her skirt as though she weren't just sobbing into my t-shirt. "Will you stop by and see your father before you go to your office?"

"Yes. But I'd like to see Alessia first."

"That can be arranged, but she's with the seamstress, I believe. She and your sisters."

I frown. "The seamstress? What for?"

Mum raises her eyebrows, as though this question is simply too stupid to require a response. "For her wedding gown, of course. As well as a gown for the engagement ball and some other scheduled events."

Her wedding gown.

The engagement ball.

My mind is still reeling as Mum pats me on the shoulder. "After visiting your father, you'll need to meet with the tailor. Photos have been scheduled for this afternoon."

"This afternoon?"

"I know you have much work to catch up on, but the sooner we gain control of the messaging with regard to your relationship, the better." She gives me a look. "Formal engagement photos will be far better than mobile phone photos of you rescuing your fiancée from the side of a hotel."

Everything she's saying makes logical sense. Or it would if Alessia and I were actually engaged. Perhaps with a little more time, this fake engagement could become a real one. But I certainly won't be rushing Sia into a decision by *this afternoon*.

My mother moves toward the door. "Allen will brief you after you visit your father, and Robert will meet with you to discuss our messaging in the media."

Have I so quickly forgotten exactly how fast my pace of life here is? Or does it seem faster now that I have simple, sun-soaked days to compare it to?

"Mum, slow down." She stops and faces me fully with a single raised brow. "We don't need to rush this—especially the engagement photos. I just got back and have many things to attend to. And with Father's health—"

"Your father's health is exactly why we *need* to rush this. In addition, your absence in the public eye hasn't gone unnoticed, thanks to our leak. A prince falling in love with a commoner is the perfect story to feed the press."

The perfect story.

I close my eyes and press a hand to my head. Guilt aside, I *must* tell her. "There's something you should know before we release a statement."

Mum laughs. "Phillip dear, Gertrude released our official statement this morning announcing your engagement and an August wedding."

CHAPTER 22

Alessia

AND FOR TODAY'S edition of *Alessia in Wonderland*, I've jumped straight down the rabbit hole and into a fitting for my wedding gown.

Yes—my *wedding gown*.

You know, for my upcoming wedding to my supposed fiancé, who is nowhere to be found.

When I woke up this morning, it was not to Nonno knocking on the wall and shouting buongiorno or even Phillip waking me as I hoped he might. No, I woke to find Phillip's Mother THE QUEEN (and I can't stop myself from thinking of her in exactly that way with all the capital letters) in my room. She was all bright smiles and big plans for my day and no mention of how I threw up on her shoes last night.

I was so thankful for that small boon, I didn't even have

231

the wherewithal to protest or ask follow-up questions. Like: Did Phillip happen to mention that we aren't actually engaged? The answer to that unasked question came when she announced I would proceed to a wedding gown fitting directly after breakfast.

If the queen says I'm going to try on wedding gowns, then I'm going to try on wedding gowns.

Meanwhile, according to his mother THE QUEEN, Phillip is in his office, catching up on "vitally important tasks" after his "long and unplanned absence." I've been doing my best not to feel hurt or abandoned. As the crown prince who's been MIA for the past few weeks, I can imagine the kind of work he has to catch up on. Not that I have any idea what Phillip's job entails from day to day. But I'm sure he's quite busy with whatever his princely duties are.

"Don't worry," the queen said before sweeping out of my room much the way she swept into it, "you'll see Phillip this afternoon for your engagement photos."

Apparently, I'm not the only one who hasn't had time to talk with Phillip today, since he most *definitely* didn't communicate to his mother how rumors of our engagement had been greatly exaggerated.

Which leads me to where I am now—pretending I'm not having mini panic attacks while being draped in dresses I could never afford and am not sure I would choose even if I could.

"Oh, that style on you is simply gorgeous." Juliet circles the small platform where a seamstress is quite violently pinning a strapless dress that seems to be ninety percent tulle around my middle. I'm not sure if she's angry with me, the fabric, or life in general. "The antique white really works with your skin tone. I'm so jelly."

"Don't use slang," Henri corrects. "But I do like the color. Even if it's a little death by tulle."

"Why no slang?" Juliet says, rounding on her sister. "Is it not fit for a *princess?*"

"No. It's just stupid." Henri tilts her head, and I try my best not to look the way I feel—like something pressed under the glass slide on a microscope. "I definitely preferred the first dress."

"The one with the long sleeves?" Juliet wrinkles her nose. "It was so stuffy. What do you think, Alessia?"

I think if I had a choice, I would choose something loose and soft, romantic and flowy. None of the choices—and I'm not going to even ask why there is a whole rack of wedding gowns on hand—feel like me. I would choose simple and pretty, not beaded and complicated or the kind of thing I'd need a seamstress to stuff me inside.

But it's shocking how much I already crave the approval of Phillip's sisters. I don't want to disappoint them—or anyone in his family. It's hard to get invested because any moment now, Phillip will tell his mother the truth, and I don't know where that leaves me. Or, rather, leaves *us*. I'm sweating under the layers of tulle just considering how his sisters might react to the truth. Or, more precisely—how they'd react to *me* after learning the truth.

Which is why I say, "Each one is quite lovely."

"Is that a polite way of saying you hate them both?" Henri asks, narrowing her eyes.

I turn to Henri. "No! They really are both beautiful. I just … I'm not sure."

The seamstress, a beady-eyed woman with wispy white hair who won't speak a word of English yet seems to understand our whole conversation, yanks the fabric even tighter.

"Ow!" She glares up at me like it's my fault she's practically assaulting me with the dress.

"Anyway. What kind of gown did you envision for your wedding? We've been talking your ears off, but you haven't said much."

I haven't said much because I'm afraid any moment now, I'll spill the truth to everyone and ruin everything.

As for wedding dresses, well ... I've never really let myself imagine it. A wedding in Repestro would have been a simple affair. I mean, involving the whole village obviously, but not *fancy*. Certainly not a seamstress and yards and yards of high-end fabrics. The beading on the bodice alone makes my head spin.

"I actually haven't thought about it," I answer, grateful for any piece of honesty I can hold on to.

Both girls gasp. This, apparently, is a worse crime than not having a phone.

"Never?" Henri asks.

I shake my head. "Nope."

Juliet's eyes are wide as she joins me on the small platform where I'm currently being seamstressed. "I have a whole notebook of designs," she says. "Starting from when I was five."

"Five?"

She nods solemnly. "The first one was terrible—though surprisingly not the worst. It looked like a giant bell. The truly awful ones were from when I went through my Madonna phase." She pauses and shudders. "But still. I can't believe that you *never* thought about what dress you'd wear for your wedding."

"Perhaps this one?" Juliet holds up a dress that looks like the whipped topping for a gourmet hot cocoa.

"Too much drama," Henri says. She grabs a strapless,

sequined mermaid gown. "This would look killer with your curves. I wish I had the butt for that dress."

"I wish I had a butt, period," Juliet says, craning her neck to look at her backside.

Despite the way it's getting hard to breathe as the seamstress tightens the bodice into oblivion, I can't help smiling. I hate the misunderstanding, but I love *this*. And for a moment, I imagine it is all true: the wedding gown, the instant family, and especially the part where I get to marry Phillip.

What should feel ridiculous and too fast instead feels oddly ... *right*. Even with the whole prince thing—which I would get used to, right? I mean, Phillip is still Phillip, whether he's wearing a crown or up to his elbows in a sink full of dirty dishes.

The seamstress moves from my waist to my bust, and I try to pretend it's not weird to have a total stranger standing eye level with my breasts. But she's glaring at them as if they're too small. Or too big? Definitely NOT just right. I start to ask if she can help me out of the dress instead of continuing to adjust this one, but the look in her eye holds me in place. Or maybe it's just her proximity to my breasts with a cushion full of straight pins.

"Oh!" Juliet exclaims, laughing. "We should ask Brit to make a dress!"

Henri chuckles. "Not a chance. I actually *like* Alessia."

I don't know who Brit is or what kind of dresses she designs, but I almost don't care because Henri *likes me!*

"Who's Brit?" I ask.

"Callum's ex—or one of them," Juliet says. "An American 'designer.' You should see her stuff. It's ... something."

"He was dating her when he was supposed to be

announcing his arranged marriage to Fi—Queen Serafina of Viore," Henri says.

"Callum had an arranged marriage? Is that ... typical? Do the two of you have arranged marriages?"

Did Phillip?

"No, thank goodness," Juliet says.

"Callum and Fi were great friends, and our parents decided it when they were just kids. It would have helped solidify something or other with our two countries." Henri rolls her eyes, as though the idea of solidifying two countries' relationships through a marriage is just everyday boring talk.

"Until Callum torpedoed the whole thing," Juliet adds. "Anyway, we're in modern times and can marry as we please. Though up until you, Mum has been doing her very best to shove Phillip into some loveless relationship with a duchess or something."

Jealousy rages through me like a stream of fire shot from a flamethrower.

"Don't worry," Henri says. "Phillip had no interest in any of them. I've never seen him look at any woman the way he looks at you. It's adorable."

Juliet giggles. "I've got the best idea. Let's ask Brit to make something for Callum to wear."

"Do it," Henri says decisively.

"On it!" Juliet is already on her phone, typing away. "Sending her a dm on Insta. Are you on Instagram, Alessia? I need to follow you."

"I'm not on any social media," I say, and both girls stare like I've sprouted a second head. "I don't have a phone."

Now they're looking at me like I have at least a dozen heads, none of them human.

"I don't ... understand," Juliet says slowly, clutching her

phone to her chest like she half expects it to disappear. "How do you function?"

She doesn't mean the question rudely, and I want to laugh because she is completely serious.

"Rude," Henri says. "I think it sounds refreshing."

Henri continues flipping through the rack. "I wonder if there's something like the first dress but without the long sleeves. They'll be too hot for a summer wedding," Henri says.

"Like *next* summer?"

That would actually give us some time to work this out. For me to make sure I can handle what life would be like as Phillip's wife in this whole royal world. I could discuss with Nonno and find a way to ease my mind about leaving him alone.

Juliet frowns. "I think Mum said August."

"August?"

It's currently JUNE.

I'm not sure if it's the tightness of the dress or this new information, but I'm suddenly in desperate need of a paper bag to breathe into. I should ask if anyone has one handy. I bet it would have the royal crest, just like the air sickness bags on the plane.

"Don't worry," Henri says. "It might seem impossible, but Mum will get everything done. That's her specialty: planning and micromanaging."

"That and meddling," Juliet adds, giving up on the dresses and pulling out her phone.

"She does love a good meddle," Henri says, and both girls laugh.

"It's too bad you don't have social media. Your following would be blowing up." Juliet grins down at her phone.

"You're trending on Twitter! Hashtag—Secret Royal Bride, hashtag—Prince Phillip Bagged a Babe."

Henri wrinkles her nose. "Ugh, Twitter. Why are you even on there? And don't you hate how women in the headlines are always described in relation to men? Gross." She pauses and looks me over. "But you *are* a babe."

"Total babe," Juliet agrees. "But a babe who stands on her own—with or without our brother." She pumps a fist in the air. "Feminism! And the official royal announcement has *one million* retweets. Epic."

That hot, panicky feeling returns with a vengeance. And with the added fun of little black dots obscuring my vision. "I'm sorry—did you say a royal announcement?"

Juliet turns her phone so I can see the screen. But I can't see anything right now.

"Mum's secretary posted about the engagement this morning on the official Royals of Elsinore account."

I sway, reaching to grab Henri's and Juliet's arms. "I don't feel so well. I think I'm going to faint."

The seamstress shouts something in Elsinorian, probably about me ruining the very expensive dress with my not-perfect breasts and clumsiness as I stumble. Henri shouts something right back while she and Juliet help me to the couch. I collapse in a veritable snowdrift of tulle as my vision goes fully black.

The girls pepper me with questions I can't answer because I can *hear* them but I can't speak or see anything. It's like overhearing a conversation from the depths of a well while half asleep.

"Do you faint often?"

"Alessia, can you hear us? Nod once if you can hear us!"

"Was that a nod?"

"No, I think she just slumped over. Put a pillow under her head. We don't want her to choke on her own vomit."

"Ew! Why would you even think about that?"

"It's what they're always saying in movies and stuff when people pass out—you roll them on their sides so they don't choke if they puke."

"That's if they're *drunk*."

"I definitely don't think she's drunk. Though she did throw up last night."

"She was just motion sick from the plane. Unless ..." There's a gasp. "What if she's pregnant?"

"I mean, she doesn't look pregnant, but no one does at first. And did you see how much she ate last night?"

"No more than you. But I could totally see it. Maybe Mum's not just pushing the wedding because of Father, but because Alessia's pregnant!"

"She's *what?*"

This new voice does NOT belong to either of the girls. It's also not the seamstress. I may have only been in a room with her twice, but I'd recognize that voice anywhere. It is Phillip's Mother THE QUEEN.

Hers are the last words I hear before I fall fully into the darkness.

239

CHAPTER 23

Phillip

THOUGH I'M TRULY CONCERNED for Alessia's well-being, it's hard not to admire her, even while she's asleep. Which, admittedly, feels *slightly* creepy.

But no one seemed to have a problem with that sparkly vampire watching a girl sleep for months. And he also wanted to eat her. Comparatively, me sitting at the edge of Alessia's bed watching her sleep is perfectly acceptable.

Though perhaps I shouldn't base my moral compass on a fictional vampire from a young adult novel.

What's less acceptable is the fact that she fainted during a dress fitting. And that someone other than me carried her back to her room after, where she was checked out by the physician and then fell asleep.

What's completely *unacceptable* is that I didn't hear about any of this for at least an hour. I understand I have a lot of work to catch up on. I'm practically swimming in papers to sign and phone calls to return.

But Alessia's well-being is far more important. I can only imagine how exhausting—emotionally and otherwise—the past day has been for her. I know I'm dragging, especially after our late night, but I'm also accustomed to life here in the palace. For her, all of this is new.

Not to mention the fact that she's been swept up in my mother's wedding plans. A fact made obvious by the wedding dress Sia is still wearing. I can't see much of it because she's tucked under the duvet, but even getting a glimpse of the beaded white straps on her shoulders puts an image in my head of Sia walking down the aisle toward me.

Did she think about actually marrying me while trying on dresses?

Was she thinking, wondering, maybe hoping that this could be true?

I'm beginning to wonder if anything at all between Alessia and me can happen according to plan. Perhaps I should give up on the idea of making plans where she's concerned altogether.

"What if we just went along with it?" I whisper, brushing her hair back from her cheek. "Of course, I'd still ask you to marry me. Officially speaking. But what if we didn't clear up the misunderstanding? What if we make this fake engagement a real one?"

Her dark locks are wild and untamed, escaping the confines of their hair tie, reminding me so much of Alessia herself. In a palace so polished that more than one person's full-time job is cleaning the doorknobs, Sia is completely and refreshingly real.

I lightly trace her dark eyebrows with a finger, then run my fingertip over the apple of her cheek and along her jaw, stopping just short of touching her perfect, full lips. THAT would definitely put me into total creeper and murky lack of consent territory. I don't think even the sparkly vampire crossed THAT line.

"I kept you up too late, threw too many surprises at you. Your exhaustion is all my fault, and I'm sorry."

When her lips part and she speaks, I jolt.

"I thought it was customary for the prince to wake the sleeping love interest with a kiss," she murmurs.

I smile. "But you're already awake. No need for a kiss to wake you."

"My eyes are closed. Maybe I'm sleep-talking."

"Hm. You're a very lucid sleep-talker if that's the case."

"Back to the kiss—did I watch too many movies as a child to think that's how this worked, or are you the only prince who doesn't understand the power of a kiss?"

"It sounds like you're challenging my princehood," I say.

"Is it prince*hood* or prince*dom*? Maybe princiness?"

"Definitely not the last one. Let's stick to princehood."

Her eyes are still closed, but her lips curve into a tiny, teasing smile. "Semantics aside, I'm questioning your title, considering I'm still lying here, clearly asleep, waiting for a kiss from my prince."

"My apologies. Let's see if we can remedy this and reassure you of the validity of my princehood."

"Less talking. More kissing," she says.

I can't argue with that request.

Placing my hands on either side of her head, I lean down slowly, drawing the moment out. Her breath catches, and her lips part. I pause, my mouth barely a breath away. Just as I sense she's about to lose her patience with me, I press my lips to hers. She makes a little humming sound, one that draws a rumbling response from my chest.

Sia pulls back, her eyes flying open. They sparkle with amusement. "Did you just purr?"

"What? No. I'm not a cat."

"It sounded like a purr," she says, grinning. "Admit it—you like kissing me so much, it makes you purr like a big jungle cat."

"I did *not* purr." I'm not sure why I'm arguing, since she clearly liked whatever sound—which clearly was not a purr—just came out of me.

"Maybe we should try it again, just to settle the argument."

"Are we having our first fight?" I ask, leaning close and brushing my lips against her cheek.

"I think our first fight involved more water and less kissing."

"Ah, yes. And who came out more soaked? I believe it was you."

"Debatable."

"But back to the purring debate ..." I let my words trail off as I kiss her jaw, then trail a row of kisses down her neck. She makes a little sound the likes of which I've never heard. I'm not even sure what word to describe it. "Who's making sounds now?" I tease.

Her hands come out of nowhere, sliding into my hair, her nails lightly scratching my scalp as she tilts my head, turning the tables to kiss my jaw, then my neck. My heart is racing, and I barely hold back another rumbly sound.

"Has our argument turned into a contest?" she asks, pressing a kiss to the base of my throat. "One to see who can draw the most noisy responses out of the other?"

I'm barely able to process her words, definitely not able to respond to them, as she kisses and nips—*and vainto, did she just lick me?*—her way back to my lips. I can't hold back the rumbling sound now, and though I think of it more as a growl than a purr, Alessia laughs triumphantly, at least until I take her lips with mine. Her laugh quickly disappears as our mouths move and our heads tilt. Her hands grasp my hair, tugging lightly in a way that awakens nerve endings I didn't know I had. My hands grip the comforter on either side of her as I do my best to hold myself in check.

"Well, you certainly must be feeling better," a voice says, forcibly yanking us from the moment.

Sia freezes, and I lift my head only enough to rest my forehead on hers with a sigh.

"Haven't you heard of knocking, Mum?" I ask.

"When have I ever had to knock?" she asks brightly, her voice growing closer.

Alessia's hands leave my hair, pushing lightly on my chest. I can see the panic in her eyes. Right—because to her, this isn't just getting caught by someone else's parent while making out (bad enough, though we *are* consenting adults), but getting caught by a queen (far worse).

I sit up fully and take Alessia's hand before turning to face my mother. "Is there something you need?" I ask, trying to be polite.

Mum stops near the bed, and I don't like the way she looks over Alessia, as though searching for faults. Sia seems to sense this as well, as she clears her throat and shifts until she's fully sitting up. Then, she seems to realize she's still in a wedding gown and tugs the duvet up a little higher.

I refuse to let go of her hand, giving her fingers an encouraging squeeze.

"I just wanted to check in and see how your fiancée was feeling. If we absolutely must, we can move the engagement photos, but with such limited time, we should really press on if possible."

"I'm feeling better," Alessia says quickly. "I think just all the travel and the excitement got to me. I'm not usually a fainter."

Mum smiles, a real one this time—soft and maternal. "When I was pregnant with Callum, I fainted frequently. I like to joke that he redirected my blood flow directly to him."

"That sounds like Callum," I say.

"Hopefully it will pass soon," Mum continues. "How far along are you, exactly?"

Wait—WHAT?

I frown, looking at Alessia, whose eyes have gone wide, glancing back and forth between Mum and me.

"I, um … think there's been a bit of a misunderstanding," Alessia says.

More than one, it seems. And one was quite enough.

"I'm not pregnant," Alessia says, looking only at me. "I'm not."

"Are you *sure?*" Mum asks.

I glare at Mum. "I think Alessia would know. Why would you even make the assumption?"

"It's what Henri and Juliet told me. I assumed Alessia told them today, and that's why your engagement was so sudden."

Alessia drops her head in the hand I'm not holding, saying something in Italian that sounds a lot like a prayer for patience.

"If not," Mum continues, "your constitution may not be suited for this life."

Alessia sucks in a breath.

"*Mother.* This is absolutely uncalled for."

Again, her features soften, but it doesn't change the tense mood in the room. "I'm not trying to be rude. I simply mean that your fiancée should know what kind of life she's getting into. I'm only saying this life requires a lot of inner strength and—"

"Please go. You're being rude, and we have a lot to discuss."

Mum blinks innocently as though she didn't just drop the equivalent of a word grenade in the room. "Take your time. Just not *too* much time, because I do need to let the photographer know about this afternoon—"

"Mum, *please*. My very last concern right now is the photographer."

Her polite voice disappears as quickly as her smile. She glances at the slim gold watch on her wrist. "You have an hour to let me know."

The moment the door closes behind her, I turn back to Alessia. "I'm so sorry. She can be ..." I search for an adequate word.

"Ruthless? Honest to the point of pain?"

I give her a tight smile. "Yes. Especially since my father's health dipped this year, she's become intently focused. Which has the side effect of making her act more like a queen than a mother most days."

Alessia picks at the edge of the duvet. "Is that how it is? You royals learn to just separate your life like that?"

Her question isn't pointed but curious. Nervous, even. And her question gives me pause.

IS that how it is?

Unsure how to answer and bothered by that more than I care to admit, I ask a question of my own. "Why did my sisters think you're pregnant?"

"I'm guessing it was the throwing up last night paired with passing out today." Sia pulls her hand away from mine and massages her temples. "How did all of this get away from us? First, we're engaged. Now I'm

246

pregnant. I mean, it would be laughable if it weren't so ... so ..."

"So very *real?*" I ask.

"Phillip, I tried on *wedding dresses* today!" She glances down. "I'm still *wearing* a wedding dress."

"You look lovely, by the way. What I can see of you, that is." I try to tug away the duvet and am rewarded with her smirk as she holds it tight against her chest.

"That's bad luck," she says.

"I don't think that's quite how this works. That's only on the wedding day."

"It's only early afternoon," she says lightly. "Given the speed at which things have been moving, perhaps we can look forward to an evening wedding."

It's on the tip of my tongue to say what I did when I thought she was sleeping—to suggest that maybe we drop the idea of pretense and make the engagement real. But I don't want it to seem like it wasn't my idea in the first place to marry her, like I'm just some overgrown child, shrugging and going along with someone else's plan. I did want to marry her, even before I knew her.

Do I need to confess that too? Should I come clean about the whole thing and why I was in Repestro?

Before I can come to a conclusion, she continues.

"Your mother already has a wedding date picked out—for *this summer*. I thought royal weddings took years to plan! I'm trending on Twitter! There are hashtags!" Her expression changes, and my chest constricts when her eyes fill with tears. "Where were you?" she whispers.

I take her hand again. She lets me, but her fingers are limp in mine. "I'm so sorry. There was a mountain of work waiting for me at my desk, and I was pulled into meetings from the start of the day. I was trying to finish things up quickly so I could get away to see you. Mum said you were trying on dresses and I didn't think I should disturb you. But I absolutely should have sought you out first thing."

This is something I've never given much thought to, as no one has ever consumed me in this way. I have no idea how to balance my kingdom work and a relationship. None at all.

Other than being honest. At least about my failures, even if I'm not yet sure how to tell her about Claudius's rubric.

I lift her hand to my mouth and press a kiss to her fingertips. "This is all new to me—finding the balance between my job and my personal life. I've really never had to do so before. I've never had to, as I've never had anyone like you in my life." I give her a rueful smile. "Turns out, I'm rubbish at balance."

She sighs, and when she squeezes my hand, relief washes over me. "This is new for me too. And the past twenty-four hours has been overwhelming. To say the least."

"Are you sorry you came with me?"

"No."

Her voice is firm, and warmth expands in my chest at her determined look.

"I will never be sorry for that. But I think I will need a mobile phone."

She winces, as though this request is akin to asking for the eradication of an endangered species. It makes me smile.

"You're finally ready to join modern times?" I tease.

"Not remotely. But I'll need to make sure I can call Nonno and Luci to explain. Neither of them paid much attention to royal gossip before, but I'm sure they are now. They probably think I'm engaged and also pregnant." Her face falls. "What are we going to do? About the wedding, the rumors—all of it? I don't want to disappoint anyone—your father, your sisters, least of all *you*."

Alessia's dark eyes are pleading, and the expression on her face tugs at something in my chest. I realize I'm clutching her hand too tightly and loosen my grip just a little, brushing my thumb lightly over her skin.

"Forget disappointing anyone. What do *you* want?"

I wait, hoping as my heart pounds that she'll say she wants it to be real. That I'm not the only one wishing it was all real.

"I don't know," she says, her eyes pleading with me to understand.

And I do. It's a lot to take in, and beyond the obvious royal world she's been thrust into, there are all the misunderstandings. And my mother tossed Sia onto a conveyor belt hurtling her toward a wedding. I can't expect her to be ready to say yes to this life. Not when she's had less than twenty-four highly emotional and confusing hours to get used to the idea that I'm a prince.

I get to my feet, letting her hand slowly slide out of mine. "I'll take care of it."

She frowns as I take a step away from the bed. "What does that mean?"

"I'll tell my mother the truth."

Alessia throws back the covers and jumps out of bed. "If you're going to tell your mother the truth, I want to go with you. She doesn't think I have the constitution for this? I'll show her my constitution."

I want to agree, but I'm too distracted by the sight of Alessia in a wedding gown. It doesn't even matter that I can see pins and some kind of giant clips hanging off the side, or that it's wrinkled from her lying in bed. She is an absolute vision.

I can only stare and imagine. Wish. Hope.

A flush crests her cheeks, and her hands tug at the fabric. "Do you like it?"

"I like *you* in it. Sia, you are extraordinary." My throat tightens, keeping me from saying more. From telling her that I would marry her this instant, in this room, in this ill-fitting dress if she'd have me.

Her chin dips, but not before I see her smile. "Thank you. It feels like too much."

"It's hardly enough." I step closer, sliding my hands around her waist. "*You* are what's beautiful, Sia. Not a dress you wear."

She gives me a shy smile before clearing her throat and regaining the fiery look she had in her eyes moments ago. "Well, I better not wear this to see your mother. Do you mind waiting outside while I change?"

I step closer until my lips are hovering over hers. "I mind very much, actually. Given your delicate constitution, I might need to stay. Just in case you need help."

Laughing, she puts both hands on my back and pushes me toward the door. "I'll show you a delicate constitution. Out!"

I appreciate the teasing as I let her propel me to the doors. I'm glad to see her fire, her passion. It feels like sliding back into what's comfortable, what we know.

Who we were *before* we flew to Elsinore.

Then I remember our midnight time in the kitchen and how well Alessia fit in with my siblings—joking and laughing and looking beautiful with egg yolk in her hair. The memory gives me a tiny surge of hope.

This really *can* work. What we have is real, even if the engagement—for now—is not. Which means for now, we must face my mother.

CHAPTER 24

Alessia

WE MEET Phillip's Mother THE QUEEN in what looks like a formal parlor. This time, I remember to properly curtsy, while Phillip nods and gives her a quick kiss on one cheek before returning to my side.

It's hard to focus when every room in the palace—honestly, even the hallways—are like expensive galleries or museum exhibits: opulent, excessive, and rich in history.

This room has high ceilings, plush rugs my feet practically sink into, and massive windows overlooking beautiful gardens with rows of hedges and flowers. The sight makes me ache with longing, and I realize that I haven't been outside breathing real air since the moment we arrived.

When is the last time I've been inside a building for this long?

Maybe never.

I'll have to ask Phillip to show me the gardens later. I'm surprised he hasn't already suggested it, but then, from the moment we arrived, it's been as though we were both tossed onto a treadmill set to the highest speed. Except I've already given up and have been thrown off the back while Phillip is still running.

We sit down, facing his mother on a sofa so uncomfortable I can't help but grunt. Are the cushions stuffed with the bones of Elsinore's enemies?

Does Elsinore *have* enemies? Have they fought in wars? Probably things I should know.

Phillip slides his arm around my waist, and I get the sense he's trying to be my shield. I wish I didn't need one, but this meeting feels akin to standing before a firing squad. It is nice to know I'm facing it with him. It's also nice to see that the queen has no weapons in hand. Unless she plans to use the cup and saucer she's holding as projectiles.

Doubtful. Though her expression is dubious.

"I had some tea prepared," the queen says. "Please help yourselves."

Suzette, I remember. At some point, someone—maybe Henri?—told me the queen's actual first name. But using it (even in my head) feels like breaking some kind of inherent moral code.

"Thank you." Phillip makes no move to take a cup from the silver tea tray on the coffee table.

I hesitate. I don't want tea. I *do* want to be polite. I want to stand with Phillip like he's standing with me. I *also* want the queen to see that I can stand on my own. Essentially, I'm a mess.

"Do you not drink tea, Alessia?" the queen asks.

"We prefer caffé," Phillip says.

I notice the *we*. So does she.

As much as I appreciate his protective instincts, Phillip answering for us both won't do me any favors. I need to show his mother THE QUEEN that I'm not some wilting flower who vomits and faints at the first sign of ... well, anything.

"I'm not normally much of a tea drinker, but I'm happy to have this. Thank you." Nodding politely and mirroring her pose—knees to the side, legs crossed at the ankle—I pour a cup, add a bit of cream, and take a small sip.

Unlike the mint tea from the night before, prepared by the jovial Bertie, this tastes like bitter, boiled grass. Swallowing this tiny sip takes an enormous amount of willpower.

"You drink coffee now?" the queen asks Phillip, one eyebrow raised.

"I do. But can we set aside the beverage discussion and focus on the more important matters at hand?"

She gives a curt nod. "Yes, I think that's a good idea. The first and most pressing matter is obviously—"

I interrupt. "We aren't actually engaged."

I'm shocked hearing the words spill from my mouth, even though I silently practiced saying them the whole walk here. My voice seems to echo across the room like I've spoken through one of those Swiss horns they use in the old Riccola commercials. Beside me, Phillip doesn't react, but one finger traces what feels like a little heart on my back.

I want to melt into him, but I'll wait. Right now, I need to be strong. No melting allowed.

His mother sets her mug and saucer delicately on the table. My proclamation does not seem to have ruffled her feathers in the slightest. Or maybe she has no feathers. I'm the chicken in this room, trying to hide my shaking hands by holding my teacup tighter.

"I see," the queen says, looking from me to Phillip, her

hands demurely folded in her lap, several large diamonds glinting on her fingers. "And this is relevant how?"

I sit in a cocoon of stunned silence, trying to decide if I misheard. Because this fact is relevant to EVERYTHING. I glance at Phillip, seeking help or answers or heck—maybe a laugh at the absurdity of this, but his jaw is tight and his eyes are locked on his mother.

"No," he says.

No WHAT? I wonder.

The queen's question about relevancy can't be answered with a simple yes or no. But Phillip seems to have understood some meaning I completely miss.

Normally, I'm so good at reading people. Assessing tiny details and gestures like I did the first night Phillip came into Nonno's restaurant. But I'm struggling to do so with his family, perhaps because my desperation for approval is numbing my normally sharp observational skills.

Phillip and his mother continue the conversation while I feel like I'm floating above it, squinting to read the subtext. They might as well be speaking Elsinorian.

"An engagement couldn't have been timed more perfectly," the queen says. "Your father is thrilled. Your siblings are similarly delighted. You're obviously smitten, and I can see why. I fail to see the problem."

The problem seems VERY clear to me. (Even as I'm reveling in the fact that she said she can see why he's smitten. I barely avoid asking her to expound on this point.)

The problem is a misunderstanding that snowballed into an avalanche.

She goes on. "If I'm being fully honest, Alessia seems like the perfect solution."

Now, I'm not a person—I'm a *solution*?

I manage to find my voice, which sounds a little too soft, a little too unsure. Definitely not full of constitution.

"Phillip?"

He doesn't respond because he and his mother THE QUEEN are locked in some kind of intense staring battle. I suddenly get the sense I'm watching a live-action, weirdly internalized version of two elk going horn to horn. I mean, in those scenarios, it's usually two males fighting over a female, not a mother and son fighting over ... what *are* they fighting about, exactly?

Right—that our fake engagement isn't a problem because I'm actually a *solution*.

"I'm confused," I say.

"Catch up, dear," the queen says, without looking away from Phillip. "I'm playing the hand I was dealt and offering you both a choice."

"An *ultimatum*," Phillip practically growls.

"Alessia is a person, not a PR opportunity." Phillip's voice is deadly calm. His hand on my back is no longer drawing hearts but clutching at the fabric of my shirt.

"It's quite simple, really," the queen says to him. "You left us at a very key time. The media is hungry for answers— about your absence and about your father's health. An engagement is the perfect story to feed the vultures. It's high time you married, and everyone loves a love story. Especially between a commoner and a royal."

"I thought you wanted me to marry someone with a title," Phillip says with no small amount of bitterness.

I'm pretty sure I just developed an instant ulcer the size of Rome in the pit of my stomach. Until yesterday, I didn't know Phillip was royal, much less the expectations of his family regarding the kind of woman he'd marry.

"I still believe that choosing someone who understands

this life will be easier for you. But there are benefits to this arrangement as well."

"It's not an arrangement," I whisper. I can almost hear Luci shouting at me to pick any Sean Astin character—*any at all*—and channel his ability to be both strong and kind. Humble and resilient.

"Alessia is beautiful in that ..." The queen studies me and I try not to wither under her assessing eyes. "Unassuming, girl next door sort of way."

"Alessia is beautiful, *period*," Phillip says. "Especially because her inner beauty shines through. Her character. Unlike the titled women you've tried to set me up with."

I mean, there PROBABLY are more awkward things than listening to your boyfriend argue with his mother about the kinds of women she wishes he'd date instead of you. But at the moment, I can't think of any. I continue to feel like an errant candlestick whose worth is being debated while I sit motionless on an end table. Sean Astin is nowhere in sight.

"Good to know," the queen says in a tone that sounds more like, *we'll see*. "The stories so far—even from *The Royal Bugle*—are positive. Glowing, even. Other than the confusing balcony incident, which thankfully is being discussed as a rescue and not some kind of drunken incident. The whole of Elsinore is happy you've found love. It gives them hope."

"But the story they've been told isn't true," I manage to say.

The queen's gaze swings to me, almost making me wish I'd said nothing at all. "And what would you propose we do about it? Should we issue an official statement saying we lied? Or were confused? How do you think that might play out in the press?"

I look to Phillip, whose beautiful blue eyes stare back at me with intensity. I can't be quite sure what he's trying to convey, but his silence seems to be his way of allowing me to step forward. To make the choice. To step out from behind his shield and stand on my own. His hand on my back presses softly, tenderly, and the tiny touch fills me with warmth.

I place my hand on Phillip's thigh, which seemed like a natural move until I wonder if thigh-touching is improper in the presence of a queen. You know what? I don't care.

I don't care what's proper. Or protocol. I don't care about PR.

Even if all of these are things I'll have to care about if I stay here and marry Phillip—in August or another time of our choosing. For now, what I care most about is the man whose thigh I'm currently squeezing and suddenly picturing as it was yesterday—was it only yesterday???—in Nonno's tiny bathing suit.

Smiling, I turn back to the queen. Take a breath. Straighten my shoulders. Make a choice.

"What if we go along with it?"

If she weren't queen, Phillip's mother could be a professional poker player. She gives away nothing with her expression.

"You want to continue in a fake engagement?" Phillip asks. Slowly. Carefully. "You want to lie?"

I tilt my chin and widen my smile for him. "It's not exactly fake though, is it? More like ... presumptuous. Jumping ahead a few steps."

More like being shot out of a cannon from one continent to the next, but *whatever*.

I search Phillip's deep blue eyes, remembering how they looked under the warm sky over Repestro. As gently as I can, I ask, "Was it lying when you didn't tell me you were a prince?"

Silence. Pure, thick, stunned silence.

When I glance at the queen, I catch the tiniest flicker of something crossing her face. Obviously, she didn't know the details of Phillip's trip to Repestro. The triumph of pulling even a teensy tiny reaction out of her feels like laying down a winning hand.

I lean into Phillip, wanting him to know I'm not trying to hurt him with the point I'm making.

"You didn't lie," I assure him. "I know you, Phillip. You were yourself with me." With a rueful grin, I add, "You simply saved some key details until later."

"Is that what you propose?" the queen asks, now fully composed. "To save key details ... like the fact this engagement is—how did you say—*presumptuous*?"

"That's exactly what I'm proposing. If Phillip agrees, of course."

"I do," he says quickly.

With more confidence and gaining steam, I meet the queen's gaze once more. "I'd like to be here with Phillip on his terms, just as he was for me when he came to my village. I'd like to get to know his family and his country, his culture, his history. Most of all, I'd like to continue to know *him*. But" —I add quickly as I see her mouth begin to open—"there are conditions."

The queen says nothing but raises a single, perfectly sculpted eyebrow. Invitation or challenge? I'm not sure, so I keep going.

"No photo shoot—yet. No more formal statements or dress fittings or wedding dates chosen without consulting *us*. We need less pressure."

Her smile is small, and I'm not sure if it's patronizing or simply amused. "This life, if you weren't aware, comes with an inescapable amount of pressure."

I nod. "I understand. What I mean is we need less pressure specifically from *you*."

Next to me, Phillip shifts and I swear I see the tiniest corner of his mouth lift. He's pleased with me.

More importantly, I'm pleased with myself. Though I feel quite sure I'm going to collapse after the adrenaline currently pinging around in my system wears off.

"Phillip?" the queen asks, turning her gaze to him. "This is what you want?"

"Yes."

I get the sense he wants to say more, but he gives me a quick glance as though to say, *later*. For now, the happiness coursing through me from Phillip's one-word answer is enough.

"Then it's settled."

The queen stands, and when Phillip stands as well, I join him, sliding my hand through the crook of his elbow.

"I'll take the liberty of canceling the photographer this afternoon, and I'll do my best to make sure the press doesn't get wind of the pregnancy rumors. We can release a statement asking for privacy and limit your public engagements for a brief time. She'll need a ring."

"Oh, I don't—"

The queen interrupts my protest. "What we won't have is rumors questioning the reality of this engagement. If we release a statement, it's as good as true and needs to look that way. Does anyone else know the truth?"

"Only Callum."

The queen clears her throat. "Not who I would have chosen to confide in. But no one else must know."

Now I've really flipped our roles, with me being the person keeping the truth from the people in Phillip's life. But at least he and I are finally sharing openly. Given the strangeness of the circumstance, I think we're doing our best.

"Do we have an understanding?" the queen asks.

"Yes," Phillip and I say together.

"Alessia, your tutoring will begin tomorrow in Elsinorian history, language, and royal etiquette. I'll have a schedule sent to your room."

"Thank you," I say, offering a small curtsy.

Her eyes move to Phillip, and I can breathe again. "You have until the ball to make a final decision. It can be a celebration of your engagement or"—she glances at me and I do NOT like this look—"it can go on as originally planned: as a ball for you to choose your bride."

A ball to choose his bride?

So much for no pressure.

Her eyes, the same blue as Phillip's, zero in on mine. "And if this does not work out, I cannot promise to shield you in the press," the queen says. "They'll need someone to blame."

"Mother." Phillip looks ready to throw something.

"These are *my* terms."

I have to respect the way power practically seeps from her pores. Of course, I'd prefer if this power were used for things like disarming nuclear warheads, raising the working wage, or saving the whales (if they're still in need of saving, that is). NOT wielding this intimidating force in a way that directly impacts my life.

I allow myself for only a moment to consider how I would handle her role as queen.

Nope—still not ready for that thought.

"I agree," I say.

The moment she's gone, Phillip throws his arms around me, and for a moment I shove away the myriad of lingering questions about Phillip and his bride-choosing ball and the worries about being torn apart publicly.

"That was absolutely brilliant," Phillip says. "I've never heard anyone speak to her that way. Not even Henri."

My heart is pounding, and my knees tremble. "I didn't break any laws?"

"Maybe a bit of light treason," he murmurs, chuckling. "But we don't even execute people for that anymore."

"Glad to hear it."

Pulling back enough to dip his face to mine, Phillip studies my face. "Are you sure this is what you want?"

At the moment, I'm sure of very little. Only that I'm not willing to leave or to give up without giving Phillip a real chance.

"I meant what I said."

Phillip kisses me until my heart *really* is pounding and my knees *really* are trembling. The adrenaline is definitely slipping out of my system, and I'm grateful for his strong arms keeping me upright.

After a moment, Phillip slows the kisses and then cups my face in his hands. "I need to clarify something," he says. "When Mum asked if this was what I wanted, I said yes, but that's not my whole answer."

He pauses, long enough to make me want to take him by his fancy shirt and shake him. Phillip's smile is a slow sunrise, blinding and warm and overwhelmingly hard to look away from.

"I. Want. You. Only you, Alessia."

Tightening my arms around his waist, I press my cheek to his chest once more as he drops a kiss on the top of my head. I want nothing more than to echo his words, to assure him that *he* is what I want.

I *do* want him. But this life ... leaving Nonno ... one day having to become like Phillip's mother THE QUEEN—I cannot yet say I want all *that*.

But if I truly love Phillip, I know any price would be worth it.

I lean away, needing to see his eyes, for him to see mine. "I want to try. I want more time. I want to get to know you here, in your home."

It's all I can offer right now. From his expression, it seems to be enough.

For now.

"And now maybe it's time you tell me about the original plan to throw a ball and Cinderella yourself a bride?"

CHAPTER 25

Alessia

WHILE I SUSPECT Phillip has already ruined me for all other men, by only the second night sleeping in the palace, this mattress has absolutely ruined me for all other beds. It's amazing enough that when Phillip wakes me (this time, with a proper kiss like a good story book prince), I try to convince him to join me and do all his work from here.

"I'm afraid I cannot relocate my meetings to your bed," he says. "As much as I love the idea."

"What is this mattress even made of? Is it even legal?"

Phillip, already fully dressed in a smart navy suit with shower-wet hair, kisses me once more then steps out of reach, away from my grabby hands.

"We don't have much time," he says. "I'll be waiting."

"And you're sure this is worth leaving this bed for?"

"I certainly hope you'll think so. But if not, I do also have espresso."

I throw back the covers. "Sold. To the man offering espresso."

Twenty minutes later, there is still no coffee as we walk at a brisk pace through a wing of the palace I've not been to yet.

At least ... I don't think I've been here. Honestly, I have no idea as all the gilded wallpaper and gold sconces and crystal doorknobs have started to look the same. I'd need a map to be sure, and when I asked Phillip about procuring one, he only laughed.

We reach a set of double doors with two guards standing on either side. Though they don't greet us or make eye contact, the guards open the doors as we approach. I'm not sure what I expected, but definitely not a set of stone stairs curving down into darkness.

Phillip immediately starts down at the same quick pace, but I pull my hand from his, peering down from the top.

"Are you sure there's no dungeon in the palace? Because this creepy staircase absolutely looks like it would lead to a dungeon."

He grins at me, stepping back up a stair until we're eye level. His hands find my waist, and I slide mine up his chest to his shoulders—quite a lovely path to travel.

"I'm sure. Though ... I can't say I wouldn't mind a few hours alone with you in a dungeon."

When he kisses me, I have to agree. Perhaps dungeons get a bad rap.

He hops down a step. Then another. "So, are you coming?"

"You won't tell me what's down there? It's not catacombs or something, is it?"

I swear, I hear one of the guards at the door snort.

"Not catacombs. Or anything else creepy. I promise. I'll tell you if you insist, but I'd love to keep it a surprise." Phillip steps back up to where he stood a moment ago, frowning now. "Wait—do you like surprises? There are still some very basic things I don't know about you."

"I *love* surprises."

"Good." Phillip kisses my neck, right below my jaw, in a place that has me gripping his shoulder for dear life.

"So many things yet to learn," he murmurs, his lips brushing over my skin. Pulling back abruptly, he glances at his watch. "And so little time. Will you join me going down the creepy stairs to a surprise I promise will be worth it?"

I glance behind him, where the stone steps curve around and disappear out of sight. Even the air here feels draftier and cooler. "You did promise me espresso, which has yet to appear."

"Creepy stairs, surprise, *then* espresso."

"Fine."

We go down and down and down. Two stories? Three? There are no exits, no doors or windows or anything at all until we reach another set of double doors, these made of metal and with no guards—only an electronic keypad, which looks completely out of place against what must be centuries-old stone.

"Close your eyes," Phillip says.

"Are you serious?"

Phillip looks taken aback. "Yes. Why?"

"You realize that every protective instinct I have is telling me to run away, right? We're like in some kind of dim, sub-basement level, completely alone. No one would ever hear me scream."

"Your mind is a much darker place than I realized," Phillip says.

And then spins me so my back is pressed against the cool metal door. His mouth is on mine immediately, like this is the surprise and he can no longer keep it to himself. "Maybe the whole point was to get you alone. Somewhere away from watching eyes and listening ears."

Honestly, I don't mind that at all. It seems since we've arrived, time alone is nonexistent. Or, at best, short-lived. Various family members always seem to be around, and the man I like to think of as Redbeard always seems to be hovering about. Though I suppose it *is* his job to watch over me.

I point to a small camera in the corner. "Not quite alone."

Phillip sighs. "Never really alone."

I hear a beeping as Phillip types in a code. There is a deep, echoing sound of a lock turning in the door behind me.

"Sneaky," I say. "Distracting me with kisses so I don't see the code. Don't you trust me?"

"I do. But right now you don't have the security clearance, so ..." Phillip presses a last, quick kiss to my lips. "Are you ready?"

He swings open the metal door, gesturing for me to enter ahead of him. I'm still nervous and now flustered from his kisses, but curiosity propels me through the doorway.

The only light comes from what must be hundreds of candles in the circular room resting on glass cases lining the walls. I imagine with the overhead lights on, the room would look like a museum. But the effect of the flickering candles makes it seem like something out of a dream. And it reminds me of the hotel suite back in Italy.

"Did Graves and Martin help?"

Phillip smiles. "Not this time."

"What is this place?" I ask.

Phillip steps close, his chest warm against my back. "Welcome to the royal treasury."

He urges me forward, toward the largest glass case in the center of the room. I realize as we move closer, it holds a series of jeweled crowns on dark blue velvet. I've never been particularly into jewelry—something Luci can't get over—but the sight of these crowns practically steals my breath. There are about a dozen of varying sizes and with different stones and gems. All like works of art. Probably priceless.

"Do you ever wear one of these?" I ask, my eyes bouncing from one crown to another to another, each more beautiful and intricate than the last.

"Only on special occasions," Phillip says. "They're more uncomfortable than you might imagine. Heavier too."

I'm so distracted by the exquisite crowns that I don't notice what's on top of the case until Phillip picks up a small box and drops to one knee right there on the stone floor. I gasp.

He takes my hand, and I blink down at him, trying to steady my racing heart to no avail.

"I decided that since our engagement was already announced—however incorrectly—I would like your permission to officially ask you to marry me."

I bite my lip to hold back a smile. "Wait—you're asking my permission to ask me to marry you?"

"Yes." He tilts his head.

I'm not sure what kind of expression my face is making, but I imagine it's one of complete shock.

"You don't need to do this. I mean, just because your mother said I should wear a ring—"

Phillip shakes his head, and the tenderness in his gaze melts me a little. "This has nothing to do with my mother. And in all honesty, it doesn't even have to do with what

Callum said." He pauses. "I spoke to your nonno about my intentions the morning after we talked all night at the cliffs."

Now, I'm definitely in shock.

"You hardly knew me," I whisper, my mouth suddenly a dry and barren wasteland.

His eyes shift away for a moment in a way that makes me feel like he's keeping something back, but then they find mine again and they're so sincere, it makes my chest ache.

"I knew enough to *know*. I know this is ridiculously fast. You might not be ready, and I fully expect for your answer to be that you need more time. But will you let me ask you?"

"Will I ... *let you* ask me to marry you?"

The idea is absurd. Absurd and *completely* romantic.

"Yes."

"A pre-proposal?"

He considers. "I suppose it is, yes. A placeholder proposal. But there's a catch."

I like surprises. Catches, not so much. I wait.

"I'm going to ask you to marry me," Phillip says. "I mean every word. But I don't want to add to the pressure you're feeling. So, at the end, I want you to only say yes to *considering* my proposal. It's not a yes to actually marrying me."

"And what if I feel ready to say yes? Are you going to take away my choice?"

"Are you ready to say definitively yes?" he asks gently, and I don't even need to think about it.

"No," I whisper honestly. "I want to be, but I'm not. Not yet."

"Then let me ask you to consider marrying me."

My hand trembles a little in his, and he must feel it because he squeezes my fingers. Phillip lifts my hand to his lips, kissing each finger while holding my gaze. I swear, I feel the brush of his lips everywhere, not just on my fingertips.

I draw in a deep breath. "You can ask me."

His face, cast in flames, is achingly beautiful as he smiles. "Alessia Maria Elana Rossi Romano, I knew you were different from the moment I met you, when I saw you across the restaurant. I don't believe in ..." He pauses and frowns, as though searching for the right English word. "Instant love."

I grin, and as I do, I feel a tear dripping into the corner of my mouth. "Instalove?"

"Yes. These feelings took me by surprise, just as *you* did. You were this beautiful, vibrant woman who made me realize how colorless my life had been before. How joyless and rote and duty filled. Though my circumstances have hurried us along perhaps faster than I would like, it's not because of my father or because of Callum's mistake that I'm asking you to marry me. It's because I don't want to spend any more of my days without you in them. You make me a better man."

His praise and his kind words make my skin feel prickly and tight, like I've stayed out in the sun too long. I'm hot and uncomfortable and yet so, *so* happy.

"I know I come with a lot of baggage. My life is complicated. Saying yes to me means saying yes to this life. It is a massive undertaking, one many wouldn't wish for, and some would desire for all the wrong reasons.

"When I saw how you cared for your nonno, how you saw the needs of the people in your village and found ways to meet them, I could imagine you doing the same on a larger scale. A kingdom scale. For my people as well as yours."

Phillip pauses, and though I know he has more to say, I fight the urge to blurt out something. A yes. A no. A premature *I love you*.

I bite the inside of my cheek to keep myself from saying anything at all.

Shut up and let the man finish his ridiculously romantic pre-proposal.

"You are all I could ever ask and hope for, Sia. As a wife first, but also as a queen. One who is humble and kind, who serves her people rather than clamoring to be served. And now we've reached the part that I'm really scared of."

Phillip smiles, and I attempt to smile back, but my whole face feels wobbly.

"I didn't mean for you to cry, mi bellina."

"Then you shouldn't have said such sweet things."

His eyes darken. "Would you like me to say some things that are also true, but less sweet?"

Before I have even finished nodding, Phillip says, "I want you to wear my ring, because I want everyone who sees you to know that you're spoken for. By me. I want you to be *mine.*"

Luci likes to say that possessive men are only sexy in books and movies, whereas, in real life, it's red-flag behavior. Typically, I agree.

But this sudden and unexpected show of possessiveness from Phillip fills me with heat and a matching desire for the same thing. I need his ring on my finger not just so I can be his, but so I can show everyone that he is MINE.

"Ask me," I demand, my voice husky, and he grins.

But when Phillip lifts the small box I'd forgotten about, I go still. Because what's inside the box is nothing like the crown jewels. Nothing large or fancy, though it is priceless.

It's my mother's ring.

"How did you ..." I trail off, emotion eclipsing my ability to speak.

"Your nonno gave it to me, along with his blessing."

"When?"

"Right after we returned from our swim. I think maybe he

just felt sorry for me after I had to walk through the village in that tiny bathing suit."

A laugh bubbles out of me, even as a fat tear rolls down my cheek. Phillip catches it with a finger.

"But if you want something else, something bigger or fancier, there are dozens of rings here or stones we could have reset or—"

"Put it on." I hold out my hand. *"Please."* The please is an afterthought and does nothing to diminish my demanding tone.

Phillip doesn't seem to mind in the least and quickly slides the ring on my finger. It's a perfect fit.

For a moment, we both pause, letting the moment sink in. I'm thinking of the mother I never met, the father I don't remember, and Nonno, who I wish was here. But the ring in and of itself is his way of being here, his blessing on this moment.

And maybe it's my heightened emotions, but I almost— ALMOST—tell Phillip to ask me to marry him for real. I'm not entirely sure what stops me, but instead, I take his face in my hands, admiring the simple ring on my finger before I capture his mouth with mine.

FROM THE ROYAL BUGLE, EUROPE'S #1 SOURCE FOR ROYAL GOSSIP

Little Orphan Alessia

While the palace's press release was (as usual) dry and lacking in details on Prince Phillip's surprise engagement, we at *The Bugle* have got you covered with all the dirty details!

And in this case, there is actually dirt! But we'll present the facts and let you decide if Phillip's choice is a wise one for Elsinore.

Alessia Maria Elana Rossi Romano hails from the tiny village of Repestro along the coast of Italy. After losing both her parents at a young age (her mother in childbirth and her father in a car accident), she was raised by her grandfather, Enzo Romano, whom she lived with up until this week, when she moved into the palace.

That's right—Phillip's new fiancée already moved into the palace. (See the photo of her bedroom and her grandfather's home in Repestro!) Our sources report that Alessia's current suite is larger than her grandfather's home, and every item of clothing and all personal effects are brand new.

An upgraded wardrobe with Elsinore footing the bill? Smells like diva behavior to us!

Prince Phillip allegedly met his new fiancée while on a secret diplomatic visit to Italy where Romano waited on the prince in her grandfather's restaurant. She doesn't speak a word of Elsinorian, but when you get hot and heavy this quickly—words aren't always necessary. Palace insiders even tell us there are rumors of pregnancy after Romano passed out several times and showed signs of morning sickness.

With such a short timeline, we hope Prince Phillip insists on a paternity test!

As for the rest of the royal family, tension is running at an all-time high. King James's health is still in peril, and palace sources say that he and Queen Suzette are not in agreement about Prince Phillip's sudden engagement. Meanwhile, Princesses Henrietta and Juliet have had at least one catfight with Romano during a dress fitting.

Meanwhile, the royal ball scheduled for next month (rumored to be an event for Prince Phillip to choose a bride) is still on, which begs the question—does the royal family already know this engagement will fail?

Don't give up your hopes of snagging—or snogging—a prince yet, ladies!

CHAPTER 26

Alessia

I QUICKLY FALL into a predictable daily rhythm I enjoy—
even if it looks nothing at all like my routine in Repestro.
Bertie is a bright spot every morning when she brings a
breakfast tray with espresso and pastries similar to what
Nonno always serves. Phillip hasn't admitted it, but I think
he asked the chef to make them just for me. I'm even starting
to understand pieces of Bertie's chatter, thanks to my
lessons, which occupy most of my morning.

Before the tutors arrive to teach me everything from the
language and history of Elsinore to which fork to use (which
made me feel completely vindicated!), Phillip joins me. Our
visits are much too brief for my taste and involve entirely too
little kissing. I'm usually still in my pajamas while Phillip has
lived half a day already—he's had breakfast and a fencing

lesson and gone for a swim *and* showered *and* gotten dressed in a sharp suit, which is his daily work uniform.

My new palace uniform consists of clothing that, just based on the feel, is way too fancy and definitely way too expensive—the antithesis of the basic slacks and shirts I wore serving in Nonno's restaurant. A personal dresser was assigned to me, and along with a lot of suggestions from Henri and Juliet (and minimal responses from me because I don't really care about clothes) filled up my palatial closet with enough clothes to last until the apocalypse. I could dress every person in Repestro several times over.

A mental image of Ernesto in one of the flowy, flowered dresses makes me collapse in laughter one evening when I'm trying and failing to fall asleep.

I texted Luci about it, and she sent back a series of gifs that made me laugh until I cried. Now that I have a phone, I'm just like everyone else in the world: completely addicted. Nonno has scolded me several times to stop calling so much, though Luci has been delighted by this change. I never knew how much I was missing before I entered the world of memes and gifs.

"There was no catfight," Juliet grumbles, looking up from her phone screen to give me an apologetic smile. "We really like you, Alessia. Promise."

"What's that about catfights?" I ask.

At least once a day, I can't understand something Juliet says —even in English—and Henri has to explain. Usually a slang term or some pop culture reference I don't know, though sometimes it's related to something Elsinorian. And often, she explains things I do know while I simply nod along. I honestly think that as soon as they found out I had no mobile phone, both girls assumed I've been living in what amounts to a nunnery.

"She's reading *The Royal Bugle* again." Henri tosses a throw pillow from my seating area's couch at her sister. "Could you stop?"

"It's not like I believe any of it," Juliet says, turning in her chair so her legs dangle over the side. "I just like to stay ahead of whatever rumor they're spouting."

"It's an endless cycle," Henri explains to me. "They make things up. Then we sue them. Then they stop for a few months before the whole thing starts over again. You'll get used to it."

Will I, though?

Juliet and Henri, whom I think of as my little shadows, especially now that Phillip has been in Paris for three days, definitely like me. But the press had suddenly decided they very much *don't*. My fairytale story of a commoner marrying a royal has shifted into one where the gold-digging waitress orphan tricks the prince into marriage with a pregnancy scare.

Their "exclusive source" inside the palace has given them a wealth of ammo.

That I have thousands of euros' worth of clothes—true, but not because I *wanted* them.

That I keep myself shut up in my suite—only true because I'm in tutoring most of the day.

That I have had numerous clashes with the queen—not true at all. Though I very much would like to have a clash with her about my suspicions that she's intentionally keeping Phillip from me with a ridiculous schedule.

I'm not sure what's worse—the results of a reader poll wherein most of Elsinore said they believe Phillip is the father, or the number of photos that have surfaced, taken from telephoto lenses or perhaps from space, of me with circles drawn over my stomach to show my growing baby bump.

"Remember when they said I have cankles?" Henri leans back on the couch next to me, lifting one leg and examining her ankles.

Juliet, lifts her leg as well, turning her feet this way and that. They both have enviable legs—long, thin, and toned.

"Definitely not cankles. If anything, they were closer to the truth that time they said I had chicken legs," Juliet says with a laugh. "Just wait until they start on your body, Alessia. It's the worst."

Technically, they already did, labeling what I thought was a pretty normal stomach as the start of a baby bump. But I don't point this out.

"It shouldn't be allowed for them to say things, especially considering your age." When both girls give me a look, I add, "Only considering you're not legal adults. It feels wrong."

Henri shrugs. "It's just how it is. Oh! Remember the time they said you had elf ears?"

Juliet touches her ears, which are completely perfect, grinning. "They thought it was an insult, but I'd be perfectly content marrying a fae prince. Or even a fae lord."

Is this really how they live? Teenage girls being criticized body part by body part in the media?

Is this really how *I* want to live?

I twirl my mother's ring on my finger, still not used to feeling its presence there after nearly a week. "Not all of the information in that article is correct, but some pieces of it are very close to the truth."

"Just good guesses," Juliet says with a shrug, but Henri frowns.

"Someone *is* leaking stories. I heard Phillip talking to Callum about it." Henri sighs. "I'm sorry they got inside your grandfather's house by the way. It has a lovely view. I'd love to go sometime and meet your grandpa."

"You would?"

Juliet rolls her eyes-hard enough for both her and her sister. "Of course we would. Will you take us?"

"I'd love to ... if you're allowed."

"You mean, if Mum will let us out," Henri says. Nudging my knee with hers, she adds, "She hasn't always been like this. Father being sick has made her ... different. More controlling."

Juliet pipes up. "More uptight and over-involved."

I want to feel compassion. Some part of me does. The other part feels like Phillip's mother THE QUEEN has set sail on a course of separating me from her son.

Or is this really how busy Phillip's life is? Will a few minutes a day with him be all I can expect?

I'm not sure which possibility is worse.

"Is your grandpa—your nonno—okay?" Henri asks softly, and I nod.

The photos of Nonno's cottage, both inside and out, are disturbing. I've never felt quite so violated. Nonno tried to brush it off when I spoke to him, saying that people have had to start locking doors, but it's not a big deal. He also said Zia Agnesia threw a bucket of compost on a group of paparazzi, which made me smile.

And feel ridiculously homesick for my simple life in my simple village with people who simply love me.

"Actually, I should probably call my nonno," I say, getting up. "I think I'll go for a walk in the gardens."

"Just like Queen Elizabeth, may she rest in peace," Juliet says. Henri and I share a confused glance. "It was part of her everyday routine—a walk in the gardens. What? She's one of my heroes."

Henri squeezes me into a tight hug. "I'm sorry about all the gossip and lies. We're here if you need anything at all."

The offer is so sweet. For just a moment, I get a sense of the woman Henri will be in just a few years' time. She and Juliet both. Strong, smart, and with a true spark of life. They remind me a little bit of Luci.

When I slip off my shoes at the edge of the garden and call Nonno, he doesn't answer. He's at the restaurant by this time of day, but I'm still disappointed. I consider calling Luci, but instead decide what I need is a walk. Alone.

Almost alone. I glance up to see a topiary elephant whose eye (maybe a walnut?) seems fixed on me.

"What are you staring at?"

The elephant doesn't answer—*obviously*—and though it has no feelings—*also* obviously—I still feel guilty. This painstakingly beautiful bush doesn't deserve my quickly darkening mood.

"Sorry," I mutter, stomping by.

Amazingly beautiful gardens, as it turns out, aren't the best place to go when you're in the mood to glower and mope.

I need somewhere cold and dark and rainy. Not a warm, sunny day where I'm surrounded by flowers and songbirds and a veritable zoo of topiary creatures.

Even the air smells amazing—light and fresh and invigorating.

Ugh. It should smell of something like stinky cheese. That's the kind of smell to accompany a bad mood.

"I know," I sigh, passing a bush shaped like a leaping horse. "I shouldn't complain about living in a palace. I sound like a spoiled brat."

I take the horse's lack of response as agreement. Yep— totally a spoiled brat.

Woe is me—I'm (sort of) engaged to a prince, enjoying five-star meals made by request at almost any hour I wish, having two sudden sisters by way of Henri and Juliet, and working with daily tutors on fascinating subjects.

Okay—fine. Royal etiquette is less fascinating and more *infuriating*. I'm pretty sure many of the so-called rules need to be shipped back to the thirteenth century from whence they came. (A fact I learned in my history lessons.)

I've got all the reason in the world to be happy. At the very least, *content*. Not stomping through a garden, talking to judgy topiary animals. I wonder if Queen Elizabeth ever talked to the plants in her garden.

A couple of birds burst into song nearby, startling me.

"Don't try to cheer me up with all your happy songs," I grumble, and they take flight deeper into the gardens, probably where they're less likely to be accosted for singing.

But I *do* feel better. Marginally. Or, at least, more like myself now that I'm outside the palace. My feet are bare (definitely a violation of royal etiquette), and the pea gravel is surprisingly soft as I make my way along the garden path. If I close my eyes, the sun on my cheeks can almost convince me I'm at home.

"Whoa there!"

When walking around with my eyes closed, I shouldn't be surprised to run into something—or, in this case, some*one*. But as my eyes fly open, I let out a gasp and can't quite stop myself from smacking into a firm chest.

Callum steadies me, his hands on my arms reminding me so much of his brother. I jump back, stepping out of his grasp. We're at an intersection where two paths cross. He must have been turning the corner when I walked right into him.

"Oh! I'm sorry. I was ..." I trail off, not sure how to explain our collision.

Don't mind me—I'm just trying to decide how I really feel about being the heroine starring in a real-life fairy tale. One which might not have the requisite happy ending because I'm not sure I have the constitution or desire to be part of this royal world.

Callum grins. "Looked like you were wandering the gardens with your eyes closed."

I sputter out a laugh. "Basically, yes."

"Who were you talking to?" Callum glances around, and I very much hope he doesn't realize I was carrying on a one-sided conversation with bushes and birds.

"Just talking to myself."

"Ah."

There's a drawn-out pause, in which we stare at each other, both nodding like oversized bobbleheads. About what? No idea. Just ... nodding.

"Care to walk and talk together?" Callum smirks. "With our eyes open, perhaps?"

"Sure."

He takes me by the elbow, steering me away from the path he was on and further down the one I was traveling. He drops my arm, then glances behind us.

"Worried we'll be followed?" I ask.

He casts another look over his shoulder, then lowers his voice. "Actually, yes. There's a mob of angry peacocks following me."

I can't help but laugh at the absurdity of this, even though Callum doesn't sound like he's joking. He smiles back, even though I notice him scanning the area around us as we walk.

"First of all, I need to know why you're being pursued by

peacocks," I say. "Second of all, a group of them is called an ostentation."

"An ostentation? Really? How very *ostentatious* of them."

"It's quite a perfect name. And before you go thinking I'm some random collector of obscure trivia, there's a children's book with that name."

"Hm. I'd check it out, but I'm currently trying to avoid all ostentations of peacocks."

"Back to my first question—*why?*"

Callum hazards another glance behind us before answering. "Do you want the long or short version?"

"Definitely the long version."

I'm in dire need of a distraction, and Callum provides exactly that. As he launches into a rambling story involving international pranks and birds, I find myself laughing easily, letting myself forget—for a few minutes—the heaviness hanging over me. He has a way of making me feel at ease. His personality would best be described as warm and sunny. His smiles are frequent and sincere, and something about the way he carries himself—probably the way he resembles Phillip—feels safe and familiar.

Even if the two could not be more different.

"So, you started the prank war by giving Queen Serafina and King Rafe attack swans for a wedding gift? It sounds like the ostentation of peacocks following you is just karma."

"First, it's not karma. I'm sure Rafe somehow planned this. He probably trained the peacocks somehow."

I can't see how that's possible, but I'm not going to argue with Callum's paranoia.

"Second, I didn't give them *attack* swans," he clarifies. "Those particular swans are still living here. Don't go too near the pond, by the way. Bit of friendly advice."

"Thank you. I'll steer clear."

"I gave Fi and Rafe *regular* swans—which are quite beautiful, actually. A lovely and thoughtful gift."

"But you sent them as a prank."

"Well, yes." Callum laughs and bumps me lightly. "You don't let a guy get away with anything, do you? I like that. Phillip needs someone like you."

And ... *pop!* goes the little bubble of happy forgetfulness. I can feel the stress tightening up my muscles in an instant.

"Uh-oh," Callum says. "I said the wrong thing, didn't I? I do that a lot. Is my brother why you're out here wandering barefoot with your eyes closed?"

"It's a little bit Phillip, a little bit your mother"—Callum groans at this—"and a whole lot of overwhelm."

"Now *that* is a potent cocktail. Can I help?"

I'm about to tell him no—because, how could he?—but then I really consider his offer. Maybe Callum is the *only* one who could offer any advice. He may not understand peacocks, but he does have experience with royal relationships.

I lick my lips before starting. "Your sisters mentioned that your parents actually had some kind of marriage plans for you and Queen Serafina?" I ask, hoping I'm not stepping on his toes.

"Ah, yes. Topping the long list of my sundry missteps and failures," he says with a self-deprecating smile.

"I'm sorry if it's a sore subject," I add quickly.

"It's fine. Fi is married to a better man than I am, and I couldn't be happier for them both. Ask me anything you'd like."

As Callum steers us down another path, finally seeming to relax about the peacocks, I consider what exactly I want to know.

"I guess I just wonder what's normal when it comes to being royal and having relationships."

Callum laughs softly. "Nothing at all is normal. At least, not compared to the general population. You've got arranged marriages for political gain, marriages that are nothing more than a show with secret mistresses and ... uh ... misters? Is that what you'd call the male counterpart to a mistress?"

Now I laugh. "I've never given it much thought, to be honest."

"Good." His tone grows serious. "I think that particular idea is rubbish."

"Doesn't an arranged marriage just lead to that— mistresses and misters?"

Callum shakes his head. "Our parents had an arranged marriage. Their love is very real, even if it started out as an agreement." He shoots me a sideways glance. "I think that's what Phillip anticipated with you. But plans changed, and he's utterly smitten."

Something worrying about his words tugs at my thoughts, but I'm distracted by the utterly smitten part. I thought it was true. I still do. But with so little time spent together, how can we know if this will work between us? I have a very strong suspicion this week's schedule is typical for Phillip, no matter what he's said.

We reach a low fountain with multiple sprays of water and large fish bobbing up to the surface. Callum hops up onto the low wall surrounding it, wobbling precariously as he balances. Though I'm sure the fish are koi, not piranha, they look hungry.

"Don't doubt that my brother is wild about you."

"Is he though? Because I've hardly seen him since the first night we arrived."

"Ah. So, you're becoming acquainted with Phillip the Dutiful." Callum almost loses his balance, swaying precariously over the water before righting himself. "My brother's biggest fault might be one of his greatest assets—his intense focus. It's why he'll be an amazing king."

Callum's voice catches on the last word, and my heart pinches, thinking of King James. He seems to have improved at least a little since we arrived, even joining us all for a rousing card game called Sliago a few nights ago. It was the first time I saw the queen laugh, which made me realize she might not be so monstrous.

At the end of the night, Phillip and Callum practically had to carry him back to bed while Suzette, Henri, and Juliet all tried to hide their wet eyes.

Though I know a lot about losing loved ones, I never knew my mom, and my dad's death was sudden. Plus, I was so young. It's impossible to compare losses, but watching your father slowly get sicker ... I can only imagine how acutely painful it would be.

"Don't take it personally," Callum says, drawing me from my morose thoughts. "Phillip has never needed to balance work and a relationship because he's never cared for someone like he cares for you. He might need a little help from you in this area."

"How can *I* help? I barely know what I'm doing. I got lost earlier today in the palace and wandered around for forty-five minutes trying to find my way to the kitchen to return a dish. Redbeard had to help me find my way back."

Callum chuckles. "Redbeard?"

"He's the one usually posted outside my door. Follows me dutifully everywhere. Looks grumpy at all times. Listens a little *too* intently."

"Ah, yes. Billy?"

"I think it's Bill, but I prefer Redbeard."

"So do I. In any case, you're not supposed to return the dishes," he says with a smile. "That's your first mistake."

"I don't like having servants do something I could do myself."

"Which is why you'll make an excellent queen."

I suck in a breath. What Callum just said is one of the things I try my very hardest NOT to think about dozens of times a day. Because when I think about the reality of it, I want to hitch the first ride I can back to Repestro. Yet Callum sounds so confident.

"You barely know me."

He grins. "I see I scared you a bit."

"Scared doesn't quite cover it. I'm terrified. I love Phillip, but I just don't know that I can do all ... this."

"You love him, eh?"

My feet stop moving of their own accord. Did I really say love?

I did.

What's more—I *meant* it.

But I also meant what I said after. I don't know that I can do this. Or if I want to. Even for love.

Callum turns to me, perching on the balls of his feet along the ledge. His smile is gone, replaced by sincerity. "Alessia, don't let the title overshadow the man."

It takes a moment for those words to sink in, and when they do, it's like a blow to my gut.

Don't let the title overshadow the man.

Guilt nags. Because if I *do* love Phillip, I'd want to be with him regardless of his job or station. Even if it means leaving my simple life for this unfamiliar, ill-fitting one.

Even if it means leaving Nonno? Dealing with an invasive press? Phillip's mother? A life so busy I hardly see the man I love?

"There's a lot more to you than what you let people see, Prince Callum."

His smile returns, perhaps a little rueful now. "If so, you're the first to see it. You want my advice?"

I nod. "Please."

"When Phillip is back, find him in his office. Interrupt his work. Ruffle his well-kept feathers. Remind him of what's more important than his royal duty."

"Am I allowed?" I ask, and Callum laughs so easily it makes hope start to unfurl little by little in my chest.

"Yes. You're allowed. My older brother will always struggle to turn off the logical side of his brain, but he's better with you. You are his heart."

I'd like to slide his words into a little wooden box I can keep in a drawer and pull out whenever I'm feeling low. "Thank you."

Once again, Callum laughs. "And to think—his ridiculous rubric worked."

"Right," I say, the hope I felt only moments ago receding with alarming speed. "The rubric."

"I thought he and Claudius were so ridiculous, talking about data points to find a wife. But it worked—the spreadsheets and rubrics to find the perfect woman for Phillip gave him you. And you are perfect for him."

Callum shakes his head, but I'm the one shaken. I don't fully follow what he's saying, but I can piece enough together to make some semblance of sense.

The key point seems to be that Phillip didn't just happen to walk through the doors of Nonno's restaurant that night. It wasn't a happy accident or fate that brought him there. Though it makes my stomach sour, it was not attraction that kept him there.

It was data points. Spreadsheets. Whatever a rubric is.

Strangely, the panic I felt when I learned Phillip was a prince has nothing on the shattered feeling I have now.

Because I willingly accepted that he couldn't tell me certain things. I knew generally what he was holding back. I even said not to tell me yet, like when I kissed him in the ocean.

But this ... it's a complete blindside. It's something I didn't know he was keeping from me.

Did he ever even plan to tell me? He put a ring on my finger without telling me, so I have to assume no.

"Alessia," Callum says softly, in almost a whisper. "Don't run."

"I wasn't planning on it," I lie. Already, my brain is considering who I can ask to help me get back to Repestro. If there were a trellis to climb down, you best believe I'd be over the railing and making a quick escape.

"Move slowly," Callum says. "Take small steps."

"What?"

"They've found us."

"Who?"

But as soon as the question is out of my mouth, I know. From Callum's terror-stricken face to the sound of gravel lightly crunching behind me, even before I turn, I *know*.

Three male peacocks stalk toward us. Their plumed tails drag along the path, but as they near us, they pause and lift them in unison, fanning out their gorgeous plumage behind them. And for the moment, my emotional upheaval is forgotten.

I've never been close to a real peacock, and with their tails up, they are massive. The deep blue spots really do look like a hundred eyes watching. I suddenly understand why Callum was so nervous about being followed.

"You must go," Callum says. "Save yourself."

"I'm sure they're not really going to attack," I say, and I've never been less sure of anything in my life.

Especially as the peacocks begin to shake their tails,

vibrations that sound like rattling bones. The horror movie franchise has been missing out on peacocks for years. I know with absolute certainty that in this situation, Sean Astin would RUN.

"When I get to three, you need to go," Callum says. "They want blood."

I'm not laughing at his paranoia now. The peacocks step closer, still rattling their feathers in warning. Their small heads and sharp beaks bob as they eye us both.

"On my count," Callum says, crouching on the wall.

I take a step back, even though it feels wildly selfish to do so. "I don't really think—"

"*One.*"

I take another step away, so I'm no longer between the birds and Callum. They're so focused on the man standing frozen by the fountain that they don't spare me a glance.

"*Two.*"

I glance around for a fallen stick or perhaps a burning torch, but the gardens are so immaculate, there isn't so much as a leaf out of place. "Callum, are you sure—"

"*Three.* Run!"

When someone shouts at you to run and there are large, angry birds with hundreds of false eyes shaking their feathers in warning, you *run*.

Behind me, I hear a scream and a splash. When I glance back, all I can see are thrashing arms, giant feathers, and water flying.

"I'll get help," I call over my shoulder as I sprint toward the palace.

I really do hope the peacocks don't drown Callum before I can find someone inside to assist him.

CHAPTER 27

Phillip

FRANCE IS OVERRATED.

Or maybe I should say travel of any and all kinds is overrated when the person I want to be with isn't beside me.

If Alessia were here ... I'd have walked her through the gardens at the Château de Villandry, holding her hand and listening to her exclaim about flowers.

You haven't even walked her through your own gardens.

The accusing voice in my head is one hundred percent correct, filling me with guilt and an even greater irritation with this trip. Getting through meetings and official dinners has never felt more dreadful. My room at night has never felt so barren. My need to get home never felt so urgent.

If for no other reason than to do better. Though it's been days since I've seen Sia, even when I was home, my time with her has been limited. I've lost myself in tasks, which seem to multiply without ceasing, and as a result, I haven't carved out enough time for her.

That will change, I vow.

"Don't worry—we'll leave first thing in the morning," Graves assures me as we make our way down the hall to my rooms for a brief rest before dinner.

It's a little frightening how attuned to me he's become. I grunt because *first thing in the morning* is not *right now*.

"I have an additional breakfast with the trade secretary," I grumble.

"Ah. Well, first thing in the morning after your breakfast, then."

Graves attempts a cheerful tone, one which I know is meant to lift my spirits. The other PPO walking with us isn't Martin, whose sullenness I'd appreciate over the silence.

When we reach my suite, I feel my phone buzzing in my pocket. *Alessia*. Already, my heart has decided to double its pace. But it's only a video call from Callum.

I answer, slipping into my room with a nod to Graves. I'm all set to say hello, then stop, staring at the screen.

Callum is shirtless and covered in scratches. One in particular runs from just below his eye to his chin, pink and angry looking.

Inexplicably, Callum is grinning. I catch sight of the royal physician's puffy white hair peeking into the frame as he rubs something on one of the cuts.

"Brother!" Callum says brightly, then winces. "Ow! Is this really necessary?"

The physician mumbles something about infection.

"What ... happened to you?"

"Rafe's peacocks," he says.

"This pranking has gone too far," I announce, frowning as I approach the bed and sink down. I loosen my tie but still feel choked somehow.

"Well, the attack was not methodically planned out," he says, like planning a coordinated peacock attack were ever in the realm of possibility. "Turns out, the peacocks just wanted to mate with me."

He laughs, like peacocks wanting to have their way with him is vastly better than peacocks wanting to murder him.

I'm pretty unclear on which is preferable.

Despite myself, I smile. The physician demands that Callum be still. My brother ignores him.

"Do you require stitches?"

"Not a one. Superficial cuts. I appreciate the brotherly concern, but don't look so worried," Callum says. "Women love scars."

"Well, in that case ..." my sarcasm flies right over Callum's head.

"The good thing is that now we know how to fix this. If we add a few peahens to the ostentation—"

"The what to the what?"

Callum laughs again, and the physician grumbles, his tufty white hair lifts and flutters as Callum waves dismissively.

"Peahens are the females, of which we have none. Hence the attack. And an ostentation is what you call a group of peafowl. I learned that from Alessia." His eyes brighten, and the physician has to grab his face to hold him still. "Listen, we had a good talk today in the gardens."

Though it shouldn't, jealousy burns through me. I want to be the one walking with her in the gardens, having good talks.

Callum smirks. "I've never seen you jealous, brother."

"I'm not jealous." But the growl in my voice reveals my lie.

The physician dabs something on Callum's cheek, and he winces.

"Was Sia with you when this happened?" I demand. "Is she okay?"

"The peacocks only had eyes for me. Don't worry. Ouch!"

Callum swats at the physician, who curses under his breath and then disappears from the frame.

"About time," Callum mutters. "As I was saying, Alessia and I talked. She seems discouraged and lonely. *Someone* has been all work and no play."

I swallow past a knot in my throat then reach up to unbutton my collar. It's already unbuttoned.

"Don't worry," Callum continues. "I assured her that you've never learned to balance your work with a woman before. I have hope for you yet!"

I'm torn between feeling grateful and humiliated.

"Thanks?"

"I encouraged her not to give up on you either," Callum says.

Was she—is she—thinking of giving up? Maybe I need to cancel the morning breakfast and return tonight. Maybe I need to clear my whole schedule to spend the kind of time with her she deserves.

Or maybe that's not what I need at all. Maybe what I truly need is to learn how to do both, as Callum said. I need to find balance.

A text comes through, flashing on the screen with Alessia's name. Only a part of it is visible at the top of the video chat, but it disappears before I can see more than *I'm sorry*. Another text pops up and another and another, a long string coming too fast for me to read. Sia has never texted me so many times in a row, and it's all I can do not to hang up in the middle of whatever Callum is saying.

A heavy weight presses into me when the last text lingers before fading.

I wish things could be different…

I stand and begin to pace, foreboding replacing my excitement. "I need to call her."

"That's a good start. And then you need to find a way to better manage your duties and your love." He says *love* in a teasing, little brother kind of voice that has me wanting to smack him until he says, "I'm happy to help. I hated shouldering it all whilst you were gone, but I'd be happy to shoulder *some*."

"Thank you," I say, meeting his eyes. "Truly."

"Of course. Like I told Alessia, it's unbelievable how well the rubric worked to find you a woman who truly is perfect for you."

I stop pacing. "You … what?"

But the physician has returned and isn't messing around this time. He orders Callum to sit still and let him clean the cuts.

Callum sighs. "I'm afraid I must go and be disinfected. Let me know if I can do anything," he says before disconnecting the call.

He's already done too much. He told Sia about the rubric.

I sink down on my bed, torn between wanting to read her texts immediately and terrified of what I suspect they'll say.

Not telling Sia that I'm a prince was one thing. It felt, for so long, like the only thing. Of course it crossed my mind that I should tell Alessia how I found her. But it almost became a moot point for me, because I feel certain if I had walked through the doors of Nonno's restaurant without the existence of a rubric of any kind, I would be exactly where I am, feeling this exact ache of longing in my chest.

Only—without the regret and guilt.

Because I didn't tell Sia. And I absolutely should have. I've made mistake after mistake, I realize, cupping the phone in my hand and looking at its dark screen.

I love her. I put a ring on her finger, and I failed her.

Of this, I am quite sure, and though it doesn't ease the sting when I read her texts explaining why she must return to Repestro and her life there, it's what I deserve.

Alessia: I'm sorry to do this over text rather than in person, though I'm not sure I could do it in person.

Alessia: Juliet tells me my texts are far too long and they should be shorter. I'll work on that.

Alessia: Sorry, that was an aside.

Alessia: I'm stalling because this isn't easy to say.

Alessia: Or type.

Alessia: Callum let it slip that you didn't find me by accident, and though I didn't fully understand the details, I understand enough.

Alessia: I could handle you keeping your identity from me. I even understand why.

Alessia: But I can't understand why you would keep this from me.

Alessia: I've been lonely here, and I am not sure I'm fit for this life.

Alessia: In fact, as every day goes by and I see less of you, I'm more and more sure that I am not princess or queen material.

Alessia: I need to return home to consider, but I'm not certain I'll return.

Alessia: Perhaps your spreadsheets or rubrics can spit out another choice.

Alessia: I wish things could be different. I wish you the best. Goodbye, Phillip.

Alessia: Oh, and my powers of observation make me strongly suspect your palace leak is the man I call Redbeard.

CHAPTER 28

Alessia

"WRONG TABLE, TESORO," Nonno chides gently, clucking his tongue. He steers me away from the big group in the center of the room and toward the smaller table in the corner.

"Sorry," I say, feeling like I'm a little girl who spilled a full glass of milk across a tabletop.

He gives me a soft smile, but there's a strangeness to it. There's been a strangeness to *all* of his smiles since I arrived back in Repestro. Maybe it has something to do with the fact that there's been a strangeness to *me*. If I expected to reenter my old life and rediscover myself, I was sorely mistaken. I'm not sure where myself is, but it isn't here.

I flew back on the royal jet with only a few necessary staff members, and a private car arranged for by the queen drove me back to my village. Shockingly, Phillip's mother didn't seem pleased when I asked her for passage home a few hours after Callum's peacock attack. There was a challenge in her eyes, but she said nothing. I'd have preferred gloating that she was right about my weak constitution after all.

When I walked in through Nonno's front door, I called out, "I'm home," and promptly burst into tears that lasted two days. It's been almost two weeks now, and the tears are more like a stubborn, leaky faucet, coming and going as they please, always with a near-constant drip.

It's hard when I'm reminded of Phillip—more like his absence—on Nonno's patio with all the plants Phillip bought for me. And when trying to sleep on the new mattress that was waiting for me at home. (Nonno has a new one as well.) It should make sleep easier instead of making it harder because the softness reminds me of the palace and also makes me think of the man thoughtful enough to do such thoughtful things.

If the mattress weren't so comfortable, I'd donate it to someone else in the village. Just out of principle.

"That's the third time tonight," Gianni says when I pass his table, his white brows knitting together in disapproval. More than likely, it's concern. But it's hard not to read disapproval into everything. I'm not sure what I expected coming home, but it definitely wasn't feeling like everyone I love is disappointed in me.

Luci glares at me from her seat at the bar with Marco. No mistaking how she feels, because she takes every opportunity to tell me I've made a huge mistake. Based on Antonio's expression, she's even converted him to her team—the team of being mad at me for not staying with Phillip. Marco only gives me sad eyes, which is just as bad. Maybe worse.

I've lived here my whole life—now everyone is taking Phillip's side without knowing any details?

According to the websites and blogs, I am a heartless heartbreaker. It's partially true. I'm not sure if I broke Phillip's heart, because I struggle to see how I ever had it. I thought this whole time that we were equally falling or stepping or stumbling into love. But it turns out I was just part of a plan.

Heartbreaker? No. Heartless? Yes. Because I'm pretty sure the organ is completely missing from the cavity inside my chest.

Not meeting Luci's or Antonio's gazes, I give the bar a wide berth, which means I walk right by a table of very annoying women who are on some kind of bachelorette trip, based on the veil and sash one of them wears.

One of the women grabs my arm as I pass. A bold move, one I'd normally have more reaction to, but I'm like a book that's been left out in the rain, all my pages damp. Soggy, sad, and limp—that's me.

"Excuse me," she says, though she's already stopped me at this point. "Are you that girl?"

My sigh feels bone deep. I am now "that girl"—the one who was briefly engaged to the prince. I wish I could go back to being the woman who had never met a prince and who didn't read royal gossip sites, drinking the headlines up like a poison I'm addicted to.

Which is how I know the ball is still happening. Tomorrow.

According to rumors, Phillip will choose a wife. The tabloids are calling it the Cinderella ball. Thanks to Henri and Juliet, I know not to trust everything I read.

And yet ... I know at least this much is true, because I heard his mother say it.

Will he really choose a wife?

Is it too late to call Phillip and tell him I'd like it to be a ball to celebrate an engagement—*our* engagement?

"I recognize you," the woman says, reminding me that I'm still standing here in Nonno's restaurant, as substantial and cheerful as a ghost. "You fell off the balcony, and he rescued you. But were you *really* engaged to a prince?"

"No," I answer truthfully. "I wasn't. More wine?" Less wine for this table would probably be better, but anything to extricate myself.

"No—it *is* her!" One of the other women says, waving her glass. Red wine sloshes over the rim and stains the sleeve of her white blouse, but she doesn't seem to notice. "I recognize her from Twitter."

"What's it like dating a prince?" the bride-to-be asks, her pencil-drawn eyebrows arching.

She adjusts her veil, and for a brief moment, I absolutely hate her. I'd like to rip off her veil and sash and hold them over a burner in the kitchen until they go up in flames.

"The better question is, what's it like to—" Her voice drops to a whisper in the middle, but I catch the gist when she waggles her eyebrows.

The women cackle and clink their glasses together in the center of the table. Rage bubbles over in me, like an unwatched pot of pasta. As I open my mouth to say something I'm very sure I'll regret (though maybe not for fifty years), a hand clamps down on my arm and yanks me back.

"Share the load," Luci mutters to me, nudging me away from the table. It's a line from Samwise Gamgee in *The Return of the King*. Her eyes gleam, and I know she's looking forward to taking on this table of women. Even if she's also mad at me.

I have never been so grateful for Luci's obsession with Sean Astin and what he would and would not do.

"I've got this," she says again. Her smile turns wicked. "It's my pleasure."

When I push through the door into the kitchen, I hear raised voices behind me, and I only smile. Nonno looks up from the stove, where he's stirring a sauce.

"Is Luci scaring off more customers?" he asks.

"Probably."

"Do they deserve it?"

"Definitely," Luci says, striding into the kitchen.

"That was quick," I tell her.

She gives a little bow. "I'm *that* good. But they did leave without paying. I'm sure Lessy will be glad to cover the cost of their meals."

"Hey," I protest.

"I'm still mad at you," she says. "Because I love you, and you're being an idiot. A coward. A dummy."

Forget being grateful for my best friend. She's the worst.

Nonno turns off the burner and wipes his hands on his apron. He's giving me that strange smile again. When he turns to Luci, his expression shifts into something totally different, so I know I'm not imagining it.

"I'm meeting Marco," she says, giving Nonno a look.

I don't like when the two of them exchange glances. It means something.

"What are you two planning?" I ask.

"Planning? Nothing, of course." Luci cackles and disappears through the swinging door, leaving me alone with Nonno and Marcello, who's humming as he chops tomatoes.

Nonno hands me a bag. "Why don't you head out early tonight?"

It's as good as a *get out of my restaurant before you drive all my customers away.*

"Are you sure?"

His nod is decisive, but he softens it with a kiss on my cheek. "Yes. Will you be okay, tesoro?"

"Sure."

One day. Maybe when I'm as old as Nonno and don't care if my pants and shirt match. Or maybe when I'm dead.

Turns out a depressing breakup results in me becoming overly dramatic AND morbid.

After hugging Luci goodbye (and enduring her fierce whisper to stop being a coward), I head out the back door of the restaurant. The streets are quiet, even though it's early. They're quiet because Phillip isn't walking beside me, asking about my day, asking me for facts about myself, his hand brushing or holding mine as we walk.

What became my favorite part of the day with him is now the part of the day I dread most. People talk about loss like it's an emptiness, but I swear, this loss has its own heartbeat. It's loud and strong and I cannot ignore it.

I kissed Phillip there, outside the bakery. He made me laugh as we passed by that tree. I tripped over that curb, and he pulled me back by my waist. I can still remember the cascade of tingles that moved up my spine.

The thing about falling in love where you live is that if that love ends, the place you live is forever ruined. Just like the way one moldy orange in a bowl infects all the others.

I feel like the moldy orange.

How do I exist in Repestro now alongside all these memories tied to Phillip? Our village hasn't ever felt this confining, this small, this ... hopeless. My old life fits like the wool sweater I accidentally shrank. Too small. Too itchy.

I know I'm just morose over this loss and I'll get over it *sometime*, but it's hard at the moment to see any way around it.

303

The night drags. The bags feel too heavy, even when they're almost empty.

The deliveries have been lighter since I got back, maybe because Nonno knows this is hard for me and is packing up less each night for me to give out. I've been too self-focused to ask, but I make a mental note to do so tomorrow.

I decide, even though there is no delivery for the DeSantis, to make the trek up the hill. I'm curious—usually we have several deliveries a week, and since I came back there have been none. I tell myself that walking releases endorphins and will help my mood, but really, I'm torturing myself, remembering the first time Phillip and I walked up here together—the fit prince all out of breath from a small hill.

The air is cooler as I near the top of the hill. I'm ready to head home. But when I reach the trailhead, my feet become rooted right where I am.

Because ... I'm not looking at the same house.

The run-down home I last saw has undergone a transformation so complete, I can only stare, trying to come up with an explanation. The walls are sturdy wood now, no rot in sight, and the scent of fresh sawdust hangs in the air, tickling my nose. The door is new and sturdy, painted a cheerful red. It even looks like the roof has been replaced.

How is this possible?

"Alessia?"

Lina DeSantis peeks out from the door. Before I can manage to respond, she's pulling me into a tight hug. Right now, a hug is the kind of thing that can too easily send my leaking faucet into a gushing torrent of tears, but I can't escape, so I hug her back. She smells of cinnamon.

When she pulls back, she's beaming, and her eyes glisten

with tears. "Isn't it wonderful?" She gestures to the house. "We still can't believe it."

"What happened?"

Her brow furrows. "I thought you knew."

I shake my head. "I don't know anything." *Fact.*

"Your prince," she says simply, and the words cut away at a piece of my heart because he isn't mine anymore. "He did this."

"Phillip?" I say his name in a reverent whisper, and she nods, laughing.

"Who else? He also bought the vineyard and hired Vinny as the full-time manager. We'll be moving up to the main house as soon as the renovations are done." She shakes her head, tears now falling into the corners of her smile. "We're so grateful. When will you go back?"

"Go back?"

"Aren't you moving to Elsinore to be with him?"

"Oh." I try to wrangle a smile onto my face, but I'm sure it's more of a grimace. "No. We—no. I'm here."

The pause that follows is awkward, and Lina hugs me once more, a little harder this time, and tells me to thank Phillip the next time I see him.

I cry all the way home, noting all the little changes I'd seen in the village—repaired windows, repainted shutters, new signs in store windows—wondering just how hard it's going to be to forget Phillip when he follows me through the village like a stubborn shadow.

And even though I let my phone die and refuse to charge it, I fall asleep that night clutching it to my chest, crying into my ridiculously, unfairly soft new mattresses purchased by the prince I still love.

CHAPTER 29

Phillip

IT'S BEEN WEEKS. Which means I shouldn't still feel a spark of hope every time the door opens that it might be Alessia.

And yet, I do.

The spark turns into an altogether different kind of emotion when Callum peeks his head inside my office. Before I've said a word, he's already talking.

Typical. There seems to be no circumstance in which my brother can keep his mouth closed.

"I know you don't want to see me but—"

"Out."

When the door is flung open fully, I pick up the sailboat paperweight, ready to send it sailing on its final voyage toward my brother's head, but Claudius steps inside. He's followed by King Rafe, his dark hair gleaming like a crow's wing and his smile as mischievous as a court jester.

I should stand and greet them, especially considering Rafe's title as King of Viore, but if they can all come storming into my office, I can remain seated.

I was aware guests were arriving in anticipation of the ball tomorrow night, but so far, I've let my brother do all the diplomatic greetings and social functions. While I've done what I do best these days: bury myself in paperwork and civic duties that don't require me to leave my office.

That and leaving Sia voicemails. But I don't want to think about those. Especially not when today, I finally heard the automated voice say her voice mailbox was full.

I decided I would keep trying until that moment. The moment is here. With perfect timing, as my mother is ready for me to choose a bride tomorrow.

"Come in, why don't you," I say with no small amount of sarcasm after the door has already been shut behind them. "Make yourselves at home."

"I told you. He's a mess." Callum raises both hands when I glare. "It's true."

"Just because things are true doesn't mean you should say them out loud," I say through gritted teeth.

Callum nods. "A thinly veiled reference to me telling Alessia about your rubric. I deserve that. But can we talk?"

I glance at the three men, then wave toward the chairs opposite my desk. "Why not?"

Rafe grins at me. I glare at him.

I have no issue with the man who married my brother's once-intended bride. Not when Callum made a mess of that as is his signature move. Rafe is utterly devoted to Queen Serafina and is a man of decent character.

Peacocks and pranks aside.

"I know that look," Rafe says. "I've seen it before."

"The look where I'm irritated to be interrupted?"

Slowly, Rafe shakes his head. "The look of someone lovesick."

I hurl the sailboat—this time at King Gerald's head. It's a resilient paperweight and bounces harmlessly off, landing on the plush carpet. Wholly unsatisfying.

"I'm not interested in being coddled or psychoanalyzed or fixed." I pause and point at Claudius, who has been suspiciously quiet. "And no more rubrics."

"That's what we came to talk to you about," Callum says, leaning forward, eyes bright. "The rubric."

"Or lack thereof," Rafe says.

"If I never hear the word rubric again, it will be too soon," I say, massaging my temples. The headache I've had for days is throbbing now.

"You must hear it just a few more times," Claudius says. "Because I must tell you something. There will be no more rubrics because a rubric never existed in the first place."

"What do you mean? I saw it." My voice is sharp, and the throbbing in my head pauses while I try to make sense of what the advisor is saying.

"No." Claudius shakes his head. Once. Decisively. "You saw a lot of documents. A dossier. And you heard a lie."

"Explain."

Claudius clears his throat and moves to adjust his glasses, but they're already perfectly in place. "When you approached me, what did you want?"

"A wife," I grit out, my jaw tense. "Someone who would be suitable for me and as a queen."

"And how did you think you would best find this?"

"I don't want to play twenty questions. Speak what you came to say and say it now," I say.

"Fine. You wanted a suitable match but didn't trust someone else to choose for you. You also didn't seem to trust yourself."

I'm set to argue because that's wholly untrue but decide instead to hear him out before I throw them all out. Perhaps even charge the three with some kind of crime of conspiracy. There must be some law they've broken.

"I gave you what you thought you needed, but also what I believed you really needed."

"Why do I feel like Frodo Baggins, dealing in riddles with Gollum in the cave?" I ask.

Callum laughs. "In this situation, then, that would make *you* Gollum."

"Alessia is my cousin," Claudius says.

I go still. I stare.

"She doesn't know me—there was a rift between her father's side of the family and long ago, they emigrated here. In any case, family drama aside, when I could, I tracked her down. I visited Enzo's restaurant. I watched her, probably much like you did."

My mouth has gone so dry, I'm not sure I could speak even if I had the words.

"I planned to tell her, but something held me back then. It threw me," Claudius says, and I see his emotions cracking through his veneer for the first time ever.

He rubs a hand over his jaw, but I still see his lip tremble. After a moment, he clears his throat.

"When you came to me, asking for help, I planned to do just that. But as you gave me your list, I kept thinking of Alessia. She had all the qualities you listed. And others I thought would suit you well. But you were overly tired of people playing matchmaker. Logic and reason seemed the

309

only way to appeal to you. So I lied. There never was a rubric. Only her."

I sit in stunned silence, processing. I swear, I can almost hear the synapses firing in my brain as I try to make sense of his words.

They're true.

Of course they're true.

I should have realized from the start how impossible it would be for Claudius—brilliant though he is—to find a single woman in a tiny village using a rubric.

As though he's following the path of my thoughts even now, Claudius smiles softly. "I am humbled by the trust you placed in me. And I understand if you will never place it in me again."

Maybe I won't. But for the moment, I'm less concerned with my future relationship with the advisor. "How did you know? How did you know I would feel the way I felt? That I would ..." I trail off, swallowing hard.

"That you would fall like a bag of rocks," Callum says with a grin.

"More like a great tree in the forest," Rafe says.

"I didn't know," Claudius says, and his interruption is the only thing that saves me from leaping over my desk and showing my brother and the king of Viore what falling feels like. "You said love was a choice. I thought if you chose Alessia, surely, love would grow. She's exceptional."

"She is."

"But I didn't expect you to give up so soon," Claudius says, his features turning hard.

"She gave up on me," I say.

"It could be argued that you both gave up on each other," Callum says.

"Classic case of miscommunication," Rafe says.

What does he even know about it?

"I've called," I say defensively. "And I would have gone to her."

I tried, actually. But my mother has me essentially under lockdown. When she caught me trying to convince Graves to help me find a pilot who would take me in secret, even for a few hours, she caught me and swore the only way I was leaving Elsinore was in a body bag—a rather effective threat.

"I can't go to her. Even if I want to."

Which I do. I ache for her. I long to apologize about keeping the whole story from her, to assure her that rubric or no rubric (turns out definitely NO rubric), I love her.

Did I give up?

I think of how many times I called today, listening to the automated voice saying her voice mailbox was full. It was supposed to be my sign, telling me it was time to give up.

"You can't go," Callum says, "but I can."

"The ball is tomorrow."

"I'll go in the morning and be back in plenty of time for the ball."

I lean back in my chair, staring at a point above my brother's head where a tiny hairline crack in the plaster has spread like a lightning bolt.

"What if she won't come?" I whisper.

"I suspect she's just as lovesick as you are," Callum says.

At that moment, the door flies open yet again. I really must install a deadbolt, or perhaps a better guard outside.

My sisters fly into the room, Henri yelling before she's all the way inside. "If you think you're choosing any woman at that ball tomorrow besides Alessia—Oh."

She stops, seeing that my office isn't empty. Juliet runs into the back of her, and both of them almost pitch forward onto Callum's lap.

"Hiya," Juliet says. "Sorry for interrupting. But also, you're not choosing anyone else tomorrow."

"I'm glad that so many people are so invested in my happily ever after," I say. My tone is dry, but I actually mean it.

I'm grateful for all the meddling because it means they care, even if it's also incredibly annoying.

"Callum is flying to fetch Alessia," I announce, and everyone but Claudius cheers. The advisor, Sia's cousin—still trying to wrap my head around that—only smiles. "If she'll have me."

"Operation Acquire Alessia," Callum says, and I want to both hug and hit him, "commences now."

FROM THE ROYAL BUGLE, EUROPE'S #1 SOURCE FOR ROYAL GOSSIP

Exclusive Details about Tomorrow's Cinderella Ball!

Shine those glass slippers, ladies--our palace source has confirmed that the ball set for tomorrow evening has one theme, and it's all about finding Prince Phillip a wife!

Rumors had been running rampant since the exclusive invitations were issued. Briefly, the event was assumed to be an engagement ball celebrating Prince Phillip and Alessia Romano, the native Italian who has returned home. But now, the *Bugle* has learned that the royal family hopes Prince Phillip will choose and announce his bride at the ball—a real life fairy tale!

No one can confirm what Prince Phillip might be looking for, especially after the brief engagement with Romano ended as suddenly as it started. Though the palace's official stance was that things ended amicably, our source tells us that Romano returned home without saying goodbye, leaving poor Prince Phillip devastated.

Who's ready to offer the crown prince some solace???

We're eagerly awaiting news from inside the ball tomorrow evening.

And stay tuned as our longtime inside source gives an exclusive interview this weekend on our YouTube channel. You'll want to meet this handsome ginger who, up until he was recently sacked, worked directly inside the palace walls. If you've ever wondered what kind of pajamas the princes wear, you won't have to wait long to find out!

CHAPTER 30

Alessia

YOU ARE A COWARD.

Waking with a gasp, I glance around my small bedroom, looking for whoever just spoke. It takes me all of two seconds to realize it was me.

Or, rather, my subconscious, which is obviously smarter than my conscious. How do I know? Because only a cowardly idiot would leave a man she loves without giving him a chance to explain in person something which upset her, even if it was something he should have told her about.

I scramble around my room, trying to locate the charger belonging to my phone—the phone I sleep with every night, curled to my chest like a teddy bear. I start muttering to myself. It feels very refreshing to call myself out.

"So what—the man used a rubric to find you. Isn't that just like Phillip?"

I had to search what a rubric was after making sure Callum was safe from the peacocks, and if a rubric isn't the exact epitome of Phillip's logical brain at work, I don't know what is.

"What kind of wife would do this? What kind of queen? Ducking out like a coward. Running without looking back. Flying home after a series of texts. I'm no better than one of the Costas' children."

I think of how it must have felt for Phillip to return from his Paris trip and find me gone. He probably hoped I wouldn't go—because who leaves someone after only sending texts???

"I should never have been allowed use of a phone. Clearly, I can't be trusted."

I locate the charger. It takes three tries to plug it into the phone. My fingers aren't awake yet apparently, and it keeps sliding between the phone and the case rather than in the tiny hole. Finally, success!

I wait for the screen to light up. It doesn't. I push the button on the side and a faint image of a battery with a tiny red strip appears on the screen.

"Yes, yes. I know I neglected you. But see? I've given you a cord. I'm making up for it now," I say in soothing tones like I'm speaking to a pet I've left alone all day. Still, nothing. I groan. "A watched pot never boils and a watched phone never charges!"

I turn the phone face down on the table. Maybe if I look away …

I realize when I do that the light is on under my door. And Nonno hasn't banged on my wall yet, though surely, all my talking aloud has woken him.

"Nonno?" I call. Not waiting for a reply, I test out the words. "I need to get to Elsinore before tonight's ball. I have to take on every eligible, titled woman in the kingdom in a cage fight."

A laugh bubbles out of me at the mental image.

But I have complete faith in my scrappiness and desire. I *would* take them all on. And win.

"Nonno?"

I check the phone quickly—still the red low battery icon —and head out of my room. Nonno's door is open, his bedroom empty. The house is lit up, despite the lazy sun barely peeking over the horizon, and I smell caffé.

Before I've fully opened the patio door, I'm speaking, because time is of the essence. "Nonno, I don't know how to arrange it, but I need to get to Elsinore so—"

I stop at the sight of the full patio. Nonno, Sal, Gianni, Luci, and even Marco (who looks slightly embarrassed) are gathered around the scarred table like it's some kind of war room meeting.

"Tesoro," Nonno says, getting up and urging me to sit in his chair. He rubs his lower back with one hand and strokes my hair with the other. "I'm so glad to hear you say that. It will make this intervention all the easier."

"Intervention?" I glance around, realization dawning. I laugh. "I've had my own self-intervention this morning."

"And what did you intervent?" Luci asks. "Intervene? Whatever—what did you determine?"

"Besides the fact that I am a coward"—a few nods and grunts of approval at this— "and an idiot"—Nonno tsks at this and tries to shush me— "I have to fight for the man I love."

Nonno kisses the top of my head, whispering sweet words of affirmation. Luci claps her hand. Marco nods. Sal giggles.

And Gianni—Gianni stands. "Then we must go. We must get you to your prince."

"I think I have a pretty good idea of how to make that happen," a familiar voice says from the doorway.

I gasp. "Callum? How are you here?"

"The door was unlocked," he says, like that's an answer, stopping just short of my chair and giving a lock of my hair a playful tug before dropping his hand to my shoulder. It's a comforting weight. I do wish I were wearing a bra though.

"I've never had such a perfect dramatic moment." He grins and gives a little bow. "Thank you all for that. In any case, I came to drag you back to Elsinore. Kicking and screaming or willingly. Guess it will be the latter, which makes my job easier. Though I did bring several PPOs and a roll of duct tape."

The patio is speechless for a moment, and Callum, clearly not processing our collective shock, waves toward the door.

"Well, come on then! We've got a ball to crash."

CHAPTER 31

Alessia

NINETY MINUTES LATER, I'm on a plane—now with a bra and normal clothes even if I didn't have time to shower—with Nonno and the grandpas, Luci and Marco. Plus Callum, a small security team, and the staff for the plane. Who right now are not Callum's favorite people.

"What do you mean, an engine issue?" he demands, and though he's generally a sunny person, at the moment, he's turned on the authoritative princely thing.

The pilot clutches his hat, working it in his hands. "Yes, I know. Things were fine when we left. There was a warning light that appeared and—"

"How long of a delay?"

"We're having it looked at now, sir."

"Be quick about it." Callum drags a hand through his hair and turns back to all of us, who are looking at him like we expect a summation even though clearly, we all heard. "We've got a bit of a delay."

"How much time do we have?" Nonno asks.

"The ball isn't until the evening, and it's only about an hour and a half in air. We should still have plenty of time to get there."

I look down at myself. "I can't show up like this to the ball."

Callum gives me a soft smile. "Phillip wouldn't care if you showed up wearing a burlap sack."

"Which is lovely, but I don't want to show up like this. Or in a burlap sack."

Not when I already feel like I don't belong. It was hard to fight back those feelings of not belonging when I was wearing the fancy clothes my personal dresser picked out. Arriving at a formal, *royal* ball dressed like this would be utterly humiliating.

Luci grabs my arm and pulls me to my feet. "Didn't you say this place has a shower?"

"It does," Callum says.

"Come on then." Luci starts tugging me to the back. "Let's get you as ready as we can. I always come prepared with makeup." She pats her bag, and I know full well she has a complete stash of cosmetics.

"And I'll alert my sisters," Callum says, already tapping away at his phone. "I told them to have a few dresses ready to go."

I yank my arm from Luci's and turn to face Callum. "They aren't angry with me?"

The smile Callum gives is so kind, I almost crumple right there on the royal crest on the jet's carpet. "Of course, they're not angry with you. They just want you to come home."

320

Home.

I can't help but find Nonno's eyes, feeling a flash of guilt as strong as the bolt of desire. Nonno's eyes are wet, and I bite my lip. But then he smiles.

"I meant to tell you as part of your intervention this morning, Lessy. You're fired."

I gape at him. "What?"

"And ... you're kicked out. I'm planning to rent out the cottage and travel the world." He pats Sal's and Gianni's arms, and the two men nod. "I am letting Marcello cook, and we are going to take a man trip."

A guy's trip, I mentally correct. Out loud, I ask, "You want me to leave?"

"I want you to *live*." Nonno's words are quiet but backed with an intensity that makes me ache. "I want you to have your dreams and to chase them. To expand your boundary lines outside of our village. Tesoro, it's time for us both to get out of our rut."

I sniff. "I like our rut."

"I love you too. Now, go! Shower and let Luci fix you up."

With tears in my eyes, I smile and walk over to place a kiss on Nonno's forehead. "Thank you."

"Enough talking," Luci says, stamping her foot. "We have much work to do. When's the last time you shaved?"

"Um, I don't know." I do know. It was in Elsinore. My legs are a veritable forest of hair—something I'd really love to not discuss in front of a plane full of mostly men.

I grab my phone out of my bag. It finally charged, but I haven't had a chance to look at it. Callum sees me powering it on, and his eyes light up. "Have you been listening to your voicemails?" When I shake my head, his grin widens. "I might suggest doing so."

"Lessy, even waterproof makeup has limits," Luci says, groaning as she steps away from me, makeup brush in hand. "You must stop this crying."

"But they're happy tears."

"Happy tears, sad tears—all the tears ruin your makeup," she says. "Come on. We're almost there and then we'll need to rush with your dress and hair! Give me your phone." She holds out a hand.

I clutch the phone tighter to my chest, sniffling. "No."

"Give. Me. The. Phone."

"Can I listen just one more time?"

It turns out that every day until my voicemail ran out of storage, Phillip left me messages. Sweet, kind, and sometimes sexy messages. Declaring his love. Asking my forgiveness. Begging me to return. Listing all the things he misses about me. Telling me all the things he'd like to do with me if I came back. Promising how he will take care of me if I do.

If I'd listened to them, I might have come back sooner. And yet, I'm glad I didn't. Because I might have been swayed by his sweet words, but I now feel *sure*. I made the decision to fight for him, for us, without hearing his words. Now, I feel more confident in the choice I'm making.

Though I'm still terrified I might arrive too late after the plane was delayed by several hours because of some issue with the engine. His mother wouldn't force him to choose someone else, would she?

I remember how she looked at me when I told her I was leaving. Honestly, I haven't figured her out. I'm still not sure.

Luci snatches the phone from my hands, opens the door of the plane's bedroom and tosses the phone out. "There. Now it's time to finish your makeup."

"Hey! That's my phone!"

"I liked it better when you hated phones," she grumbles, coming at me again with a makeup brush. "Now sit still."

If I was worried about Henri and Juliet being mad at me, the way they greet me with massive hugs before rushing me up to my suite assures me of their forgiveness. And though I'm slightly claustrophobic by the room completely stuffed to the gills with people, I've never felt more loved.

I choose a turquoise gown that reminds me of the one I wore on my first official date with Phillip, and Henri has just finished zipping me up when Luci steps out of the bathroom in a sparkly pink dress. Marco comes out behind her in a tuxedo that looks as though it's been thoroughly rumpled.

"I can't believe you just have all these extra dresses and suits lying around," Luci says, eyeing the nonnos, who all have been suited up as well.

"Being royalty comes with a lot of burdens," Juliet says. "Might as well balance those out with some solid perks."

The door to the suite is thrown open once more, and I grumble, "Who is it now?"

"Never fear, I'm here!" a deep voice calls as a dark-haired man in a tux sweeps into the room with dramatic flair. He holds open the door for a woman in a beautiful white gown and a small crown.

She's laughing. "I think they've got more than enough help," she says, giving the man a pointed look as she hesitates just inside the room, scanning the faces and looking a little nervous.

"Fi!" Phillip's sisters bolt for the door, hugging the woman much as they did me when I arrived.

"King Rafe and Queen Serafina of Viore!" Sal exclaims, bowing low.

"How come I didn't get a bow?" Callum asks.

"Because he knows you're a lesser man," the dark-haired man says as he and Callum engage in a back-slapping hug that looks nothing like the way one might expect royals to greet one another. "Sorry about the scar."

"The ladies love it," Callum answers. "And I'll find a way to return the favor."

"How about a temporary truce on all pranking so we might enjoy the ball, hm?" Serafina says, giving both men a look that has them nodding their assent. "Now, who is going to introduce me to the woman who's won Phillip's heart?"

"Alessia," Henri says, coming to stand beside me. "I'd like to introduce you to Queen Serafina of Viore."

I try to get to my feet so I can bow or curtsy, but Serafina, who looks only slightly older than I am, waves a hand.

"Please, no formalities. We're among friends." She glances around, smiling. "I'd love to meet each and every one of you"— Sal looks ready to pass out at this— "but time is of the essence as the ball just started. Alessia, it's lovely to meet you."

"It's wonderful to meet you too, Queen Serafina," I say, trying to shove away my nerves. She makes me feel more at ease than Phillip's mother, thankfully. But I'm a ball of nerves right now about all of this, which doesn't help.

"Please, just call me Serafina. Or Sera. Or Fi." Serafina laughs. "I've accrued a lot of nicknames."

"But only I get to call you Seraf." Her husband, King Rafe, drags his fingertips over Serafina's bare shoulder before pressing a soft kiss there. She bites her lip and smiles before pushing him away—but only an inch or so before he slides a hand around her waist.

"So, *you're* Rafe of the peacocks," I say, and he laughs. "King Rafe," I correct, realizing my error.

He only laughs, waving me off as his wife did. "I am Rafe of the peacocks. Perhaps I should have my title officially changed. What do you think, Angel?"

Serafina rolls her eyes. "We're trying to get the national budget under control. No need to add a revolving door of nameplates to it."

Rafe holds out a hand to me. "I'm Rafe. It's wonderful to meet the woman who proved Prince Phillip has a heart and isn't, in fact, a robot running on a computer program he designed."

Callum snorts, and I can't help but smile.

"Rafe!" Serafina slaps at his hand. "That's rude. I'm sorry," she says to me. "I have zero control over the man."

"You can control me anytime you'd like," he murmurs into her ear, and this time, the queen gives him a hearty shove.

"Why don't you and Callum go distract Phillip," Serafina suggests.

"We'll make sure Mum doesn't foist some duchess on him," Callum says, throwing an arm around Rafe's shoulders.

My eyes go wide. "Is that a possibility?"

"No," Callum says firmly. "I wouldn't joke if it were. Despite what you might think, my mother approves."

Doubtful, but I appreciate Callum's words as he and Rafe leave.

"I'm so sorry about my husband," Serafina says. "He learned his manners in a barnyard. Do you mind if I sit?"

I shake my head, and she smooths down her beautiful gown and takes a seat on a chair near the dressing table. My stomach clenches with nerves, and Juliet appears, kneeling to slide my feet into fancy slippers.

She grins up at me. "They're more comfortable than glass. Also more comfortable than heels. Just—promise you won't run?"

"Not again," I assure her. "I'm sorry again for doing so the first time."

She nods, and I know I'm forgiven. Even if I'm not sure I deserve it yet.

"Now, what about this hair, Lessy?" Luci asks, picking up my hair, which we washed on the plane. While we worried about makeup and then getting into a dress here, it dried as it usually does—wild and wavy.

Gianni is suddenly there, looking as grumpy as ever, but also handsome in a suit that mostly fits his stout frame. "I will do the hair," he says.

"You know how to do hair, Gianni?" I ask, trying to do so in a tone that isn't soaked in disbelief.

But he's already behind me, working the tangles out of my hair. "I always did my Lia's hair." He chuckles, a low, gruff sound as he switches from his fingers to a brush Luci hands him. "Every morning, I would wash and brush her hair before styling it. This was before YouTube and TikTok, so I was on my own."

There are soft laughs around the room and a few sniffles as well.

"I dreamed of having daughters," he says, and raw emotion coats his voice. "Of fixing their hair the same way, morning by morning. But it was only us. Then, only me. You are the daughter I never had, Lessy. And I need you to know this—don't walk away from love."

I reach up and gently grasp his wrist, not wanting to disturb his work. I meet Gianni's gaze in the mirror a few feet in front of me. His cheeks are wet, but his eyes glow with happiness. I bite my lip to keep it from quivering too much.

"You know," Serafina says. "I'm sure all of this must be quite overwhelming."

"I'm not sure *overwhelming* covers it," I say with a wavering voice.

Serafina gives a soft laugh, then leans closer to take my hand.

"There are two important things to know about being a royal," she says. "First, you don't live just for yourself. You live to serve a whole people. A country, a kingdom. It's a massive role."

Gianni begins twisting my hair into braids as Serafina continues.

"But at the end of the day, the second thing to remember is you're just as human as anyone else," she says, squeezing my hand. "You have likes and dislikes. You have friends and family. Those are really the foundation. If you have a solid foundation of love and support, the things that seem so overwhelming, the tasks of ruling and decision-making and being in the public eye, those things are manageable. Small, even."

Serafina stands, giving my hand a last squeeze before letting go. Surveying the room, she nods. "I look around this room, and I see love. I see support. I see your strength, Alessia. You have everything you need to be a successful queen. Everything else will come in time. Being a king or queen is an acquired skill set. Anyone could do it. But those who want it the least are often those most worthy of it."

And then, shocking me so much my mouth falls open, Queen Serafina of Viore curtsies to me. Luci doesn't even try to smack me with the hairbrush she's clutching, because she's looking just as dumbfounded as I feel.

Serafina stands back up with perfect posture, looking regal and beautiful and also so very human. "It was lovely to meet you, future queen of Elsinore. I look forward to getting to know you better."

And then she's gone. Gianni steps back, and Henri places a small tiara on top of the braided crown of hair.

"Perfect," she says.

"È perfetto," Gianni agrees, wiping his eyes.

"Tu sei perfetto," Nonno corrects, touching my shoulder. "It's time, beautiful."

"I'm scared, Nonno."

"I know, tesoro. But the best choices in life require you to stare fear right in its ugly face and to take the leap. Say yes to your prince."

"Say yes," Juliet says.

Henri nods. "Please, please, say yes."

"Say yes," Sal and Gianni say in unison.

Say yes, a small voice inside me says, the one that I hear every so often, the one that makes me think of the mother I never met.

The door flies open, which seems to be the theme of today, and Graves pops in, out of breath. His eyes skate over the room and then land on me. "You must come," he says, panting. "They've just said Prince Phillip is about to make an announcement."

CHAPTER 32

Phillip

SHE ISN'T HERE. I'm probably a fool for thinking she would come, for hoping that after two weeks of silence, she would come.

Still, I hoped. And she isn't here.

I saw Callum enter the ballroom with Rafe moments ago. And that was the moment my hope died. Because Alessia didn't walk in with him.

Every other woman in Europe seems to be here though, and my mother has looked less pleased than I thought she would be watching me dance with them all. I wish dance cards were still a thing so I could have pointed to mine and said it's full.

I've taken the liberty of a quick break, drinking water and instructing two security officers to keep everyone back, just for a moment. The orchestra stops playing, and my mother

329

takes the stage, father beside her. He looks well—better than he has in weeks, his cheeks flushed and his eyes bright.

"Thank you all for joining us," Mum says, smiling out at the room, which hushed the moment she stepped in front of the microphone. "We're so pleased you could be here. Please take a glass of champagne because in just a moment, Prince Phillip will be making an announcement."

Oh, will I? It's so very like my mother to make an announcement about an announcement, trapping me into the action she wants.

Her eyes meet mine, giving me a look I interpret to mean, *Oh yes, you WILL be making an announcement.*

Did she really think I would just pick a woman out of the crowd tonight and get down on one knee? I suppose she must have.

Sighing, I trade my water for a champagne flute when a server appears with a tray. Scanning the room one last time (because apparently my hope isn't *quite* dead), I wonder if there have ever been so many dark-haired women congregated in one place.

None of them, of course, is the one I want to see.

I walk toward the stage, where the orchestra is playing a celebratory song and Mum and Father have stepped back, waiting for me. When I reach them, I give them each a quick hug, careful not to spill the champagne.

"Really, Mother," I murmur as she hugs me back. "You really want me to do this?"

"Every baby bird needs a mother to kick them out of the nest," she says. "Consider this my very loving kick."

"Oh, come now," Father says, and I don't miss the twinkle in his eyes.

"What are you up to?" I ask. Because they definitely are up to something.

I glance out over the room one more time, and my eyes catch on long dark waves. Sucking in a breath, I watch, heart pounding, only to feel the bitter sting of disappointment when the woman turns. It's not Alessia. Of course it's not.

Mum steps closer, taking my arm and pulling me close again. "Phillip, you know I want what's best for you first, and what's best for Elsinore second. But in this case, what's best for both is for you to choose a woman to marry." Mum's eyes fill, and while this is an oft-used tool in her toolbox, right now, her tears seem sincere. "We want you to be happy. And I know that's a cliché statement, but your father and I know what it's like to rule a country. More than ever now that he's been sick, I see how difficult this is to do alone."

I swallow, and she cups my cheek. For a brief moment, the sound fades from the room, and it's just my mum and me. Not a queen and a prince. A mother and her son.

"I want that too."

But only with Alessia, I think.

"Love can grow from friendship, Phillip. It can start with choice rather than some silly feeling that will just fade over time."

I want to laugh. I used to think that. I suppose I still think it can happen that way. But in my case, it didn't.

It's what I first thought when I asked Claudius to set up the rubric. I thought it would be as simple as finding a woman who fit my criteria, making a commitment, and spending the rest of our lives not falling in love, but choosing it. Daily.

Instead, I found myself falling in love, feelings and all, offering her everything, and watching her choose to walk away.

"I'm ready," I say, stepping away from her.

I glance at father, but his eyes are on the crowd, scanning as though he, too, is waiting for Alessia to show up.

As difficult as it might be to rule alone, as much as I'd love for my father to see me happily married before his illness overtakes him, I know that I can't choose anyone but her.

The orchestra leader nods to me, signaling for the song to reach its conclusion. Clapping fills the room as I step forward, taking the microphone stand in a hand I hope can keep from shaking. Whoever is in charge of the lighting turns a spotlight directly on my face, assuring I can see nothing.

Which, honestly, is fine. The one face I want to see isn't here.

"Good evening." I squint as the applause dies down. "I want to thank everyone for being here tonight."

More applause. I wait, trying not to feel irritated by people who will clap for anything I say just because it's me saying it. I clear my throat, hoping I remember the speech I prepared but didn't want to give.

"Prince Phillip!"

Someone calls my name from the back of the room, but I cannot make out who the voice belongs to. Neither can I recognize it over the way my heart is beating in my ears. I've never been this nervous to give a speech before.

"I'm sure many of you heard the rumors in the press about this being a so-called Cinderella ball."

There are a few cheers, a wolf whistle, and someone shouts, "Choose me!"

There are murmurs in the crowd, and I feel my lower back start to sweat. I press on.

"I have, uh, decided that—"

"JUST PHILLIP!"

This time, the words land. It's Alessia's voice, and it's *her* nickname for me.

I shade my eyes with my hand, trying and failing to see beyond the blinding light. "Sia?"

I step to the side in hopes of getting a clear view. But the genius running the lights moves the spotlight with me so I still can't see. There's a commotion, and then I hear Sia's voice again, rising above the murmurs in the room.

"Phillip!"

I must get to her.

Whether it's the lights or the surprise or just my desperation, I lose my footing and step right off the edge of the stage.

I expect to hit the floor an instant later and am shocked when I'm caught. By arms and hands and bodies. I've never been to a concert, but I've seen videos of crowd surfing, though a video could not have prepared me for this bizarre feeling of being carried along like a leaf in a current.

Also—I bet that leaf didn't have someone grab its butt while traveling downstream.

I'm sure my PPOs are losing their minds, and I catch sight of Graves, a hard look on his face as he pushes his way through the throng just as I'm deposited back on my feet, a little more unsteady than I was moments ago.

But I hardly care, because Alessia stands before me.

I can only stare as our security team pushes everyone back, leaving me and Sia alone in the middle of a crowded room. She looks beautiful with her hair up in some complicated style and a gorgeous blue dress cascading over her curves. It reminds me of the sea we swam in the day we first kissed.

"You came back," I say, because I have no brilliant words right now, no speech prepared for this.

"I couldn't stay away," she says, smiling.

"Callum brought you back?"

"He did, which was very convenient as I wasn't sure how I was going to manage arriving on time on my own."

I have so many questions, so many things I want to say, but Sia steps forward, closing the distance between us as she places a hand on my chest, right on top of my quickly beating heart.

"Just Phillip," she says, then gives her head a little shake and smiles again, a little nervously now. "*Prince* Phillip. Before I so cowardly ran away, you asked me a question. You said it was a placeholder question of sorts."

She reaches into a pocket of the dress, pulling out something in her closed fist.

"You asked me a question and told me to let you know when I was ready to answer. Even then, I knew the answer. I knew it the moment you asked—maybe even before that, when I saw you on your knees. But I was too afraid of the changes it would mean and the sacrifices it would take. Too afraid I wasn't enough for the job. Enough for you. But I'm not afraid anymore. If you'd like to ask me the question again, I'm ready to answer."

Holding out her hand to me, she opens her fingers to reveal her mother's ring. My hands are shaking as I pluck it from her palm.

With a soft smile, she leans closer and whispers, "If it helps with the nerves, my answer is going to be yes."

I laugh, feeling warmth and happiness and relief bubble up inside me. "Thank you. Now, let me make it official."

I drop to my knee and take her hand in mine. "Alessia, I'm sure this was more eloquent the first time, when it was just you and me. Now, we're surrounded by half the kingdom and your most-welcome arrival has shocked the words right out of me. I hope you're okay with simple."

"I am," she says.

"Good." I draw in a deep breath, then say the Italian words I've been practicing. "Alessia, mi vuoi spostare?"

The yes is out of her mouth almost before I'm done with the question, and then the whole room erupts into cheers and the orchestra is playing as I stand and gather Sia in my arms. Hugging her to me, I see a whole row of familiar faces in the crowd: Luci and Marco, Gianni, Sal, and Nonno. I grin, and Nonno gives me an approving nod. Gianni points to me and then back to his eyes by way of warning, and Sal wipes tears from his eyes.

Claudius stands nearby with Kat, and his eyes are damp as well. Fi, Juliet, and Henri are hugging and smiling through tears, and Callum and Rafe stand shoulder to shoulder. I hope this means the prank war is over.

"Phillip," Alessia whispers, her lips near my ear. I can feel her smile. "You forgot to give me the ring."

"Oh, right." I set her gently back down, hoping I haven't wrinkled her dress too badly. For the second—and final—time, I slide the ring on her finger. She glances down at it, and I wipe a tear from her cheek with my thumb.

"Thank you," she says. "I'm so very sorry I left."

"It's okay," I assure her. "We'll have time to talk later. I also need to introduce you to someone." I glance at Claudius and give him a quick nod. "But first, I really need to kiss you."

"I was hoping you would," she says, and then, not waiting for me, Sia throws her arms around my neck and kisses me first.

After a few moments of kissing that my mother would

definitely not deem appropriate, I press a more chaste kiss to Alessia's lips and lean my forehead against hers.

"Ti amo, Sia," I tell her.

"Te me amorre," she says, surprising me with her Elsinorian. Grinning, she leans closer, her lips brushing my ear. "And as much as I love that you've been brushing up on your Italian, you should know that you asked me to *move* you, not *marry* you."

"I did?"

"You did." Alessia pulls back, grinning. "But moving, marrying—with you, Just Phillip, the answer is yes."

EPILOGUE

Alessia

I HEAR the crunch of gravel behind me, but I stay still, staring down at my favorite view in Repestro. As the heavy steps grow closer, my skin tingles in anticipation. *I know those footsteps!*

When Phillip's hands brush my hair away from my neck, I shiver. He presses a soft kiss right to the top of my spine, his breath warm as it ghosts over my skin. I close my eyes.

"I thought I'd find you here in your thinking place," he murmurs, settling both hands on my shoulders, lightly rubbing. "Having second thoughts, mi bellina?"

"Not a single one. I just wanted a moment alone."

"Should I go, then? So you can be alone?"

I place my hand on top of his, keeping it in place on my shoulder. "Don't you dare. Just stay with me for a quiet moment."

He does. And it's one of my favorite things about Phillip —his ability to be still, to be quiet, and yet so very present. That said, we don't get many moments like this. Especially leading up to our wedding.

The past week in Repestro has been a flurry of activity. And though it's been lovely to be home after living in Elsinore, the villagers have hardly given me space to breathe. I feel as though I'm living inside a beehive someone has taken a stick to. Only the bees are happy not angry. Happy I'm here, happy for me and Phillip, happy we chose to have our wedding here in the village, not at the palace.

"Do Elsinorians consider it bad luck for you to see me in my wedding dress?" I ask, done with my quiet moment. I still haven't looked at Phillip, and the anticipation is making me feel as fizzy as a bottle of shaken champagne.

"Traditionally, yes."

"So, you're causing bad luck on our wedding day?" I tease, squeezing his hand, which still rests on my shoulder, a warm comfort.

"What if I told you my eyes are closed?"

"Then I would tell you it's not just bad luck but dangerous to stand near a cliff without looking where you're going."

"I can trust you to keep me from going over the edge, can't I?"

I smile. "Yes. Always. Though I also might be the one driving you right up to the edge."

"That's just one of the things I love about you, Sia. Also, my eyes are open, and you are stunning. Fiele." He presses another kiss to my neck, and again, I shiver. "Aren't you going to look at me, Sia?"

"One of us has to uphold tradition," I say through a smile.

"We'll make our own traditions," he says, the words as firm as any promise he's ever made to me.

Yes. We will. And buck some traditions as well.

Like this: hosting our wedding in my tiny village rather than at the palace in Elsinore. Though his mother THE QUEEN (whom I'm now *mostly* calling Suzette except in my head) was less than pleased, Phillip and I insisted. We also insisted on pushing back the wedding a month, waiting to see how a new treatment would help King James's health. At least for now, it's helped immensely, making travel possible even if they will both leave soon after the ceremony.

Claudius agreed to help with security and logistics of this village wedding—I think partially out of guilt for not revealing himself to me earlier. But mostly, I think, to connect with our tiny part of the family tree. Over the past few months, he spent some time here with Nonno. Apparently, Gianni got Claudius tipsy on homemade wine. I've been saving a particular video Nonno sent me of Claudius singing a Lady Gaga song and falling out of his chair on the patio.

I'm sure at some point, I'll find a way to leverage it against my newfound cousin.

"How about a new tradition," I say, bending to pick up two tiny yellow flowers growing from a crack in the stone wall.

I stand, turning to finally look at Phillip. He is chest-achingly handsome in a navy blue suit, even without the jacket. Maybe *especially* without the jacket since he cuffed his sleeves, revealing his strong, tanned forearms. He is like my old, once-a-week daydreams come to life. Only better.

Handing one of the flowers to Phillip, I gesture over the wall to the rocky cliffs leading down to the sea. "For our new tradition, we'll throw these flowers over the cliff and make a wish."

Phillip holds the flower up to his nose and sniffs, his eyes never leaving mine. "And we'll do so every time we come home to visit?"

The question makes warmth unfurl in my chest. Phillip has always been so conscientious about making sure I have enough time back here. He's even been able to visit several times. When he calls it home, I know he doesn't just mean for me.

"Yes. Every time."

Phillip's smile comes slowly, hitting his eyes first and softening the blue into a summer sky, then tilting one corner of his lips at a time. "What if all my wishes already came true?" he asks.

I step closer, lifting up to press a kiss to one side of his jaw, then the other. "Then I'd say you need to dream bigger."

I toss my flower, and it's almost immediately caught by the wind, carried out over the cliff's edge. Phillip does the same, not looking to see where it goes, because his gaze is pinned only on me.

———

"Are you ready, gioa della mia vita?" Nonno asks, holding out his arm. "Don't be nervous!"

"It's not nerves," I tell him, sliding my hand into the crook of his elbow. But I can't find another word to describe how I'm feeling, so I only shrug. There isn't a word—not in Italian or Elsinorian or even English. "Are you ready, Nonno?"

"I've been trying to get you out of my house for years," he says, his eyes shining with mirth but also with tears.

I glance around the small room. This still feels more like

home than the palace does—at least in terms of buildings. But home isn't about a building. It's about the people who make you feel most happy to be yourself. Phillip is my home, more than I ever knew a person could be. But so is Nonno and Luci and Sal and Gianni and now even Phillip's family ... which only means I am blessed enough to have many homes.

Graves pokes his head in the door. "It's time." Then his eyes land on me, and he blinks rapidly, his mouth opening and closing. "You make a beautiful bride," he says, and Nonno hands the big man a tissue from his pocket. "Phillip and all of Elsinore will be so pleased to have you."

"Thank you, Graves."

The big man sniffs, wiping at his eyes. Not for the first time, I'm grateful to have a personal protection officer who could keep me safe with little more than the strength in his pinky finger, but also is such a romantic. If Luci weren't still with Marco, I'd have set her up with Graves long ago.

Nonno kisses my cheek, smiling. "Shall we?"

"We shall."

We step outside into a warm, sunlit September afternoon. Garlands of flowers hang across the street, and people line the sidewalks, many tossing flowers in front of us as we walk. We go slowly, as I told Nonno I want to look at every face I can. To meet every set of eyes, to share my gratefulness by way of acknowledgement. It isn't easy, but I do my best.

The entire village is here, of course, as well as many people from Elsinore. Our chapel is small, so most won't fit inside, but the reception will be something of a street party, with the entire village closed down for the event. Security teams have blocked off the roads leading in and out, and Phillip actually came up with a device that can be used to deactivate drones, keeping the most invasive tabloids from intruding on our special day. We've sold the rights to our photographs to another newspaper—NOT *The Royal Bugle*—and all the money will be given to Repestro, which is slowly revitalizing itself into a true tourist destination.

Today feels exactly how I wanted it to: intimate, yet inclusive. Suzette didn't love it when I told her how I wanted this day to be, but in the end, she gave in to most of what I asked for. I do feel badly for Henri and Juliet, who won't be so lucky when their time comes.

I don't know some of the people we pass who have come from Elsinore, but I hope one day to know as many as I can. It's special when my eyes connect with people I've known since I'm a girl—Maria and Ernesto, Antonio, Zia Agnesia. The closer we get to the chapel, the more familiar the faces become.

There's Luci—on Marco's arm and sporting her own ring. Claudius and his wife Kat—who I expect to be Luci's new best friend by the end of the night—stand nearby. Callum looks as handsome and sunny as ever with Henri and Juliet on either side. The two of them look so beautiful and suddenly much more like women, even with their girlish excitement. Rafe beams at us before giving Serafina—who has become a trusted friend and ally—a kiss that almost makes me blush.

Closest to the chapel, the king and queen stand on one side with Sal and Gianni on the other. I smile at them each, but my eyes are drawn quickly back to my groom.

Though I loved seeing him earlier with his shirtsleeves rolled up, now in his full suit and holding a white rose to match the one I carry, Phillip makes my heart race. He always does, just as he did the moment he first walked into Nonno's restaurant and into my life.

"There is your boy," Nonno says. "Your prince, Lessy. Mr.

Perfect. Ah, look at his tears! Sal will have to pay me twenty euros."

"Sia," Phillip whispers as Nonno and I ascend the few steps to the chapel. "You are so beautiful, mi bellina, amore mio."

Nonno gives me a quick kiss on the cheek before shaking Phillip's hand and stepping down. We're surrounded by hundreds, and yet in this moment, it feels as though we're the only two people in the world.

"No thorns," Phillip says, handing me the rose as I hand him mine. "I cut them off myself."

"Remember the time I cut my palm trying to climb down the side of a hotel?" I ask, smiling through my tears.

"Remember the time I beat you in a water fight?"

"Remember the time you got out of breath walking up a tiny hill?"

"Remember the time you met my mother?" he asks.

I gasp in mock outrage. "Remember the time you thought you could choose a wife by a rubric?"

"Remember the time I was a fool?"

"I remember several. Remember the time you wore Nonno's tiny bathing suit?"

Phillip leans close, his lips grazing my ear. "What do you think I'm wearing under this suit?"

I burst out laughing at this, and though no one else could have heard the joke, my joy seems to bubble over into the crowd. Laughter and cheers rise all around us.

"I hope you're kidding," I tell him.

Phillip's eyes gleam. "Guess you'll have to find out later."

"I can't wait," I tell him with a wink.

"All right, all right," Nonno says, climbing back up the steps to take my arm. "Let's make this official, tesoro."

I loop my hand through Nonno's arm once more. With Phillip close behind, we lead the way inside, followed by our family and friends, royals and commoners alike—and thankfully, exactly zero peacocks, swans, or any other fowl—ready to celebrate a love greater than either of us could have imagined.

THE END

A NOTE FROM EMMA

Readers! We made it!

If you're someone who has followed me on social or is in my email or ALL UP IN MY BUSINESS (I *love* it when you're all up in my business), you know that I wanted to release this book in September 2022.

In the end, I loved Phillip and Alessia's story. It's totally different from Rare and Serafina (if you read Royally Rearranged), but it was so fun to write a royal in hiding kind of book. Even if that means dealing with the inevitable criticism for having characters be deceptive.

IT IS WHAT IT IS. And I'm so happy to bring you this book, which made me think of *Return to Me* (one of my fave movies) and *The Prince and Me*, which I admittedly haven't seen in a long time. There's just something about the Cinderella story and the royal + commoner trope that I love!

(Also, I hope you all got the nods to Cinderella inside. One scene I REALLY wanted to recreate was when the birds and animals helped her get ready for the ball—only in this case, it was friends and nonnos.)

The pressure as I was working was UNREAL. You'd think that after something like a bazillion books the pressure would go away. It doesn't. For me, it's worse. I have to shove away worries like, "What if they don't like this as much as the last book?" Or "What if this one isn't funny?" Or "What if the people who say they love everything I write finally realize ... they don't?"

It's silly, but also serious in terms of the toll it can take on mental health. (Go give your fave author a hug or kind email! We're all a mess over here!)

Pressure was part of what slowed me down, making this book take longer than I wanted. I'm glad it did though, because all that percolating added some of my favorite things to the book. (I'm pretty sure I wrote one of my favorite scenes in the whole book a day before I uploaded to Amazon —the "Unchained Melody" one, in case you're wondering.)

In addition to dealing with pressure, we also moved and my husband got a new job—not in that order.

It's been a lot of transition.

This book, like *Royally Rearranged*, took way more research than my typical books set in small town, USA. It's been YEARS since I've been to Italy, and I am so grateful for Jill and Antonello for all the info on Italy. (Thanks to Jenna for connecting us!) Even in making up a country, it's still more setting and research. I did my very best to stay true to life in ways that I could, even as I was constantly bothered by thinking about what language people would REALLY be speaking in at the moment. I took some liberties, but hope that I gave this book my best in terms of the research I did.

This cast of characters was also *massive*. I loved the nonnos (even if Jill and Antonello suggested another name might work better) and the whole royal family—except maybe the queen, who is understandably not her best self right now.

While I really hope one day to write some other royal stories, I'm going to focus on my other open series for now to get those out in the world. But I hope to come back to the royals. I am 100% shipping Graves and Henri, and I think Callum has been sufficiently humbled so as to deserve a second chance. Don't you???

(The best way to find out about books, royal or otherwise, is to connect via email—https://emmastclair.com/romcomemail)

I'm so relieved to give this book to you, and I hope you love it as much as I do.

I hope it makes you want to travel again, to hug your family, to kiss the person you love—on both cheeks or even on the lips.

Do stay away from peacocks, though! IRL I've had a peacock chase down my family's car when I was a girl and hop on the hood like some kind of avenging dragon, so thanks for that moment, which inspired Callum's amorous peacocks.

As always, thank you for being my readers. I'm so grateful to you for being here, for being supportive, and for reading this far.

You're really fetch. And you're TOTALLY going to happen.

-Emma

TRANSLATIONS

Elsinorian

- Fiele- beauty, literally the light from a distant star
- Vainto- mild curse word most like crap
- Te me amorre- I love you
- Mi bellina - my beauty

Italian

- Ti amo- I love you
- mi vuoi spostare- will you move me
- mi vuoi sposare- will you marry me
- Che cavolo- literally what cabbage (mild curse)
- Porca miseria- damn misery (mild curse)
- Tesoro- treasure, a pet name
- Buongiorno- good morning
- Gioa della mia vita- joy of my life
- Mortacci tua- an insult to dead relatives

ACKNOWLEDGMENTS

A giant thank you to Jenny Proctor. You read my words. You hold me together when I fall apart, and you help me believe I can finish things.

Thank you to Jenna for reading and improving *The Royal Bugle* scenes. I'm sure you didn't think all those times at *The Bullet* would be prepping you for helping with a romcom.

A massive thanks to Jill and Antonello for letting me pester you with questions and helping me find words that weren't cussing in Italian, among other things. I loved incorporating some of the things you shared, like your wedding day photo and tradition of meeting outside the church. I was so happy to incorporate that.

Thank you to Alisa for hanging out with me, keeping my head on straight, and reading through and providing encouragement.

Thanks to Rita and Vivian and Bernie for the typos you caught!

Thanks to Jordan, Haleigh, Alisa, Rachel, and Rita for your early beta read!

WHAT TO READ NEXT

The Appies
Just Don't Fall- Emma St. Clair

Absolutely Not in Love- Jenny Proctor

A Groom of One's Own- Emma St. Clair

Romancing the Grump- Jenny Proctor

Runaway Bride and Prejudice- Emma St. Clair

When Alec Met Evie- Jenny Proctor

Love Stories in Sheet Cake
The Buy-In

The Bluff

The Pocket Pair

Sweet Royal Romcoms
Royally Rearranged

Royal Gone Rogue

Love Clichés
Falling for Your Best Friend's Twin

Falling for Your Boss

Falling for Your Fake Fiancé

The Twelve Holidates

Falling for Your Brother's Best Friend

Falling for Your Best Friend

Falling for Your Enemy

Oakley Island (with Jenny Proctor)

Eloise and the Grump Next Door

Merritt and Her Childhood Crush

Sadie and the Bad Boy Billionaire

Izzy and Her Off-Limits Love

ABOUT THE AUTHOR

Emma St. Clair is a *USA Today* bestselling author of over thirty books and has her MFA in Fiction. She lives in Katy, Texas with her husband, five kids, and a Great Dane who doesn't make a very good babysitter. Her romcoms have humor, heart, and nothing that's going to make you need to hide your Kindle from the kids. ;)

You can find out more at http://emmastclair.com or join her reader group at https://www.facebook.com/groups/emmastclair/

Emma is represented by Kimberly Whalen, The Whalen Agency.

* 9 7 9 8 9 9 2 3 4 7 0 1 2 *